THE GODLESS MAN

THE GODLESS MAN

A Mystery of Alexander the Great

PAUL DOHERTY

CARROLL & GRAF PUBLISHERS
NEW YORK

Carroll & Graf Publishers
An imprint of Avalon Publishing Group, Inc.
161 William Street
16th Floor
NY 10038–2607
www.carrollandgraf.com

First published in the UK by Constable,
an imprint of Constable & Robinson Ltd 2002

First Carroll & Graf edition 2002

ISBN 0–7867–0995–2

Printed and bound in the EU

To the Clooney family, with every good wish

"That Godless Man"

Euripecles, *The Bacchae*,
L.991

"Εν ολιγω σ χεονω μεγαλας πφχξεις ουτος ὁ Βασιλευς κατειφγασατο."

"The King [Alexander] accomplished great things in a short period of time."

Diodorus Siculus, *Library of History*,
Book 17, Chapter 1

THE GREEK WORLD, 334 BC

ILLYRIA

MACEDONIA

THRACE

BLACK SEA

•Pella

THASOS

SAMOTHRACE

SEA OF MARMARA

Sestos Lampascus

Elaeus Zeleia Granicus Dascylium

Troy Abydos

TROAD

HELLESPONTINE PHRYGIA

ASIA MINOR

THESSALY

AEGEAN SEA

Chaeronea•

EUBOEA

LESBOS

Delphi

Thebes•

•Sardis

CHIOS

Athens•

SAMOS

•Ephesus

Corinth•

Olympia• Argos•

•Sparta

RHODES

MEDITERRANEAN

CRETE

SEA

N

Historical Personages Mentioned in the Text

The House of Macedon

PHILIP   King of Macedon until his assassination in 336 BC. Father of Alexander.

OLYMPIAS OF MOLOSSUS (Born Myrtale):   Philip's queen, Alexander's mother. Co-Regent of Macedon during Alexander's conquest of Persia.

EURYDICE   Philip's wife after he divorced Olympias: she was niece of Philip's favourite general, Attalus. Eurydice, her baby son and Attalus were all executed after Philip's death.

ARRIDHAEUS   Philip's son by one of his concubines, poisoned by Olympias. He survived but remained brain-damaged for the rest of his life.

The Court of Macedon

BLACK CLEITUS   Brother to Alexander's nurse: Alexander's personal bodyguard.

HEPHAESTION   Alexander's boon companion.

ARISTANDER   Court necromancer, adviser to Alexander.

ARISTOTLE   Alexander's tutor in the Groves of Mieza: Greek philosopher.

SOCRATES   Athenian philosopher. Found guilty of "impiety", forced to drink poison.

PAUSANIAS   Philip of Macedon's assassin.

APELLES   Ephesian artist, court painter to Alexander.

Alexander's Generals

PARMENIO, PTOLEMY, SELEUCUS, AMYNTAS, ANTIPATER (left as Co-Regent in Macedon), NEARCHUS, ADMIRAL NICANOR.

The Court of Persia

DARIUS III   King of Kings

ARSITES   Satrap of Phrygia. Persian commander-in-chief at the Granicus: executed afterwards by Memnon.

MEMNON OF RHODES   A Greek mercenary in the pay of Persia, one of the few generals to defeat Macedonian troops.

CYRUS AND XERXES   Former great Emperors of Persia.

BAGOAS   Formerly Vizier, executed by Darius III.

GREEK PLAYWRIGHTS   Aeschylus, Aristophanes, Euripides, Sophocles.

HOMER   Reputed author of the two great poems the *Iliad* and the *Odyssey*.

DEMOSTHENES Athenian demagogue, ardent opponent of Alexander.

HIPPOCRATES OF COS   Greek physician and writer, regarded as the father of medicine.

The Mythology of Greece

ZEUS Father god.

HERA His wife.

APOLLO God of light.

ARTEMIS Goddess of the hunt: Ephesus was regarded as the centre of her cult.

ATHENA Goddess of war.

HERCULES Greek man-god. One of Alexander's reputed ancestors.

AESCULAPIUS Man-god; a great healer.

OEDIPUS Tragic hero, king of Thebes.

DIONYSIUS God of wine.

EYNALIUS Ancient Macedonian god of war.

CENTAURS Half-men, half-beasts who allegedly ravaged Thessaly and Thrace before crossing the Straits to Asia. They were, according to legend, wiped out by the man-god Hercules. Nessus was the last of their tribe.

HYARA Poisonous snake of Greek legend.

MEDUSA A fearsome goddess of Greek legend.

The Gods of Persia

AHURA–MAZDA   The All-Creator, Lord of the Fire, of the Hidden Flame.

AHIRMAN   The Power/Lord of Darkness.

Preface

I n 336 BC, Philip of Macedon died swiftly at his moment of supreme glory, assassinated by a former lover as he was about to receive the plaudits of his client states. All of Greece and Persia quietly rejoiced – the growing supremacy of Macedon was to be curbed. The finger of suspicion for Philip's murder was pointed directly at his scheming wife – the "Witch Queen", Olympias – and their only son, the young Alexander, whom Demosthenes of Athens dismissed as a "booby". Macedon's enemies quietly relished the prospect of a civil war which would destroy Alexander and his mother and end any threat to the Greek states as well as the sprawling Persian Empire of Darius III. Alexander soon proved them wrong. A consummate actor, a sly politician, a ruthless fighter and a brilliant general, in two years Alexander crushed all opposition at home, won over the wild tribes to the north and had himself proclaimed Captain-General of Greece. He was to be the leader of a fresh crusade against Persia – fitting punishment for the attacks on Greece by Cyrus the Great and his successors a century earlier.

Alexander proved, by the total destruction of the great city of Thebes, the home of Oedipus, that he would brook no opposition. He then turned east. He proclaimed himself a Greek ready to avenge Greek wrongs. Secretly, Alexander wished to satisfy his lust for conquest, to march to the edge of the world, to prove he was a better man than Philip, to win the vindication of the gods as well as confirm the whisperings of his mother – that his conception was due to divine intervention.

In the spring of 334 BC, Alexander gathered his army at Sestos while, across the Hellespont, Darius III, his sinister spymaster the Lord Mithra and his generals plotted the utter destruction of this

Macedonian upstart. Alexander, however, was committed to total war.

He crossed to Asia and shattered the Persian army at the battle of the Granicus. He marched south, capturing vital cities but searching for a port his fleet could use. Alexander then took "Golden Ephesus". Like many Greek cities, both on the mainland and in the Persian Empire, Ephesus was riven by partisan politics: the rich, conservative Oligarchs supported Persian rule and bitterly opposed the Democrats. Alexander entered this maelstrom of violence, blood-chilling intrigue and treachery. Darius and Lord Mithra watched: perhaps Alexander would become enmeshed in Ephesus's bloody politics as well as forget his warlike dreams amid the luxury of that opulent city. Persian and Greek secretly conspired against each other. Darius hoped to trap Alexander once and for all and utterly destroy him, while the Captain-General of Greece plotted his own way out of the net closing around him . . .

Prologue

———◦◦◦◦———

"Alexander reached Ephesus within three days . . . The people of the town, freed from the fear of their political masters, were eager to put to death the men who had called in Memnon."

Arrian, *The Campaigns of Alexander*,
Book I, Chapter 18

E phesus the Magnificent, the city of Artemis of the Greeks and the Persian goddess Anahita, had become the house of mayhem and murder. Once described as "a silver jewel under a golden sun", Ephesus was now the camp of Ares the god of war. Soaring columns of black smoke rose up against the blue sky, spreading out like a pall of mourning over this great city of Darius, King of Kings. A time of settling accounts, of resolving grievances and grudges, of gruesome killings and senseless slaughter. Corpses littered the broad avenues fringed by plane and olive trees. The grey-green sheen of its cypress groves was tarnished by flickering flames and acrid smoke. No place was safe. The living even settled grievances with the dead – in the great cemeteries to the west of the city the gorgeous tombs, ornamented with brazen bulls or long-necked marble jars, were ransacked and pillaged. Corpses were dug up to be burnt or hanged from the nearby trees. Hate lapped like a river through the city. The powerful ones, the Oligarchs, barri-caded gates and fortified the high walls of their mansions. Others, putting their trust in the gods, fled into the places of sanctuary, up the steps through the porticoed entrances of temples: they threw themselves before the statues of the gods, who gazed stonily down at these refugees fleeing from the malice of their fellow citizens.

1

The dry market stench of fruit and meats, spices and herbs, mingled with the iron tang of blood and decomposing flesh. Houses lay empty: the doors to their courtyards hung open. Looters and ransackers bathed in their fountains or rested beneath their vine-covered columns.

The source of all this horror was the abrupt flight of the Persian garrison. Messengers had arrived, covered in dust, shouting that Alexander of Macedon, the barbarian from across the sea, had annihilated a Persian army at the river Granicus. The victor had swaggered south along the Ionian coast, taking one city after another. Sardis, with its massive walls and soaring bronze gates, had fallen like a ripe fig: its Persian commander had gone out to meet the conqueror, offering him the keys to both the city and the imperial treasury.

News of all this had swept like a storm through the city of Ephesus. Alexander, King of Macedon, Captain-General of Greece, conqueror of Persian armies, was coming to claim his own. The rivalries and tensions had surfaced like dirt in clear water. The two great political factions had emerged like swordsmen, eager to settle accounts. The rich and powerful, the Oligarchs, who had collaborated with their Persian rulers, had to confront the fury of the Democrats, who believed their hour had come. Two years earlier Parmenio, a Macedonian general, had been despatched by Philip, Alexander's father, across the Hellespont to establish a bridgehead. Parmenio had launched a lightning attack on Ephesus, removed the Oligarchs and put the Democrats in power. He had raised a statue to Philip in the half-finished Temple of Artemis, but then withdrew when the Persians counter-attacked. The Oligarchs had resumed power: Philip's statue had been destroyed and bloody reprisals carried out against the Democrats. Now fortune had spun its wheel again. Macedon's hour had finally arrived. Once the Persian garrison had gone, the cry of "Eynalius! Eynalius! Eynalius!", the name of the ancient Macedonian god of war, rang through the streets of Ephesus. Hidden weapons were dug up, the mob from the slums armed, and retribution began.

The eye of the storm, the place of bloody execution, was the broad agora, the main marketplace. At one end stood the half-finished Temple of Artemis, which had been mysteriously burnt down on the night Alexander of Macedon had been born. On the two sides, the meeting-house and civic halls of the city. At the other end, the great portico, the Painted Colonnade where, in calmer times, the Ephesians would walk and enjoy the perfume of the flower baskets, admire the ornamental pools glinting in front of their marble buildings and savour the fragrance of the lotus blossom. All this had gone. Corpses, blood gushing from their wounds, bobbed, face down in the pools of purity. Cadavers, necks twisted, swung from the iron brackets which had once held flower baskets. The market booth and stalls had been cleared away, a tribunal of summary justice set up. In the Painted Colonnade leaders of the Democrat party, Peleus, Agis and Dion, sat enthroned behind a broad trestle table: further down, armed with bronze stylus and folding pad of black wax, sat their principal scribe and clerk Hesiod, a powerful silversmith now called to record the judgments of this court. The sun-swept square below the steps was packed with a mob which served as both jury and executioner. The three judges sat behind their table while ruffians from the city dragged up prisoners. The trials were both short and brutal.

"This man," an accuser would yell, "supplied the Persians and the Oligarchs with food and wine!"

No proof would be needed, because the victim's name had been long recorded on a secret list: death was a foregone conclusion. The principal self-appointed judge, Agis, would rise to his feet, a powerful, bull-necked man with the voice of a born orator. He would scream at the mob: "How say ye? Guilty or not guilty?"

The answer was always the same – "Guilty! Guilty! Guilty! Death! Death! Death!"

The unfortunate would be hustled away to be hanged from one of the iron brackets, beheaded at the foot of the steps or, depending on the whim of the executioners, have his throat cut and his corpse thrown on to a pile of others or into one of the pools of purity. The executions had begun just after dawn. One of the ledges in the Painted Colonnade was already lined with severed heads, and the pile of decapitated corpses stank under the midday sun. Blood flowed everywhere, dark pools trickling down the steps, following the line of the paved stones of the agora, staining the sandals and bare feet of the mob.

The executions were watched by a unit of Macedonian guardsmen in their silver corselets, red tunics, great rounded bronze shields with greaves of the same colour. They wore Phrygian helmets, their high coned tops decorated with white plumes, a sign they belonged to the elite unit of the Royals. They did not interfere or move from their vantage point on the steps which swept up to the Temple of Artemis but stood in battle order, shields up, lances half-lowered. On either side of them were ranged two units of Alexander's mercenaries, their ornate Corinthian helmets decorated with red horsehair plumes: the ornamental face-guards revealed nothing but staring eyes, moustached mouths and bearded chins.

Alexander's soldiers were growing impatient with the blood-letting. When a young woman was led up to be accused and, after a short while, taken away to be strangled, a murmur of protest swelled from the Macedonian ranks. Their general Amyntas, however, was under strict orders.

"If I've told you once, I've told you for the thousandth time," he whispered to a grumbling staff officer, "the king's orders are quite specific. Let the blood-letting continue. Only intervene at his command!"

The staff officer, suitably rebuked, stepped back. Amyntas, cradling his helmet, stared cold-eyed as one judicial murder followed another. Macedonian troops had reached Ephesus the night before: Alexander now lay camped outside the city walls. He had been greeted with fruit, wine, garlands and the bloody demands of the Democrat leaders. Vengeance was the meal they had been yearning for, and vengeance would be served. Amyntas only hoped Alexander would not wait too long, otherwise the mob would get out of control. Amyntas did not relish a fight to regain the city, a bloody hand-to-hand struggle as they fought for one house after another.

"Occupy the temple!" Alexander had ordered, his different-coloured eyes gleaming passionately. "The Temple of Artemis is sacred to me, traitors aren't. Blood must flow, so flow it will. Only intervene when I send Telamon."

Amyntas licked dry lips. He only hoped the black-haired, dark-faced personal physician of Alexander would not tarry long. One of Alexander's most trusted counsellors and confidants, Telamon had been present when the order was issued. He, like others, had protested, but the king was insistent: punishment would be carried out and only end on his orders. Amyntas felt the burning heat and squinted up at the midday sun. He had drunk and eaten more than he should the previous evening and, beneath the cuirass and the leather war kilt, his body was soaked in sweat, wafting away the perfume he loved to wear. He walked over to stand in the shade of a column, shielded his eyes and stared across the square. This time an entire family were on trial.

"When will he come?" The rebellious staff officer had followed him over.

"If you don't shut up . . . !" Amyntas growled. The staff officer fell quiet.

Across the square another figure, hidden in the shadows, watched the grisly executions. He was dressed in a beggar's garb, a ragged tunic covered by a patched military cloak, its hood pulled well across his face. To any passer-by who might be curious, he was just one of those road wanderers, covered in dust, who came to beg or filch what they could. Only the silver chain round his neck, hidden by the thick serge cloth of his tunic, betrayed his true status. The chain carried a silver wasp, the emblem of the centaur, that mythical half-man, half-horse creature wiped out by the god-man Hercules, who had a temple in this very city.

The Centaur, as he called himself, studied the executions, his face betraying no emotion. He did not flinch as the men, women and children in the Oligarch's family were all found guilty and thrust down into the square for summary execution. He only had eyes for the judges. From his vantage point he could study their faces. The scribe Hesiod, fat and sweaty, those black eyes hidden in rolls of fat. Agis, in his white tunic, the silver rings on his fingers and wrists glinting as he gesticulated for a fresh batch of prisoners. A tall man with a beak-like nose and sunken cheeks, Agis had his head shaved, a sign of mourning for those wasted years, bowing to the Persian rulers and their collaborators among the Oligarchs. Next to

5

him, Peleus, with his thick shock of black hair, cruel eyes, podgy nose and full fleshy lips, a man who revelled in these slayings – Peleus's kinsmen had been butchered by the Oligarchs only two years previously. Finally Dion, the lawyer among the group, with his clever face and deep-set eyes. A young man with powerful ambitions. He too had lost kinsmen in the Persian blood-letting. Dion was present to give these hideous proceedings a legal facade.

The Centaur scratched at the sweat on his neck and wondered if his master was one of those bloodthirsty judges. He moved and stared across at the Macedonian soldiers. He was about to go back to his original vantage point when a group of horsemen debouched from an alleyway. The Centaur narrowed his eyes. The cavalrymen ringed a man in a white tunic and blue mantle, a red-haired woman riding next to him. The Centaur had been out to the Macedonian camp and recognized the new arrivals. Alexander had sent his physician Telamon into the city. The killings were about to end. The Centaur bit his lower lip: Alexander would not get off too lightly. Darius, King of Kings, and Lord Mithra, the Persian ruler's keeper of secrets, had not yet finished with Ephesus, and neither had the Centaur and his master.

Across the square the Macedonians were now stirring: a soldier ran up the steps gesturing that the summary trial should end. The crowd roared its disapproval, which faded away as Macedonian troops, armed for battle, debouched out of side streets. The watcher in the shadows had seen enough: the blood-letting was over. Those Oligarchs in hiding would now flee for sanctuary to their favourite shrine, the Temple of Hercules. The watcher smiled grimly – that wouldn't be the end! So much work to do, so much planning, but – he licked dry lips – the rewards would be so great.

The Apanda, the King of King's Hall of Audience, lay silent. The Immortals, the personal bodyguard of Dairus III, stood like graven images, spear and shield in hand, their gorgeous clothes studded with precious gems in the shape of rosettes or lozenges. They were there to guard the royal presence and the approaches to the Red House, the Imperial Treasury. They stood, eyes fixed on the roaring fire which burnt on its raised platform in the centre of the hall. This was the Holy Fire, the manifestation of Ahura-Mazda, the Persian God of the Hidden Flame. The imperial throne was empty. Courtiers and chamberlains, fan-bearers and fly-swatters, the Carrier of the Imperial Perfume, the Bearer of the Royal Axe, were no longer needed. The hall looked sombre, its wall paintings subdued. These exquisite frescoes proclaimed the glory of the King of Kings, the destruction of his enemies and his adoration by a myriad subject peoples: Jews, Elamites, Medes, Egyptians and even strangely garbed people from beyond the Hindu Kush. One young guard stirred nervously, grasping the long spear with its iron blade, its base shaped in the form of an apple. He peered through the soaring pillars of cedarwood at the corpse stuffed with sawdust which knelt on a footstool; this had been turned so the glazed eyes of the grisly mummy were for ever fixed on the imperial throne. This had once been Bagoas, formerly king-maker in the Persian Empire, Grand Vizier and mighty lord. Bagoas had poisoned the way to the throne for Darius and, when he turned against his protégé, had been poisoned in return. Darius would never allow anyone to forget Bagoas's treachery.

"He wanted glory," Darius had jibed, "and glory he shall have! He wanted to be a member of my court, and so he shall be!"

Bagoas had been denied sacred burial. Instead, his poisoned corpse had been cleaned and mummified by an Egyptian keeper of the dead, stuffed with sawdust and for ever fixed in a posture of obeisance before the imperial throne.

The guardsman breathed out. He dared not move. He was an Immortal, one of the hand-picked soldiers of the King of Kings, yet he felt uneasy, staring at this corpse with its sightless, glassy gaze. He could make out every feature of the grisly cadaver: tufts of hair springing up as in life, the scrawny moustache and beard, the dark eyes and high cheekbones. The corpse knelt, head slightly forward, hands joined as if in eternal prayer. The more the guardsman stared, the more certain he became that the corpse had a life of its own. Hadn't the head moved? The eyes flickered? The lips begun to speak? The guardsman shifted his gaze as he heard the soft footsteps of his officer, who walked up and down guarding the gallery leading down to the Red House where

7

Darius, King of Kings, sat closeted with his Keeper of Secrets, the Lord Mithra.

"Are you nervous, man?"

The officer was now standing just behind him. The guard nodded imperceptibly.

"Don't be," the officer reassured him. "This is a divine place, the Holy of Holies. Nothing of evil can walk here. The divine flame purifies all and keeps the demons at bay."

Inside the Red House, Darius would certainly have disagreed with this. He sat in the principal office of his treasurer, behind the green baize-covered table where the accounts of his empire were drawn up, staring across at Lord Mithra, his thin bony face shrouded in a cowl. Darius usually felt comfortable here, among the wealth and power of his empire, but today he did not. The doors were firmly closed and their bronze sheeting glowed like bars of gold in the dancing light from the oil-lamps. The walls of the treasury were of carved limestone with a facing of blood-red enamel brick which gave the place its name. A place where no eavesdropper or spy could enter. Darius himself had constructed the treasury, to guard not only his wealth but also his secrets: now he regarded it as a place of refuge from the terrors which haunted him. He stared up at the star-studded ceiling, supported by columns, their capitals carved in the shape of bulls' heads, their bases strange winged creatures, a hybrid of lion, dragon and griffin. Leading off from this chamber were the vaults containing sixty thousand talents in gold ingots, thirty thousand in gold darics, coffers and caskets full of jewels and precious stones, Median shekels, every type of coin in the empire. Darius picked up the royal seal and stared at it as he reflected on what Lord Mithra was saying. The seal was emblazoned with the God-King's sign of the sun-disc borne by eagle wings.

The Lord Mithra spoke, just above a whisper, describing what was happening in the western provinces. Darius tried to control his fear. He stared across at a frieze on the wall, depicting himself offering sacrifice before a fire altar and slaying creatures of the Underworld. The more Mithra spoke the deeper Darius's agitation grew. He felt hot and stuffy and, without a thought, took off the cidarias, the smooth tiara round his black, curly, oil-drenched hair. He regretted wearing the candice, the beautiful embroidered Median robe of purple and gold satin. Darius wished he were out hunting, riding some fleet-footed horse through the green coolness of his hunting parks. Yet this meeting was vital: the Lord Mithra was saying things which no Persian courtier would even dare think. Darius wiped a bead of sweat from his brow. Lord Mithra finished speaking.

"Is it so bad?" Darius murmured, putting down the seal. "Has the Lord Ahura-Mazda deserted us completely?"

"We have been fooled and misled," Mithra replied. "We expected the Macedonian to wander about like a child lost in an orchard. Instead he has struck fast and ruthlessly, like a raging panther. Sardis has fallen, other cities are opening their gates. Ephesus is now his."

Darius picked up the seal and clenched it in his hands.

"The fruits of the Granicus," Mithra added.

Darius nodded in agreement. "Granicus." The name haunted his every waking moment and drove his dreams into nightmares. He had ignored the advice of his Greek mercenary Memnon and sent an army out to meet Alexander: the army had been annihilated and Memnon's mercenaries either massacred or taken as slaves to work in the silver mines of Macedon.

Darius muttered a prayer. He should have followed Memnon's advice and never allowed his army to meet Alexander in battle. It gave him cold comfort to know that outside, in the place of execution, the Persian commander's severed head, coated in wax, was thrust on a pole.

"What can we do?" Darius demanded. "If we meet Alexander in battle, a second Granicus? Yet we cannot allow the panther to roam unchecked."

Mithra studied his master. He felt confident and calm. Darius trusted him completely. Hadn't he been the one who had dis-covered Bagoas's treachery, as well as warned this proud and arrogant King of Kings not to confront the Macedonian in battle? Darius wanted to know the truth, so the truth he must face.

"Alexander is elated." Mithra leaned against the table, eyes on his master. "He has taken Sardis and its royal treasury. Memnon has withdrawn to the port of Miletus, and the Greeks have no fleet." He laughed sharply. "Well, none to boast of. Our ships can support Memnon for as long as they wish."

"But Ephesus?" Darius protested. "Ephesus has fallen, only a few miles from Miletus."

"My lord," Mithra replied, "Ephesus regards itself as Greek and the Macedonians as barbarians. The Democrats will seize power, but they want that power themselves. They don't want to replace one master with another. A Greek poet, my lord, described their cities as beehives: each man has a sting which he uses against his neighbour."

"I am not interested in Greek poetry," Darius retorted.

"And neither am I, my lord, but when it comes to taking heads or causing confusion, to stirring up riot and dissent . . ."

Darius leaned forward. "We can do that?"

Mithra gestured around him. "You have gold and silver. Alexander may control the city, but our spies are there."

"In Ephesus?"

"The Centaur, my lord." Mithra smiled slightly. "Well, that's what we call him."

"You have met this spy?"

"No. One of the few who truly hides in the shadows." Mithra decided to tell his master only what he had to: the Centaur's identity was his secret. He would give that secret to no one.

"Why does he take that name?"

"He, my lord? It might be a woman."

"The Centaur!" Darius snapped.

"A mythical race," Mithra answered. "Half-man, half-horse. They reputedly live in Thessaly but crossed the Hellespont. The Greek god Hercules wiped them out."

"There's a temple to Hercules in Ephesus?"

"Yes, my lord. It contains a sacred relic. Hercules fell in love with a beautiful woman and, taking her home, had to cross a river. She was helped across by one of the last remaining centaurs, Nessus, who tried to rape her. Hercules killed him with one of his poisoned arrows. The woman took some of the centaur's blood which contained poison from the Hydra, a venomous snake."

10

"Why did she do that?" Darius asked.

"Because she suspected Hercules was going to betray her. When he did, she gave him a tunic as a gift but soaked it in the blood of the Hydra. Hercules wore this tunic and his body was consumed by fire. On his death, he was taken up to Olympus."

"And what has a Greek legend to do with Alexander?"

"Everything," Mithra murmured. "Hercules was a god-man. Alexander believes he is a god-man. Now, in the centre of the temple at Ephesus stands a silver vase which contains an earthenware vase. According to legend, that vase holds the Hydra venom. Folklore has it that the poison was dedicated to the temple as a votive offering. It stands on a stone plinth surrounded, as usual, by a bed of fiery charcoal."

"And?" Darius asked tersely.

"Let us stay in Ephesus," Mithra said quietly. "Many years ago our governor waged a cruel war against a group of assassins who called themselves the Centaurs. They were bandits, thieves, murderers. They robbed wayfarers and travellers but their principal task was to carry out assassinations, which they did with considerable skill and ease. They always notified their victim of their intentions by sending him a silver medallion with an image of a wasp on it: the wasp was regarded as an emblem of the Centaurs."

"And these were wiped out?"

"According to the evidence, yes, my lord. However, when trouble with Macedon broke out three years ago, I searched for spies in the city." He shrugged. "The usual, merchants, city officials. I tried to buy spies in both camps: the Oligarchs, those wealthy families who believe Ephesus should be ruled by them, as well as the Democrats."

"The rabble?"

"No, my lord, just the powerful and rich who want to control the rabble. It's common in Greek cities – that's why I quoted the poet. I found a spy, a very good one, who took the name of the Centaur." Mithra paused: he would not tell the full truth, that this spy had been in his pay even before Darius Codomanus had usurped the throne.

"And what will this Centaur do?"

11

"I don't know, my lord, not yet, but let's turn to Alexander. He is mighty in victory, the powerful Captain-General, the liberator, yet he leads an army of no more than forty-five thousand men. Memnon still holds the nearby city of Miletus and our fleet patrols the sea. Alexander has taken other cities." Mithra measured his words. "In each city, my lord, he leaves a garrison."

"So his army grows smaller?"

"Precisely. The other side of the coin is that these cities can become beds of intrigue and conspiracy. They may not like our rule, but they don't want a Macedonian princeling lording it over them, so we encourage revolt and dissent to distract and weaken the great conqueror. Every city he enters will greet him with wine and garlands, food and precious gifts. However, once the citizens see Macedonian troops swaggering through their streets they'll soon grow tired of being liberated." Mithra sucked on his lips. "They'll revert to habit, waging war against each other."

"Like bees in a beehive?"

"Of course, my lord. Each with their sting."

"Will Memnon be successful?" Darius mused. "They claim Alexander's favourite book is the *Iliad*, that he sees himself as a descendant of Achilles. In that poem didn't Achilles kill a warrior called Memnon?"

"Aye, my lord, but in the end Achilles was killed – an arrow through his heel, the only part of his body which could be wounded. Ephesus could be our enemy's Achilles' heel. Alexander loves the city. On the night he was born a madman burnt the great Temple of Artemis to the ground. Olympias, the witch-queen, Alexander's mother, claimed it was a divine sign: the temple was burnt because Artemis was busy in Macedon at Alexander's birth."

"What nonsense!" Darius breathed.

"Alexander believes it."

"And this Centaur will stir up trouble?"

Mithra gazed down at the floor.

"What's the matter?" the king asked crossly.

Mithra raised his head, pushing back his cowl, rubbing his hand along his shaven pate. Darius could never really assess the man's age: a youthful face, despite the lean, hungry look, the eyes bright with life.

"I am not sure, my lord, if the Centaur is one person or two." Mithra intended to confuse his master so as to distract him.

Darius sat up in his throne-like chair.

"What makes you suspect two?"

"The assassins at Ephesus took their name because they always worked in twos: a parody of the half-man, half-horse centaur, a hybrid creature. The Centaur sends messages to our governor at Ephesus written in a cipher. The scribe Rabinus sends them on to me. The Centaur reports on the different machinations of both Oligarchs and Democrats."

"So, this Centaur," Darius sneered, "could be both Democrat and Oligarch?"

"Possibly," Mithra replied evasively. "The Centaur is also a killer. He wages war against both Oligarch and Democrat: individuals from both parties have been brutally murdered."

"Why?"

"To keep both factions at each other's throats." Mithra shrugged. "Though there may be deeper, more personal reasons. Whatever, the Centaur, not any garrison, army, or fleet, is our best hope of impeding Alexander from striking further east."

Darius leaned his arms on the table and stared at the glowing bronze doors behind Mithra. Here he was in his treasury, surrounded by the wealth of his empire. Outside, his elite corps of troops, the Immortals. Guards patrolled the grounds. On crosses at the far side of the palace hung the corpses of his victims, those who had dared to oppose him, guilty of treason by word or deed and, on a few occasions, even look. Nevertheless, Darius felt vulnerable. Ephesus and Sardis were many days' journey away, yet this Macedonian panther was already lording it in those cities, once jewels in Darius's crown. Had Ahura-Mazda deserted him? Did the sacred fire outside hold nothing? Had the Divine Presence gone? Darius closed his eyes. Sometimes at night, after the ladies of the harem had left and his sheets and bed still smelt of their heavy perfume, Darius would lie awake, tossing and turning, staring into the darkness. He would glimpse the ghosts of those he had

13

slaughtered in his seizure of the Peacock Throne. Was this his punishment? Would Alexander one day break open those bronze doors and swagger in to plunder his treasury?

"What will you do?" Darius asked quietly.

Mithra had been sitting with eyes closed, lips moving as if in prayer.

"How shall we act?" Darius demanded.

"You have done great wrong, and I warn you once again!" Mithra closed his eyes. "A quotation, my lord, from another Greek playwright, Euripides. 'You have done great wrong'," he repeated, "'and I warn you once again.' That is what we will do to Alexander – warn him again, wage secret war by all means possible, stir up trouble in Ephesus, bring him into disrepute."

"Why not kill him?" Darius asked. "Once and for all. A knife to the heart, poison in the belly."

"It may come to that, my lord," Mithra agreed. "But the question is how. It must be someone close, someone we trust."

"Could this Centaur do it?"

"Perhaps, but our spy must not be detected. The beehive." Mithra smiled. "Each man has a sting. Let the Macedonian be stung by someone close."

"But Alexander keeps himself safe? His own father was assassinated: those about the Macedonian love him deeply. There are his physicians. One in particular," Darius continued. "A man who once worked in our empire, a native of Macedon . . ."

Mithra picked up a scroll and unrolled it. "Telamon, my lord. His father once fought with Philip, but gave up the sword for the plough."

"Could he be bribed?" Darius leaned across the table.

"Oh no." Mithra shook his head. "If Alexander is to go into the dark, Telamon must go with him."

Darius sighed. "And so the panther will be killed?"

Mithra nodded. "If it is the gods' will, my lord."

Darius picked up the seal and stared at the insignia. He muttered his own prayer that Alexander of Macedon would be delivered into the hands of Ahirman, the Evil One.

★   ★   ★

14

Callisthenes, captain of the unit of shield-bearers known as the Eagles, patrolled up and down outside the great sealed doors of the Temple of Hercules in Ephesus. Once again he turned and was relieved to see the sky lighten, a faint flush of pink marking the rising sun. He took off his Phrygian helmet and rubbed his eyes.

"I hate night watches," he muttered.

Callisthenes was pleased he would be relieved within the hour. His men, in various states of dress, lounged against the wall, some asleep, others eating dry rations. Callisthenes heard a bell tinkle. He walked to the table along the portico, picked up a small hand-bell and rang it in answer, the agreed sign that all was well. He undid the scarlet cloth round his neck, the colour of his unit, and used it to wipe the sweat from beneath his tunic. Once again he went down the steps and stared up at the tympanum above the portico, which depicted Hercules in one of his many battles against the wild tribes of Thrace.

"Quite a place, isn't it, sir?" One of his unit had come down the steps to stand beside him. "How old do you think it is?"

Callisthenes narrowed his eyes. The temple was carved out of limestone and covered in a shield of brilliant white plaster. The tympanum above was exquisitely carved: the soaring pillars, dark portico, cedarwood doors and the broad sweeping steps leading upwards, gave the temple a sombre majesty. At first Callisthenes had been impressed, but now he was tired of the place and the people inside it. In fact, Callisthenes disliked Ephesus, with its porticoes, theatres, temples and broad dusty avenues. He was a Macedonian who dreamed of lovely tree-filled valleys, rushing rivers and flower-decked water meadows. Ephesus was so different: the constant sunshine which shifted the shadows, the busy, cramped markets, the smelly alleyways, gorgeous temples and fertile parks, a mixture of majesty and meanness.

"How old is the temple, sir?" The guardsman broke his reverie.

"I don't bloody know!" Callisthenes retorted. "They're always building temples in Ephesus. Certainly older than you or me, perhaps a hundred or a hundred and fifty years. Now," he balanced his helmet, "I just want to make sure it's secure, so you can help me."

The guardsman stifled a curse: he regretted leaving his comfortable seat, but Callisthenes was a stickler for discipline. A good officer, Callisthenes had let his own men eat and sleep while he prowled up and down like a guard dog. They went down the narrow alley at the side of the temple, Callisthenes patting the outside walls as if searching for some hidden door or entrance.

"What are you worried about, sir?" the guardsman asked. "They're safe inside." He gestured up towards the cornices. "Even a monkey couldn't get through those windows – too high, too narrow."

Callisthenes, cradling his helmet in his arm, stepped back and peered up.

"You're right, soldier," he agreed. "Six windows along this side, two at the back, six along the other side. Still, we have to be sure."

He walked on round the corner and paused at the rear door, which stood behind the sanctuary. This was still bolted from the inside and sealed with the king's own insignia in great purple blobs of wax. The two windows high in the wall were small and circular. Callisthenes studied the ground as he had the previous evening: no marks, no footprints, no one had been here. He continued his patrol along the far side wall and back into the temple forecourt.

"Why is this so precious, sir?"

"For two reasons," Callisthenes replied. "Bring me a cup of water and I'll tell you."

The soldier hurried off and brought back an earthenware beaker. Callisthenes rinsed his mouth and poured the rest over his face. He would have loved to undo the cuirass, take off the heavy leather kilt, while the greaves and heavy marching sandals made his legs and feet itch.

"You see, lad, this is a temple to Hercules and our king, may the gods bless his golden head, believes he is a descendant of Hercules so, in a way, this temple is his."

The guardsman stifled a yawn. He had filched a few jewels and golden darics after their great victory at the Granicus. In Ephesus he had found himself a handsome young woman in the Perfume Quarter: dark-eyed, foul-mouthed, but a proper handful in bed.

16

The guardsman couldn't care if Alexander called himself Zeus as long as the good times continued.

"And is he going to make this temple his home, sir?"

"No, no," Callisthenes laughed. "First, the temple has a shrine. You saw it last night."

"Oh, that silver vase surrounded by a bed of charcoal? Why is it so sacred?"

"I don't bloody know!" Callisthenes retorted. "But Alexander doesn't want it stolen. If you and I helped ourselves to that, we'd be on a cross quicker than you can say 'Darius's balls'."

"And those men?" the guardsman asked. "The ones who've taken sanctuary?"

"They're the leaders of the Oligarchs' party," Callisthenes said. "They once ruled like kings in Ephesus until our noble king arrived: those who were riding high now have to run after the dung cart." He recalled the bloodstain he had seen on the step the previous night.

"They really hate each other, don't they?" the guardsman wondered. "We're still finding corpses."

"Well, that's over." Callisthenes walked forward, searching for the bloodstain. "Our king has said there's going to be peace and reconciliation, but those buggers in the temple don't believe him, that's why they've taken sanctuary. Alexander has sworn sacred oaths they will be safe. He wants it that way. These men have money and power. Think of two dogs, lad, constantly squaring up to each other – that's what Alexander wants: two dogs ruling Ephesus and he doesn't want one to get too strong or the other too weak. So he's told these Oligarchs to come out. They'll be safe, no one will hurt them."

Callisthenes stared at the cedarwood doors. He had campaigned with both Philip and his son in the wild Thessalian forest. He had also been present at the Granicus when they had smashed the might of Persia. Callisthenes prided himself on sensing danger and, although everything looked serene, he felt deeply uneasy. The guardsman detected this.

"They'll be safe, sir. They're all locked in like a group of virgins, and Procanus is with them."

"Aye."

Callisthenes wondered how Procanus had fared. The sanctuary-seekers had demanded one Macedonian to be with them, and Procanus was the best man in his unit. He didn't give a fig about shrines, relics or the gods. Procanus was only concerned with three things: his own skin, wine, and where he could find a pretty woman. Nevertheless, the temple had been so silent, so quiet. What had his officers said? That the silver vase held something sacred yet very dangerous? Alexander had promised those who'd sought sanctuary inside would leave unscathed, not a hair on their heads would be harmed. Callisthenes's commander had shouted what would happen if anything went wrong and Callisthenes fully believed him. He gazed round the temple forecourt. The entrances to the streets were all sealed off. More units patrolled there, while a squadron of cavalry were camped in the next square. Perhaps it was the silence? He stared across at a small grove of cypress trees – not even birdsong, nothing! Callisthenes recalled how, during the recent massacres, this place had seen its fair share of grisly murders. Did their ghosts still throng here?

"I'm beginning to hate this place," he murmured. "What I need is a soft bed and something softer inside it."

Somewhere deep in the city a conch horn brayed. The sun was beginning to rise, the city come to life. Callisthenes dismissed the guardsman and walked up the steps. Once again he tried the heavy cedarwood doors, which held fast. Callisthenes heard a voice, the sound of marching feet. He hastily put his helmet on and shouted at his men to stand to attention.

A group of Royals emerged from a side street and crossed the square. The rising sun glinted on their burnished armour, helmets gleamed, white plumes nodding in the morning breeze. They were led by an officer and escorted two men dressed in tunics and mantles. Callisthenes brought himself to attention as the Royals stopped at the bottom of the steps, and the two men came up towards him. He repressed a shiver. The leading one had a scrawny neck and the face of an angry bird, hollow-eyed with pitted cheeks, sparse sandy hair and the mere whisper of a moustache and beard. His face was painted like that of a woman, fingernails dyed in

18

henna; even from where he stood Callisthenes could smell the rich musk–like perfume. The man walked effeminately, rings and bracelets dazzling on fingers and wrists. He paused on the top step and looked Callisthenes from top to toe.

"You look well, Callisthenes, you haven't been sleeping?"

"Of course not, sir."

Callisthenes tried to sound offhand, but this man frightened him more than a Persian Immortal. Aristander, necromancer, magician, warlock, Master of the Royal Secrets, confidant to Olympias, Alexander's mother, now the king's personal seer: a man who wielded considerable power and loved to exercise it. Courtier and politician, Aristander controlled the king's spies: he sniffed out traitors like a dog would buried bones.

"You haven't slept, have you?" Aristander's head came forward, lips parted to show yellowing teeth.

"Of course he hasn't!" Aristander's companion scoffed. He was tall, his black hair, moustache and beard neatly cut, with dark brooding eyes in a swarthy face. He was dressed in a simple white tunic with a light-blue mantle: the only jewellery he wore was a heavy embossed ring displaying the sign of Aesculapius the Healer.

"I am Telamon." The man extended his hand and Callisthenes grasped it. "Personal physician to the king."

"He's here to check on the health of our guests." Aristander waved sardonically at the temple doors. "And to repeat the king's assurances. No commotion, Captain? No alarms during the night?"

"All's quiet, sir."

Aristander pulled a face, as if he found that difficult to believe. "Well, we have to wait for the others."

"The others?" Callisthenes queried.

"The leading Democrats: Agis, Peleus, Dion and Hesiod, not to forget one of the few remaining Oligarch leaders, Meleager."

Callisthenes stared at his men, now dressed in their armour: they stood, shield and spear at the ready, as if they had done so all night.

"They are supposed to be here," Telamon murmured.

Callisthenes noticed that the physician was more calm, reserved, his eyes certainly friendlier than Aristander's. "A friend of the king," was how the officers had described the physician: "a

19

boyhood companion whom Alexander trusts. He carries the king's seal: whatever he asks, make sure you do."

Callisthenes idly wondered at the whereabouts of the physician's assistant, the red-haired wench, what was her name? Ah yes, Cassandra. The gossips were knowledgable about her: a former Theban whom Telamon had brought out of the slave pens. Some claimed she was his mistress, a bed companion. Others, who had done more than their fair share of prying, maintained she had been a temple healer and was now assistant to this enigmatic physician.

Further speculation was ended by the sound of voices, the challenge of a guard. Callisthenes walked between the columns at the top of the steps. Five men were approaching, four in a cluster – Callisthenes smiled grimly: these must be the Democrats. One walked by himself: tall, balding, with a sensitive, bronzed face, sharp beak-like nose, large eyes and firm mouth – that must be Meleager, Callisthenes concluded. If the truth be known he could tell little difference between them. To Callisthenes, all politicians looked the same: wealthy, powerful and very, very dangerous.

The five men came up the steps. Meleager kept his distance, and the other four hardly spared their companion a glance. Aristander seemed to enjoy their predicament. He gathered them in the shade of the portico, gesturing at them to draw close. Telamon stood behind him.

"I won't waste time," Aristander smirked, "in introductions. I believe you gentlemen know each other very well."

Meleager smiled imperceptibly. He looked Aristander from head to toe, then his gaze shifted to Telamon. The four Democrats remained grim-faced.

"The Oligarchs should thank the gods," Agis gestured at the temple doors, "they are still allowed to walk the streets of Ephesus."

"With assassins like yourselves," Meleager jibed, turning his back, "it's surprising anyone walks the streets of Ephesus."

"Now, now, now," Aristander purred. He grasped Meleager by the elbow and turned him round to face the others. "The king's instructions are very clear. Peace and reconciliation will reign in

Ephesus. We have soldiers enough to enforce it," he added tartly. "Isn't that correct, Telamon?"

The physician stared back as if bored by the proceedings.

"Now, what we're going to do," Aristander continued lightly, "is open the temple doors. Inside reside six Oligarchs, their servant and one of the king's soldiers. The seven Ephesians have taken refuge there. Alexander has sworn their lives and goods are both safe and sacred. You," he jabbed a finger in Agis's face, "are here to guarantee that promise. Persuade these gentlemen to leave. Now, without any more fuss."

Aristander drew from beneath his cloak a leather pouch. He undid the cord and drew out a thick, brass key: he held this up as if it would provide entrance to Hades.

"Last night Telamon and I visited the sanctuary to ensure all was safe. They had food and wine. All should be well."

Aristander walked dramatically to the temple door: he inserted the key, turning it with difficulty, drew it out and beckoned at Callisthenes and the soldiers to pull back the heavy cedarwood doors. These creaked open. Inside stood a small vestibule, a stone seat on either side where the porters would usually sit. A recess led to a further set of doors, smaller, made of heavy oak and bound with clasps of iron. Another key was produced and these doors were opened. Callisthenes himself pushed them back. He had hardly taken two paces inside the temple itself when he realized something was wrong.

The light was very poor. The sun's rays had yet to pierce the windows high in the walls. The cresset torches had flickered out: all he could see was the great bed of charcoal spluttering and glowing in the darkness around the plinth which no longer bore the silver embossed vase.

Callisthenes stood, mouth open. He forgot about his companions, so shocked by the deathly silence and that odour, the smell of blood, the stench of the battlefield and, ranker and fouler, that of burning human flesh. Callisthenes had taken part in the sack of many a city and recognized that smell.

"What is it? What is it?" Aristander came up beside him. "Why is it so dark? Captain, what is the matter?"

21

Telamon walked forward, eyes growing accustomed to the gloom. "In the name of all that's sacred!" the physician whispered. "Look!"

He peered through the gloom and saw the corpses sprawled in congealing pools of blood on the temple floor. He heard the scamper of a rat, the buzz of a fly. Telamon broke free of his trance.

"Torches!" he shouted. "Bring torches!"

For a while confusion reigned. Meleager tried to go forward, but Callisthenes pulled him back.

"That's right, Captain," Telamon declared. "No one is to go forward or move around."

Torches were lit. Callisthenes grasped one and walked deep into the temple. A narrow, sombre hall, pillars and dark aisles on either side, swept up to a gigantic statue of Hercules at the far end. The torchlight revealed a chamber of horror.

Telamon moved to the first corpse and turned it over. The man was dressed in a simple tunic, no sandals on his feet, the right side of his head and face a mess of blood and brain. Someone had taken a club and smashed in his skull.

The Ephesians began to quarrel. Meleager, cursing, accused his opponents of treachery; they retorted with cries of innocence. Telamon demanded silence: when the politicians ignored him he gestured at Callisthenes to draw his sword. The sound of scraping steel as Callisthenes and his unit obeyed forced silence.

Telamon led the soldiers forward towards the statue of Hercules, and as they approached it the scene of carnage became more apparent. Corpses sprawled everywhere, and just beneath the statue lay one set of hideous remains, blackened by fire.

Aristander stood shocked, his gaze moving from corpse to corpse.

"We found him!" a soldier cried.

Callisthenes hurried forward, stepping over corpses. Beside a pillar lay Procanus. The soldier still wore his corselet and war kilt but his legs and feet were bare, his helmet had rolled into a corner: he, like the others, had his face and skull cruelly crushed, features disfigured, smeared with blood and brains.

"What is it, Captain?"

Callisthenes searched for the soldier's war belt and glimpsed it hanging from a small hook on the wall of the aisle.

"One of my men." Callisthenes swore under his breath. "I put him here with the rest."

People were now milling about. The physician came over and grasped Callisthenes by the arm.

"Captain, I am going to withdraw. I will take everyone who came into the temple this morning outside. You and your soldiers remain."

"He can't be trusted either," Aristander screeched: his words died on his lips as Callisthenes raised his head and glowered at him.

"He can be trusted," Telamon retorted. "Callisthenes was on guard. You know and I know he kept faithful vigil. The king trusts him."

Callisthenes smiled at the physician.

"What I suggest," Telamon added firmly, "is that we all leave. No corpses are to be moved, nothing is to be touched. Captain, stay here with your men: they can act as torch-bearers. I want you to inspect the temple and everything within it. We shall wait for you outside."

Aristander made to object.

"It's the only way," Telamon declared. "I don't want the waters to be muddied. This is murder, treason, and the culprits must be found."

"But what culprits, sir?" Callisthenes whispered. "Everyone is dead. I swear on my life, after the doors were locked last night, no one even approached this place, certainly no one left. Look at the windows, they're too high to scale, too narrow for the smallest man. We heard no screams."

Telamon gestured towards the blackened remains at the far end of the temple. "And yet," he said, pointing to the plinth, "the great prize has gone and eight men are brutally murdered. Captain, we will wait outside."

Aristander shouted at the Ephesians to follow. They left the temple, Telamon even locking the second set of doors. For a while Callisthenes just stood, hands on his hips, staring down at the floor.

"Some bastard," he shouted, "did this! And we are not going to take the blame!"

23

"Procanus was a good soldier!" one of his men yelled back. "He would have fought for his life, but he didn't even take down his war belt."

Callisthenes breathed in. He walked into the centre of the temple. The circle of charcoal surrounding the plinth was at least two yards wide. He drew his sword and dug into it and reckoned the charcoal must be at least nine inches deep: the bed of coals still glowed fiercely. Callisthenes flinched at the heat as he stared across at the plinth.

"How on earth," he whispered, "did someone cross this, take the silver vase out of the groove and bring it back?"

He walked round the circle. He could see no disturbance, while the light flagstones revealed no ash or dead coals. He drew a deep breath and sniffed. He had seen such temples before. Usually incense was sprinkled on the coals to provide a fragrant smell, but this was now missing: all Callisthenes could detect was the smell of human flesh. He told his men to stand with the torches and beckoned one over to examine the blackened remains which lay sprawled at the foot of the statue. Callisthenes crouched down. The man's features and body were nothing more than shrivelled black flesh: the eyes and lips had turned to water, the teeth blackened stumps, no tongue or gums. The rest of the corpse was indistinguishable. The vital organs had been shrivelled and the flesh torched. He touched the remains with his hand: cold, gruesome, like picking up a piece of meat from burnt oil. The corpse was twisted: Callisthenes concluded this must be due to the fire.

"What do you think happened, sir?" the soldier holding the torch asked.

Callisthenes pointed to the broad dark stain around the corpse. "This poor victim was covered in oil and set alight: he must have been dead first."

"Why is that?" the soldier asked.

"Well," Callisthenes replied, "do you remember when we took Olynthus and those bloody defenders poured down oil and threw torches? Men screaming, running like living firebrands. This man didn't run. He was already dead. He was consumed by fire,

24

probably oil from a wineskin poured all over him. A torch was brought . . ."

Callisthenes shrugged and got to his feet. He stared up at the great statue of Hercules dressed in the garb of a hunter, a club in one hand, a sword in the other, long hair falling down to his shoulders, a wreath about his forehead. The god's sightless eyes stared into the darkness.

"This is one occasion," Callisthenes murmured, "I wish a statue could speak. Eh, soldier?"

The captain recalled Telamon's orders. He studied the statue once again and went behind it. He examined the rear door of the temple, which was firmly bolted. From the hinges and the dust on the floor the door hadn't been opened for some time, though the bolts at top and bottom were freshly oiled. Another corpse sprawled here, almost hidden by the shadows, a jug lying beside him. Callisthenes ignored both, more determined to find some secret entrance to explain these hideous murders. He checked the small rear *cella* and the dark aisles, yet they were as he had found outside, undisturbed, the stone unbroken and unyielding. He examined the base of the statue, the flagstones around it.

"What are you looking for, sir?"

"A secret entrance?" Callisthenes swore. "Not even a fucking mouse could get in here!"

"There's something glinting over here, sir."

Callisthenes walked into the shadowy corner near the first set of doors: propped in a small recess stood the silver vase he had seen on the plinth. He picked it up and examined it carefully. It was heavy silver, and the outside bore a frieze depicting Hercules chasing a fawn. The top was fretted with precious stones, none of which had been disturbed. Callisthenes thrust his hand inside: it was empty.

He crouched down and peered into the recess. It contained nothing but earthenware jars used in the temple at times of sacrifice. They were all stoppered and sealed. Callisthenes pulled each one out, but they only contained oil.

"Well, at least we've found the sacred vase," he declared grimly.

"What was inside, sir?"

"It was supposed to contain the Hydra's poison, the venom which killed Hercules."

"Wouldn't that have disappeared over the years, sir?"

"Of course it did." Callisthenes smiled. "But you know what priests are like. If they said that vase contained Zeus's balls most people would believe them. Let's look at the corpses."

Callisthenes moved from corpse to corpse. They were all the same: features unrecognizable, foreheads and faces smashed in. Callisthenes recognized a pattern: the victims bore similar wounds, one on the side of the head, the other on the face or forehead. Each was shaped the same. Callisthenes was so disbelieving he called over his second-in-command.

"Study the corpse," he said quickly.

The soldier did so.

"I don't believe it," he muttered, getting to his feet. "Do you know something, sir, when I came in here I caught a whiff of a stable, as if a horse had been here."

Callisthenes shook his head.

"I smelt the same, sir," another soldier shouted.

Callisthenes went over to the last corpse, near the rear entrance. This man was sprawled on his side, his back to them, as if he had fallen asleep. Callisthenes pulled him over, moving away the heavy earthenware jug, and held a hand up.

"This one's different. Look!"

He dragged the corpse into the pool of torchlight. The corpse's face and head bore no death wound except for cruel claw marks along his cheeks and down his left arm, as if he had been mauled by some great cat. The corpse's face was swollen, slightly purplish, a white froth dried on his lips: the muscles were rigid, jaw clenched, the open, unseeing eyes slightly popping.

"Why is this one different?" Callisthenes murmured.

He pulled up the man's tunic to expose a muscular, sunburnt body: the stomach was now slightly distended. He examined the man's fingers: they were clean, the nails pared, the muscles, like the rest of the corpse, slightly hardened.

"Well, soldier?" Callisthenes stared up at his lieutenant. "What do you make of this?"

26

"Well, sir, it appears there were eight men in this temple. One of them was a soldier, another a servant." He pointed at the claw-marked corpse. "I would say he's the servant: his clothing is of poorer quality than the rest."

"Good!" Callisthenes got to his feet. "And the others?"

"Erm, one's been burnt. We don't know how he died."

"And the others?"

"I —" The soldier took off his helmet and scratched his sweat-soaked hair. "I don't know how to put this."

"I'm waiting."

"Well, sir, the others look" — the soldier stared sheepishly at his officer — "they look as if they've been stomped on."

"Stomped?" Callisthenes mocked. "What do you mean?"

"You know full well, sir. Each corpse bears two blows: one to the side of the head, one to the front. Now an axe or sword cuts deep. A club?" He shrugged. "Well, it just leaves a hideous mess."

"But?" Callisthenes insisted.

"Well, you can trace a pattern here. Each blow is in the same shape, of a horse's hoof. Yet I can't believe that."

"Why not, soldier?"

"Sir, these are men of fighting age: one or two rather old, but still capable of defending themselves."

"Go on," Callisthenes urged softly.

"It looks as if a horse came in here and stamped on each man as he lay asleep: one blow to the side of the head, one to the face."

"And this horse," Callisthenes added testily, "then set fire to another corpse, clawed this man to death, crossed the bed of charcoal, took the silver vase from the plinth, stole what was inside and disappeared into thin air."

"Well, er, yes, sir."

"And who is going to report this to Aristander?" Callisthenes pushed his face closer.

"You, Captain, you're the one in charge."

Callisthenes groaned and stepped away.

"There's more to it than that, sir. Why didn't these men resist? Fight back? Scream? Yell? Shout for assistance? Procanus wasn't a new recruit. He didn't even draw his sword."

"Perhaps they were drugged?" another soldier called out. "Sir, there's a table over here with wine and food on."

Callisthenes had glimpsed this before but ignored it. He walked across and pulled back the linen cloth. It covered a number of cups and two large jugs. He sniffed at these: one bore water, the other wine: some bread, now stale, cheese and what remained of dry fruit, dates, figs and some cherries. Callisthenes examined these carefully.

"This was brought in last night," he said.

He picked up the food: the cheese had turned rancid, and most of the wine and water had been drunk; the cups were still stained. Callisthenes picked up the jug and filled a goblet.

"I wouldn't do that if I were you, sir."

Callisthenes pulled a face and lifted the goblet. "It's good wine." He drank it in one gulp, filled the goblet with water and did likewise.

"What are you doing, Captain?"

Callisthenes slouched down at the base of the pillar and stared across at his helmet on the other side of the temple.

"I'm looking for a way out," he declared grimly. "If I fall asleep, or have convulsions," he grinned at his lieutenant, "then you have to make the report. By the gods, I don't know what to say!"

Callisthenes sat but, apart from a slight discomfort in his stomach at having drunk so quickly, he could feel no ill effects. He became engrossed in a faded painting on the far wall depicting two centaurs, armed with clubs, rearing up against each other. Callisthenes shivered. Was that what had happened here? Had a Centaur, one of Hercules's enemies, entered this temple last night to wreak such bloody havoc?

Murder had made its home in Ephesus. The porter at the House of Medusa, an ancient rambling mansion in the Street of Sighs near the Pottery Quarter, wasn't yet aware of this. He sat in his little booth just inside the main gateway watching the sun rise, squinted up at the sky and chomped on toothless gums, wiping away the saliva with the back of his hand. The porter didn't sleep much, as he told friends in the beer shops and wine booths: "When you sleep you are close to death, and the two might get confused." Instead he would stay awake, reflecting on the past, staring up at the skies or wandering the overgrown garden. In spring he would watch for the buds to bloom, and in late summer and autumn, collect the fallen fruit. He had been porter at the House of Medusa for many a year: he knew all its legends and grisly stories, but no one really believed him. The house passed from hand to hand, one purchaser after another. All its occupants complained that the place was haunted, possessed an eerie, ghostly atmosphere which chilled the blood even as it quickened the heart. The old porter laughed. If there were ghosts, they were his friends. The mansion was old, the plaster flaking; its timbers creaked, and when the wind sprang up the old building seemed to sing, but that was just the passing of the years.

The porter sniffed. The air was sweet with the freshness of grass, leaves, the scent of olives and figs. He relished the odour. He loved his own small lodge, so he always made himself welcoming and industrious to whoever occupied the house.

"Indispensable", that's how one occupant had described the porter. He could always tell the new occupants which was the best market to visit, where the cheapest oil could be bought. Above all, the porter always kept his mouth shut. What he saw was best kept a secret. After all, he didn't want to frighten people off.

Nevertheless, something had disturbed him. A few days ago, while the massacres were taking place in the city, he had heard a commotion, gone out and glimpsed the beggar for the first time for many a month. Scraggy hair and beard almost hid the man's face. He wore a tunic which hung like a tattered sack, battered sandals on his feet, staff in one hand. The beggar had been further down the alleyway, studying the gateway as if fascinated by the picture of Medusa painted on the front, from which the house gained its name. The porter liked the painting: a severed head with staring eyes and gaping mouth, the hair twisting up like snakes. Well, it was a token of good luck, wasn't it? It kept away the evil spirits, or so he told each new purchaser. What he kept to himself was that the House of Medusa needed every piece of good luck it could acquire.

The porter rocked backwards and forwards. He recalled the stories about the hideous society of Centaurs who used to meet here when Malli owned the house. The porter never told anyone about that, not even Leonidas, but there again, the old veteran probably knew more than he did. Now, what should he be thinking about?

"Ah yes, the beggar," the porter murmured sleepily to himself.

The fellow had just been standing there, so he had gone up and asked him his business. The beggar's face was disfigured, a deep scar down his right cheek, one eye permanently closed, the other gleaming expectantly.

"What's your name?" the porter had asked.

"Why," the fellow replied in a rough accent, "my name is Cyclops, but that's my business."

"And why are you standing here looking at the house?"

"Ah well, that's my business too, isn't it?"

The porter would have asked more questions, but the beggar had a sinister appearance. His chin jutted out in a threatening manner, he looked strong and wiry, and he twirled the staff as a soldier would a spear. The porter had retreated to the safety of the gates and slammed them shut. Nevertheless, over the last few days, he had glimpsed Cyclops again, either outside the gates or along the curtain wall, staring up like a cat ready to jump. The porter's suspicions had deepened.

"I'm sure I've seen him before," he murmured.

Well, he was safe enough now. The house had been empty when the Macedonians entered the city and the Persians fled; now his old friend Leonidas had returned. The grizzled veteran took over the house, as he had when the Macedonians entered Ephesus before. Leonidas looked older but still as cheerful and blustery as ever. He had brought out a jug of wine and shared it with the porter, asking him how the house had fared since he had last been there. The porter had acted stupid, as if he knew nothing about the stories of Malli, the Centaurs, the rumours of hidden treasure or what might have happened here two years ago. What was all that to him? He did not want to alarm Leonidas, who had brought two other soldiers with him. The porter screwed up his eyes. He had forgotten their names: young men with cruel eyes, men of iron and blood, warriors. They had not been so friendly. In fact, if they had had their way Leonidas would have dismissed him, but the porter was useful. He told the old Macedonian all the gossip of Ephesus, or at least what he knew, and how the House of Medusa had lain fairly quiet for the last two years.

Leonidas and his two companions had set up house. They had brought a maid and, because they were conquerors, soon had food and all the other comforts of life. Leonidas still liked his wine. He and one of his companions had gone out the previous evening and returned long after midnight.

"Drunk as cats on milk," Leonidas's companion had slurred as he helped the old soldier through the gate and along the side of the house. The porter had sat and watched the lamps glow in the upstairs window. He had heard singing, a filthy song about a young girl who had taken up with a soldier, but afterwards, silence.

In a drunken stupor more likely, the porter reflected. Yet Leonidas, for all that, could hold his wine. The porter had glimpsed him leaving, only a short while ago, out of the side door and across the orchard. The cold morning breeze made the porter shiver. He climbed off his high wooden stool, left the booth and walked across the grass. In fact, he hadn't seen Leonidas return. He had left by the side entrance as if he were searching for something. The porter ambled across the dew-wet grass. The cold water made him flinch, but now he was curious.

"Leonidas, sir!" he called.

He entered a small grove of trees and peered through the murky half-light. He could glimpse no torch glow. He went through the trees and across to the long, rectangular pool surrounded by brambles, its edges overgrown, the water dirty. The porter called Leonidas's name again – the only answer was the angry chatter of some bird high in the trees. He pushed through the brambles. Perhaps Leonidas was sitting by the pool.

He paused at the edge and stared in horror: floating face down was the old soldier, cloak billowing out around him. The porter flapped his hands.

"Sir!" he called, crouching down.

Leonidas didn't answer. He floated like some dead fish, his steel-grey hair spreading out, gnarled hands clenched, his great water-logged cloak moving slowly with the ripples of the water.

Chapter 1

<hr />

"In Ephesus . . . all things were tending to turbulence and effusion of blood, when Alexander, interposing, arrested the outrages of the rabble."

Quintus Curtius Rufus,
The History of Alexander The Great, Book II, Chapter 7

"**I** tell you," Telamon declared, "the method works."

The other physicians shook their heads. They were seated around a cloth in the gardens of the Persian Governor's residence on the outskirts of Ephesus: an oasis of greenery with watered lawns where gorgeous peacocks strutted and cried. The garden was dotted with apple, pomegranate and cherry orchards as well as shaded, vine-covered pergolas and summer houses. A lake, covered with lotus blossoms, glinted in the centre: lazy fat carp made its silvery surface ripple in their constant hunt for flies.

Telamon's declaration was greeted with silence and disbelieving looks. Such debates were now common among Alexander's retinue of physicians. Telamon felt as if he were always challenging the accepted wisdom, although he suspected his colleagues enjoyed teasing him. Perdicles, the cynical Athenian, sharp-faced under his thinning, black hair; Nicias of Corinth, a grey shadow of a man with deep-set eyes and a mouth ever ready to question; finally, the blond-haired, bland-faced Cleon, whom everyone regarded more as Alexander's spy than as his physician. Cassandra, Telamon's assistant, sat beside him, carefully peeling an apple before dividing it into slices.

"I've seen it done as well," she declared, stuffing her mouth.

The three physicians dismissed her remark.

"I've seen as many skull fissures as you." Her angry green eyes challenged each of them.

"So, what you are saying," Cleon drawled, "is that you shave a patient's skull and cover it with a thick, inky substance?"

"Of course," Telamon agreed, "you make sure none goes into his eyes or mouth. Usually the substance runs off but, like water on hardened mud, where there is a crack or fissure, it will settle."

"I must try that," Perdicles declared. "Though my patients will probably sue me!"

"Another method" – Cassandra would not be dismissed – "is to make the patient chew hard and watch the bones of the skull. If there is any fissure it will become obvious. You should do it quickly," she added. "Lesions at the front of the skull are more dangerous than those at the back. Moreover, if the patient shows symptoms of fever or dizziness, it means the brain has been damaged."

"Who said that?" Cleon jibed.

"Hippocrates," Cassandra taunted.

Cleon nearly choked on his roast goose.

"I can give you chapter and verse," she teased.

Cleon shook his head.

"I have also tried," Telamon intervened quickly, "an ingenious method to heal fractures below the knee. Take twigs from a cormel tree . . ."

"The same wood sarissas are made of?" Nicias referred to the eighteen-foot spear carried by the Macedonian phalanx.

"The same," Telamon agreed. "Wrapped and padded around the patient's leg, one just above the ankle, the other just below the knee. Take four twigs" – he spread his hands – "a little longer than the distance between the padded rings, and force these between the rings as if you were making a basket."

"What happens then?" Perdicles asked.

Telamon heard voices from behind a clump of bushes.

"The slightly bent twigs have a tendency to spring into a straight line, so they constantly force the two rings apart."

"And?" Cleon demanded.

34

"The body weight is moved from the ankle to the knee, allowing the broken bone to settle and heal properly."

The cries of disapproval died on their lips as Aristander appeared, surrounded by his bodyguard, burly Celtic mercenaries dressed in a motley collection of armour: even in the heat, they still wore their fur-lined robes. Telamon found it hard to distinguish one from the other with their long, blond hair, moustaches and beards. Aristander called them his "lovely boys". Telamon secretly considered them a gang of murdering rogues, though they always treated him with great affection: he tended their minor wounds, scrapes and constant belly ailments caused by their heavy drinking.

Aristander stopped in front of the physicians and glared down at them. He was dressed in the light-blue robe and mantle of a woman, edged with gold and silver bands, plundered from some Persian wardrobe: heavy make-up painted his face.

"I have taught them new verses," he declared. "We are rehearsing Euripides's *Hippolytus*, marvellous work!" Aristander loved to teach his bodyguard the works of the great playwrights: he always insisted everyone listen and praise his "lovely boys'" scholarship.

" 'Gifts from enemies'," Telamon murmured, " 'are no gifts and they bring no good.' "

"What was that?" Aristander demanded.

"Nothing," Telamon grinned. "Just a line from Sophocles's *Ajax*."

"Have you forgotten your Aristotle?" Aristander taunted. "Chapter Two of the *Poetics*?"

"I know what you're going to say," Telamon replied. "According to Aristotle, Sophocles claimed men could be as they wanted to be, but Euripides accepted them as they are."

Aristander sniffed and turned away. "Right gentlemen, form a chorus."

Telamon sighed: whatever the physicians wanted, Aristander would have his way. The chorus stood in a line, hands extended, faces all mournful.

" 'My tongue swore though my mind was still unpledged' . . ."

They would have continued their chanting but a page boy, as

35

fleet as a deer, came racing across the lawn, shouting their names. Telamon sprang to his feet.

"The king!" the page gasped, slithering to a stop. "The king wishes to see you now!"

Aristander's hand shot out like the claw of a hunting bird. "Whom does the king wish to see, boy?"

"Why you, sir, and the physician Telamon."

A short while later Aristander and Telamon, the chorus sweeping behind them, entered the royal quarters at the far end of the Governor's palace. They marched along the polished oak floor, whitewashed walls on either side hung with bright cloths. They were stopped halfway down by members of the royal bodyguard, Foot Companions dressed in full ceremonial armour, purple breastplates and kilts over snow-white tunics, their helmets decorated with plumes: they had drawn their swords as if expecting a sudden attack by all the might of Persia. The officer recognized them but insisted on protocol: despite Aristander's loud protests, he searched them for hidden weapons before allowing them through.

Alexander had taken lodgings in the Hyacinth Chamber, an exquisitely decorated room, its unshuttered windows opening on the gardens below. It was filled with delicate furniture: tables, chairs, stools and quilted foot-rests cushioned with precious fabrics, the costly acacia, sycamore and terebinth wood inlaid with onyx, silver or gold. Blood-red roses decorated the ceiling, dark-blue hyacinths the gleaming walls. The floor was of highly polished wood. In the centre of the room was a small pool of purity served by hidden pipes: rose petals floated on the surface, spreading their own cloying fragrance. Over these buzzed the busy wasps which plagued this palace: the king had protested about these and members of his bodyguard were gingerly searching out the nests which hung under the eaves, in cellars or any available recess.

Alexander had transformed all this into his headquarters: one adjoining chamber served as his chancery, another as his sleeping quarters. He was sprawled in the throne-like chair, turned to catch the breeze from one of the windows. On a stool beside him sat his bosom friend, the dark-featured, anxious-faced Hephaestion. He held the king's right hand, rubbing the fingers gently between his own, talking quietly. Alexander seemed unaware of either Hephaestion or the approach of Aristander and Telamon. He slumped halfway down in the chair, plucking at the light-green tunic he wore. He beat his feet in a silent tattoo on the floor and waved away the occasional marauding wasp.

Hephaestion rose to greet them. He looked heavy-eyed from lack of sleep. Like the king's, his face was unshaven, his dark hair ruffled. He brought up two camp stools so Aristander and Telamon could sit facing the king. Alexander kept staring at the window, one finger in his mouth: a small trickle of saliva coursed down his chin and dropped unnoticed onto his tunic.

"Are you well, my lord?"

Alexander blinked.

"My lord, are you well?" Telamon repeated.

"It's some evil spirit," Aristander whispered. "The king has been cursed."

"Nonsense!" Telamon leaned forward and grasped the king's wrist. He felt the irregular pulse and noticed the beads of sweat beneath the red-gold hair.

At times Alexander could look what he pretended to be, the man-god, with his beautiful eyes and clean-cut, regular features: when his face was shaved and gleaming with oil, a fillet round his hair, he looked as fit and keen as any athlete in the Olympiad. He now looked, as Telamon secretly knew to be the truth, drunk, with a heavy hangover and a bad night's sleep: this in turn had provoked a sudden panic attack, a deep anxiety state when Alexander became frenetic and quarrelsome. The king's face looked flushed, slightly swollen, his eyes more deep-set.

Alexander moved his head slightly to the right, a favourite gesture which even his courtiers now imitated. "Let go of my wrist, physician!"

"Well said, sir," Telamon replied. "I am your physician and you are my patient."

Alexander pulled his hand away. "I have immortal longings," he complained.

"Haven't we all?"

Alexander's face changed, creasing into a smile. He pulled

37

himself up in the chair, looked hard at Telamon then, throwing his head back, bellowed with laughter.

"Sober, dour Telamon, practical as ever! Where's that red–haired bitch of yours? Have you bounced her yet? I bet she takes to bed–wrestling like a bird to flying."

"My assistant Cassandra is outside in the garden," Telamon replied.

" 'Not to be born is the best of all,' " Alexander replied, quoting a line from Euripides. "Next best," he continued, "is, having been born, to return as quickly as possible from whence you came."

Telamon glanced quickly at Hephaestion, who shook his head. When Alexander began to reflect upon mortality, especially after too many cups of wine, his mood became positively dangerous.

"Why do you put me down, Telamon? Why don't you pander to me?"

"Hephaestion doesn't either. I don't like to talk about sex," Telamon said. "What happens in my bedchamber is a matter for me, not for you!"

Alexander's head went to the side again. "Have you read Plato's *Republic* recently, physician?"

"You know I haven't."

"Someone asked Sophocles the playwright," Alexander murmured, " 'How do you stand in matters of love? Are you still able to have sex with a woman?' 'Keep quiet,' the playwright replied, 'I have left all that behind me very gladly; I have escaped from a mad and savage master'."

"He had a slave girl brought to him." Hephaestion pulled a face.

"And were you impotent?" Telamon asked bluntly.

Alexander's head went down and he laughed softly. " 'Always to excel and be distinguished above all others,' " he replied, quoting from the *Iliad*.

Telamon pushed back the stool. "Oh, don't be dramatic, Alexander! It's well known that heavy drinking interferes with sexual prowess. You know it, I know it, your soldiers know it. Even the baboons in the royal menagerie know it."

"My lord," Aristander intervened, "Telamon tended to you this morning. You'd been sick, unable to stand. You were trembling and, despite the heat, complained of the cold."

"I've had a letter from Mother!"

The words cut like a whiplash through the room. Telamon closed his eyes and sighed. Olympias the Witch Queen! She could upset her son, with one line, more than a charging troop of Persian cavalry.

"She says the treasury is empty, that she has already spent the wealth I sent her after Granicus. She wants me to come home."

"But you can't," Hephaestion soothed. "You have business, my lord, business here and in Persepolis."

Alexander leaned forward, resting his elbows on the arm of the throne. "I drank too much." He glanced sheepishly at Telamon. "I'm sorry for that. I apologize for my remarks about Cassandra. I'll send her a gift. No, no." He lifted a hand. "A silver flute, I know she'll like that. I have also had dreams."

"Your father Philip?"

"Who?" Alexander's mood changed abruptly.

"Your father Philip?" Telamon repeated.

"Was he my father?"

"You know he was."

"He's entering the ampitheatre at Pella." Alexander licked his lips. "And the shadows are all about him, the assassin's racing forward. I see the knife glinting in his hand. Philip falls to his knees; his eyes beg me for life even as he spits the lifeblood from his mouth."

"Olympias mentioned Philip again, didn't she?" Telamon leaned forward and grasped the king's cold hand. "She hinted once again, as she always does, that you are not really Philip's son but the offspring of a god. That Artemis left her temple here in Ephesus to assist your birth. It's all dreams, sire. Nothing but vapour in the air. If you drank some good clear water, ate hot oatmeal, went for a walk and smelt the flowers, you'd feel a thousand times better!"

The king abruptly sprang to his feet, pushed past them and walked off to his bedchamber. Telamon stared at Hephaestion, who raised his eyes heavenwards and shrugged.

"He drank too much," the king's companion whispered. "Three-quarters wine, one quarter water. He fell asleep on his couch. I had to take him to bed myself. The rest you know. I am sorry you have been waiting so long. There is other news?"

"We have other news," Telamon replied. "The Temple of Hercules?"

Hephaestion nodded. Telamon recalled that long macabre temple room: its murky gloom, the narrow shafts of light, those corpses, battered and mauled, lying about. The blackened remains beneath the statue, the strange smell, the confusion and consternation of Callisthenes who reported accurately on what he had found, totally mystified about how such a massacre could have taken place. The news had swept the city. Alexander, when he'd heard it, had fallen into a royal paroxysm of rage which accounted for his heavy drinking bout the previous evening.

"He's also heard," Hephaestion said, looking over his shoulder, keeping his voice to a whisper, "about the death of one of his father's companions. You remember Leonidas?"

"Leonidas!" Telamon exclaimed. "One of Cleitus's old drinking friends! Every second word was a curse."

"A brave fighter," Hephaestion remarked. He paused at sounds from outside.

"Oh, don't worry," Aristander explained, "that's my chorus! They don't like being kept waiting and they're probably showing off to the royal bodyguard."

"Whether they like it or not," Telamon grinned, "they'll be quoting every line from Euripides they know."

Two wasps, buzzing like the Furies, came to hover over a wine stain on the floor. Hephaestion lashed out with his foot. "A damn nuisance!" he muttered. "They have nests all over this palace, in the cellars, the lofts . . ."

"We should search out their nests." Aristander flapped a hand as a wasp circled his head.

"Your perfume attracts them," Telamon laughed. "They like . . ."

Alexander appeared in the doorway. He had changed his tunic and splashed his face and hair with water. He clapped his hands and strode forward.

"Enough of self-pity." He retook his seat. "I've had my little tantrum. Hephaestion, is Ephesus under control?"

"The citizens love you, sire."

"Aye, as they do Darius's bollocks!" Alexander quipped. "But the massacres have stopped?"

"There's no more killing, sire. Your order has been proclaimed. Any disturbance is to be punished, under martial law, by instant death. The markets are open, the streets are clean and cleared, everyone is going about their normal business."

"And my lads?" Alexander rubbed his face. "My golden boys, my soldiers?"

"Some are camped in the city, where the officers have their quarters, the rest are beyond the walls. They are all living on the fat of the land, filling their bellies with milk and honey, meat and beer."

"And wine," Alexander added drily, winking at Telamon. "Now."

He sat back in the chair, rocking himself gently. Telamon watched curiously. Alexander's moods could shift in the blink of an eye, from being full of self-pity to an imperious ruler, cunning general or astute politician. Alexander could be mean-fisted, petulant and foul-mouthed. Yet, if the mood suited him, he'd give up this entire palace to some poor widow woman. Telamon only hoped the king was not in one of his fickle moods.

"We'll rest here." Alexander's different-coloured eyes narrowed as if he could see something outside the window and was studying it carefully. "We will rest here," he repeated, "and then we'll strike south-west to Miletus. What's the problem there, Hephaestion?" Alexander had decided to lecture them on strategy.

"It's a port," his companion replied. "It possesses a good harbour."

"But?"

"But," Hephaestion agreed, "it's heavily fortified by our old enemy, Memnon of Rhodes, who can be provisioned from the sea by the Persian fleet."

"So how do we take it?"

Hephaestion gazed blankly back.

41

"Ah well," Alexander sighed. "Before we march, Ephesus must be quiet. Now, Telamon, the Temple of Hercules. He was my ancestor, you know. Mother said . . ."

"I know what your mother said," Telamon retorted. "What's more important, sire, is what you said. You swore great oaths that the men who took sanctuary there would not be harmed, not a hair on their heads."

Alexander's eyes flashed angrily. "I know what I said," he grated. "Now the Ephesians think I can't, or won't, keep my word. I want to know what happened."

"They claim a centaur entered the temple." Aristander spoke up. "Half-man, half-horse, the old enemy of Hercules. He stamped those men to death, clawed the face of one and burnt that unfortunate with fire from his mouth."

Alexander looked solemnly at his Master of Secrets.

"Did you know Artemis was my mother?" Telamon asked. "And that she suckled me at her breast?"

The king began to laugh: Hephaestion joined in; Aristander sat all prim and proper.

"What are you saying, Telamon?"

"I'm saying that if a centaur entered that temple and committed those murders, then Artemis is my mother."

"I know who your mother was," Aristander added peevishly.

This only brought fresh bellows of laughter. Alexander held a hand up.

"Physician, tell me your story. Aristander, for the moment, please" – he glared at his necromancer – "keep your mouth shut!"

"Two weeks ago," Telamon began, ignoring Aristander's sniff of annoyance, "a few Macedonian troops entered Ephesus: the blood-letting began. You, my lord, allowed that to continue."

"I had no choice!" Alexander snapped.

"You had every choice. Instead you chose to let the Democrats have their vengeance. Executions were carried out, as were massacres, rioting, pillaging and looting. A week ago you stopped it. However, leading members of the Oligarchs, with their leader Demades and his servant Socrates, took refuge in the Temple of Hercules."

"Why should they go there?" Hephaestion demanded.

"Because it was a temple frequented by their party. A sort of shrine, a chapel, it's quite common here," Telamon explained. "Certain citizens pay their devotions to Artemis, others to Poseidon, Apollo."

"You don't believe in the gods, do you?" Alexander taunted.

"I am not too sure, sire. Even if I did, I'd have fresh difficulty in accepting that they believe in us. Anyway, the temples were safe. No one wishes to incur the anger of the gods. The Temple of Hercules was different. Its principal priest was assassinated on the steps, his assistants and helpers were given a good beating and fled." Telamon held a hand up to fend off questions. "We don't know why, but I suspect the priest was considered a member of the Oligarch faction: he had been party to their councils and deliberations and so paid the penalty. Nevertheless, Demades and his followers knew that once inside the temple they were safe."

"How did they escape the massacre?" Aristander asked.

"We don't know. They probably hid out in their houses or the countryside. Once the massacres ended, they gathered at Demades's mansion, made their way to the temple, guarded by Macedonian troops, and got themselves safely inside. They took very little with them and sent a message to us explaining that they feared for their lives and safety. They declared they would shelter in the temple until they received fresh assurances from our king."

"By that time," Alexander declared, "the city was safe and secure. The other Oligarchs had emerged from their hiding-holes: powerful men, merchants, city officials, a few priests. I need their help as much as they need mine. They, too, were vociferous in their demands that Demades and his party be respected. Go on, Telamon."

"They were in the temple about seven days. They took no weapons in accordance with the ritual, and were only provided with food, drink and a change of clothing."

"How did they relieve themselves?" Hephaestion demanded.

"I broached that." Telamon smiled. "They claimed to have good bowels and bladders. During the day they would demand an escort to the nearest privy — that was the last thing they did before the temple doors were sealed at night."

"And they *were* sealed," Alexander agreed. "There's an inner and outer door. The rear entrance is bolted from the inside and hasn't been opened for some months." He stared at Telamon.

"Sire, you are correct. The windows are high and narrow. I have had the place searched: no secret entrances or passageways exist. The temple is a very simple building, stark and solid – perhaps that's why Demades chose it? It's an ancient place, quite simple in design. The roof is heavily beamed." Telamon used his hands to describe it. "Columns down the sides support this. The aisles are bare. At the far end stands a majestic statue of Hercules."

"And the shrine?" Alexander asked eagerly.

"Oh yes, the shrine. I have visited similar temples throughout Lydia and Greece which hold sacred objects. In this case it was a silver vase which, allegedly, held a simple pottery jar containing some of the poison which killed Hercules."

"The Hydra's blood!" Alexander's eyes sparkled like a child's. "I always wanted to see that! I remember Mother telling me the story. How Nessus the Centaur gave it to Hercules's lover. If I had . . ."

"We don't know what was in it," Telamon intervened smoothly. "But the silver vase stood on a stone plinth in a bed of concrete. A recess at the top of the plinth kept the vase secure. It was protected by a circular pit two yards wide, full of glowing charcoal, the heat from it quite intense."

"So no one could cross it?" Hephaestion murmured.

"No, that's how the vase kept its secret. Knowledge of its contents was passed from priest to priest. The last incumbent died abruptly, so the true contents of that silver vase cannot be discerned."

"How did the priest cross over?" Aristander wondered.

"Apparently, when each new priest was installed," Telamon explained, "the charcoal was allowed to die, the ashes to cool, the pit was cleared." He pulled a face. "The priest walks across. He takes the vase down and, in the sanctity of the temple, is allowed to inspect its contents."

"And the murders?" Alexander demanded.

"The temple was ringed and guarded by soldiers," Telamon continued, choosing his words carefully. "I trust Callisthenes.

There was no reason for any Macedonian to become involved in city politics."

"I agree. I agree." Alexander looked absent-minded, as if still wondering about the contents of that silver vase.

"The night before last," Telamon tapped Aristander's arm, "both of us went down to the temple on your orders. We met Demades and the rest. We repeated your solemn assurances. We described how we would return the following morning together with leaders of the Democrats. Meleager, who'd been so insistent that Demades leave the temple and retake his position in civic life, would also be present."

"They all seemed hale and hearty enough to me." Aristander spoke up. "They claimed to be missing their families, said how they wished to have a bath and change their clothes."

"They accepted your assurances?" Alexander asked.

"Oh yes. They said they would leave the temple the following morning, provided we two returned," Aristander explained. "On previous nights the captain of the guard had locked the temple and kept the keys on his person. Demades asked if we would take the keys with us. I agreed and asked if they wanted anything else. They replied, their freedom."

"Were they all the same?" Hephaestion asked. "No one sullen or withdrawn?"

"No."

Telamon licked his lips. His throat and mouth were dry: he recalled the refreshing fruit juices he and Cassandra had been drinking out in the garden. But, as was his habit when the king was absorbed in a problem, everything else, including food and drink, was forgotten.

"They all seemed eager to leave, especially Socrates. Demades's servant. He claimed the temple was haunted, full of shifting shadows."

"Did he explain?"

Telamon shook his head. "Demades snapped at him, said he was too superstitious for his own good. Moreover" – Telamon held a hand up – "one of Callisthenes's guards, fully armed, also stayed in the temple, as he had the previous two evenings. Demades appreciated that. He said he trusted Macedon's word but not that of Agis and the other Democrats."

"The temple doors were secure," Aristander explained. "I locked both the inner and outer. They were sealed in."

"And the next morning?" Alexander asked.

"There were eight men in that temple," Telamon said. "It was protected and well guarded. Apart from the soldier, no one carried arms. Foodstuff, bread, cheese and wine, had been sent in."

"Is it possible other items were smuggled in?" Alexander leaned forward, face screwed up in concentration.

"It's possible," Telamon conceded. "But they'd be small, innocuous items. Anything out of the ordinary would have been stopped."

"Weapons?" Alexander demanded.

"Perhaps a small dagger but, according to Callisthenes, he saw nothing. Nor did his men."

"And were there visitors?"

"Members of the Oligarchs' families visited them, but these were searched. Again nothing suspicious was found. Callisthenes sampled what remained of the wine and food: neither was tainted. In fact, he said the wine was very good and shared what was left with his men. No weapons were discovered except those belonging to the soldier. No sign of a struggle, yet all eight men were killed." Telamon paused. "Callisthenes searched that temple for me, an objective witness. When he finished, Aristander and I did the same. We studied each of the eight victims. Some had been clubbed to death." Telamon used his hands to explain. "In the main, a blow to the side of the head and one to the front which shattered part of the skull and most of the face."

"A powerful blow?" Alexander asked.

"Very powerful. Six were killed in such a manner. They lay in pools of blood, cold and congealed, so the deaths must have occurred some hours earlier, I would guess shortly after midnight. The seventh victim was burnt beyond recognition. I don't know how he died. I have examined the skull, perhaps he was also struck on the side of his temple. Why and how he was burnt remains a mystery."

"And the marks of the blows were the same on each victim?"

"In my view, yes. They'd been struck with a heavy club."

"I disagree with that," Aristander intervened. "I have never seen a club carved in the shape of a horse's hoof."

"Is that true?" Alexander asked. "Did it look as if these victims had been killed by the hoof of a heavy war horse?"

Telamon stared past the king at one of the paintings on the wall: a beautiful girl, dressed in the finest drapery, one sandal slipping off as she performed a dance, a hyacinth in each hand: her face was long, she had sloe eyes and a full red mouth. Telamon's heart skipped a beat – in some ways she reminded him of Anuala, the heset girl, the woman he'd so passionately loved, and so despairingly lost, in Thebes in Egypt. What would she make of all this?

"Physician, I asked you a question." Alexander clicked his tongue in annoyance.

"According to the evidence," Telamon agreed, "it did look as if the hoof of a horse had smashed each of these victims in the side of the head and on the face."

"But there were no horses in the temple," Aristander taunted.

"The eighth victim –" Telamon chose to ignore the interruption "– was a much more curious case. He was scratched on his cheek and left arm. The marks were very similar to the claws of a cat."

"But no cat was in the temple," Aristander added mischievously.

"I don't think the claw marks killed him," Telamon continued lightly. "He was poisoned."

"What?" Alexander edged forward, head slightly to one side. "But you said the bread and wine were untainted?"

"If he had been clawed, the poison could have been on the claw," Telamon declared. "He was certainly poisoned, by what I don't know. However, the rigidity of his muscles, particularly the face, the tightness of the jaw, the colour of the tongue, his belly hard and distended, a milky-white froth staining his lips – all these indicate poison: a venomous snake, a certain sea fish or the extract from some plant or mineral."

"I want to discuss this further!"

All signs of heavy drinking and panic had disappeared from Alexander's face. He reminded Telamon of the young boy he had gone to school with at Aristotle's academy in the Groves of Mieza. Any problem intrigued Alexander. He liked to worry it as a cat would a rat.

"Could this man have been the assassin?" The king asked. "Killed the others and taken poison himself?"

"It's possible," Telamon conceded. "But that creates as many problems as it resolves. First, why? Second, how did one servant kill eight able men? Third, what weapon did he use? Fourth, what clawed him? Fifth, why should he take poison?"

The king remained silent.

"There are other questions. Demades's servant was called Socrates, wasn't he?"

Aristander agreed.

"How did Socrates burn one of the victims? How did he kill the others? Where was his weapon? How did he cross those fiery coals and take down the silver vase? What did he take out? We found nothing in the temple. Finally," Telamon sighed, "if Socrates had been the assassin, how was he going to explain it all when the temple guards broke in?"

His questions were greeted by surprised looks and shrugs.

"The same problem exists," Telamon continued slowly, "if we apply it to any of the other victims. I don't suppose the man consumed by fire killed everybody and committed an act of self-immolation."

"It grows ever more ridiculous," Alexander declared, getting to his feet, stretching till his muscles cracked. "If we work on the hypothesis that someone broke into the temple?"

"An impossible feat," Aristander replied. "No one was hiding there. We searched every nook and cranny of that temple."

"So who killed them?" Alexander wondered. "How and why? Where are the weapons? Where is the poison? How did the killer cross a bed of glowing charcoal?" He sat down and glanced sharply at Telamon. "I'm repeating your questions. So, there was no disturbance? No sign of any struggle? Nothing untoward? Are you sure the food and wine were untainted?"

"I am certain."

"Questions! Questions!" The king chewed his lip. "Nothing

untoward?" He raised his hand to his face and peered through his fingers at Telamon.

"One of the guards claimed that, during the night while he was patrolling, he caught the smell of burning, but that could be an illusion. Even if it were true, there have been fires in Ephesus, people burnt."

"Anything else?"

"One of the guards said he could smell horses, like a stable."

"And so we come back to the matter of centaurs," Aristander spoke up, preening himself. "You know the legend, sire, half-man, half-horse. The centaur had hooves, claws on his hands. He could call up magical fire, his blood was poisonous. He was surrounded by poisonous wasps."

"And could he go through stone and masonry?" Telamon pleaded.

"Perhaps." The necromancer played with a ring on his bony finger. "But we always come back to the centaurs. You may disagree, Telamon, but those murders could have been the work of a magician, a warlock."

"Like yourself?"

"Hush now," the king intervened. "Eight men dead," he whispered. "A bed of glowing charcoal crossed, the vase taken down, the relic stolen. More importantly, my assurances have turned out to be nothing but straw in the wind. Was the roof examined?"

"Callisthenes sent for the engineers," Telamon replied. "They could find no opening or gap, it is as solid and sturdy as the rest of the building."

Alexander grasped Telamon's wrist, his eyes cold and hard. "This is Ephesus, Telamon, the city of light and dark, life and death, blood and sunshine. It houses the shrine of Artemis. I have been mocked, and even more, but we'll discuss that in a short while. I am going to hate the name Centaur. No one ridicules Alexander of Macedon. Soon I leave for Miletus. I want Ephesus quiet behind me. I don't want the pot bubbling over and spoiling the rest. You pride yourself on being a physician, a man who studies symptoms and signs — then discover what's wrong here, who made a fool of me. Who dared mock my promise? Find him! Them, her, whoever!" He let go of Telamon's wrist.

The physician nursed his arm. Alexander made a face.

"I'm sorry, but in this case, physician heal thyself."

"We don't know the who, how or why about these murders," Telamon replied. "The Democrats could be settling final grievances with the Oligarchs, but to what point? They've had their revenge and are now in power. Perhaps it could be the work of a coven of Persian spies and assassins. But why should they turn against their former collaborators? Perhaps it was some private grudge or grievance." Telamon shrugged. "I know very little, except these murders are the work of man, not some mythical beast."

"In this case," Aristander huffed, "the centaur may not be mythical."

"Oh, don't start," Telamon groaned.

"I have seen men murdered by magic." Aristander couldn't resist the jibe. "But the Centaurs were more than mythical beasts as far as Ephesus is concerned. They were a group of assassins, professional killers."

"I have heard the story," Telamon agreed.

"However" – Aristander was now enjoying himself – "we know the Persians had a spy here." He crossed his legs and smoothed his mantle out as if he were a woman. "A very valuable spy who told Lord Mithra everything that happened in this city."

"How do you know this?" Telamon demanded. "Why didn't you tell me before?"

"We didn't know ourselves till yesterday evening." Aristander preened himself. "The Persian Governor and his staff fled; as we came in one gate they left by another. However, their principal scribe, Rabinus, moved a little too slowly. He decided to hide out in the house of a courtesan. Unfortunately for him, this love-nest was visited by one of our officers. Rabinus was detected. He tried to flee but was betrayed, captured, and now resides in the palace dungeons."

"Rabinus is a very frightened man," Alexander added. "I feel sorry for him. One of the little men caught up in great trouble. He doesn't want to die. He doesn't even want to be questioned. All he wants are assurances that he will go free, safe and unharmed."

"We are going to question him," Aristander replied. "You and I, Telamon, the king's eyes and ears. However, Rabinus has already talked. He has mentioned the Centaur."

"Does he know anything about the murder at the Temple of Hercules?"

Aristander shook his head. "No, he doesn't, and I for one believe him." The necromancer got to his feet and walked over to a water clock by the far corner of the room. "Agis and the rest will be arriving shortly to answer certain questions." He flounced back, sat down and stared at the king.

"And there is something else, isn't there, sire?" Telaman guessed.

Alexander turned and snapped his fingers. Hephaestion brought his cloak. The king swung this round his shoulders and fastened the clasp.

"Yes, there's something else, Telamon. I want to show you a corpse."

Chapter 2

"Darius is a man of folly, as he knoweth not the power of God Almighty."

The Alexander Book in Ethiopia

A rella the courtesan was, as customary at midday, preparing to take her bath. Arella regarded herself as one of the most beautiful whores in all of Ephesus, and one of the most expensive. Hadn't the great painters chosen her as a model for Artemis and Aphrodite? A woman no more than twenty summers old, Arella only sold her favours to the high and mighty, the rich and powerful of the city. She had risen late that morning: her maid had brought the usual breakfast of fruit and the light barley beer for which Arella had a liking. Now her maid hovered close to her, busy in the bedchamber, waiting for her mistress to go out into the garden and swim in the pool of purity. Afterwards Arella would dine, then retire for the afternoon to sleep, attend to business affairs and wait till the evening.

Arella believed in beautifying herself: her golden hair shimmered with oil and the most costly perfumes coated her snow-white body. Finger- and toenails had to be painted, teeth cleaned, mouth sweetened, robes selected, sandals chosen, while Arella could spend an hour over her jewellery casket deciding which item to wear. Arella's customers always came in the evening. No more than two at any one time, though of course, as Arella confided, laughing behind her fingers, one would have to wait while the other patron took his enjoyment. Arella was most selective. Only those who could engage in intelligent conversation and be sensitive to her shifting moods were invited to her small, expensively decorated house on the Avenue of Plane Trees leading down to the Temple of Aphrodite. Today was no different.

Arella walked out into the shade of the portico overlooking the lush green garden, a gift from a powerful merchant who had imported rich, black soil from Canaan before planting bushes, shrubs and flower gardens and constructing the long ornamental pool where Arella always swam. Clothed in a white diaphanous robe, she sat on a wickerwork chair in the portico and watched the birds swoop over the grass. Nothing but silence! Arella smiled. Conquerors may come and go. One party could seize power, another could fail, but the courtesans of Ephesus always remained. A wasp buzzed angrily before her face and she waved it away.

"Bring the fly-swatter!" she cried crossly to her maid.

The girl grasped this and hurried across. Arella grabbed it and smacked the girl on the bottom. "Don't wander too far," she murmured.

The girl simpered and withdrew. Arella laid the fly whisk on her lap and ran her finger round her lips. So much excitement! Rabinus had been a fool to come here looking for protection and safety. Arella laughed to herself. Courtesans weren't interested in politics, only in power. What use was a high-ranking Persian scribe when Darius's writ no longer ran in Ephesus? She recalled Rabinus being arrested, the congratulations and thanks of the handsome Macedonian officer. Arella leaned her head back and stared up at the cloud-free sky. He had been so handsome! Face of a falcon, slim-waisted, strong legs, muscular arms. Arella sighed: but was he rich and powerful? That was the rub. A trickle of sweat ran down her neck. Arella dabbed at it. Try as she might she couldn't remove Rabinus's frightened face from her memory. The Persian had squealed like a puppy, calling to her for help. Arella had simply turned on her heel and walked away. Nevertheless – Arella's eyes narrowed – Macedon had taken Ephesus before and retreated; what if that occurred again? Was she in any danger? And what about those secrets Rabinus had whispered to her as they had lain among perfume-drenched sheets? Like all men, the Persian scribe had opened his heart to impress her with the power he exercised.

He had chattered like a magpie on a branch. But what would happen if the Persians came back? Ah well. Arella got to her feet. Tonight, who was her guest? Ah yes, a goldsmith. He would certainly bring her a gift. A gilded statue of Aphrodite? Perfume in a pure alabaster jar? He was rather crude, Arella considered: perhaps it would just be golden darics in a leather pouch.

"I will bathe now."

Arella slipped on her sandals and walked across the dry grass, through a line of bushes, and stopped at the edge of the pool of purity. It was constructed of polished limestone which gave the water a soothing freshness, with green tiles around the rim; beneath the water, a brilliant mosaic caught the light of the sun. It rippled and moved as the water gushed in from a hidden spring, the gift of another customer, an engineer in the Persian army. Arella slipped off her robe and, walking across, laid it gently over the table next to the pool which bore a silver tray of cosmetics, sponges and perfumes.

Arella kicked off her sandals and slipped like a fish into the water. The daughter of an oyster merchant, she had learnt to swim as a child, but had soon decided that there was more to life than a hand-to-mouth existence, a poor marriage and childbirth every year. The courtesan smiled to herself: now she was believing her own fables. Her father, Malli, had been an oyster-merchant, but something had happened when she was a child. A hideous, terror-filled night. Soldiers arriving at that old house with the painting of Medusa on its gate: Malli seizing her, bundling her in blankets and hastening through the streets to hand her over to Basileia, self-styled Queen of the Moabites, once the leading whore in Ephesus. Ah well, that was all in the past!

Arella swam gracefully through the water, across to the far steps. She grasped the side of the pool and turned; her maid was standing by the pool staring at her. Arella smiled back. She knew that look: the fascination in the eyes, the slightly half-open mouth, the way the girl loved to help her mistress cream her body and drape it in the finest robes. Arella lifted a hand: perhaps one day, she was comely enough. Arella decided to tease her even more. She left the steps and slowly swam the length of the pool, face to one side. The movement soothed her, cleansed her body. She heard a sound but continued, reached the end and turned.

She glanced back towards the table and started in horror. The maid was now lying on the edge of the pool. Blood gushed from her cut throat, trickling along the tiles to stain the water with dark-red blushes.

Arella's shoulders prickled with a cold fear. She felt unable to move, half convinced that if she left the edge, let her fingers slip, something would happen. The maid had been attacked, though there was the porter at the gate. A shadow moved across the pool.

She turned, too late; the attacker was behind her. He grasped her drenched golden hair and, even as she struggled and screamed, Arella knew she was caught, trapped like a fish.

Telamon stared down at the corpse laid out on the dirty table in one of the cellars of the palace. The man had been stripped and covered with a white linen sheet, which was already stained with dark patches where it touched the water-soaked corpse. Alexander pulled back the sheet. Telamon recognized the face immediately: the half-open eyes had once crinkled in amusement; the fleshy nose still bore the marks of heavy drinking; the iron-grey hair, moustache and beard were now tangled and dirt-stained.

Telamon took the sheet and pulled it further back. The muscular corpse of the soldier bore the scars of at least a dozen battles: the stomach was slightly swollen but the thighs and legs were firm and strong, the shoulders, arms and wrists sinewy after years on the drill ground or in the mad pitch of battle.

"It must be a dozen years at least," Telamon whispered, "since I met him. He's hardly changed." He gently caressed the dead man's scarred cheek. "Poor Leonidas!"

Telamon sniffed the mouth. Beneath the rankness of the water where the body had been found, Telamon could still detect the heavy wine fumes.

"Why are you showing me this?" he asked.

Alexander stood, arms crossed, tears in his eyes. "He was my friend, Telamon, and my father's friend. At the battle of Chaeronea he helped me, and never mentioned it again."

56

"An accident?" Telamon demanded. "Is that how he died?"

"See for yourself."

Aristander had walked away and was sitting on a stool in the shadowy corner: this matter apparently did not concern him. Telamon examined the corpse, turning the body over, examining the skull, massaging the wet grey hair with his fingers.

"I can find no bruise," he declared. "No recent wound. Leonidas undoubtedly drowned. You said he fell in a pool?"

"I've told you the accepted story."

Telamon again examined the corpse. He found callouses, bruises, old scars, but nothing suspicious. He covered the corpse and walked round the table.

"Alexander, why don't you accept it as an accident? Leonidas was well known for his drinking. He was in his cups, staggered out into a garden with which he was unfamiliar, stumbled into a pool. He was so drunk he was unable to rise so he drowned: a common enough accident."

"Leonidas could drink Dionysus under his altar," Alexander retorted, "and still walk a straight line, drill the troops till they dropped, march twenty miles and drink again. He was an old fox, sly as a mongoose. I think he was murdered. He was also a fighter, a warrior: Leonidas would have fought for his life."

Aristander in the corner sighed noisily, as if bringing his presence to their attention: Alexander ignored him. He went and sat on the steps leading down to the cellar.

"Let me tell you a story, Telamon. Two years ago General Parmenio marched on Ephesus. He took the city and, for a few weeks, held it against the Persian counter-attack." He gestured at the corpse. "Leonidas and six of the Royals formed part of the army of occupation. He took quarters in the city."

"At the House of Medusa in the Pottery Quarter," Telamon said. "You told me that."

"Now, I don't know what happened," Alexander continued, "but Leonidas and his six companions became self-absorbed, isolated from the rest. They very rarely turned up in the mess and kept to themselves. They hardly seemed to move from that house. Now, when Parmenio retreated, Leonidas was the last to leave the city. When he rejoined the main army, he was by himself. He claimed he and his companions had been ambushed by a troop of Persian horse, he was the only one to escape." Alexander sighed. "No one really knew what happened. After Granicus, Leonidas volunteered to be in the expeditionary force which reached Ephesus first. Our troops were hardly within the city . . ."

"When Leonidas seized the House of Medusa?"

Alexander nodded. "He went there straight away. From what Aristander has told me, the house has a bad reputation. Some people claim it's haunted. Now, Leonidas went with two companions, young officers, Agathon and Sallus. Like typical soldiers, they helped themselves to food and wine from the local markets. They reported for duty, faithfully carried out any tasks assigned to them, but once again, Leonidas became absorbed with that house." Alexander picked at a cut on the back of his hand. "According to Agathon and Sallus, Leonidas insisted on going out and drinking until he could hardly stand. On the night in question Agathon went with him to a wine shop and on to a brothel. Leonidas was in no fit state to walk. Agathon brought him back. They were admitted to the house by an old porter. Agathon took Leonidas up to his chamber, threw him on his bed, made sure he was comfortable and retired for the night."

"That's all we know," Aristander spoke up, "until just before dawn. The old porter said Leonidas came back down into the garden. When he didn't reappear, he became curious and found Leonidas floating face down in an overgrown pool."

"Well, why not accept that story?" Telamon snapped. "It's logical enough. Leonidas was befuddled, he wakes up, staggers out and falls into the pool. No one saw Leonidas leave the house, did they?"

"Oh yes, the old porter did. He was alone."

Alexander, eyes closed, nodded. "I want you to investigate, Telamon."

"Oh no," the physician protested. "There's no evidence here of murder. We're busy enough."

"There is a connection." Aristander rose and walked forward: he now held a piece of parchment taken from the leather wallet at his waist. He handed this to Telamon, who unrolled it and took it over to a small lamp. The drawing was a centaur, roughly etched: Telamon could make out the face and beard, the horned head, the upper torso of a man and the hindquarters of a horse. Around the figure swarmed a protective cloud of wasps.

"That was found among Leonidas's papers," Aristander whispered. "There are similar drawings, references to centaurs."

"Where's the rest?" Telamon demanded.

"In a casket in my chamber. They are much the same: strange diagrams, drawings of centaurs. The word 'centaur' is common to them all, or sometimes just the letter 'C'."

"But Leonidas was a soldier," Telamon objected. "He liked wine, women and song. What would he have to do with a Persian spy and the politics of this city?"

"I don't know." Alexander got to his feet. "All these mysteries, Telamon," he gestured with his hand, "are linked, beads on the same string. I want you to rethread these beads, make a pattern, draw sense from them. I want to know what happened in the Temple of Hercules: why an old soldier was found drowned in a pool. Now," Alexander rubbed his hands together, "Hephaestion is busy on other matters. You and Aristander interview Rabinus then, mid-afternoon, report to me in the council chamber. We will enjoy the company of our friends from Ephesus, Agis and his group. They are going to meet Meleager. I want to know if they were involved in any murder or treachery. I also want to knock their heads together so, when I leave, Ephesus will know peace: a loyal, faithful city, not a boil on my backside!"

Alexander strode out of the cellar, shouting for his bodyguards gathered at the far end of the passage.

"You are very blunt with the king."

Telamon openly yawned.

"It's dangerous," Aristander taunted.

"No, it's not." Telamon closed the cellar door and leaned against it. "Alexander is a despot."

Aristander gasped in surprise.

"Oh, don't act the innocent!" Telamon snapped. "Philip was a despot! Olympias is a despot! She loves power as Leonidas loved

59

wine, her son is the same. But I am always safe. Do you know why, Aristander?" He walked across and pushed his face close. "I am not safe because I am the king's boyhood friend. I am safe because I can say what I like and do what I like. The danger arises when you don't do what Alexander wants. And that situation" – he opened the door and gestured the seer forward – "thankfully has not yet arisen."

Aristander didn't move but stood, lower lip jutting out. "Will that situation ever arise, Telamon?"

"Why, Aristander, you're jealous of me! You are hoping it will happen. I am concerned about today. Tomorrow can take care of itself. Now, our Persian scribe awaits."

They went down the corridor which snaked through the palace and reached the line of cells where prisoners were kept. Rabinus was lodged in the far one: a comfortable room with a grille high in the wall which allowed in light and air. He had a bed, stool and table. The air smelt savoury, of some spice-laden food: platters and dishes were piled on the table over which flies now buzzed. Rabinus sat on the edge of the bed. A middle-aged man, in a dirt-stained tunic, his black hair, once oiled and ringleted, now hanging lank to his shoulders: his beard and moustache were unclipped and stained with food. The Persian was frightened, eyes watchful as they came in and introduced themselves. Aristander took the stool while Telamon leaned against the wall.

"Do you want to die, Rabinus?" Aristander began. "Our king can crucify you. Now, don't sit there like a boy who's been caught stealing cherries from a bowl. You understand Greek very well. You were a high-ranking scribe in the Governor's chancery. You have things to tell me and my friend."

"I am a subject of the great king." Rabinus's dark, liquid eyes never wavered, but there was a tremor in his voice. "I worked for my masters. I should be allowed to go free." He enunciated the words carefully, slowly.

"You are a Persian caught in a Greek city," Aristander snapped, poking him viciously in the shoulder. "You had no right to be here. You were found hiding in the house of a courtesan. You are a spy. Spies are crucified."

"She betrayed me!" The words were spat out. "Arella is nothing but a whore!"

"No, she's a sensible girl." Aristander grinned. "I must visit her. Perhaps she can give me some advice on how to dress . . ."

Rabinus looked perplexed.

"My little joke," Aristander murmured. "But come, Rabinus, don't let's talk about being crucified along the Great Highway, your naked body straining against a cross, the sun drying your flesh while the vultures cluster round."

The Persian's eyes grew fearful.

"Instead, let's talk about what you know, about what you did."

"And will I go free?" Rabinus demanded.

"You'll not only go free but you'll be clothed, given money, a horse and safe passage. You can ride like a hero back to Persepolis and tell them whatever story you want."

Rabinus smiled bleakly. "I know very little."

"No, no, no." Aristander shook his head. "You know a great deal. You told us that. We've been among the records your master left."

"He took the secret ones . . . !" Rabinus closed his eyes at the mistake he had made.

"You see," Aristander exclaimed sweetly. He slapped the man's face. "How do you know what he took and what he burnt? Because you are a scribe who worked in the secret chancery! We are busy men, Rabinus. If you don't confess there are guards outside. They do love to play with a handsome Persian like you." Aristander leaned closer. "Our Thessalians," he whispered menacingly, "are cannibals who first bugger their victims. Have you ever been sodomised, Rabinus?"

"Think of a passage," Telamon said. "You stand at one end."

Rabinus looked up expectantly.

"You have only one way out," Telamon explained. "Tell us what you know. I am the king's personal physician. You have my solemn promise: a horse, a bag of coins, a change of clothing and safe passage out of Ephesus."

Rabinus sighed, his shoulders slumped. "I have a wife back in

Persepolis," he replied. "A house with a garden where my two children play."

"Then you shouldn't have been visiting ladies like Arella, should you?" Aristander taunted.

Telamon leaned forward and dug his fingers into Aristander's bony shoulder. "I think our friend is going to tell us something," he confided. "Aren't you, Rabinus? Who is the Centaur?"

Rabinus ignored him.

"Who is the Centaur?" The question was repeated. "You've mentioned him before."

"I don't know."

Telamon jumped as Aristander slapped the Persian's face, the rings on his fingers drawing blood along the high cheekbones.

"Ah well." Aristander made to rise.

"I don't know who the Centaur is," Rabinus began. "But yes," he added quickly, "I have heard of him. I was the scribe who dealt with secret ciphers."

"And where are those now?"

"The Governor burnt them all."

Again the slap. Rabinus nursed his cheek.

"We must have answers," Aristander sighed. "So, I'll give you one more chance."

"I was senior scribe to the Secret Chamber." Rabinus blinked. "I worked directly for the Governor and Lord Mithra. We had spies here in Ephesus and beyond. When the news of our great defeat at the Granicus reached us" – he held up his hands as if to fend off a further slap – "the Governor immediately ordered certain archives and records to be burnt. I can give you names," he added, "but most of them have fled."

"Most?" Aristander queried.

"Those who stayed," came the answer, "were petty officials, collectors of scraps of information. Two important ones remained. The first was the priest at the Temple of Hercules . . ."

Aristander sighed. "You've heard what happened there?" he asked.

Rabinus nodded. "When I was hiding, Arella told me the news."

62

"Arella? So we hear about her again?"

"She was the second spy," Rabinus added spitefully. "Oh, didn't you know that?" He enjoyed Aristander's look of consternation. "She used to bed the high and the mighty, the rich and the powerful, and pass on their babble and chatter to me."

"We'll be paying her a visit," Aristander declared.

"I think you should," Rabinus agreed. "Did you also know that, while Demades and the rest were in sanctuary at the Temple of Hercules, Arella visited them?"

"Was she a friend of Demades?"

"A bed companion perhaps, but there again, Arella didn't really mind the politics of her customers: she bestowed her favours on both Oligarchs and Democrats."

"Well, well, well!" Aristander rubbed his hands together. "I do look forward to questioning her."

"She shouldn't have betrayed me," Rabinus spluttered, wiping the blood from his cheek. "She thought I'd keep my mouth shut. It's finished, isn't it? The Persians have left Ephesus . . ."

"Does the name Leonidas mean anything to you?" Telamon asked.

Rabinus glanced up quickly.

"It does, doesn't it?" Telamon insisted.

Rabinus nodded. "He's a friend of the king, isn't he? An old soldier. When Parmenio's forces occupied Ephesus two years ago, Leonidas was the last to leave. He also visited Arella."

"Why?"

Rabinus shrugged. "Why do men visit courtesans? She is a skilful and energetic bed companion."

"No." Telamon crouched before Rabinus. "Leonidas would sleep with a donkey or a she-goat. A typical old soldier, he'd seize some serving wench and tumble her." He chucked Rabinus under the chin. "Come, come," he urged. "As you have said, Persian, everything is finished. Alexander is the new master of Ephesus. You must make a decision: life or death? The House of Medusa, where Leonidas lived – he died there last night, found floating face down in a pond."

"Very well," Rabinus murmured. "It's true what they say. The

Lord God waits for his moment. Everything is connected." He coughed and cleared his throat. "Arella told me about her own family. Her father, Malli, was an oyster-merchant who belonged to a secret society called the Centaurs. You'll find the like in many cities, here and elsewhere, professional murderers, assassins. They were devoted to the cult of Ahirman . . ."

"The Persian god of darkness?" Telamon asked.

"They were assassins," Rabinus explained. "They carried out murders for this person or that. About eight to ten years ago, when Meleager the Oligarch was chief magistrate, the authorities struck. A trap was laid, two Centaurs were arrested. They were tortured, you could hear their screams for days. Eventually they gave names; one by one the Centaurs were taken up and imprisoned. Some died of fever, others died under torture, a few were crucified along the king's highway. It's our custom for the entire family to be put to the sword for such crimes. Just before he was arrested, Arella's father killed his own wife, gave Arella a small fortune and handed her over to one of the principal courtesans of Ephesus to be trained for a house of pleasure."

"What has this got to do with Leonidas?"

"The House of Medusa was once owned by Malli, Arella's father, who destroyed everything. Leonidas, like an old hound, nuzzled among the rubbish, and came down to ask her questions."

"What questions?"

"Arella never told me. She confessed she must have been no more than ten when she left the house, she never laid claim to it. She drew a curtain across the past and said such things should remain secret."

"Was Arella a murderess?" Telamon asked, getting to his feet.

"No." Rabinus shook his head. "She loved power and wealth. Shortly after the news of Granicus, she did claim she had been visited by a stranger: a man who wished to buy her favours for someone else."

"Would that be costly?" Telamon asked.

"Very much so. I was one of Arella's customers. She knew tricks and games" – Rabinus smiled, a faraway look in his eyes – "other

64

men only dream about. You could become infatuated with her. Arella was very particular about her clients. You could offer her a casket of pearls, but if she didn't take a liking to you, you might as well bay for the moon." Rabinus spread his hands "And that's all I know. Arella still wishes to become the principal courtesan of Ephesus." Rabinus laughed sharply. "The Queen of Whores!"

"We'll see about that," Aristander taunted.

"If I were you," Rabinus's eyes grew hard, "I'd arrest her as swiftly as possible. Arella knows many secrets. I urged her to flee. She has one weakness, arrogance. She believes we men are fools and can be easily persuaded. She sees no difference between Macedonian and Persian."

Telamon listened, fascinated. Throughout his travels in Egypt, southern Italy, even here in the Persian Empire, he had met the likes of Arella: women who exerted considerable power not because of their position or status, but due to their skills as a courtesan.

"And so we come to the Centaur." Aristander moved on his stool.

Somewhere down the passageway a voice cried, deep in pain.

"Another prisoner," Aristander smiled. "A rogue who thought he could make a profit out of the chaos in Ephesus. Our king has issued a decree: food must not be hoarded, the markets must be opened, trade must be resumed. You don't want to cry out in terror, do you, Rabinus?"

"Will I go free?" The Persian anxiously dabbed at the cut on his cheek.

"The Centaur? You told us the Society of Assassins had been wiped out."

"So they were, so they were," Rabinus hastily agreed. "A few years ago the Governor began to receive secret messages which I was not allowed to look at. They were sealed in a small silver cylinder and despatched immediately to the King of Kings at Persepolis."

"You mean to Mithra, Darius's Master of Secrets?" Telamon asked.

"You have heard of him?" Rabinus asked, surprised.

"Of course we have," Aristander sniggered. "We have crossed swords before and will do so again. Who is the Centaur?"

"I don't know," Rabinus wailed. "Whoever it is took the name Centaur: his messages were brought here and the Governor despatched them immediately to Persepolis."

"And the replies?" Aristander said. "There must have been a reply?"

Rabinus's head went down; he shuffled his feet. "The Temple of Hercules," he murmured.

"What was that?" Aristander forced the Persian's head back.

"I saw one message." Rabinus had, apparently, decided to confess everything. "Before it was put in the silver cylinder and sealed in the secret chamber. It was written in a cipher I couldn't understand. No" – he flinched as Aristander raised his hand – "I swear by the God of the Hidden Flame I tell the truth. The Governor made me take these messages to the Temple of Hercules, usually at noon, in the heat of the day. I would enter the temple and kneel just within the inner doorway, the silver cylinder in my hand."

"And?"

"The Centaur, whoever he or she was, came up behind me. The message would be plucked from my hands. Sometimes I was given one to take back."

"And you never saw this person?"

"I was aware of sandals, a shabby cloak, but that's all."

Again the cry, full of terror, echoed down the corridor. Telamon steeled himself.

"Anything else?" Aristander asked softly.

"My freedom?"

Aristander patted Rabinus on the shoulder and got to his feet, kicking away the stool. "We shall see! We shall see!"

Aristander and Telamon left the cell and walked along the passage. "Who is being tortured?" Telamon asked.

Aristander stopped by a cell door and pushed it open. Inside a soldier squatted on the floor, his back to the wall.

"Did I do well, sir?"

Aristander took a coin from his pouch and spun it through the air. "You did very well, soldier."

He walked on, grasping Telamon by the shoulder. "In these circumstances it's always useful to have a cry of terror, a shout of pain. It shows people like Rabinus we mean business."

Telamon broke free of his grip "I'll remember that, should we ever meet in different circumstances."

Aristander laughed, a loud neighing sound: he sardonically waved Telamon up the steps and along the portico leading into the palace.

"You talked of papers?" Telamon demanded. "Found in Leonidas's chamber?"

"Oh, you'll see those by and by."

"What will you do with Rabinus?"

Aristander stopped halfway down the portico and stared out at a statue, an athlete preparing to throw a discus, the white marble shimmering in the warm sunshine. He breathed in noisily.

"Smell it, Telamon, the scent of hyacinths. It always reminds me of my mother's garden." He glanced at the physician out of the corner of his eye. "I did have a mother, Telamon. We lived in a small village about ten miles to the north of Pella. They thought she was a witch. One night they battered down our door. They killed my mother and my elder brother. I escaped out of a back window. I had an aunt whom they also accused of witchcraft: she was a friend of the young Olympias. She took me in and trained me in both the black arts and loyalty."

"And you've never looked back since?"

Aristander smiled thinly. "To answer your question, I don't really care what happens to Rabinus. He's a traitor both to his own master and to us. I'll let him cool his heels for a day. Then I'll give him a horse, a change of clothing, some food and a bag of silver. He'll ride to Persepolis pretending to be a hero. I'll send an anonymous message to the governor of the nearest Persian city. I'll tell them how Rabinus chattered, like a child being offered a sweetmeat."

"You are wicked," Telamon retorted. "So, when he gets to Persepolis he'll be arrested and Lord Mithra will wonder how much he told us. He'll become worried about his spy Centaur. Perhaps he might panic, do something?"

Aristander waggled a bony finger in Telamon's face. "You'd make a very good Master of Secrets, physician, no wonder the king wants you to help him in these matters. Come, sit down."

He steered Telamon to a stone bench against the wall, then walked back to the steps leading down to the cells. Telamon sunned himself: through half-open eyes he watched a butterfly move across a flower bed, wafted here and there by the soft breeze. In a few weeks, he reasoned, such a breeze would disappear. The summer sun would be strong. He idly wondered how long they would stay here. What Cassandra was doing. How he was to resolve the mystery confronting him. He heard footsteps and glanced to his right. Aristander came carrying a tray, a jar with three goblets, and behind him was Rabinus between two guards.

"In Apollo's name!" Telamon whispered to himself. "What is the serpent up to now?"

Rabinus, dishevelled and rather shaken, was ushered to the seat beside Telamon. The guards were told to walk away. Aristander poured the wine. He filled each goblet to the brim and shared them out. He raised his own in a toast.

"To secrets, eh? The finest Chian. Cool and fresh." He took a deep gulp. "Go on, Rabinus, drink it. It's not poisoned."

The Persian obeyed. Telamon sipped at his.

"Shall I tell you something?" Aristander smacked his lips. "I have decided to free you, Rabinus."

The Persian would have sprung to his feet, but Aristander pushed him back and bent over him. "You have forgotten to tell us something, Rabinus?"

Telamon turned sideways in the seat.

"What do you think of the sunshine?" Aristander continued quietly. "Smell the flowers. Can you hear the fountain splashing? How does it feel to have the sun on your face and good wine in your mouth?"

"It is good," the Persian whispered.

"Let's go back to the last few days. The Governor comes into the Secret Chamber with his trusted scribe Rabinus. The Macedonians are marching on Ephesus. The Democrats are stirring up the mob.

The Persian garrison is about to leave and their Governor with them. What does he do?"

"He burns all his secret papers," Rabinus replied.

"You are very nearly free," Aristander murmured. "He also talks about the Centaur?"

Rabinus became agitated, shuffling his feet, changing the goblet from hand to hand.

"And the Governor has one last task for you?"

"How do you know?"

Aristander pinched Rabinus's cheek. "Because I, too, have spies in Ephesus. You took a money belt, didn't you? Little pouches stitched along the edge. Full of what? Half a talent, a talent of gold darics?"

"I don't know what you're . . ."

Aristander banged his goblet against the Persian's face: blood spurted out of Rabinus's nose.

"You were given an escort: four Syrian mercenaries dressed in dark robes. They hurry you through the streets as the turmoil begins. You reach the Temple of Hercules and go up the steps. So far you have nothing to be frightened of. The mob is not yet on the streets. The blood-letting hasn't begun. You kneel inside. The Centaur appears behind you. What was the password?"

Rabinus coughed on the blood and wiped his face on the back of his hand.

"The password?" Aristander repeated.

"Mithra."

"Good!" Aristander soothed. "That was the word you used all the time, wasn't it? Why didn't you tell us before? You don't turn round, you undo the belt and the Centaur takes it."

"How do you know this?"

Aristander splayed his fingers. "Four mercenaries. Two were killed, one got out with the Governor, the fourth wasn't paid. He went into hiding and, when the bloodshed was over, he swaggers into Alexander's camp: he offers him his sword as well as what information he can bring. One of my scribes chattered to him. I'll tell you the truth. He never saw the man who met you in the temple, he was standing on the steps outside, his back to the door.

However, when you left, the belt which clinked had gone. Now, Rabinus, aren't I a clever boy? So, tell me, why should the Persians fleeing Ephesus, probably for the last time, send a belt full of gold to their principal spy?"

Beads of sweat broke out on Rabinus's brow: his nose was slightly twisted from the blow, a thin trickle of blood seeping down to his mouth.

"You're an intelligent man, Rabinus. You must have asked why? Persian governors are not known for their generosity."

Rabinus cradled the cup and his shoulders began to shake. "It is as you say," he sobbed. "It was my last task. I took the belt; it was heavy with gold and one silver cylinder. The Centaur was waiting for me."

"No, no," Aristander intervened. "What happened before you left the palace?"

"I asked the Governor why. He replied that it was a good investment. The Centaur would still provide valuable information."

"And?" Aristander demanded.

"He would rid us of our problems once and for all."

Telamon felt a slight chill, as if a cold wind were blowing down the portico. He grasped the Persian by his shoulder.

"What do you think he meant by that? You asked him, didn't you?"

Rabinus nodded. "The Centaur will carry out sentence of death," he whispered through blood-stained teeth. "The Governor's last order from the Lord Mithra," he glanced up fearfully, "was to have your king assassinated."

Telamon gazed into the Persian's dark eyes. He could detect no guile, no double-dealing: this man was genuinely terrified.

"You see," Aristander's voice was gleeful, "the papers may have been burnt, the treasury pillaged, but there's nothing like a pair of sharp eyes, is there, Rabinus? Guards!" he bellowed down the portico. "Take this man back to the cell but treat him well. He's to be given food, wine and clothing."

He dragged Rabinus to his feet and pushed him towards the soldiers. "When I say, he is to be escorted to the city gates: a horse, a bag of silver and a letter of safe passage."

Telamon waited until Rabinus disappeared through the door-way. "The Centaur has been paid to assassinate Alexander?"

"Yes," Aristander replied. "I suspected as much. After the Granicus Alexander was safe, surrounded by his soldiers. But here, in a city half-full of traitors?" He sipped at the wine and, taking the goblet used by Rabinus, refilled his own.

"They are hunting our king, Telamon. So we must hunt them!"

Chapter 3

———>●○●<———

"On his father's side, Alexander was a descendant of Hercules."

Diodorus Siculus: *Library of History*, Book XVII, Chapter 1

A rella's assassin, the Centaur, watched the courtesan's corpse, arms extended, float beneath the surface of the pool in an ever-widening scarlet cloud.

"So beautiful," he murmured.

Even as he had killed Arella, he had admired her firm pointed breasts, the beautiful sinuous body. He could imagine her in bed, twisting and turning, her skin oiled with the costliest perfume.

"Ah well!" he sighed. "The task is to be finished."

He stared sadly across at the bunch of hyacinths growing at the base of a statue of Aphrodite, beyond it, a flower-covered gazebo, a shady arbour from the summer sun. He recalled the line from Aristophanes's play *The Peace*: "You'll never make a crab walk straight." He was now an assassin, committed to killing, he could not stop. To kill or be killed. To strike before one is struck, that was the way it had begun and that was the way it would end. Alexander of Macedon would make no difference. Despite the killings, the sense of urgency, the Centaur would not be moved but stood relishing the moment. He had entered the City of the Damned and, to quote a line from *The Bacchae*, he had no choice but "to walk amongst the ruins he had made".

Beyond the garden walls a cart trundled by, its wheels crashing on the rutted track, which startled the Centaur from his reverie. He adjusted the mask over his face and, kneeling down, pulled the corpse from the pool. He dragged it into the house, laid it in the vestibule and, going back, brought in the maid's corpse and that of the porter. He ensured the gate was on the latch and kicked dust over the pool of blood and brains where he had committed his first murder. He crossed the gardens, so richly sweet with the fragrance of flowers, and entered the coolness of Arella's small mansion. He examined its stone-flagged kitchen, the dining chamber with cushions piled around the walls, its exquisitely coloured friezes extolling the achievements of Aphrodite. He went up the staircase of polished sycamore and searched every room. The downstairs floor was of hardened stone, the upstairs of polished sycamore and elm. The Centaur was relieved; it would be easy to find hiding places.

He pillaged the velvet-draped bedchamber of Arella, a fragrant, beautiful place, its walls depicting love scenes, banquets, a young woman entertaining an old man on a couch. In each of the small paintings the young woman adopted a different posture. Behind his mask the Centaur smiled: no wonder men had desired this young woman's body! During his search he discovered how valuable she had been: caskets and pouches full of jewels, precious stones and pearls, strips of silver, small ingots of gold. Coffers and chests with false bottoms concealing coin from every part of the empire and mainland Greece. He examined the wainscotting at the base of the wall and found a secret compartment. Most of the letters were from admirers, and the Centaur learnt a little more about the failings and foibles of some of the leading citizens of Ephesus. He stripped the gorgeously decorated bed, dragging the feather-filled mattress to the floor, ripping it open with his dagger. He checked the bedposts for secret compartments or caches. Satisfied, he went back downstairs and coolly continued his foray. He knew Arella's routine. In the afternoon she would sleep, rest, the house would be quiet. He found nothing interesting, so he went out into the garden. Statues and paving stones, fountains and even a small flower-filled arbour were carefully inspected. He returned to the house, his hard-soled marching boots crunching on the gravel. A beautiful afternoon; butterflies hovered from one flowerbed to another, bees buzzed in their search for honey.

"I have done what I have come for."

The Centaur picked up a bulging wineskin and plucked out the stopper. He soaked all three corpses, the staircase, the gallery and the rooms above. He came downstairs and was about to enter the kitchen for an oil-lamp when the crunch of footsteps on the gravelled path outside made him pause.

The Centaur hid behind the half-open door and stared through the crack. He became aware of his heavy breathing, of his own sweat-drenched body. At first he could see nothing, then the city scribe Hesiod came into view, dressed in a white tunic, a dark mantle over his arm. The scribe was apparently puzzled and stared up at the house, dabbing at the folds of sweat on his neck with a rag. Hesiod took a step forward: his black eyes, almost hidden by rolls of fat on his podgy face, betrayed curiosity but no alarm.

The Centaur drew his dagger. He glanced quickly to where the corpses lay. Hesiod must walk forward, not take alarm and flee. What was the fat fool doing here? Another killer, a man who liked to enjoy the deaths of others, Hesiod had been on his list: now was as good a time as any.

Hesiod placed his mantle over the small marble bench to the left of the porch and rolled the heavy gold bracelet on his left wrist.

"Arella!" His voice was squeaky. "Arella, you have no porter! Are you at home?"

The assassin watched as a spider would a fly hovering near his web.

"Can I come in?"

Hesiod half turned. The assassin gripped the dagger tightly. If necessary he would strike before Hesiod left. The scribe changed his mind: he picked up his mantle and strode through the front door.

The Centaur slammed it shut. The scribe whirled round. He opened his mouth, fingers all a-flutter at the hideous vision confronting him: a man garbed in cloak and hood, a horseskin mask covering his face and that long, sharp blade coming up, its point nicking his fat chin.

"What is this?" Hesiod backed away.

He slipped on the oil and crashed to the ground, falling on his bottom with a jarring thud. He sat, mantle and tunic soaked in oil.

He rolled over to get up and glimpsed the corpses just by the wall in the shadow of the stairwell. He crouched on hands and knees, squeaking like a pig. Surely he was having a nightmare? A boot tapped him on the backside.

"Get up, little pig!"

Hesiod clambered to his feet. The vision of terror still stood there, the blade still out, this time turned, the flat against his hot cheek. The Centaur forced Hesiod to move until he stood with his back to the door.

"What are you doing? Why are you here?" The voice from behind the mask grated.

"I . . . I have a meeting . . . at the Governor's palace."

"With the Macedonian murderer?"

"With . . ." Hesiod's voice failed. He blinked. He couldn't stop the trembling. His legs felt like water and, unwittingly, he began to urinate. The Centaur noticed this and laughed softly.

"Well, well, well! Our city scribe! Not the conquering hero now, eh? The brave, stern judge watching men, women and children being dragged off to death?"

Hesiod fell to his knees, hands clenched. He tried to grasp the folds of that dirty, heavy cloak, but the Centaur lashed out with his gauntleted hand, smacking the scribe full in the face, splitting those fat lips. Hesiod began to blubber.

The Centaur crouched over him. "How many do you think you've killed, scribe? Five or six? Or was it thirty-six?"

"I had no choice," Hesiod wailed. "Agis was the keenest. He, Peleus and Dion."

"Turds from the same arse!" the Centaur growled. "But tell me, Hesiod" – his voice became softer – "why are you here? Are you a client of Arella?"

The tip of the dagger pricked Hesiod's fleshy throat.

"I . . . I came . . . I came to take her to the Governor's palace."

"Why?"

"She may have information."

"About what? Come on, Hesiod! You're not a philosopher, a sophist engaged in a dialogue of question and answer. Tell me or I'll cut your throat!"

"Arella was friendly with the Persians," Hesiod gabbled. "She knew a great deal. She was also involved with those Oligarchs, the trai . . ."

"Which Oligarchs? I am growing impatient."

"Demades and the rest: the ones who took sanctuary in the Temple of Hercules."

"Is that so? How do you know that?"

"I saw her go there on at least two occasions. One time she entered the temple. I think she took wine and foodstuffs. The other she stood in a doorway opposite the temple door: she must have been there to see someone."

"Who?"

"I don't know." Hesiod's hands began to shake. "She may know something about the mystery. She certainly knows a great deal about the Persians."

"Ah, I see." The Centaur got to his feet. "Anything else, Hesiod?"

"You know me! How do you know me?"

"Everybody knows you, Hesiod. The brave, noble judge, the savage persecutor of the Oligarchs and their families. Come, get to your feet."

He stretched out a gauntleted hand. Hesiod grasped it. The Centaur pulled him to his feet and, as he did so, thrust the dagger straight into the man's heart. He watched the life-light die in the scribe's widening eyes, pulled the dagger out and let the corpse slump to the ground.

The Centaur picked up the oil and drenched Hesiod's corpse, then went into the kitchen and picked up a small oil-lamp, a night-light which had not been extinguished, and walked back to the door. He tossed the alabaster lamp jar over his shoulder, opened the door and left.

For a while the Centaur stood under the shade of a solitary palm tree, watching one of the ground-floor windows. At first nothing, then wisps of smoke: a short while later, flames as the oil caught light, and Arella's luxurious mansion became a blazing furnace.

The Centaur walked towards the orchard near the curtain wall. Behind him the roar of the flames was growing, but he didn't hurry. This quarter was fairly deserted, many of the citizens would be resting from the noonday heat. Arella and her mansion were now beyond all help.

The small pomegranate orchard was cool and sweet-smelling. The trees ringed a small grove, in the centre of which a fountain had been built, boasting a statue of Poseidon and two sea nymphs. The Centaur stopped, took off his gauntlets and mask and splashed water on his face, licking the small drops in the palm of his hands. He noticed a few streaks of blood on his fingers, cursed, and began to rub at the stains, snatching up clumps of grass. He took a little of the water and wetted the back of his neck, allowing the cool drops to seep under his rough robe. He put on his mask and gauntlets. The smoke from the house drifted towards him and he sniffed in satisfaction.

He was about to continue through the trees to the curtain wall when he paused and stamped his heel in anger. He had been too rash, too quick; he should have interrogated that fat scribe more closely. Hesiod hadn't just arrived to take Arella to the Governor's mansion. He could have sent a letter, a servant, or arranged for some of the city guards or market police to arrest her. Why else had that fat, sly pig come sliding in here? To offer protection? To threaten, blackmail? Did he know more than he had confessed? Did he suspect something?

The Centaur's throat went dry. He walked to the wall and stood, one hand against a buttress. Hesiod was a bachelor, a man who liked the pleasures of the flesh. He lived alone, but there would be servants in his house. He liked to be pampered, did Hesiod, being carried round the city in a litter or his fat legs astride a donkey. Was he acting by himself? Or was there someone else? The politics of this city teemed like a nest of spitting, writhing vipers. No, he had done enough work for today. He would wait and see.

The Centaur was about to climb the wall when he heard a sound and, turning, glimpsed the figure standing just inside the gateway.

Telamon was busy in his own chamber, a small room in the centre of the palace overlooking a sun-washed courtyard. He stood at the window, staring down at the small pool of water. The fountain had been smashed when Alexander's troops had entered the palace, and now the water just gushed up from uncovered pipes. The king's engineers had promised to mend it, but Telamon knew they were too busy for that.

"A pity," he murmured.

"What is?" Cassandra sat at the table, a pestle in her hand. She was busy crushing herbs in a small earthenware bowl.

"The fountain."

Telamon flinched as two wasps, like small winged demons, shot through the open window. "They are a nuisance!"

"They have nests all over this palace."

Telamon walked back to the small writing desk filched from another chamber, so small the cushioned chair before it seemed like a throne.

"There wasn't much destruction." Cassandra pushed back her red hair and tied it once again with a piece of ribbon. She plucked at the dark smock she wore. "It's so hot."

"Have you drunk red wine?" Telamon asked. "You've read Hippocrates. Never at midday, particularly in hot weather; it flushes the skin and makes you sweat."

Cassandra whispered some obscenity about Hippocrates.

"What was that?" Telamon demanded.

"He wasn't right about everything." Cassandra's green eyes glared across at the physician. "He said there were ninety-one bones in the human body."

"Well, aren't there?"

"With the addition of nails it should be one hundred and eleven," she retorted.

"Nails aren't bones," Telamon argued.

"I think they are. When I worked as a temple healer in Thebes, the physicians always considered the nails to be bones and treated them accordingly."

"You might be right." Telamon picked up the scraps of parchment from the desk.

"What are you doing?" Cassandra glared crossly. "We were all enjoying ourselves in the garden. The king summons you. You're gone for hours and return with that evil-smelling, ugly-eyed Aristander."

"I wouldn't let him hear you say that. Aristander buys the costliest perfumes."

"You can cover manure with rose water. It's still manure!" Cassandra snapped. "What is the great killer planning?"

Telamon got up. He checked the door was closed, came across and crouched down beside Cassandra. She turned and winked, holding the pestle like club: she studied the solemn, dark face of this physician who had taken her from the slave pens.

"It always agitates you, doesn't it?" she whispered. Cassandra leaned closer. Telamon could smell the mint and thyme being crushed in the bowl. "Alexander," she repeated softly, "is a great killer. He wiped out Thebes and, after the Granicus, showed no mercy to the Greek mercenaries who fought for Persia." She waved the pestle in Telamon's face. "If needs be, you, Telamon, and any one else who frustrated his will, would either go up on a cross or down to the execution yard. He has an ungovernable temper: when he's drunk, he's very dangerous."

"He has mood swings," Telamon explained, getting to his feet and standing over her. "The king becomes depressed or excitable, but that is rare. On most occasions he's generous and open-handed."

"He might not be Philip's son," Cassandra retorted, "but Olympias is his mother. Where are we off to now? Which is the next city to be plundered and pillaged?"

Telamon tapped her on the tip of the nose and walked back to his desk.

"This business of the Temple of Hercules?" Cassandra asked. "It's all over the city. The troops say a centaur entered the temple and slaughtered those men."

"I don't think so," Telamon replied. "Those slain at the Temple of Hercules were the victims of a very cunning murderer. I doubt whether we'll ever know the full truth."

"But Alexander wants to know the truth, doesn't he?" Cassandra taunted. "They say he's furious, he gave his word and couldn't keep it. He's been humiliated, mocked, the great conqueror who can't even control a Greek city."

Telamon refused to reply. He had returned to his chamber, where he and Cassandra had eaten bread, cheese and grapes with a goblet of watered wine. One of Aristander's scribes had brought the documents taken from Leonidas's chamber as well as a note: it reminded Telamon that he would have to attend the king later in the day when he met certain leading citizens of the city.

"What are those scraps of parchment?" Cassandra asked. "Why are they so interesting?"

"Wouldn't you like to go for a walk in the garden?" Telamon sighed. "Or perhaps there is some soldier you can tease, or a page to flirt with?"

"I don't flirt with pages."

Cassandra began to bang the pestle into the bowl. Telamon closed his eyes and gritted his teeth. She'll begin to sing soon, he thought, either that or whistle. As if she could read his thoughts, Cassandra began to croon a lullaby; the more she sang the louder it became.

"Leonidas!" Telamon shouted.

"Ah good, you're going to tell me." Cassandra put down the pestle and folded her arms, eyes wide, a false grin on her face.

Telamon took a deep breath and told her everything about Leonidas and the House of Medusa: his character, his love of wine, and how he had apparently drowned himself.

"Good," Cassandra murmured, rubbing her hands together. "One Macedonian killer the less!" She ignored Telamon's warning look. "And tell me, master, what are those parchments the cruel spider sent up to you?"

"Aristander is not a spider."

"He's got legs like one, that's why he envies mine. Do you think he'll ever invite me to one of his supper parties? When he gets dressed like a woman and that bunch of cut-throats who accompany him everywhere sing love songs to him?"

"These pieces of parchment," Telamon continued, ignoring her outburst.

"Yes master."

"Please don't call me that." Telamon got up and brought over the scraps of papyrus. "See." He moved the mortar and pestle and laid them out on the table. "Some have the letter 'C' which, I suppose, stands for Centaur. A few have three rectangles connected to each other, some have two." He picked up another piece of parchment. "While this one has four."

"What do they mean?" Cassandra asked.

"I don't know."

Telamon placed the parchments back on the table. A breeze wafted through the window, lifting them gently. Telamon picked up a wooden carving of a marsh bird, the work of some Persian craftsman, and placed it on top of the parchments.

"It's exquisite, isn't it?" Telamon pointed to the carving. "The work of a Persian craftsman in a Greek city once ruled by Persians and now ruled by Macedonians. That's the root of all this mystery, Cassandra, violent change! Ephesus is like the rich mud at the bottom of a pool: it's been stirred, and all sorts of foul things have come floating to the top."

"Do you often speak in riddles?" she snapped.

Telamon shrugged apologetically. "Leonidas was an old rogue. I met him out in the Groves of Mieza. Our military tutor was Black Cleitus. You've met him?"

"The one-eyed man with the face of a twisted quince?"

Telamon laughed. "Cleitus used to come swaggering out. Now and again he'd bring what he called a real soldier."

"Your father?"

"He did, on occasions, but that was before Father saw his vision, left the House of War and took me out of the Groves of Mieza to train to be a physician. Anyway, Cleitus and my father Margolis were friends. Now and again they'd bring Leonidas with them. He'd stand on the edge of the drill ground and yell out obscenities: 'Lift your sword that way! Hold your shield this!'"

Telamon paused as the wail of a conch horn echoed across the palace grounds, the sign that the watch was being changed.

"Leonidas liked war but he also liked wealth," he continued. "He had dreams of finding lost treasure trove. He used to sit round the camp fire at night and tell us macabre tales. How the ancient graves and monuments hid fabulous wealth." Telamon picked up the wooden duck and cradled it in his hands. "I used to think of

82

Leonidas when I was in Egypt and visited the Necropolis on the west bank of the Nile. Hundreds, maybe thousands, of tombs filled with treasures, not to mention the haunted Valley of the Kings with its hidden royal graves. Rumour claims it's a veritable treasure house full of gold, silver and precious jewels."

"You think Leonidas found something similar here?"

"Yes I do. He took over the House of Medusa, a malevolent-sounding name. He and members of his unit fought with Parmenio but, when the Persians returned, Leonidas and his companions had to leave in a hurry."

"You think there's treasure there?"

"The house was once owned by a Centaur, a member of the assassins here in Ephesus." Telamon shuffled the parchments. "Leonidas probably went back there looking for hidden wealth."

"But that doesn't mean he was murdered."

"No, it doesn't. He may have got out of his bed, drunk as a sot, and decided to search the garden, tripped and drowned himself." Telamon paused at the knock on the door.

Aristander slid into the room. Cassandra immediately moved away.

"All alone with your redhead, eh?" Aristander minced forward, his narrow eyes leering and rapacious.

Cassandra ignored him and went across to a small alcove where her truckle bed stood, hidden behind thin white veils hung from a wooden bar. Cassandra pulled these apart and disappeared inside.

"She doesn't like me," Aristander purred as he came and sat down on the stool next to Telamon's desk.

"Very few people do, Aristander. How's the king?"

"He was going to go hunting, but envoys arrived from other cities bearing tokens of submission. So he's not in a good mood." Aristander pointed to the parchments. "Did you find anything interesting?"

"Nothing at all." Telamon collected the parchments together and thrust them into Aristander's hand. "I believe Leonidas was searching for hidden treasure."

"I believe the same," Aristander agreed: he said it so offhandedly Telamon's suspicions were aroused.

"Is there treasure, Aristander? Greed glints in your eyes."

"Well, there must be, mustn't there?" the Master of the King's Secrets retorted. "That's why Leonidas went back to the House of Medusa."

"And have you searched the place?"

Aristander shook his head.

"You are a liar," Telamon taunted.

Aristander lifted his hands to his face and sniggered behind his fingers. "Well, I've been there and looked round, but I could find nothing suspicious. Any treasure trove found," he added warningly, "belongs to the king. Oh well, the day draws on."

Clutching the parchments, Aristander got to his feet and walked to the door.

"Goodbye Cassandra!" he cooed. "We'll certainly meet again." And he was gone like a cat into the night.

Telamon sighed, got to his feet and walked over to a small couch, its arms carved in the form of crouching lions. It was covered by costly fabric decorated with silver lozenges and golden suns. He lay down on this and stretched out.

"I can't stand that nasty creature!" Cassandra's voice echoed from behind the curtain. "He's always touching my hair and plucking at my flesh."

"He sees you as a bride for the leader of his chorus. All of his beautiful boys adore you, Cassandra."

A stream of invective greeted his words. Telamon stared up at the ceiling. The white plaster was cracked and stained. He idly wondered who had occupied the room before, Rabinus? He stared at the cornices. A craftsman had carved the likeness of an ibis, which brought back memories of Egypt. The Nile, like a green snake, curling through the hot sands: the white marble city of Thebes, the refreshing oases, soaring palm trees protecting cool pools and lush grass. He was there with Anuala, the love of his life, the temple girl who served the Goddess Isis. She was kneeling beside him, a carnelian necklace round her throat, precious stones gleaming in her ears. A rich, oil-drenched wig circled by a golden fillet framed her lovely oval face, those marvellous eyes, light green, her lips bending down to kiss his.

"How you used to tease me!" Telamon murmured.

The tears pricked his eyes. He remembered that day so clearly: one of the great feast days of Isis. They had laughed and talked, eaten and drunk; that same evening, when the shadows grew long, Anuala had been raped and killed by a Persian officer, drunk and rapacious, acting the almighty lord. Telamon had confronted him in a wine booth. He had killed him with one blow, driving the knife deep into his heart. Telamon wondered was that the end of Anuala? She always claimed her ka or soul would travel into the west across the far horizon but, if anything happened, she would come back to him. Telamon laughed sharply. She wouldn't come here, not to this place of intrigue and murder. Perhaps she was only alive in his soul? He summoned up her face as he drifted in and out of sleep.

Memories of Anuala were replaced by sharper, more recent images of war: Alexander and his generals, eyes gleaming through the slits of their helmets: blood-red horse plumes nodding in the breeze; the neighs of sweat-lathered horses. Marching phalanxes, in the different colours of their regimental sashes, great pikes up against a blood-red sky, the bray of trumpets shrilling through clouds of dust . . .

He was roughly shaken awake by Aristander bending over him, members of the chorus grouped round the couch. Telamon pulled himself up, rubbing his eyes. The sunlight pouring through the windows was fading.

"You are needed," Aristander snapped, clicking his fingers.

"I need to relieve myself!" Telamon retorted.

"We'll be waiting outside."

A short while later Telamon joined him in the passage. Aristander no longer acted foppishly. He stood surrounded by his bodyguard, dressed as if they were going into battle. They even carried shields and had drawn their swords. They clustered about their master, smelling richly of the kennel and stable.

Aristander plucked at Telamon's arm. He told his "lovely boys" to wait and took the physician into a window embrasure overlooking the gardens. Telamon was grateful for the sweet smell and cool breeze. Further down the gallery stood members of the Foot

Companions dressed in ceremonial armour. They, too, were tense, wary of the armed and vicious-looking Celts so close to the royal quarters.

"What's the matter?" Telamon asked. "Why couldn't you speak to me in my chamber?"

"Red Hair has big ears!"

"She's called Cassandra."

"Well, that's what she says," Aristander retorted, "but she's a Theban with a new name. God knows who she really is."

"Oh, for the love of Apollo! Aristander, you're suspicious of your own shadow."

"Yes, I have good cause to be. We've had corpses brought in."

"More killings?"

"More murders. You remember the Persian Rabinus mentioned a courtesan, Arella?"

"Oh yes, a woman," Telamon grinned, "with a foot in either camp. I am afraid I couldn't put it more elegantly."

"Well, she has a foot in no man's camp now. Early this afternoon someone visited her. They killed her porter, her maid and finally Arella herself. She must have been swimming. The pool is laced with blood. The assassin dragged all three corpses into the house, then set fire to them and everything the courtesan once owned." Aristander's face was white with fury.

"You are sorry you didn't arrest her immediately, aren't you?"

"Yes. I would have done, but that fat scribe Hesiod told me he wanted to see me about her. Said he had something interesting, very interesting indeed."

"You didn't tell me that."

"It was none of your business."

"Ah, but it is now . . ."

"No, listen." Aristander tried to be tactful. "Apparently Hesiod disturbed the killer. He too was murdered. Anyway, you'd best come and look for yourself."

Aristander walked away, gesturing at Telamon to follow. The physician had no choice. The chorus swept him up and marched along the gleaming wooden passage. The guards at the far end stood aside. They went down the stairs out into the garden. Alexander's companions were there. Sly-eyed, dark-featured Ptolemy with his monkey face and cheeky grin; Seleucus, blond-haired, round-faced, with hard, agate-blue eyes; grizzled Parmenio, the one-eyed favourite of Alexander's father Philip, Amyntas and Hephaestion. They were standing, goblets in hands, discussing some news. Ptolemy called across but Aristander made a cutting movement with his hand. Ptolemy shouted something about the company Telamon kept, but Aristander was already striding down the path. He took him across a cobbled yard into the stable area, long buildings of grey stone with dark-red tiles. The place was quiet; most of the horses had been taken out to the fields for exercise.

Aristander led them into an outhouse. The chorus thronged at the door, blocking out the light, till Aristander screamed at them to stand aside. Oil-lamps illuminated a garish scene. Telamon felt sick as he looked at all four corpses, blackened and twisted, burnt beyond recognition.

"How do you know these are Arella and the rest?"

"Well, it can't be anyone else in her house!" Aristander retorted. "Or wearing her jewellery. Hesiod wore a ring, the insignia of the chief scribe of the city."

He handed Telamon a pomander drenched in rose water. The physician ordered the lamps to be brought closer.

"Tell me what you see," Aristander asked thickly.

Telamon tried not to reflect, to imagine, just to observe and report. He went round all four corpses.

"Two men, two women," he began. "Blackened and burnt. They were probably saturated in oil, lying on a hard floor." He turned one corpse over to reveal patches of burnt skin. "The floor protected their backs. Three of them had been clubbed to death. Well, at least I think so, from their shattered skulls. Hair, eyes, lips and noses have disappeared, ears shrivelled, tongues turned to liquid, but the teeth are relatively unmarked. There is very little skin on any of the cadavers. Faugh!" Telamon groaned and walked to the door. He leaned against the lintel gulping in the cool afternoon air before returning to examine the grisly remains. "Three of the victims have had their skulls smashed. One, two blows to the side of the head."

87

"As in the Temple of Hercules?" Aristander asked, his voice muffled by the pomander.

"As in the Temple of Hercules," Telamon agreed. "But, there again, I've seen similar wounds on many a battlefield. This fourth victim" – he pointed to one, head twisted, mouth open in the snarl of death – "his skull is complete. He has been stabbed, in the throat or chest. There's nothing else. Once they were dead, they were saturated in oil and consumed by a fierce fire. They could be the people you describe: Arella, her maid, the porter and Hesiod the scribe."

"Look again," Aristander demanded.

Telamon made to object but he sighed, held the pomander to his nose and examined the corpses once again. The remains belonging to Hesiod were ghastly: the flesh had bubbled and shrivelled leaving no recognizable feature. The ribs protruded through fragments of charred skin; Telamon could detect no fracture. Arella's corpse, strangely, had a few golden locks at the back of the head untouched by the fire. The front and side of her skull were completely shattered, the damage of the blow worsened by the fire. The maid had a clean blow to the right side: a whole piece of her skull was missing and a deep fissure ran from the gap down to the base.

"She was struck violently," Telamon declared. "A terrible swinging blow by this mysterious assassin. He crept up behind her. She turned slightly but it was too late: her skull was shattered, brains and blood oozing out before she ever fell to the ground."

He moved to the corpse of the porter: this, too, was blackened and shrivelled. The front and side of his skull bore no contusion or fractures; the killing blow was to the back of the head. He examined this carefully.

"Again," his voice sounded muffled, "you are talking of terrible violence, a strong person wielding a war club." Telamon's interest quickened. "Do we know anything about Arella's habits?"

"Why?"

Telamon dropped the sponge and walked out into the cobbled yard; Aristander followed. The chorus grouped round like school-boys. They had seen the hideous cadavers and knew enough Greek to follow Telamon's explanation. They had a deep fascination and reverence for this physician. He could tell so much from a corpse and was so often consulted by their exalted master. Moreover, he was kind and gentle when he tended their scrapes and bruises or made them drink herbal potions after they had consumed too much beer. Telamon gazed at their faces.

"Aristander," he murmured, "why do they look the same? Are they brothers or cousins? Blue eyes, blond hair, their faces are even shaped the same!"

"They come from the same tribe." Aristander waved his hand. "Telamon, stop keeping me waiting!"

"Arella was a courtesan," Telamon began. He smiled. "If I understand correctly, they sleep late, rise and spend the rest of the day preparing for the evening. A little," he winked at Aristander, "like yourself, eh?"

"That's my secret."

"No it isn't, everybody knows!"

"I am waiting, Telamon."

"Well, courtesans tend to be lonely people, the keepers of secrets, like yourself. They indulge men's fantasies, pamper them, make them feel like powerful princes. So they tend to have few servants who can eavesdrop or become busy-bodies. Arella has a maid and a porter. Now" – Telamon gestured back to where the corpses lay – "whoever came into that house must have known Arella's routine."

"He could have come across the wall?"

"Yes," Telamon agreed. "And he could have been unfortunate. Arella might have been entertaining your chorus, or half of Alexander's army."

"That's highly unlikely."

"No, but he had to make sure, didn't he? You can't just walk into a house, slay the mistress and her servant. You have to be sure there is no one else there."

"So he must have knocked on the door?"

"Yes, he knocked on the door. The porter opens it and allows him in, which means her killer was recognized as a former customer, or someone quite powerful with the authority to impress. The killer would ask: 'Is your mistress at home?' The porter replied: 'Yes.' 'By herself?' Again the porter would answer: 'Yes'."

"But Hesiod was there?"

"No, I'll come to him in a while." Telamon wiped his lips. "The porter apparently let this man through without resistance or raising the alarm."

"How do you know that?"

"Well, that's what porters do, don't they? I am sure Arella's man was a burly young oaf, quite capable of defending himself or raising the alarm. Now, Aristander, shut up and let me continue. I wager the walls around Arella's house are high and the gate is barred. The first conversation would have taken place through the grille. The porter unbars the gate and admits the killer. What does he do then, Aristander?"

The necromancer's eyes crinkled into a smile. "The porter would bar the gate again."

"You can imagine the scene. 'Stand there, sir, and I'll take you up to the house.' He turns to bar the gate and push back the bolts at the top and bottom. He crouches down; as he does, the assassin strikes. One killing blow with a club to the back of the head."

"Why not use a knife?"

"That requires getting a little too close, the risk of a fumble or a mistake. No, a club is the best weapon to use. The porter is slain, the killer is now free to act as he wishes. He knows the house only contains two young women who will find it difficult to resist him. He walks across the grass. Arella is in her pool, her maid nearby. He comes up quietly behind the latter. The girl half turns and takes a hideous blow to the right side of the head. Arella is preoccupied. Perhaps she was swimming or drying herself, her eyes full of water? The killer seizes her at the edge of the pool and kills her. He drags all three corpses into the house, then ransacks it from attic to cellar."

"We have no proof of that," Aristander intervened. "The place is now nothing but blackened ash and charred timber. Only the stone base survives."

"Ah yes," Telamon replied. "The assassin didn't arrive to kill and leave. He was searching for something: manuscripts, letters, a pledge, a bill of sale." Telamon spread his hands. "He may have found it. He may not, but he wanted to make sure. The house is doused in oil: he's preparing to burn it when Hesiod arrives."

"But wouldn't the assassin have locked the gate?" Aristander asked.

"No, I don't think he would. He'd keep it closed but with the bolts pulled back. If someone did visit, he would prefer them to come in rather than stand and raise the alarm; that's what happened to Hesiod. The scribe turned up, not just to discuss matters but for something else." Telamon sighed. "But I have no evidence for this. Nevertheless," Telamon continued, "Hesiod walked to his death. The assassin was waiting for him inside the house: unlike the others, Hesiod wasn't killed by a club, probably a knife thrust to the throat or heart. So much killing," he added, "and only the assassin knows the true reason for it."

Chapter 4

———————◇◇◇◇———————

"At Ephesus, Alexander frequently recreated his mind, after the fatigues of government, by visiting the studio of Apelles."

Quintus Curtius Rufus:
The History of Alexander the Great, Book II, Chapter 6

Aristander's further questions were silenced by a commotion at the entrance to the stable yard. A group of Foot Companions, swords drawn, strode in, Alexander behind, his arm on a man's shoulder. Telamon didn't recognize the stranger: he was tall, willowy, with black curly hair and a coloured band round his forehead. He was dressed in a long dark-brown tunic which looked more like a woman's smock, his mantle slung over one arm. He and the king were chattering like two boys.

Alexander paused, his arm slipping from the man's shoulder; he grasped his hand and stared across.

"Aristander, Telamon, come here!"

The king was excited, face flushed, eyes gleaming. He was dressed in half-armour, as if he had come from the drill ground. Telamon recalled he had planned to go hunting.

"Come on! Come on!" Alexander strode forward, almost dragging the man with him. "Aristander. My, er, counsellor. Telamon, my physician, or so he claims," Alexander added mischievously. "This is Apelles."

Telamon's hand went forward. "I have heard of you, sir, and admired your paintings."

The artist's long, rather horsey face broke into a smile that transformed his ugliness. He blushed slightly as he grasped Telamon's hand.

"It's very flattering to meet a stranger" – Apelles's voice was low and cultured – "who has both seen and admired your work. I have also heard of you, Telamon. Your work at the Temple of Aesculapius in Corinth, drawing poison from a lung?"

"Isn't this flattering?" Aristander spoke up, stretching out his hand. "We've all heard about each other. What clever people we are!"

Apelles's smile faded as he grasped Aristander's hand. "I've heard of you, too, Aristander." The artist paused, searching the Master of Secrets' face. "I would love to paint your eyes, the expression there, but it might be beyond me."

Aristander, discomfited, stood back. Alexander, however, was full of the occasion. He embraced Apelles, hugging him like a long-lost brother.

"Apelles is a great artist." The king's eyes gleamed. "I have persuaded him to paint me astride Bucephalus. I'm not too sure what I shall be holding, the spear of Artemis or Zeus's thunderbolt."

"You could carry both," Telamon remarked. "Possibly balance a third on your head?"

Alexander blinked. "I don't understand . . .?"

Apelles began to laugh, a chuckle which began deep in his chest, shoulders shaking. Telamon studied him curiously. The man was regarded as a genius, not only for his use of colour but also sometimes the way he could catch an expression, a movement. Anyone who looked at his paintings long enough became part of them; the figures and the beasts in his murals possessed a life all of their own. What sort of man could work such magic? Apelles's face was neither young nor old; his clever eyes were full of mockery; the brows met over the bridge of the long pointed nose: he had a generous mouth and broad chin. His face was deeply furrowed, testimony not only to a life dedicated to his art but to years of suffering.

"Apelles didn't want to come to Ephesus, last time he was here the Persians ill-treated him," Alexander explained in a hushed whisper. "However, he is my guest." The king held his hands up. "Apelles will do my painting and have it placed in the Temple of Artemis: a broad, breathtaking mural which will excite the eye and gladden the heart."

"You will have to get permission for that," Apelles said. "The rulers of Ephesus —" He bit his lip. "I am sorry, my lord: you *are* the ruler of Ephesus."

"No, no." Alexander went across and tapped the corselet of one of the Foot Companions. "You haven't put that on properly," he said crossly. "Look, the gap between the front and back is too wide. In battle that might cost you your life." He came back. "No, Apelles, in everything you are right."

Once again the king grasped Apelles's hand, holding it like a father would a favourite son's. Telamon noticed how long and sensitive the artist's fingers were; streaks of red paint still stained his wrist and thumb.

"Captain!" Alexander called over to the officer of the guard. "Take Apelles to his chamber. He must have everything he needs." The king grasped the painter's face between his hands and kissed him full on the lips. "You are Alexander's friend," he declared, standing back. "You are my guest."

Apelles thanked him, nodded at Telamon and Aristander and strode away, escorted by the guard. Alexander watched them go, brow furrowed. "A great artist," he whispered. "He's going to paint me. Father may have had his statue in the Temple of Artemis, but I'll have my painting!"

He spun on his heel, head slightly to one side as if he were examining Telamon and Aristander for the first time. He clicked his tongue noisily, a mannerism copied from his mother Olympias.

"You have news, I hear?" He gestured to where the chorus stood, some distance away. "I don't like standing downwind of them. Moreover, their Greek is better than they pretend."

He walked over to a horse trough and sat on the edge, patting the rim on either side. "Well, you'd best sit down. We are meeting the powerful men of Ephesus in a short while. So, tell me every-thing."

Aristander did. Alexander sat, legs apart, hands resting on his thighs, head slightly down. He never interrupted, though now and again he whispered to himself. When Aristander finished he stared up at the sky, its dark blue now shot with the red-gold rays of the setting sun.

"It's going to be a beautiful evening," he murmured. "I've got the palace cooks to prepare a banquet. You are all attending."

Telamon stifled his groan. He knew Alexander's drinking parties; he only hoped nothing untoward would happen.

"We'll have venison, boar's meat and something sweet with plenty of honey: that will help me digest what you've told me." He played with his leather wrist-guard.

A groom led across a horse, hooves scratching on the cobbles.

"Don't hold that halter too tight!" Alexander shouted. "You can see it's been sweating, so dry it well. No, don't bring it over here for water, you fool! Let it cool first!"

"Are you well, my lord?" Telamon asked. Alexander's excitability was apparent; his face slightly flushed, the strange-coloured eyes darting here and there.

"I am not well, physician. I have just ridden through Ephesus. Oh, all is quiet, but my word has been violated. Murders have been committed and, apparently, they are going to continue."

He turned and slapped Aristander on the knee. "You should have arrested Arella immediately, she was the link in all this. So, what do we have?" Alexander stretched out his hands. "The Oligarch party is almost destroyed, the Democrats are in power. We have those grisly murders at the Temple of Hercules. A whore, who possibly knew a great deal about what happened, is also murdered. The scribe Hesiod may have suspected Arella was a fount of knowledge. He goes to her house and is killed. I want this to end." Alexander added warningly, "There will be no faction fights in my Ephesus. Now we come to the Centaur. He's undoubtedly an assassin and a spy. He takes his orders directly from Persepolis and he's probably been bribed to murder me." He paused. "'Must he die in his own house?'" he quoted. "'Of a painful sickness?'" He glanced at Telamon. "Book eleven of the *Iliad*."

"No, it's Book thirteen," Telamon replied.

"I was just testing," the king grinned. "If I am to die" – he stared down at his hands – "let it be in battle, like Achilles."

"Achilles had his vulnerable heel," Telamon retorted.

"Aye." Alexander got to his feet. "And I have councillors who fail me."

"That's not fair!" Telamon glowered up at him.

"No, it isn't," Alexander agreed. "But it's the way things are. I wish they were different."

He would have continued, but a chamberlain came hurrying into the yard, lifting up his gorgeously embroidered robe, disdainfully stepping round the pools of urine and mounds of horse manure.

"Sire," he gasped, "your guests have arrived. They await you in the council chamber."

"Are you Persian?" Alexander asked.

The man bowed deeply. "No sire, Median, though my grandmother was Greek."

"We'll be there," Alexander replied. "And, for pity's sake, watch as you go back. Horse manure is very slippery."

Escorted by Telamon and Aristander, he walked back into the palace. The king paused to wash his hands and face and sent for Hephaestion. They waited for the king's friend in the vestibule. He came hurrying up, a wine goblet in one hand, a small figurine in the other.

"I found this in a chamber." Hephaestion's face was wine-flushed. "It's the God Apollo, my patron. May I keep it?"

Alexander plucked it from his hand and studied it. "Pure alabaster," he declared, and dropped it. The statue smashed into pieces.

"Why did you do that?" Hephaestion gasped.

Alexander kicked the pieces away with his sandalled foot. He grasped Hephaestion's arm and pushed him further down the passage. "You are my friend, Hephaestion, my sword companion. Never ask for anything, just take it."

Aristander glanced at Telamon and raised his eyebrows.

"Come on!" The king clapped his hands.

Guards came out of the shadows, forming a ring around the royal party as they made their way through the palace. They crossed empty marble hallways, walked down exquisitely furnished passageways, through great doors of leather-covered cedar into the great council chamber. This was an oval-shaped room on the ground floor. The large windows looking out on the garden had been shuttered. Oil-lamps had been lit, winking like a myriad fireflies in their niches along the marble wall. Telamon smiled as he heard the buzzing – the wasps were even here.

The men waiting for them, grouped beyond the circle of high-backed chairs, immediately came forward. Being Greeks, they paused only a few inches from the royal party and bowed. Alexander immediately strode forward to shake hands and exchange the kiss of peace, greeting them as friends and allies, offering wine and refreshments. The leader, Agis, shook his head.

"We have eaten well," he said sharply, "and waited long enough!"

"Then we'll wait no longer," Alexander answered, waving them to the circle of chairs. "Hephaestion." He turned his back on the Ephesians and came back to his own group. "Hephaestion, stay near the door. Telamon, you sit next to me. Aristander, try not to give offence, so watch your tongue and keep your ears sharp."

They took their seats. Alexander insisted his chair be moved so he looked like the king flanked on either side by his councillors, a subtle move to re-emphasize his power and authority among men who regarded him simply as a successful general and nothing else. Telamon made himself comfortable as the formal introductions were made. All the men were dressed in white robes trimmed with red or blue. They exuded power and self-importance: their faces were freshly oiled, costly rings glittered on fingers, expensive mantles lay on the floor beside them. They tapped their sandalled feet as if impatient to finish the business and be gone. Although the group was small, it divided into two. Agis, leader of the Democrats, Peleus and Dion the lawyer. The remaining two were Meleager, leader of the Oligarchs, and his fresh-faced son with untidy blond hair and a plump, pink face. Apparently nervous, he kept close to his father, who glared across at his inveterate enemies.

"Why are we here?" Agis demanded, brushing aside Alexander's second offer of wine.

"If you wish to be like that," Alexander retorted, "then so be it. You are here, Agis, because I asked you to be. My troops control Ephesus. My army lies camped beyond these walls. I am the conqueror, the victorious Captain-General who destroyed the Persian army at the Granicus."

"Darius has more armies."

"Aye, and a tree has plenty of leaves, but they'll still fall when the wind blows."

Agis allowed himself a slight smile.

"Will you rule Ephesus?" Dion kept his voice to a drawl, hands folded on his lap. "Will you act the tyrant here in a Greek city?"

"No, I am not so stupid while you are too stiff-necked to accept me," Alexander said. "You will have a governor."

Agis sighed and shook his head in disbelief.

"The liberties of this city will be fully restored." Telamon enjoyed the surprise on Agis's face. "Ephesus will be self-governing," Alexander continued. "It will pay tribute – or shall I say make an offering to my treasury?"

"Why?" Peleus demanded.

"Because I am Captain-General of Greece. The city governor will be restored: he will answer to you."

"But the important offices will be held by Macedonians?" Dion asked.

"I didn't say that. Agis will be Chief Magistrate."

Alexander's pronouncement caused a stir.

"Meleager will be your subordinate. Dion shall be Treasurer: you, Peleus, will be in charge of the city secretariat."

Peleus's face broke into a smile. He rubbed his hands.

"You are pleased?" Alexander teased. "Do you think I'm here like a satrap or a tyrant? Ephesus will be a free, self-governing city. I have come to liberate all citizens, be they Greek or Persian."

"But how will it work?" Meleager spoke up.

"It will work because you make it work." Alexander turned to face him. "No more faction fights. No Oligarch against Democrat. No more blood feuds, no rioting, burning or executions!" His voice rang through the chamber. "That's what you came here for, wasn't it?" he insisted. "To obtain your liberties? Well, you shall have them!"

"And the Macedonian troops on the streets?" Agis mimicked Alexander's words.

"They will be withdrawn, a small garrison left, nothing else. Now" — Alexander leaned forward — "let us turn to other business: the killings which took place in the Temple of Hercules."

"It was not our doing!" Agis replied.

"Don't sit there so innocent!" Meleager snarled, pointing accusingly at the Democrat leader. "You murdered and you slaughtered!"

"No more than you did!" Agis threw the accusation back. "My head is shaved because our kinsmen died, stabbed in the market-place, hacked down on the steps of temples by Oligarchs. For years, Meleager, you and your party had the run of this city. Now its liberties have been restored, justice will be done."

"Justice has been done," Alexander interrupted. "It is finished. But tell me about these killings. The ones which occurred before I arrived" — he emphasized the words — "to restore order."

Agis and Meleager, in turn, described the litany of assassinations: death by poison, by the knife or the garrotte. Killings in the full light of day: victims being hunted out beyond the walls at dead of night. Threats and menaces, attacks, assault, rape and robbery. The more he listened, the more repelled Telamon became. These were men who truly hated each other: he wondered if Alexander's charisma could bring such bloody vengeance to an end.

At last both spokesmen finished their litany of shouted accusations and counter-accusations: Alexander never interrupted but listened intently.

"It's a wonder." The king straightened in his chair. "Yes, it's a wonder anyone in Ephesus survived. How long have these killings been going on?"

"Three to four years," Agis replied.

"And what is the tally?" Alexander asked. "Eight leading members of your party, Agis. Meleager?"

"Including those killed in the Temple of Hercules" — the

Oligarch shook his head — "sixteen or seventeen deaths in all. That doesn't include those slain in the recent massacre."

"And no one was brought to justice?" Telamon spoke up.

Agis gazed back, stony-faced.

"These were murders!" Telamon exclaimed. "Whatever the cause, they were still murders! You have priests, you have magistrates, informers, spies! Yet no one has gone on trial?"

Silence greeted his words.

"Events are as we described them." Meleager grasped his son's hand. "Blood for blood! Life for life! Everyone here has lost kinsmen. During the recent terror even women and children died."

"Did any of you order these deaths?" Telamon asked. All he received were dark looks and muttered curses. "Someone must have begun the blood feud," he insisted. "You had two parties here in Ephesus. The Democrats, I believe, wish to have elected officials, a register of voters, a council and magistrates. On the other hand, the Oligarchs believe all power should be held by certain families, and were supported by the Persian Governor and his troops. The situation is not so different in many Greek cities, be it here or on mainland Greece, except for these blood feuds."

"Answer the question!" Alexander ordered. "Is any man here guilty of ordering another person's death?"

"I cannot answer for my colleagues." Agis's voice was full of sarcasm. "But they will agree on one thing. Time and again Demades and I met to establish a truce, to bring an end to these killings. Isn't that true?"

Agis, Peleus and Dion nodded.

"I can speak for Demades," Meleager continued. He gestured at Agis. "Did you not meet in his house and in yours? Did you not share the loving cup and break bread? Each of you take vows? Solemn oaths, witnessed by the priests, that neither of you were party to these killings?"

Agis, a little crestfallen, nodded.

"Were you sincere?" Telamon asked.

"Yes and no," the Democrat replied. "Every time we met I was committed to peace. Then another murder would take place and the truce would be shattered."

101

"And Demades, the leader of the Oligarchs?" Telamon persisted. "Was he sincere? Telling the truth?"

"He was." Meleager spoke up. "To the very end he wanted these killings to stop."

"Did you believe that, Agis?"

The Democrat stared up at the ceiling.

"Did you believe him?"

"Yes, I think so. I wanted the same, but the killings continued."

Alexander tapped Telamon's foot with his own, a sign to continue the questioning.

"And the murders in the Temple of Hercules?"

"The commoners believe it is the work of a centaur, the vengeance of the gods."

"Against whom?" Alexander's voice was dangerously low. Meleager remained unruffled.

"My Lord King, you swore they would be safe and secure. Those who remain in my party still feel nervous: they barricade themselves in their mansions, their servants are armed . . ."

"And I have offered guards," Alexander interrupted. "Soldiers from my elite corps. You are safe. No mythical beast is responsible for the murders, but who, why and how remain a mystery, at least for now."

"Did any of you approach the temple," Telamon asked, "in the days before the massacre took place?"

"I did." Meleager's son spoke up. He was still nervous, moving restlessly, plucking at the mantle across his lap.

"Why?"

"I sent him," Meleager replied, "with secret messages to Demades." He turned, his face full of pride, and grasped his son's shoulder. "Albiades is a brave young man. He volunteered. I sent messages of comfort and reassurance to Demades. I even told him to trust you, my Lord King, and that the sooner he left the temple, the better."

Telamon could sense Alexander's growing anger. "You approached the temple." He pointed at Albiades. "You went in disguise?"

"I dressed like a commoner," the young man replied. "A dirty, sweaty tunic, no sandals on my feet. I pretended to be a curious bystander. Soldiers guarded the door, but they were allowing relatives to approach the entrance."

Alexander nodded. He had permitted this.

"I went up the steps. Socrates was standing by the door . . ."

"Ah, that's right," Alexander intervened. "Callisthenes, the captain of the guard, often remarked on how Socrates seemed to be the bravest. He would come to the porch, stand just within the main door and stare out across the square."

"And you delivered your message?" Telamon asked.

The council room had fallen very silent.

"I spoke to Socrates, but he seemed distracted, as if he didn't want me to be there. He kept nodding, tapping his fingers against the wood, avoiding my gaze as if interested in something behind me. I turned round to look." The young man shook his head. "I could see nothing, just crowds milling about. I became so concerned," Albiades continued, "I returned two days later. This time I demanded to see Demades. He came out and I asked him had his servant Socrates delivered my messages. Demades shook his head and became annoyed. He was very agitated, his face was unshaven, his clothes smelt as if they had been soaked in a privy. I didn't return again."

"Why was the priest at the temple killed?" Alexander demanded.

Agis spread his hands. "We tried to control the mob but it was impossible: the priest was a member of the Oligarch faction."

"He was stupid enough," Peleus spat out, "to make his allegiance known. He was a pompous snob. He hoped, by soliciting favour with the rich and powerful, he would receive endowments for his temple."

"Most temple priests," Meleager spoke up, "do the same. As you know, my Lord King, the Temple of Artemis is being rebuilt; it is a heavy drain on the wealth of this city."

"Ah yes." Alexander now rubbed his hands together. "I wish to come to that."

"One thing." Aristander's voice cracked like a whip. "You said Socrates was standing by the temple door. You all know the whore or courtesan who called herself Arella? Well, she was present on the temple forecourt. She was seen there on at least two occasions. Did she ever approach the temple?"

"What are you trying to do?" Agis snapped. "Trap us? We weren't there. We can't tell you. You had guards. Why not ask them?"

"I have." Aristander pounced like a hunting cat, his voice full of menace. "Callisthenes recalls a young woman, swathed in a dark-red cloak, approaching the temple. Did any of you send her?"

Silence greeted his words.

"Were any of you her clients?"

Again silence.

"Were you?" Aristander demanded.

"That is a personal matter."

"Not now," Telamon declared. "You know the news. Arella has been killed; she, her maidservant and porter, and her house gutted by fire."

Dion shrugged. "So, another whore has died."

"Aren't we missing someone?" Aristander demanded.

Agis looked round. "Our scribe Hesiod, but he may have been delayed."

"For a meeting with the king?" Aristander scoffed. "You have all been given passes to the palace, a sign of great trust and honour. Where is Hesiod now? Or haven't you heard the news?" he added spitefully. "Hesiod's corpse was also found in Arella's house."

His words created consternation. Agis rocked backwards and forwards on his chair. Peleus and Dion began to chatter; Meleager smiled.

"Is this true?" Peleus asked.

"His corpse has been brought to the palace." Aristander made a face. "It could only be recognized by a ring on his finger. He certainly was one of Arella's clients. Why he was there earlier today we can only speculate. What I want to know is where were the rest of you? Did any of you visit this famous courtesan?"

"You talk of confidence and trust," Peleus blustered, "and now ask us to account for our movements."

"Before you leave tonight," Alexander commanded, "I will

104

need an answer to all these questions. According to the evidence the courtesan belonged to no faction."

"Was the attack on her house robbery?" Meleager asked.

"No, no," Aristander shook his head. "People who rob come in the dead of night. This assassin killed four people and burnt Arella's house to conceal any evidence."

"Let's move on! Let's move on!" The king was growing impatient. "Ephesus has now been liberated from Persian rule. I have appointed you as its principal officials. Persian spies still lurk in the city, merchants, travellers, but they are only chaff in the wind. I am only interested in the one who calls himself the Centaur."

The entire group became watchful.

"You know who I'm talking about!" Alexander tapped his foot impatiently. "A very important spy from the Persian court; not even the Governor knew his true identity. Do you?"

"We have heard rumours," Agis replied slowly. "We always knew that both the Governor and the court of Persepolis were fully informed of all matters." He glanced sheepishly across at Meleager.

"Whoever the Centaur is," the Oligarch added, "he knew the secrets of both factions."

"What?" Aristander demanded. "You are saying this Centaur had a foot in either camp?"

Meleager nodded. "I often met with Demades: he raised the matter of a spy in our own camp. I believe Agis had the same anxiety."

"So, here is a man," Telamon summarized, "who spied on you both and reported directly to the Persian court. How did you know?"

"I was often summoned to the palace," Agis said. "The Governor would say he had heard of this or that. Demades was also present. We were astonished at how the Governor knew all our secrets. When we asked him how, he just smiled and said the King of Kings could hear the birdsong in our gardens and the laughter of our children."

"But the name Centaur?" Telamon demanded.

"We pressed the Governor," Meleager replied. "He laughed

and said the wasps told him, that's why his palace was full of them. We all remember the legends about the Centaur, hence the name."

"Could this Centaur, the spy, also be the assassin?" Telamon glanced quickly at Aristander: they knew the truth, but did these powerful citizens?

"I don't know," Meleager replied; Agis nodded in agreement. "We now suspect he is; only the King of Kings knows the full truth."

"But now the King of Kings has gone," Alexander said quietly, "and his Centaur will also disappear. There will be no more factions. No more killings. These mysteries will be resolved."

He got to his feet, a sign the audience was over. The others followed suit rather reluctantly. Alexander waved at the goblets and jug on the table.

"You'll be our guests tonight at the banquet. I ask you to stay and enjoy the gardens. My physician Telamon will be your host. Gentlemen! Tonight we will celebrate a banquet of brotherhood, of unity. You know my wishes in this matter. Please observe them."

Alexander spun on his heel and, with Hephaestion and Aristander following, left the council chamber.

For a while there was an awkward silence. Agis and his two companions walked to one of the windows as if to admire the garden, but became engaged in hushed conversation. Albiades bade farewell to his father and almost ran from the chamber. Telamon took a chair next to Meleager. For some reason he trusted this man with his air of quiet confidence. Meleager stared at the door until his son had left.

"Do you have many children?" Telamon asked.

Meleager smiled. "Four, three boys and a girl."

"And you all survived the massacre?"

"The gods be thanked, yes. I received a warning, anonymously, a small scroll a day before the blood–letting began. I immediately sent my family out of Ephesus. I tried to warn my friends but it was dangerous even to roam the streets. I went into hiding." Meleager turned, determined that his opponents at the window could not hear what he said, and his gaze held Telamon's. "*You* are going to investigate all this, aren't you? *You* arc going to find out who the Centaur is. Who was responsible for that massacre in the temple. But why you, a physician?"

"I am a childhood friend of Alexander. I was with him when we were youths. The great Aristotle taught me to observe symptoms, look for signs."

"And you've spent your life doing that?"

Telamon paused at the sound of marching feet in the corridor. He waited until the footsteps faded.

"My father became tired of bloodshed." Telamon laughed softly. And I wasn't the best of recruits! He sent me to Athens, Corinth and elsewhere to train. I travelled to Italy, the islands, Sicily, Libya and eventually Egypt. I killed a Persian officer there and had to come home. My father's dead. Mother still lives in Pella." Telamon sighed. "So I joined the king. Alexander wants me, like a man hires a physician, to watch for signs, search for the symptoms of treachery."

"Not for his own health?"

"I do give him advice on that," Telamon replied. "But Alexander uses me more for the infection of treason, conspiracy and assassination."

"Will you solve these mysteries?"

"Perhaps. Perhaps not. Tell me." Telamon moved his chair closer. "Could this Centaur have been responsible for the assassinations in both your factions?"

"As I've said, possibly. Agis suspects the same." Meleager spread his hands. "The Persians liked it that way, to have us continually at each other's throats, to divide the powerful Greeks in Ephesus." Meleager emphasized the points on his stubby fingers. "Whatever Agis and the rest may call themselves, Democrats or mob leaders, they're still powerful merchants and tradesmen. Agis imports timber, Dion cloth, Peleus leather goods."

"And you?"

"The best wines in the empire, from Chios, Samos, the vineyards of Lydia and Phrygia."

"And your warehouses were burnt?"

Meleager became guarded. "No, they were not. I know," he

confessed, "it sounds suspicious, but my house and stores were not touched. I thought that might be the work of Agis."

"Why?"

"Ah, don't you know?" Meleager sucked on his lips. "We are half-brothers. We share the same father but different mothers. We were raised in the same household and grew to hate each other. When we reached manhood, we went our separate ways. I often believe our blood is tainted. We should be close as hairs on a man's head, but as far as I can remember it's always been hatred and fighting. No, I'm not blaming Agis. I am as guilty as he! When you are young, Telamon, the blood courses hot and violent. Grievances are nurtured, grudges settled, and, before you realize, you have built a wall of iron, then you arm it with spikes and cutting blades."

"Would Agis protect you?"

"I would like to think so, Telamon. However, what he doesn't know and I do, is that the letter of warning claimed the Democrats had marked me down for death, me and my entire family. What I suspect is that Agis wished to cut me off from the rest of my party. Already the questions are beginning to be asked. How did I escape? How did my family emerge unscathed? Why weren't my mansions and warehouses attacked and burnt? Oh, I suspect Agis hunted for me, but when he couldn't find me, ordered a change of tactics." He sighed. "In a way I am grateful, but for years I shall be treated like a pariah. Some people even suspect I had a hand in the murders at the Temple of Hercules."

"Did you know the courtesan Arella?"

"By name and reputation. I am a happily married man, Telamon. Prostitutes do not concern me."

"Was she a member of your faction?"

Meleager laughed, eyes crinkling in amusement. The group at the window turned, distracted from their own conspiratorial conversation.

"Arella, my good physician, was a member of every faction. When it comes to writhing on the bed, Arella's clients included Democrats, Oligarchs and even Persian officers."

"You know we have Rabinus, the Governor's principal scribe, in the dungeons below?"

"We've all heard of it," Meleager replied.

Telamon stared across at a painting on the far wall, depicting Medes, in their gorgeous robes, carrying gifts to the King of Kings, above them the all-seeing eye of their god borne aloft by eagle wings.

"We were talking about the assassinations," Telamon said. "They could have been the work of the Centaur?"

"Ah yes. The Centaur probably spied on us both. He didn't betray one party to another but to the Persians. Yet how could one man know the secrets of both parties? Secondly, the assassinations were carried out at any time of the day, in a house, a garden or the marketplace. I have reflected on this: the assassin always knew where his victim would be."

"As if he knew the whereabouts of all of you, whatever your faction?"

Meleager agreed and scratched his head.

"And the gentlemen at the window?"

"I am not your spy, Telamon."

"I didn't say you were. How many of them were clients of Arella?"

Meleager's gaze shifted. "Agis, no. He doesn't love anyone but himself and his child. His wife has died, he has a young daughter: she is the apple of his eye."

"And the other two?"

Meleager chewed on his lip. "Peleus likes young boys and he's brutal with it. Dion perhaps: he's a clever lawyer who has amassed considerable wealth. He's a born demagogue, a leader of the mob. He likes the ladies, does Dion. I would wager it was he rather than Hesiod who visited Arella. But, quickly now." Meleager's fingers brushed Telamon's arm. "One thing I will tell you, my son didn't mention it. He met Demades on one occasion when he was sheltering in the Temple of Hercules; Demades was highly anxious. He told my son, and kept repeating it time and time again, 'Something is wrong, terribly wrong!'"

"Do you know what he meant by that?"

"No, I do not. My son said Demades acted like a man who truly feared for his life, distrustful of everyone."

109

"Did Demades confide in you before the massacres took place?"
Meleager shook his head.

"And the Persians?"

Meleager pushed back his chair. "The Persians controlled Ephesus. I and my party collaborated with them to keep the peace and trade busy. I don't think they shed a tear over our partisan murders."

"Your party was in power when the Centaurs, the Guild of Assassins, were crushed?"

"That's public knowledge," Meleager replied. "We obtained names which yielded other names. Arrests were made, confessions forced and executions carried out." He shrugged. "Our Persian spy has nothing to do with that band of cut-throats except sharing their name."

"You've heard of the House of Medusa?"

Meleager laughed. "Yes, once owned by a Centaur called Malli. They say it's haunted."

"And the treasure?"

"Fable and legend," Meleager scoffed. "A search was made but nothing was ever found."

"Did you know Arella was Malli's daughter?"

Meleager's eyes rounded in surprise. "No. So that's what happened to the child. No one really bothered to search for her."

"What are you talking about?" Agis and the other two left the window and came across. Peleus moved chairs; they sat down facing Telamon.

"You should be careful, physician," Dion smirked. "Otherwise we will think our noble king patronizes one party rather than another."

"Your noble king patronizes neither!"

Telamon whirled round. Alexander stood in the doorway, in one hand a goblet of wine, in the other a small statue of Artemis.

"Oh no, don't stand up!" He placed the goblet on a small table, sauntered across and lounged in a chair. He held up the statue of Artemis, dressed like a huntress.

"Your temple is not yet finished. I would like to pay for the work to be completed."

110

"That's not possible," Dion retorted. "The Temple of Artemis is owned by the city. It is part of our sacred constitution" – the words were spat from his lips – "that no outsider be responsible for the temple."

"I thought you'd say that." Alexander smiled falsely back, though the tension in his voice betrayed his anger. "I do have a special kinship with that temple: a statue to my father was raised there."

"The Persians ordered us to pull it down."

"Will it be restored?"

"Time will tell." Dion was eager to taunt the king.

"I am having a painting done of myself," Alexander continued, "by the great artist Apelles. You know the story? How Artemis left her temple at Ephesus to be present at my birth, and the temple, being unguarded, was burnt down."

Telamon closed his eyes. He only hoped no one would scoff at such a legend. But these were politicians; even Dion knew he had gone far enough.

"I wish to make my devotions to the goddess. I would like my painting installed there. Agis, did you bring what I asked?"

The Democrat opened his wallet and handed across a thin, yellowing scroll of papyrus.

"My Lord King." Agis spread his hands. "We have heard the legend about your birth: however, the Temple of Artemis was burnt down on the night you were born by a madman who was later crucified against the city walls. When asked why he committed arson, he wrote that confession. The Greek is archaic."

Alexander studied the parchment and handed it to Telamon.

"Read it out, physician. What does it say?"

Telamon translated: "I burn, I am, alternately, the Beginning and the End of all things, the Child of the Immortal and the son of God." Telamon glanced up. "What does it mean?"

"We don't know," Dion scoffed. "That's what the madman wrote. I cannot see any reference," he added spitefully, "to Alexander of Macedon."

"I will keep this for a while." The king rolled up the parchment and tossed it at Telamon. "We shall see what truth it contains."

111

Chapter 5

———◆◆◆◆———

"On his arrival in Ephesus, Alexander recalled everyone
who had been expelled for supporting him: he stripped
the small ruling clique of its power and restored democratic institutions."

Arrian, *The Campaigns of Alexander*, Book I, Chapter 18

"I am terrified," Rabinus whispered a prayer. "I am alone in the
midst of my enemies. No one can help."

Tears welled up in the Persian's eyes. He rose from his cot bed,
walked over and stared through the grille of his cell door. Nothing
but blank walls. Down the passage he heard the laughter and
chatter of the Macedonian sentries, the gurgle of water and wine
being mixed in a cup. He smelt the well-roasted goose served to
the soldiers. Rabinus licked his lips: he felt more hungry in prison
than when he had been a busy scribe. He turned and leaned against
the door, staring up at the small aperture in the far wall which
allowed in some light and air. Daylight was dying, the sunlight
fading. Rabinus's body quivered in terror. Try as he might, he
couldn't control the shaking of his hands, the weakness in his legs.
Once again he cursed Arella.

"The treacherous bitch!" he spat out.

If he was ever given the chance, he'd take a dagger and gouge
out those sly, beautiful eyes ringed with their black kohl. He'd
scrape his nails along those painted cheeks. Rabinus walked up and
down. He became so restless he beat his fists against the wall and
stifled a cry. The Macedonians would only mock him, come down
and peer through the grille. Yet it was not so much the prison:
Rabinus was trapped wherever he might be. If he were released,

how could he survive in a Greek city where he had been a member of the occupying power? And if he went back to Persepolis? Rabinus sat down on the bed. He didn't trust Aristander, that sly-eyed demon with the cunning of a mongoose and all the compassion of a striking cobra. If he returned to Persepolis, the Lord Mithra would be waiting, together with the Cowled Ones. The questioning would begin again. Why had he not fled with the Governor? Why had he allowed himself to be captured? Why had the Macedonians freed him?

And what answer could he give? Rabinus moaned and lay back on the bed. He would face terror, fire and torture. The Lord Mithra's servants would strip him and beat him with rods. They would take him to a Tower of Silence where the bodies of the dead hung in wire cages, open to the skies and the pecking claws and beaks of the buzzards. They would lash him to such a cage, walk away and forget him. Rabinus recalled his soft-eyed wife, her beautiful face hidden by a veil, hair lustrous black as night, her soft plump body; his house and gardens; the small orchard beyond the fountain; his two children running towards him. Why hadn't he fled? He had been so beguiled by Arella, so confident the danger was slight: Alexander would leave Ephesus as the King of King's great army counter-attacked and thrust the Macedonian back into the sea.

"Arrogance," Rabinus whispered. "Lord Ahura-Mazda, I was arrogant: in my pride I stumbled."

Rabinus had been so used to slipping along the streets on the business of his master. He recalled that last journey to the Temple of Hercules, the heavy money-belt wrapped about his waist. The frightened priest standing on the steps, the dark cool recess and the Centaur's shadow behind him.

Rabinus sat up in his bed. He knew who the Centaur was! One piece of information he had withheld. On the one hand, if he escaped he might try and seek the Centaur out. On the other, he could use this, his last bargaining counter with Alexander. Perhaps the Macedonians would take him into their service? Rabinus had heard how Alexander was favouring former servants of the great king: the only reason Rabinus

114

was in prison was because of his former position, his close links with the Centaur, and because he had not immediately surrendered in accordance with Alexander's decree. Rabinus calmed down: he would use that information! He recalled the Governor's fat face shrouded by oily ringlets, ears and throat glittering with precious gems.

"Rabinus," the Governor had lisped in the security of his private quarters, "you are my trusted scribe, my confidant."

The flatteries had slipped out like honey from a jar. Rabinus had dutifully listened. The Governor waved plump fingers and the scribe – oh, he tried not to laugh. The Governor wished to meet Arella the famous courtesan. He had heard so much about her from that ancient whore-mistress Basileia, the Queen of the Moabites. Could Rabinus effect an introduction? Would Arella come to the palace? The shifty-eyed Governor smiled. Rabinus knew he could not refuse: he kept quiet and listened as flattery was heaped upon flattery. The Governor had a wife, but she was away in Susa visiting relatives. The matter would have to be confidential between comrades, colleagues and, the Governor had winked slowly, even friends. Hadn't the Governor trusted him with important secrets of their Great King and the Lord Mithra? The Governor leaned across the table.

"You deal with the Centaur," he murmured. "You know I have his name?"

Rabinus had stared back, owl-eyed.

"If the Lady Arella were to come here?"

Rabinus had left the Governor's chamber head up, shoulders back. He had immediately gone to see the courtesan; it had been his turn to pour flattery upon flattery. How the Governor was an important man, a kinsman of the great Darius. Arella, the little bitch, had simpered and cooed, fluttered her eyelids and acted the reluctant maid. However, two nights later, she had slipped through one of the many secret entrances into the palace. Rabinus himself had led her, cloaked and cowled, though this did not conceal the aura of exquisite perfume the bitch had drenched herself in. Down passageways to the Governor's personal quarters, to a meal consisting of the finest wines, precious fruits and superbly cooked meats and other dishes. Arella had stayed all night. She later pouted that the Governor had been hard work; the fact that the Governor did not leave his quarters the following day was a powerful witness to Arella's skill in love-making. The Governor was pleased. He was in Rabinus's debt. One day he placed the name of the Centaur on a piece of parchment and left it on Rabinus's desk.

The scribe's reverie was shattered by the raucous laughter of one of the guards. Rabinus sat up, waving away a marauding wasp. He filled an earthenware bowl with a little of the watered wine and sipped at it. Perhaps he should meet Aristander again? However, once he had given that name, once he had betrayed his masters in Persepolis, there would be no going home: no more wife and children, no more walks in their shady garden.

"Rabinus!"

The scribe started. He jumped up and walked towards the door and stared through the iron bars: the passageway beyond was empty.

"Rabinus!"

He whirled round: his name was being called through the little aperture high in the wall. Rabinus stared. The courtyard beyond was usually empty, nothing but a stretch of dirt, a cobbled area where carts and lumber were left.

"Rabinus, are you there?"

The scribe bit his lip. Whoever was outside would have found his cell easily enough, moving like a dog from one aperture to another: his visitor could tell if someone was inside simply by the smell. The Governor's gaolers had done likewise when they'd roused prisoners in the dead of night to frighten them.

"Rabinus, I know you're there! Don't be nervous. Come closer!"

Rabinus walked across the cell and stared up. "Who are you?" he whispered; he knew his voice would carry.

"I am your friend, Rabinus."

"Are you the Centaur?"

"I am your friend," the voice repeated. "You have not betrayed

116

your master, have you, Rabinus? Think of your wife and children in Persepolis! Of the king's guards arriving at your house."

"I have not betrayed you," Rabinus stammered.

His reply was greeted with a slow chuckle. "Is Aristander going to free you?"

"I am a prisoner," Rabinus wailed.

"Hush now! Hush now! I am the Centaur!"

The sweat broke out on Rabinus's back.

"Rabinus, I know this palace like the back of my hand, all its secret entrances and darkened passageways. Don't be afraid, Rabinus. Do not betray your friends. I have come to free you, but" – the voice became hard – "you must keep faith!"

"How can I be freed?" Rabinus whispered.

"How did all those fools die in the Temple of Hercules?" came the mocking reply.

"What surety do I have? What guarantees?"

Rabinus thought the Centaur had moved away: nothing but silence.

"Surety?" the voice taunted slowly. "Guarantees? The woman who betrayed you, the whore Arella: she is dead, her beautiful body burnt to ash, her soul gone to the corrosive fires of Hades. Do you see what happens, Rabinus, to those who betray? I shall return!"

For a while Rabinus just stood gaping up at the dying light pouring through the gap. Then, grasping the wine jug, he hastily filled his bowl to the brim and drank greedily.

The Governor's banqueting hall was ablaze with light: oil-lamps glowed in alabaster jars, arranged in niches along the wall. Bronze oil-lamps hung from the cedarwood rafters. Sweet-smelling braziers crackled in corners, giving off heat, fragrant herbs laid on the burning coals. The guests lounged on couches, a small table before each of them. The air was warm, stifling with the perfumed oils as well as the wreaths which had been passed round by a fruit girl before the banquet began.

Alexander sprawled on a purple and gold couch which had pride of place on a small dais. He was dressed in a white linen robe edged with scarlet, a silver wreath on his head. All the king's companions, his principal generals, were present. Alexander was deep in conversation with Apelles, his guest of honour, using spilt wine to draw a diagram on the table before him. On his left Hephaestion, who had drunk too much, lay half asleep. The guests, sprawled on couches arranged in a horseshoe fashion, had eaten and drunk well. Wheat and barley loaves had been served, followed by appetizing savouries: fresh fruit, shellfish, roasted birds and salted sturgeon, baked mackerel, meats in flavoured sauces and, finally, spit-roasted lamb. Afterwards, the tables had been cleared and a dessert of honey cakes and dried fruits was served with even more wine.

Alexander joined his companions, who were teasing each other by throwing bones and scraps of fruit. Acrobats and dancers, fire-eaters and tumblers, musicians with flutes and double pipes, dancing girls and jesters, had all been invited to grace the occasion: none had been greeted with any approbation. Led by Ptolemy, Alexander's generals acted like a group of naughty schoolboys: they had pelted the artistes with scraps of food until they withdrew in disgust, leaving the royal party to the serious business of drinking.

Telamon had eaten well but drunk little. Now he lounged against the headrest: Aristander, on his left, was also careful what he drank, especially when Ptolemy was nearby. Nevertheless, the Master of the King's Secrets had dressed for the occasion in a billowing coloured robe found among the Persian Governor's wardrobe. Sandals of the same colour graced Aristander's feet, and his toes- and fingernails were painted a deep henna. He had rubbed cosmetics into his scrawny cheeks; black kohl rings made his eyes more fearsome. His fine hair had also been oiled and prinked so it stood up, as Ptolemy scoffed, like the quills on a porcupine. Every time Aristander moved, the heavy jewellery he wore clinked and clattered.

He now pursed his lips in a spiteful pout and glared across at the leading citizens of Ephesus, most of whom were feasting to their hearts' content.

"Look at them!" Aristander jibed. "Revelling in their own

118

importance and new appointments. I wouldn't trust them as far as I could spit!"

"Neither does Alexander," Telamon replied.

The physician stretched his legs to ease the cramp and glared around. Despite the wreaths, the flowing wine, the fragrant air and the savoury food, Alexander left nothing to chance. Royal guards, dressed in full battle armour and carrying shields and drawn swords, stood in the shadows: Alexander's personal escort, ready to intervene, not only to protect the king, but even to restrain his companions. When the wine flowed freely, these could lunge viciously at each other over some half-forgotten grievance or grudge. Two of Aristander's chorus stood behind their master, watching his every move. Telamon could never understand their unswerving adoration of this sinister man: Aristander couldn't tolerate naked steel and sometimes fainted at the sight of blood.

"Just look at them." Aristander flicked his fingers, aping the gestures of a lady of the court. On such occasions his voice grew even more high-pitched.

Telamon stared across. Meleager was by himself, drinking moodily. Next to him, Dion was searching around for a dancing girl who'd caught his eye. Dark-faced Agis was in deep conversation with Peleus. Now and again the Democrat would turn his head and glare across at Telamon.

"My spies have been busy," Aristander whispered. "Arella was a popular poppet. I wish I'd met her, she could have taught me something." He banged the arm of the couch. "My mistake, I should have plucked up that little sweetmeat immediately."

"You said your spies had been busy?"

"Now, now, Telamon, don't get bitchy with your friend. I've been trying to find out where they all were," Aristander continued. "The fire at Arella's house was noticed just after midday."

"And?"

"Well, we know that Peleus was busy in the marketplace, haggling with some young boy. Meleager was at home. According to our spy, the Oligarch never left, though," Aristander simpered, "I could be mistaken."

119

"And Agis?"

"Ah, that's where it becomes interesting. Agis apparently visited Dion but Dion wasn't at home. We can't find out where the lawyer was. Now isn't that strange?"

Aristander paused as a chamberlain bustled up the banqueting hall, all a-waddle and full of self-importance. He neatly dodged a pear thrown at him by Ptolemy and knelt before the dais, whispering across the table at Alexander. The king, who had been busy caressing Apelles's shoulder, sat up in annoyance.

"What is it?" Telamon asked.

"The widow of Demades, the Oligarch leader killed at the Temple of Hercules, wishes to show her affection and thanks to our king."

"But he was killed! Murdered!"

"The woman wishes to show that she does not hold Alexander responsible. I think Meleager had a hand in it."

The chamberlain withdrew. Alexander clapped his hands noisily and got to his feet.

"Gentlemen!" he bawled. "A noble woman of this city, an honourable widow, wishes to pay her respects. She will be treated with every civility. Ptolemy, for Apollo's sake, wake Seleucus: make sure the sot doesn't vomit!"

The banqueting hall fell silent. Outside the double doors a gong sounded. Preceded by guards, the widow of the murdered Oligarch, dressed in mourning weeds, her grey hair hidden under a dark purple veil, made her way slowly up the hall. Behind her came two children and other members of her household. The young woman walking beside her held an open cedarwood casket. On the scarlet cushion inside rested a priceless goblet which shimmered in the light, drawing envious gasps from Alexander's companions.

The widow was tall, elegant, her sorrowful face almost hidden by a cowl. She walked slowly past the couches. Alexander snapped his fingers. A Guards officer hastily moved the small banqueting tables on the dais. The widow would have knelt, but Alexander shook his head and stepped forward to greet her. Telamon caught his breath.

The widow woman took the casket from her maid: in that instant her face did not look sorrowful but angry, resentful; just the twist of the lips, the way she glared at the maid. Telamon swung his legs off the couch. The woman was now cradling the casket.

"My lord." Her voice was strong and carrying. "My lord Alexander, King of Macedon, Captain-General of all Greece, I bring you this gift, this priceless goblet, as a token of my appreciation."

She handed the casket back to the maid, took the goblet off the cushion and handed it to the king. Alexander accepted it. Always a lover of beautiful things, he held it up, turning it so it caught the light.

"It's pure gold!" Aristander whispered. "I'm sure it's silver-plated inside and studded with gems!"

Telamon watched the widow. She moved quickly, one hand plucking off the scarlet cushion and delving deep into the box. Alexander, who never drank as much as he claimed, caught this sudden movement: he stepped back, even as the woman plucked up the concealed knife and, in one glittering arc, struck at the king's exposed neck.

Alexander, a born swordsman, used to the lunge and parry of battle, was faster. He used the goblet to fend off the blow. The widow was thrown off balance. Alexander caught her free hand. Hephaestion threw himself across the table, crashing into the woman, sending her sprawling to the floor, wrenching the dagger from her grip. Guards hurried forward. Tables were overturned, dishes sent clattering, there were shouts and screams. The children in the widow's entourage began to wail. Meleager was shouting. He tried to come forward but a burly captain of the guard pushed him back. Alexander stood on the dais coolly examining the goblet: his black-armoured guards dragged Demades's widow up and forced her to kneel before the king.

Alexander, his face pale, gazed at her as if distracted. "My lady, I did not tell you to kneel."

The guards pulled her to her feet.

"Nor did I tell them to hold you fast."

The widow woman stood alone, head bowed, shoulders shaking.

"I thank you for your gift." The king's voice was carrying. "I understand your grief. I gave my word and my word was broken. I think thoughts of peace and I wish you well. I accept your gift."

Alexander stepped off the dais. He plucked the dagger from Hephaestion's hand and threw it over his shoulder to clang and clatter on the marble floor. Alexander abruptly grabbed the woman by the shoulder and gave her the kiss of peace on each cheek, then, moving to one of the tables which had not been overturned, he took a dish of honey cakes and crouched before the wailing children.

"Take the cake." Alexander stroked a child's hair. "And the dish. Captain of the Guard" – Alexander got to his feet – "escort this lady back to her house. Let it be known that Alexander of Macedon does not make war on widows and orphans!"

"Magnaminous as ever," Aristander whispered. "I never know which way the boy is going to jump."

Telamon was about to reply when a conch horn brayed, raising the alarm. The wailing sound created immediate silence. The Ephesian dignitaries milled about. Two of Alexander's companions remained fast asleep, but the more quick-witted gathered round the king. More guards appeared from the shadows. Aristander's "lovely boys" came round the couch, knocking aside a table. Alexander turned and glared at them. A chamberlain hurried in, slipping and slithering, and stopped before the banqueting tables, wringing his hands.

"My Lord King, the alarm has been raised!"

"That I realize!"

Alexander strode forward, beckoning Aristander and Telamon to follow. They left the banqueting hall. The chamberlain, fluttering like a brightly coloured butterfly, gasped: "This way! This way!"

He led them through an open door where soldiers thronged in the light of torches. The courtyard was ringed on three sides by shadow-filled porticoes. An officer strode forward.

"My Lord King, one of our men has been killed."

He took them across to the portico on the left. Wooden hoardings, used in inclement weather to close the portico off, were stacked at the far end. The murdered soldier lay hidden behind these, his corpse betrayed by a sticky pool of blood oozing along the pavement.

"Pull him out!" Alexander ordered.

Aristander shouted for more torches. The corpse was dragged out. The dead soldier was dressed in a corselet and kilt, his pale young face masked by the blood which had spurted from his nose and mouth.

Telamon bent down, turned the corpse over and examined the killing blow.

"Very similar to the Temple of Hercules," he explained. "One savage blow. Look, my lord, the man has no sword belt, no shield, no spear."

Telamon peered behind the wooden hoarding. "I see no sign of his helmet." He tugged at the black sash round the dead man's waist. "A member of the Raven Squadron, this is their colour, isn't it? Why should someone kill him?" He felt the corpse's face and lightly touched the congealing blood with his fingers. "He's been dead some time," Telamon continued. "The blood is almost dry, the flesh stone cold, the limbs have hardened." He glanced over his shoulder at the officer. "Do you recognize him?"

"Not from my regiment, sir. This is a lonely place," the officer continued. "He may have wandered in here, seen someone and challenged them."

"But why isn't he wearing a sword belt?" Alexander asked. "Units from Raven are being used to guard the gates."

Telamon rose and walked along the portico. He stopped at the marble seat built against the wall. "Bring the torches!" he shouted.

Telamon crouched down and scraped at the rough stain on the edge of the marble bench. He then felt beneath the bench, found an earthenware jug and pulled it out; it smelt of cheap wine. Telamon thrust this into the officer's hands and, sitting down, peered up at the starlit sky.

"Why so mysterious, Telamon?" Alexander urged.

Telamon moved along the seat. "Think of late afternoon," he

said. "The sun has shifted. This portico is hidden in shadows: a cool, refreshing place to sit." He pointed in front of him. "This bench is almost obscured by the pillars. What we have here is a soldier who has come off duty. He goes to the barracks where he leaves his helmet and sword." Telamon pointed with his hand. "There's another courtyard further along, isn't there, that leads to the kitchens?"

The captain of the guard followed the direction of his gesture and agreed.

"What does any soldier do," Telamon asked, "after he's been on duty at the gates during the heat of the day? He goes to the kitchens, filches a jug of cheap wine, which he doesn't want to share, and comes here, away from the watchful eye of an officer, hiding in the shadows behind the pillar." Telamon took the jug back and weighed it in his hand. "Three or four good draughts in this."

"And he goes for a sleep," Alexander finished. The king barked at the soldiers gathering round to stand back.

"The assassin then strikes," Telamon explained. "The sleeping, half-drunken soldier can't resist. One savage blow and he's killed then dragged behind the hoardings."

Telamon rose and walked slowly to the hoardings. He turned and spread his hands. "What, no more than a few heartbeats?"

"But why?" Aristander demanded.

"More importantly, who?" Alexander asked.

"The Centaur, it must be." The physician pointed to the corpse. "I could examine him more carefully, but the fracture looks as if he was given a vicious kick in the side of the head by a horse."

"And why?"

"Terror, Aristander!" Telamon explained. "The Centaur is showing his power. He can wander into a royal palace and do what he likes. You've seen the passions which seethe in Ephesus? The attempt by Demades's widow to kill the king?"

"Ungrateful bitch!" Alexander snapped. "I was tempted to take her head!"

"The Centaur would have loved that." Telamon grasped the king's arm and pulled him closer. "Don't act the despot," he warned. "In this matter, don't retaliate." Telamon smelt Alexander's wine-drenched breath.

"We must still investigate her murderous attempt!" Aristander snapped.

"There's no need to." Telamon smiled ruefully. "The widow woman brought a casket, inside which rested a small precious goblet on a scarlet cushion. The captain of the guard examined it. The widow woman picked the goblet up and removed the cushion. The captain would peer in and see nothing but an empty cedarwood box."

"But the dagger?" Alexander queried.

"Stuck to the bottom of the cushion," Telamon explained. "A cunning trick. She gently puts the cushion back and places the goblet on top. After she delivers her gift, she plucks the cushion out and grasps the dagger."

"Artemis was certainly with me tonight," Alexander murmured. "But how did the Centaur get in?" He glared at Aristander.

"My Lord King, don't hold me responsible. Merchants come wandering in bringing food and wine. You have the leading citizens of Ephesus and their servants here. Look at Demades's widow. Walls can be scaled, and there's something else . . ." Aristander ran a finger round his painted lips.

"Yes?" Alexander tapped his foot.

"This palace has secret passageways. Some of them we know, some we don't."

"Just like Mother's at Pella," Alexander grinned. "And, of course, it's easy to get a pass. I've issued them to most of the leading citizens and officials of Ephesus. Ah well! Collect that corpse!"

He was about to walk back into the palace when hideous screams rent the night air.

"In sweet Apollo's name!" Telamon murmured.

Immediately the king was ringed by his guards. Aristander, looking rather comical, clapped his hands and shouted for his chorus, who came hurrying out of the darkness to protect him. The Master of the King's Secrets, stumbling like a woman, holding his taffeta gown high in one hand, the other resting on the arm of one of his bodyguard, hastened out of the courtyard. Telamon followed. They went along the side of a building which overlooked the palace gardens, and into the next courtyard leading to the large kitchens.

Telamon gazed in astonishment. Cooks and scullions, spit boys and maids, even the soldiers who guarded the entrance, were running about screaming: some of the soldiers had dropped shields and swords, waving their hands, ruffling their hair.

"What in . . .!"

Telamon heard the buzzing sound. He felt an insect brush his cheek and smacked it away. In the light pouring through the kitchen door more insects clustered, like a horde of mosquitoes above a swamp. A young spit boy came running up, his eyes all puffed up. Telamon grasped him by the shoulders.

"What is it, boy?"

The boy struggled in his grip, moaning, hands to his face. Telamon pulled him gently away from more wasps which came buzzing too close.

"We were in the kitchens," the boy gasped, "and the wasps appeared, thousands of them."

Others came hurrying through the courtyard, shouting for water. Alexander and his Master of Secrets, realizing the danger, retreated hastily to the lawn. Some of the royal escort were already using their torches as protection. A couple of them cursed as they were stung. The night air hummed ominously, as if it masked some demon with a thousand darts.

They returned to the first courtyard, Alexander storming into the palace. Telamon summoned soldiers, officers: those who had been stung were gathered into porticoes. Cassandra appeared, medicine bag in one hand, a small chest of salves and potions in the other. The other physicians joined them, as well as the leechers and apothecaries who looked after the soldiers' health. Most of the victims had been stung a number of times, their faces or bodies displaying angry red welts. Telamon gave instructions.

"Use pincers!" he ordered. "Try and take out the stings. Do not touch those in the eyes. Leave them, the eye can heal itself."

Perdicles would have begun an argument, but Telamon told him to shut up. Some of the victims had been badly mauled by the wasp attack, stung at least a dozen times; one cook had lapsed into a fever. Telamon couldn't decide whether it had been brought on by the excitement or the stings. Using pincers and small needles, working in the light of torches and oil-lamps, the line of victims slowly diminished. Most of them returned to the palace. A few were taken over to the infirmary or the hospital tents in the far gardens of the palace. Telamon walked up and down helping where he could, studying the victims closely. Bee or wasp stings were usually painful but not serious. Nevertheless, Telamon had witnessed cases where an individual, because of his or her own humours, never recovered, and this was no different. One young girl, at first listless, complaining of a heavy drowsiness, began to convulse, as if suffering from the falling sickness. Orderlies tried to hold her down. Telamon became involved, forcing her mouth open, wondering if she'd swallowed something: the girl was choking, her sharp teeth scored his fingers. Despite his best efforts and those of Perdicles, the choking continued. The girl collapsed on the floor, limbs jerking, the back of her head banging against the hard paving stones. Telamon could do nothing but watch her die. He hastened among the survivors looking for similar symptoms before returning to the kitchen courtyard. This now lay deserted. The air still hummed angrily: the light from the kitchen door revealed two bodies lying just inside.

"You'd best not, sir." A soldier came up behind him.

"How did it happen?" Telamon led him out onto the lawn.

"I don't know, sir, but I have one of the cooks. He was cleaning ash from beneath the spit when it happened."

The soldier shouted a name and a middle-aged man waddled forward, still nursing a stung cheek, his right eye half-closed. "He seems the calmest of the lot, sir, and he speaks Greek."

Telamon opened the small purse in his belt, took out a silver coin and held it up. "For your pains." He thrust the coin into the man's sweaty palm. "Tell me what happened."

The cook grasped the coin but still moaned slightly: podgy, with thinning hair, he was dressed in a shabby tunic with a makeshift apron.

"Do what the gentleman said," the soldier whispered menacingly. The cook kicked off his sandals. "My feet were stung!" He glared at the soldier with his good eye. "I will tell the gentleman. I can speak Greek, that's because I am Greek! I'm an army cook. I do for the Captain-General, as I did for his father. My pies are famous. What I can do with chicken, not to mention a shoulder of pork and sweet wine cakes, or rock eels in mulberry sauce . . ."

"Yes, yes," Telamon intervened. "I have often heard the king talk of your dishes."

The man forgot his pain, smiled at the flattery and peered up at Telamon. "You're the physician, aren't you? Ah well, what happened was this. We were all in the kitchens cleaning up. You know the drill? Washing down the tables, dousing the fires, then we eat the scraps."

"And the wasps?"

"The lamps were low. We've had terrible trouble with wasps." The cook turned and pointed to the eaves above the palace. "The little buggers nest there and elsewhere. In the kitchen, where the floor meets the wall, there are gaps. Very clever, probably built by an engineer from Greece. These allow the slops to run down into the elmwood pipes and drain away. Only the gods knows where they lead. I've seen them, one got choked up."

"So there are cellars beneath the kitchen?"

"Of course there are, that's where you build cellars, isn't it?"

"And the wasps' nests were there as well?"

"I don't know," the cook replied. "They might have been. I know as much about wasps as I do about soldiering."

Telamon tried to recall the teaching of Aristotle. The philosopher had taken him out to show him a nest in a cemetery not far from his academy. The wasps had built their nests in the shadow of a great tomb. Aristotle had gone on at great length about how the wasps were citizens of their own city. He had even lifted a nest carefully, hands and arms protected by heavy military gauntlets and with a light gauze veil thrown over his head and face.

"What are you thinking, sir?" the cook demanded.

Telamon shrugged. "That it is the easiest thing in the world to make a wasp angry. How many, would you say?"

"Oh come, sir," the cook laughed. "I didn't stay to count!"

Telamon felt the cold night air chill the sweat on his back. "No, but at a guess, what would you say?"

"Oh, there were thousands of the buggers. I only escaped because I was near the fire. I seized one of those heavy cloths used for lifting hot pans. I threw it over my face and head, wrapped another around my arm and ran like an arrow for the door."

Telamon tried to imagine the kitchen. Cooks, scullions and servants, tired and heavy-eyed: those gaps between the floor and wall. The Centaur in the cellar, maliciously intent on mischief, picking up a nest, thrusting it through into the kitchen then striking at it with a dagger. Such a disturbance, even being shaken or the nest being broken, would send the wasps up in a frenzied horde.

"It wasn't an accident, was it, sir?"

"No, I don't think it was." Telamon patted him on the shoulder. "But you saw or heard nothing suspicious?"

The cook shook his head.

"We'll soon know," Telamon reassured him. "The king will send in soldiers. I have seen bodies lying there. We'll have to discover whether they are alive or dead."

"But why?" The cook was now persistent. "Why send the wasps? Is it an omen from the gods?"

"No," Telamon replied. "Just the malice of man."

He thanked the cook and soldier and walked over to where Cassandra was putting phials and caskets back into the small coffer. Apparently asleep when the disturbance first occurred, she had thrown a small tunic on and wrapped a military cloak around her: this had slipped to reveal muscular shoulders and heavy breasts. She pulled it close and smiled self-consciously at Telamon.

"Well, thank the gods you weren't stung." She gestured at two spit boys still standing near a pillar. "You can go now, lads."

The boys wandered off. The courtyard fell silent, except for the soldiers lounging near the entrance of the palace, ever watchful for the hum of an angry insect.

"Are they in any danger?" Telamon asked. "Could the wasps mass and attack again?"

"No," Cassandra retorted. "They probably took one look at

Alexander and his Master of Secrets and decided to retreat. No" –
she fastened the strap on the medicine bag – "the night air will soon
cool their ardour. Once, in Thebes, I saw a nest fall from one of the
eaves of the temple. It had been dislodged by a madman: he'd
climbed up onto a plinth to commit suicide. Anyway, the wasps did
some damage, but it was out in the open. They soon return to a
swarm and seek a fresh resting place. The palace kitchens should be
left till about midday tomorrow."

"There may be survivors."

"If they're alive they'll come crawling out, Master."

"Telamon," the physician corrected her. "My name is Telamon.
I am slightly drunk, rather tired and not in the mood for sarcasm!"

"There's mischief here," Cassandra blithely continued. "I have
heard of wasps' nests being thrown into schoolrooms, or even
through the window of a private house. Who is the perpetrator,
Greek or Persian?"

Telamon shook his head. "I wish I knew. Those politicians, it
could be one, two, or indeed all of them. You heard what
happened at the banquet?"

"Oh yes," Cassandra agreed. "The cooks and scullions were full
of it. Our noble conqueror nearly met an ignoble end."

"Keep your voice down!"

"What do you mean," Cassandra persisted, "it could be one,
two or all of them?"

"We believe the Centaur is a spy," Telamon reasoned. "An
assassin. Or it could be the name of a group."

"Do you think this was his work?"

"Probably, the wasp was a symbol of the centaurs," Telamon
sighed. "Ephesus is full of grievances against Alexander. Persians in
hiding, families who have lost loved ones during the recent
massacre: even members of Alexander's army who, now they've
savoured the pleasures of Ephesus, don't wish to march on."

"And the business in the Temple of Hercules?"

"I am no closer to the truth." He sat down beside Cassandra and
leaned against the wall. "But this is the hour of the assassin.
Whoever he, she or they is or are, will cause mischief until they
are killed."

"And what a place to perpetrate it," Cassandra retorted. "I have wandered this palace, Telamon. It's honeycombed with cellars, passageways and hidden doors. Oh yes," she added, "the perfect place for murder!"

Chapter 6

—⫸⫷⫸⫷—

"On the night in which Olympias gave birth, the Temple of Artemis in Ephesus . . . was destroyed by fire: this conflagration was the work of a profligate incendiary."

Quintus Curtius Rufus:
The History of Alexander the Great, Book I, Chapter 1

R abinus the scribe was roused from a light sleep by the cries and sound of running footsteps. At first he was worried, but the more he listened, the more his flagging hopes revived. Was he to be freed? Had the Centaur created a diversion? He hammered on the door. Perhaps the guards had left their posts?

"What's happening?" he cried. "What's happening?"

"Shut up!" a voice bellowed back.

Rabinus bit back his disappointment. The guards were veterans. They would only leave their posts if ordered. He went back and idly played with a piece of charcoal he had found in a corner.

Across the palace the cries and yells grew. Voices sounded outside. Rabinus went to the door. An officer had come to visit the guards. Rabinus listened intently. He heard what had happened, and stood confused until he recalled the many wasps' nests built under the eaves of the palace. Perhaps it was just an accident? He returned to sit on the edge of his bed.

"Rabinus! Rabinus, are you there?"

The scribe jumped to his feet. The aperture was black; night had fallen. He recognized that voice. He stood on his bed and peered up.

"I'm here," Rabinus whispered hoarsely back. "You've come to free me?"

"Rabinus, I kept my promise. I have come to free you."

"What's happening?" Rabinus asked. "An attack by wasps?"

A hoarse chuckle greeted his question. "The Macedonians are being discomfited and embarrassed. The mighty conqueror driven from his palace by a swarm of wasps. Have you betrayed me, Rabinus?" the voice continued. "Or have you kept faith?"

"I wouldn't betray you." Rabinus strained his ears. He could hear no sound from the passage outside. "How did Arella die?"

"By fire and sword."

"What am I to do?"

"Listen now," the voice hissed. "I am the Centaur. I know this palace well, its secret galleries and hidden doorways. You must do exactly what I ask. Go and stand by the door, facing the grille."

"Why?" Rabinus asked.

"Go and stand there!" the voice repeated. "I can see from here whether you obey or not. You need to be there, otherwise I cannot liberate you. If you don't go, I shall!"

Rabinus hesitated, rubbing the piece of charcoal through his fingers.

"Shall I leave?" the voice whispered.

Rabinus walked to the door and stared through the grille, body tensed, ears straining. He looked around: the cell was still pitch black. He had a lamp, but was saving its precious oil. He closed his eyes and listened intently. Time passed slowly. He expected to hear some confusion, perhaps alarm as the guards were roused, but nothing.

Rabinus, impatient, turned. Something was trickling, like water being poured out of a jug. He walked towards the cell wall. What was it? And that smell? The odour of the kitchen?

Climbing onto the bed, Rabinus scrabbled at the wall and felt the wet stickiness. The scribe took his hand away, sniffed, and stared up in horror, even as the first fiery rag was thrust through the vent. He screamed and jumped down.

Other pieces of fire were being pushed through the gap. The oil-drenched wall caught the flame, which raced across the bed, catching the dry cloths and straw. Rabinus yelled, stamping his feet: the hem of his shabby tunic caught light. He hurried

134

towards the door, but his haste only fanned the flame; his tunic was alight.

Rabinus tried to drag it off but the cloth was stiff, the scorching pain in his legs only increasing his panic. The soldiers at the far end of the gallery were ignoring his screams and yells as those of a hysterical prisoner.

The corner of his cell was now a fiery inferno. Rabinus tried once more both to remove the tunic and douse the flame. He cursed the Centaur who had come to liberate him, not from his cell but from life itself. Grasping the piece of charcoal, Rabinus's last act was to fling himself against the wall near the door and draw the first letter of his assassin's name.

In the early hours of the morning, Alexander, Hephaestion, Aristander and Telamon confronted the leading citizens of Ephesus in the council chamber. The king was sweat-soaked. He refused to sit down, but paced the chamber like a caged panther. Agis and the rest stood in a group, Meleager next to his arch rival, their former enmity forgotten in the face of such fury. Aristander hid in the shadows near the door. Hephaestion, not yet sober, lounged half-asleep in a chair, Telamon beside him. The physician watched the king, in particular the sword he carried.

Alexander stopped and began to hack at the back of a chair, the sword rising and falling, as if it were a piece of firewood, white spittle flecking the king's lips. The sword slipped; Alexander threw it to the floor and drew off his rings, which he flung in Aristander's direction. He picked up the sword.

"My lord!"

Alexander held the sword above his head, glaring down at the hacked chair as if it were Darius himself.

"My lord!"

Alexander's head came up: sword still held high, he turned and glared at Telamon.

"My lord, that will do no good."

"It does me the world of good!" Alexander hissed. "I am made a public mockery, a fool in my own palace. My banquet is disturbed. I am attacked by a would-be assassin, my soldiers and servants stung

135

by a swarm of wasps. By dawn the news will be all over Ephesus, tomorrow Susa, the next day Persepolis: Alexander of Macedon, the great conqueror, the victor of Granicus, cannot control his own household!"

"That's one version," Telamon replied quietly.

Alexander brought the sword down but paused halfway. He glanced at Telamon.

"One version, physician! One version!" he mimicked. "What are you? The Pythian Goddess? Or perhaps Aristophanes writing a play? One version!" He repeated in a high-pitched voice.

"Alexander! Alexander!" Telamon rose and seized the king's arm; his muscles were tense, hard as stiffened rope.

"Let go of me, physician! None of your tricks. My head beats like a drum, my blood pounds, my belly churns and my sword seeks life."

"Remember where you are," Telamon whispered, "and who watches." He turned to the citizens. "Stand back! The king is in a divine fury. Artemis has visited him."

The cynical look on Peleus's face clearly showed how convincing Telamon sounded.

"Stand back!" Telamon repeated. The citizens had no choice but to retreat.

"I warned you to keep your distance!" Telamon shouted. "Do you not know that our king is a descendant of Achilles? He experiences the divine madness, the rage of Hercules, the fiery wisdom of Artemis!"

"What nonsense is this?" Alexander whispered.

"Is there a statue here?" Telamon murmured. "A statue of Artemis?"

"In the far corner, behind us."

"Turn round and go to it."

Alexander reluctantly obeyed. Telamon hastily picked up an oil-lamp. The statue of Artemis stood on a pedestal. He placed the lamp in a niche on the podium. The ancient statue gleamed with life: Artemis the Moon Goddess, the Huntress in flowing robes and hoplite helmet.

"Let's kneel before it."

The king obeyed.

"What's this?" Hephaestion half-struggled to rise but Aristander, realizing what was happening, moved quickly and pushed him back in his seat. Telamon knelt beside the king.

"You could always tell stories," Alexander whispered, staring at the statue. "Do you remember, Telamon, out in Mieza? You once convinced Seleucus that a statue of Apollo had moved?" He giggled.

"This is what you will say," Telamon murmured. "Think now, Alexander. You are doing what your enemy wants. Your rage, your panic, will only be the breeze to fan the flames."

"I don't panic," Alexander declared.

"Very good, you just have violent moods," Telamon soothed. "For the sake of the Goddess, shut up and listen!"

"I could take your head!"

"In which case I would be without a head, the king would be without a physician, and Alexander would be without a friend."

"You're beginning to sound like Mother. Thank the gods she's not here!"

"Think now."

Telamon knelt beside Alexander, staring up at the statue as if they were rapt in prayer. He kept his voice just above an audible whisper, confident no one else could hear.

"A widow woman nearly killed you. Deranged by grief and, perhaps, encouraged by someone else." Telamon quickly seized Alexander's wrist. "Stay still! But you, the great king, were warned, weren't you? You accepted that woman into your presence. Artemis intervened and mysteriously knocked the dagger out of her hand."

"These politicians won't believe that."

Alexander seemed so discomfited that a faint suspicion pricked Telamon's mind. Who, he wondered, had warned the king? "Who cares about them?" he replied. "The people will believe it."

Alexander laughed softly. "Very good. And the wasps?"

"We know how that was done," Telamon declared. "Use your wits! The Centaur knows this palace and he's used his knowledge

137

to dislodge a nest of wasps, to embarrass you. In truth, they were sacred messengers from the gods."

"And what did they come to tell me?" Alexander's voice was tense and strident.

"Only the gods know."

Alexander half-turned, eyes narrowed.

"I am trying to think," Telamon whispered. "What problems confront you?"

"The murders at the Temple of Hercules, Leonidas's death."

"Forget that! What else?"

"The manuscript," Alexander retorted. "The madman who burnt Artemis's temple. I could say it contained a secret message for me from the Goddess."

"Now you're listening."

"And there's something else," Alexander continued. "We must march on Miletus: its Persian governor has promised to open the gates."

"And?"

"He's a liar! Miletus is a powerful fort, ringed by three walls and served from the sea. The Persian fleet is not far off. My generals say we can't take it."

"And can you?"

"No!" Alexander hissed. "My fleet isn't big enough."

"But you will," Telamon teased.

"Why?" Alexander demanded.

"Because the Goddess has just told you. Remember," Telamon insisted, "how you act now will, by tomorrow, be the common gossip of this city!"

Alexander's head went down, shoulders shaking with laughter. He put his face in his hands, bowed three times towards the statue and extended his hand as if in deep supplication. Without waiting for Telamon, he sighed, got to his feet and turned round. He picked up his sword, placed it on the table and walked to the ring of chairs.

"Gentlemen, sit down! Sit down!"

The Ephesians did. They had all eaten and drunk deeply, but the events of the night and the cold air had sobered them up. Agis and

Meleager hid their feelings. Dion and Peleus found it difficult to hide knowing looks and cynical grins. I'll soon have you dancing, Telamon thought.

"What is wrong, sire?" Dion, his face a mask of solicitude, leaned forward: his expression and posture, the sarcasm in his voice, were clear indications of the arrogance, not only of these men but of their city and other cities in this empire. You are contemptuous, Telamon reflected: you are neither Persian nor Greek, but Ephesians first and last. You don't really care if Alexander defeats Darius or the Persian re-emerges as the victor.

"Do you see us as upstarts?" The words were out of Telamon's mouth before he could reflect.

Dion raised his eyebrows.

"Do you see us as upstarts?"

Aristander took the seat next to the physician. Now the king's rage had passed, the necromancer was eager to play any role assigned to him.

"Do you think we will leave tomorrow?" Aristander echoed Telamon's words.

"What are you talking about?" Meleager demanded.

"Did you think we were here for a month and a day?" Aristander sneered. "And then we'd be back across the Hellespont? Our king will march to the rim of the world."

"Before he does," Telamon interrupted drily, "a few questions. When the feast ended, did you leave the banqueting hall?"

"Of course we did," Meleager interrupted. "We left both before and after the Demades widow appeared. We are not wine jugs, physician; what we eat and drink brings a call of nature."

Telamon smiled.

"Are you accusing us," Meleager continued, "one of us, or all of us, of being responsible for those wasps? Others in the palace, Greek or Persian, could be responsible for such mischief."

Telamon had anticipated such an answer. Meleager was correct. People had left the banqueting hall to go to the privies. It would be easy for the traitor, with his knowledge of this palace, to slip down into the cellars, remove those nests and thrust them into the kitchen. It would take some time for the wasps to be disturbed and break out. All these men had had time enough, both during the banquet and afterwards, to prepare their mischief.

"So, you all left the banqueting hall." Telamon tried not to falter. "Even after the king was called away?"

"Of course we did," Agis snapped. "We were wondering what had happened."

"We knew the king was alarmed," Peleus sneered. "Some of us waited, then we, too, went searching to see what was wrong."

"Do you know this palace?" Telamon asked.

"We try to keep away," Dion drawled.

Telamon ignored the insult; further questioning would only make him sound strident and vulnerable. Alexander sat as immobile as a statue. Telamon knew the king would be thinking about what had happened. Now his rage had passed, the king's mind would be turning and twisting like a hunting mongoose.

"Demades's widow?" Telamon asked.

"That is my fault." Meleager spread his hands. "She asked me for an audience with the king. She assured me of what she wanted to say. I accepted her word. Will she be questioned?"

"Perhaps," Telamon smiled, though he knew it would be fruitless. The widow had been fortunate to escape so leniently. She would portray it as a passing madness rather than depict herself as part of some well-planned conspiracy. And what proof existed that she was?

"And Hesiod?" Telamon asked. "Did anyone here visit his house?"

"I hope not." Aristander's voice was barely above a whisper. "My agents have already been there. They have confiscated all his papers and books."

"Did you find anything?" Dion asked.

"Nothing," Aristander declared. He cackled. "Just how much he hated Meleager and your party. Plenty of lists of names, houses, men and women marked down for death."

"Oh, Hesiod loved that," Meleager remarked. "He always vowed vengeance and supped deep on blood. Now he can pay for it in the Underworld. Let the Furies tear him to pieces."

"Greek killing Persian." Telamon ignored the look of hatred in Agis's eyes. "But Greek killing Greek, eh?"

140

"Many died at the Granicus," Peleus jibed.

"Rabinus the scribe is dead." Telamon stretched his legs out while studying these men.

"Rabinus?" Agis pulled a face. "We know of him. We met him. The Governor's principal scribe, found lurking under Arella's bed."

"Consumed by fire in his cell," Telamon declared. "Somebody discovered where he was. They poured oil through a gap which looks out onto the courtyard and dropped flames within. Rabinus was burnt alive. The guards heard his screams, but at first they ignored him. It was the fire and smoke which raised the alarm."

"Could it have been an accident?"

"No, sir." Telamon smiled falsely at Peleus. "The wall had been drenched with oil. We also found a number of rags soaked in oil outside. The courtyard is deserted, anyone could have done it."

"We do not know this palace," Meleager declared.

"You were all left to your own devices," Aristander retorted. "And, if you were questioned, what would we hear, eh? How one person wandered that way and another went this?"

"We would vouch for each other," Agis declared smoothly. "Except for Meleager, he was by himself."

The Oligarch blinked and smiled.

"Of course we could examine your hands and clothing," Telamon continued, "but what use would that be? A pair of hunting gauntlets, an old tunic picked up from some hiding place. Thankfully, the cell is built of stone, except for the door, so it never spread: the guards doused it but could not save Rabinus."

"We understand the king's rage," Dion mocked.

"I was not angry." Alexander rose, crossed his arms and walked over to these powerful citizens. "I was in a divine madness."

"Alexander the actor," Aristander whispered. Telamon tapped him gently with his foot.

"Artemis was present at my birth." Alexander's voice rang through the chamber. "She saved me from the assassin's dagger tonight, those wasps were her messengers. Tell the citizens of Ephesus how I was saved from the assassins. Tell them what the Goddess's messengers reported to me. The madman who burnt her temple wrote a confession which you have handed to me,

141

that contains a secret which I shall proclaim for all the city to hear.''

The Ephesians looked uncomfortable: Alexander was playing a game, but they could not understand it.

"I received the divine madness," Alexander continued. "I have prayed before the Goddess's statue. Tomorrow I shall issue a proclamation describing how I was saved. I will soon publicize the message sent to me. As a sign that this is all true, the Goddess has revealed that the powerful Persian city, the port of Miletus, will fall into my hands! Even more" – Alexander's voice rose – "the assassin responsible for the murder and sacrilege at the Temple of Hercules will be caught, his life will be my oblation to the Goddess!"

The king spun on his heel and walked towards the door. Telamon followed him out. Once the door was closed, Alexander grasped the physician's shoulder.

"In Apollo's name, Telamon, you've led me into this! Make sure you lead me out!"

"Did you see that?"

Telamon stood outside the House of Medusa and stared down the rutted track: a tired, barren alley running under the high walls of the house, here and there a lonely, dust-laden pine or palm tree.

"I saw nothing," Cassandra replied. "Even the pariah dogs have more sense than to be out in the noonday heat. Hippocrates said . . ."

"I know what Hippocrates said about certain times of the day and how the humours are disturbed, but I feel so tired, it wouldn't make any difference." Telamon narrowed his eyes. "I am just sure I saw someone dressed like a beggar watching the house further down the alleyway. Ah well."

He stared at the peeling paint on the door. The artist who had fashioned the face of Medusa, with its popping eyes, blood-soaked mouth and hair of writhing snakes, had lacked skill but compensated with a crude vigour: the face was cruel, predatory, a phantasm from a nightmare.

"Let's wait no longer." Cassandra brushed by him, picked up the metal tongue of the Medusa and banged it noisily.

142

"Who's there?" The voice was squeaky, strident.

"I bear the king's seal," Telamon replied. "The cartouche of Alexander."

The gate was pulled open. Watery eyes in a tired face stared out above the chain still fastened to its clasp.

"What do you want?"

"Open the door!" Cassandra warned. "We can call the guards or the market police."

The chain was released and the porter ushered them in.

"You were expecting us," Telamon declared. "A messenger came down this morning. Are the two officers, Agathon and Sallus . . .?"

"They're inside." The porter walked back to his little lodge, no more than a moss-covered, stone hut.

Telamon gazed around. In Greece most cities were built all a-huddle, cheek by jowl, but this was Ephesus. Women like Arella could ring their mansions, like the nobles of Egypt, with plea-saunces, paradises, lawns, shrubberies and orchards. The House of Medusa was similar. Its garden, however, was overgrown, dotted with different trees: palm, fig, terebinth and sycamore. Once it would have been a pleasant, green, fragrant place, but nature had been allowed to develop unchecked. Bushes obscured the house. The cobbled yard in front of the gate was sprouting weeds.

Telamon moved to get a better view. The house reminded him of those Egyptian mansions outside Thebes, built of brick and wood on a hard stone base. The front had a portico approached by paved stones and crumbling steps; the light-green paint on the main door was peeling. The windows were shuttered; one shutter had broken loose and creaked noisily. An overgrown, desolate place: no birdsong, only the whirring of crickets in the long grass. The air smelt stale, rather sour.

"Why are you here?" The porter stood in the doorway to his lodge, glaring at them.

"That's our business."

"Who are you," the porter demanded, "with your green eyes and fiery hair? A man lived here who had a cat like you, red like a streak of fire, with cruel, green eyes."

143

Cassandra pulled a face, lifting her hand as if to claw. Telamon sat down on the wooden bench just inside the gateway.

"You are the porter?"

"Have been for many a year."

"Do you have some wine? Come on," Telamon urged. "Be friendly. We won't call the king's officers down."

The porter brought a jug and three rather cracked earthenware goblets: the wine he poured tasted delicious.

"It's from Naxos," he explained. "One of the officers inside gave it to me." He smacked his lips in a fine display of sore gums and yellow gaping teeth.

"How long have you been here?"

"Can't remember," the porter replied.

"So."

Telamon put the cup down and got to his feet. Cassandra, bored, wandered into the long grass, staring at the house.

"I know and you know," Telamon began, "that this house was owned by an assassin. He belonged to a secret society called the Centaurs."

The porter almost choked on his wine. Telamon grasped him by the shoulder.

"I want the truth," he threatened. "Otherwise I will take you to the king's dungeons: his torturers will hang you from hooks in the ceiling."

"That's right. That's right," the man stammered. "Years ago it was, his name was Malli. He wasn't from Ephesus. He came from further east."

"And the Centaurs were crushed?"

The porter nodded vigorously. He had misjudged this powerful visitor with his sharp face and dark watchful eyes. The porter quietly resolved he would tell them the truth, or as much of it as he could.

Telamon noticed the change in expression. He opened his purse and drew out two silver coins, which he placed near the cup on the ground. "If you tell me the truth you'll be paid well, with no trouble."

"Is the house haunted?" Cassandra sauntered back, retying her thick red hair behind her. "It looks as if it's haunted."

"That's what people say," the porter explained. "There are cellars beneath the house. They claim the assassins met there to worship some demon god. But the Centaurs were destroyed and the house passed from hand to hand. No one really likes it."

"Except you?"

The porter nodded. "I regard it as an old friend."

"Did you know Malli?"

The porter smiled slyly. "An oyster merchant: I knew him, but I didn't know his secrets . . ."

"And his daughter?"

"She disappeared."

"Is that all?" Telamon asked.

"Master," the porter shrugged, "I am a porter." He spread his hands. "Things happen."

"And so we come to Leonidas," Telamon smiled. "A Macedonian officer. He belonged to the Falcon Squadron, an elite cavalry unit. He came here two years ago when Parmenio occupied Ephesus for a while. Come," Telamon urged. "You are telling me some of the truth, so you might as well tell me the full story."

"What do you know of Leonidas?" the porter asked.

"Leonidas was an old rogue, a typical soldier. The great loves of his life were wine and money. Leonidas took this house because no one wanted it: it's dirty, not very pleasant. Leonidas, however, discovered something interesting about this place. It can't have been wine, it certainly wasn't women: that means lost treasure. Leonidas always wanted to find a secret horde. I suspect" – Telamon picked up the wine cup – "Leonidas stumbled on some story about the Centaurs hiding their wealth here. I am correct?"

"Oh yes, sir. He was only here for a short while. He found some manuscripts, a map or an inscription, I don't know what, but he began to pester me about treasure hidden in the house or the grounds. At the time six other men were with him, officers from the same squadron. They stabled their horses here, the only time the grass was cropped."

"And?"

Cassandra sat down on the bench beside Telamon. The porter looked at this strange woman's round, muscular face and high

145

cheekbones: she had a kissing mouth, but her eyes did remind him of that ferocious cat which used to hunt in the long grass here.

"I couldn't help him," the porter muttered. "I didn't want any trouble, but Leonidas and his companion began to search, then the Persians returned. I fled. Six days later I returned to the house. Leonidas and his companions had gone. They left some food, bits of armour, scraps of clothing. The Persians had broken down a door and taken off some of the shutters. I did a few repairs and settled down to my old life. Ah, I thought, that's the last I'll see of Leonidas. Me and the house went back to sleeping under the sun. A merchant bought it but his wife was nervous, she didn't like the place, so they left after a few weeks. The war broke out again, the Persians fled and Leonidas returned. This time with two companions. I asked him about the past, but he looked at me out of the corner of his eye, like he often did. Leonidas had a savage temper, especially when he'd been drinking. Oh, oh, says I to myself, the least said the better."

"Did Leonidas ever refer to the treasure again?"

"No, he never did. He came back here as if this had been his home since the day he was born. He became very busy."

"What do you mean?"

"Sometimes he'd go back out to the camp: he and the other two had duties to perform. However, whenever they could, they were out here in the garden. Well, at least Leonidas was. I could hear the other two stumbling about inside."

"Are they by themselves?"

"Oh no. They have a maid, a camp follower. What's her name? Ah yes, Harna. She looks after them, washes and cooks, not a bad cook either."

"So, Leonidas didn't find the treasure the first time?"

The porter stared into his wine cup. "I'm not sure. You see, sir, sometimes I listen to conversations. One of Leonidas's companions, an officer from Samos, seemed to have some hold over Leonidas. I suspect he was related to one of those who were here with Leonidas last time."

"You know they were all killed?" Telamon asked. "Or at least disappeared?"

"Yes, that's what Leonidas said."

"You mentioned conversations?" Cassandra asked.

"Oh, only a few scraps. The Samian asked Leonidas something to the effect, 'Didn't the others help you search?'" He shook his head. "I couldn't hear Leonidas's reply."

"So, those two officers," Telamon lowered his voice, "acted as if they knew about the treasure? And about Leonidas's visit here last time?"

"Yes, that's my impression!" The porter scratched his head. "But you must remember, sir," he gestured at the lodge, "this is my home. I eat, drink and sleep in there. I know very little. Sometimes I go into the marketplace." He blinked. "I might be old but," he smiled, "I have no wife, there's a very fat whore, she's always accommodating."

"Haven't you ever thought of searching for this lost treasure?" Cassandra asked.

"It's blood money, isn't it?" the porter replied, pushing back his stool. "What do I need it for?"

Telamon picked up his leather satchel and took out the scraps of parchment he had borrowed back from Aristander.

"I can't read," the porter warned. "I don't know my letters. I worked as a potter's assistant. I can only count on my fingers."

"This is the letter 'C'," Telamon explained, pointing to a scrap of parchment. "Probably stands for Centaur, but do these drawings mean anything to you? Look!" He laid them out on his lap. "This one shows four rectangles or narrow shapes connected, this one has two, this one three."

The porter studied them carefully, a drool of saliva running down his stubbled chin. "Could be rooms in the house," he murmured. "But no, sir, they mean nothing to me. You think it's a map for the treasure?"

"I do." Telamon picked up the pieces of parchment and handed them to Cassandra. "By the way, where are the officers now?"

"It's early afternoon, so they've probably drunk some wine and gone to bed. Harna may be bestowing her favours on them."

"They knew we were coming?"

"They're Macedonian officers," the porter smirked. "They don't care about anything."

"And since Leonidas's death?"

"Oh, they've been quiet."

"No searching or digging?"

The porter shook his head.

Telamon scratched his chin and stared at the sombre house. "When Leonidas was alive, did they ever tell you to go away?"

"Oh yes. Just after they arrived. Leonidas gave me a coin, sent me into the city and told me to visit the wine booths and beer shops, seek out my fat friend."

Telamon leaned against the hard brick wall. The wine was now making itself felt. He'd slept late that morning but still felt heavy-eyed, drowsy. He had hardly had a chance to reflect on the violent proceedings of the night before: when the king's officers finally entered the palace kitchens they had discovered three more corpses. Alexander had already drafted his proclamation and ordered it to be posted throughout the city, giving his version of the previous night's events. Telamon closed his eyes. He only hoped that he could realize what he'd promised Alexander. But – Telamon opened his eyes – for the moment that would have to wait.

"Are you finished with me?"

"No, no, I am not. Cassandra stand by the gate. Please!" Telamon urged.

She sighed, rose and leaned against it.

"Just listen," Telamon asked. "Now, sir, the night Leonidas died?"

"Ah yes, he and Agathon went out to a wine booth in the city, the other one stayed here. They came back in the early hours; both stank of wine, Leonidas could hardly walk." The porter gestured at the paved path. "They could have gone through the main door, but they went along the side of the house to the small postern door. Inside are store rooms, kitchens, whatever, and stairs built into the side of the house."

"And then what happened?"

"I went back to my lodge, I was dozing. Suddenly I heard the postern door open. Curious, I got up and walked a bit further

148

down the garden. Leonidas, wrapped in his cloak, went out into the darkness."

"How do you know it was Leonidas?"

"Well it must have been. He left but never returned: I discovered his corpse in the pool."

"But did you recognize him at the time?"

"He had his great cloak on, covered round the neck with some animal fur from which medallions hang."

"And when you found his corpse?"

"I went through the postern door. Harna was sleeping downstairs in the scullery. She has a mattress under the table. Up she jumps like a little dog. When I told her what I'd seen, she was all a-feared and ran up the stairs. The two officers came down." He shrugged. "The rest you know. The corpse was dragged out and taken back into the house. Some other officials came, sharp-faced men, they searched the house, talked to the two officers and took the corpse away."

"Ah yes. Aristander's men."

"Who?" the porter asked.

"Never mind, never mind!" Telamon stood up. "Come on, show me this pool!"

"Shall I stop here, Master?" Cassandra asked.

"Don't be sarcastic!" Telamon retorted. "Just stand, listen and watch!"

The porter led him through the garden: no paths, only beaten tracks through the grass and gorse. They passed the house with its pitted bricks and crumbling stonework, the wooden eaves battered and decayed. A cracked path ran along the side of the house to a postern door painted a dirty green. Telamon cursed as a briar scored his leg. They went through a small clump of trees, the remains of a pear orchard. The porter paused and pulled the long grass aside. The pool which lay beyond was covered with green scum and smelt dank, flies and mosquitoes buzzing above it: about three yards long and two yards wide, once built as a pool of purity, its brick edging had long crumbled.

"You see, sir, a man could easily stumble, particularly if he was full of wine."

149

"Yes, but what was he doing out here?"

Telamon picked up a fallen branch and used it to pull the undergrowth aside as he walked round the pool. He reached the far side where the grass and gorse was beaten down: Telamon deduced this marked Leonidas's final walk. He crouched at the edge of the pool and pushed the branch in; it almost disappeared before he felt the vegetation at the bottom of the pool.

"About a yard deep," he murmured.

He got up and followed the route Leonidas must have taken from the postern door: a difficult feat, for the ground was uneven, the vegetation thick and thorny. The undergrowth also concealed rubbish, shards of pottery, crumbling masonry and the occasional hole. At last Telamon reached the path outside the postern door. The sun blazed down. He ignored the porter lumbering towards him, gasping and cursing, and stared back over the overgrown garden. The pool was now hidden, and he wondered once again what Leonidas had been searching for. Telamon could understand how the old veteran had been killed, walking across the garden, searching for something. Perhaps he forgot about the pool and simply stumbled in, drunk, with that heavy cloak about him. Telamon had heard of similar cases, of men drowning in a few seconds.

"Are you satisfied, sir?"

"Not really." Telamon smiled. "Let's see the back of the house."

He followed the path round. The garden was as untidy here as elsewhere. Shuttered windows in crumbling walls looked out over a small cobbled yard which stretched to a line of bushes on which cloaks and other items of clothing were drying in the sun. Telamon stood and stared at these. He sniffed; the air smelt staler, with a stench of the privy, of dirty water. Telamon remembered Cassandra near the gate. He walked round to the front of the house, across the steps and along the path made out of long paving stones which stretched down to the cobbled area near the gate. Cassandra was still leaning against it, head back, eyes closed. She raised a finger to her lips for silence.

"There's someone there," she whispered.

Telamon quietly drew back the bolt and gestured at Cassandra to stand aside. He opened the gate quickly and stepped into the alley. The one-eyed beggar, crouching near the wall a few yards away, sprang to his feet and ran like the wind down the runnel, tattered cloak flying, battered sandals slapping. Telamon watched him go and came back through the gate.

"The beggar?" he asked the porter.

"Ah, you mean Cyclops, the one-eyed one? He's been prowling around this house since Leonidas arrived!"

Chapter 7

"In Greece alas! How ill things ordered are."

A quotation from Euripides, *Andromache*,
cited by Plutarch: *Lives*: "Alexander"

"**I** am sorry to rouse you from your slumber."

Telamon sat in the main room of the House of Medusa. Once upon a time it might have been opulent, even elegant, with its wooden columns and high ceiling, but now the plaster and woodwork were cracked, cobwebs hung from corners, dust soiled every ledge. The air was musty and stale. Built in the Egyptian fashion, with a dais at one end and a central fire on a raised hearth, it was now a soulless, tawdry room. The two officers sitting opposite him reflected their surroundings. Both wore soiled tunics, their faces unshaven. The taller of the two, Agathon, with narrow eyes and pitted cheeks, simply smirked, dismissing Telamon's sarcasm with a flick of his fingers.

"The army's orders have been posted." Agathon scratched his thin reddish hair. "We fought at the Granicus, we marched on Ephesus. We now have a month's leave to enjoy the fruits of our victory. Isn't that correct, Sallus?"

His companion was squat with a broad, ruddy face under a shock of black hair which looked as if it hadn't been washed since he had left Macedon.

"That's right." Sallus bit deeply into an apple and chewed noisily, leering at Cassandra. She glared back. Sallus laughed, opened his mouth in a fine display of half-chewed apple and bit again.

"You certainly don't keep this place tidy."

"We're soldiers, members of the Raven Squadron. It's not our job to clean someone else's house."

"Did Leonidas believe the same?" Telamon asked.

"No, poor drunken sod. He was in his cups most of the time. Couldn't walk a straight line, let alone get off a horse."

"He was a fine cavalryman," Telamon declared. "I knew him when I was a boy."

The apple chewer paused, a calculating look in his eyes. "Who did you say you were?"

"Telamon, personal physician to Alexander, a member of the royal circle. I am here to investigate Leonidas's death."

Sallus sneered. Agathon got to his feet, stretched, plucked an apple from the bowl and came back. He rubbed it on his tunic, winked at Cassandra and bit deeply.

"So why are you here?" Agathon asked, his harsh accent blunted by apple pieces. "To investigate Leonidas's death? So what? He was drunk, staggered out of his bed, went downstairs to the garden and drowned in a dirty pool."

"Why?"

"I don't know. Nor does Sallus. Perhaps he was sleepwalking. Perhaps he had a nightmare. Maybe he thought he could find a wineskin."

"He was your commanding officer?"

"Aye, and a good one. When the army came into Ephesus he seized this house and got the quarter-master's approval to stay here. We've now been released from duties and haven't to report back till the full moon. We eat, we drink, we wander the city."

"Where are your horses?"

"Oh, don't be stupid," Agathon sneered. "You know the orders. Cavalry mounts are with the army, they were too precious to waste here. Anyhow, we haven't got enough fodder for a long stay."

Telamon got to his feet. He opened a window, pulling back the battered shutters, allowing in the sunlight. He turned quickly: Sallus had his tongue stuck out, making a rude gesture at Cassandra.

"I could have you arrested!"

Agathon almost choked on his apple. Sallus threw his core on the ground.

"I'll certainly have you arrested" – Telamon retook his seat – "if you threaten me or my companion."

"I am a Macedonian," Agathon declared. "Free born. I own a farm. I fought for Philip, now I'll fight for his son. Three times I've received a golden ingot for bravery in battle. Sallus here is from Samos, but his mother was Macedonian. He, too, knows his rights. We were with the king when he crossed the Granicus. We protected his back, yet you come swaggering in here saying you'll arrest us!"

"You are very brave, skilful cavalrymen." Telamon ignored the self-satisfied sneer. "You're also lying charlatans, so don't waste my time. Leonidas came here last time the Macedonian army occupied Ephesus. This house once belonged to an assassin."

The smile disappeared from Agathon's face.

"Somehow or other, Leonidas learnt treasure was buried here. I don't know what happened last time, but when the Macedonians retreated, Leonidas withdrew with them. Only the gods know what happened to his companions. After Granicus Leonidas was probably the first into Ephesus, you two with him. He comes back to this ghastly place, the House of Medusa with its evil memories and malignant ghosts. Leonidas wanted to come back by himself but two of his junior officers, namely yourselves, were suspicious about what happened last time, especially Sallus! Wasn't your kinsman among the six who disappeared? Anyway, you demanded to accompany Leonidas here."

Both officers were staring hard at him.

"Good!" Telamon continued. "I now have your attention. What I want to know are two things. First, has this treasure trove been discovered? According to army orders, at least half of it is the property of the king. Secondly, did Leonidas stumble? Was it an accident or was he murdered? Thieves falling out? Sit down!" Cassandra jumped as Telamon shouted at Sallus. "Just sit and listen to what I am saying. Now, you can answer my questions or I can have you court-martialled. You think about your reply. I wish to talk to the serving girl."

Telamon rose and walked through the far door. The kitchen was as dingy as the rest of the house. The walls, once plastered and painted white, were grey with grime and soot. A bucket of stale water stood just within the doorway, a small fireplace full of ash was built against one wall, a movable stove stood against the other. Harna was squatting on the floor, slicing up vegetables on a piece of wood. She pushed back her black hair and stared up at Telamon: dark eyes in a thin, brown face. Telamon gently touched the bruise on her left cheek.

"How old are you? You do speak Greek?"

"As good as any." Harna's voice was harsh. She ran her finger round the high neckline of her tunic, once white, now dirty and sweat-stained. Telamon crouched down. The girl studied him, then looked at Cassandra.

"Is she a Celt? We have some Celts in the camp. Most of them are whores. Big, they are, arms as thick as soldiers'. Is she your woman?"

"Who hit you?" Telamon asked.

"Who doesn't hit me?" Harna retorted.

"Did Leonidas?"

"No, he was just an old sot. I am Agathon's, or at least he thinks I am. I cook, clean and warm his bed."

"Do you like him?"

The girl spat on the filthy stone floor. "I'm deeply in love with him."

Telamon opened his purse and took out a silver coin. The girl went to snatch it, but Telamon withdrew his hand.

"Where do you sleep?"

"Under the stairs. It's warmer there. If there's a fire it's near the postern door. I can get out safely."

"What do you mean?"

"Soldiers drink, they get clussy and knock oil-lamps over."

"And the night Leonidas died?"

"Agathon brought him back from the city. They were as drunk as each other. They could hardly walk through the door." She pointed to the stairs beyond the kitchen. "They were cursing. Agathon took Leonidas upstairs and that was it."

"Didn't Agathon call for you? Wouldn't he need your help, your company?"

156

"Not when he's drunk. He's incapable, and I'm wary of his fists!"

"And Leonidas came down again?"

"Oh yes. He had that great cloak on, the one with the fur and silver medallions."

"Show me!"

The girl balanced the knife in her hands.

"Show me," Telamon repeated, "how Leonidas came downstairs."

She led them out of the kitchen to the wooden staircase built against the wall. Telamon stood at the foot and stared up. The steps looked solid and secure, built against the wall of a house, one side protected by the plaster wall, the other by a long rope fixed into the post at the top and tied to a pillar at the bottom.

"I was under the stairs there."

The steps were wooden slats a few inches above each other.

"Go on!" Telamon urged.

Harna grasped the rope, waggling her bottom, the hem of her tunic slapping against her long brown legs. She reached the top and turned.

"What's happening?"

Telamon looked over his shoulder. The stairwell stood between the kitchen and the main room of the house. Agathon lounged against the doorpost. Telamon did not like the look in his eyes.

"If I need you, I'll call you," Telamon smiled. "Now go away!" He held up the silver coin so Harna could see it. "Come down as Leonidas did."

The girl, a cheeky grin on her face, obeyed. She descended slowly, bare feet slapping against the wood. She reached the bottom and, breathing heavily through her nose, moved towards the door.

"Are you sure?" Telamon asked.

"That's the way he came, down the stairs, opened the door and out."

Harna held out her hand. Telamon handed over the silver and she disappeared into the kitchen.

Telamon and Cassandra went up the staircase. The second floor was supported by pillars, the gallery floor scuffed and chipped, the wall paint flaking. Five chambers in all: each was the same, wet with mildew and crumbling plaster. Here and there a floorboard was missing. The beds were narrow frames covered with heavy cloaks; a few pots and some battered furniture lay about.

"A pigsty," Cassandra murmured. "Faugh, what a smell!"

At the far end of the gallery was another staircase leading up to a loft, a narrow, makeshift affair with some of the steps missing. Telamon told Cassandra to bring an oil-lamp. She found one and brought it back, the flame flickering weakly.

"Be careful!"

Telamon took the glazed piece of pottery and climbed the steps. The trapdoor at the top was missing. He pushed his head through, holding up the oil-lamp: all he could see was a long, dark chamber, the outline of rafters, mounds of rubbish, and a pool of damp shimmering under where the flat roof had cracked. The only noise was the scampering and squeak of rats. Telamon stretched his hand out: the floor of the loft consisted of planks of wood, not too strong and certainly not able to bear a man's weight. Telamon came down the steps and handed back the lamp.

"Shouldn't we search their chambers?" Cassandra whispered.

"What's the use?" he retorted. "Aristander's agents have swept through the house, and those two beauties downstairs knew we were coming. We'll find nothing suspicious."

"It's an evil place." Cassandra extinguished the oil-lamp with her fingers and put it carefully on the floor. "It's hot outside but cold in here. I've never seen a place which so reeks of evil! It's like one of those ancient temples in Thessaly with their fire altars on which children were sacrificed."

Telamon touched the side of her head. "Don't let your imagination scare you. This is a house where murders have been committed. If I find the truth, or even if I don't, I'll ask the king to raze it to the ground!"

They went down the stairs and back into the kitchen. Harna was back slicing vegetables, hacking at them with her knife.

"Agathon asked me what you wanted; I told him I knew nothing."

158

Telamon noticed the fresh bruise high on her right arm. "I'll have a word with him before I go. Is there a cellar?"

Harna pointed to the sunken trapdoor in the far corner. "Pull that up. Stairs lead down. You'll need an oil-lamp. Here!"

She went across, dressed one and, using a tinder, lit the wick. Cassandra took this, Telamon lifted the trapdoor, and they both carefully walked down into the darkness beneath the house. The cellar was as black as pitch, airless. Telamon pinched his nostrils at the sweet-sour smell. Cassandra fumbled about and lit a cresset torch fixed into a niche in the wall. Telamon was glad of its warmth and light. The ceiling was low, just above his head, the walls of rough stone, the floor of beaten earth. Telamon stretched out the torch and exclaimed in surprise. He had expected one large, cavernous room, but in the light of the torch the cellars stretched the whole length of the house. He walked slowly forward.

"Four chambers in all," Telamon murmured, recalling Leonidas's rough drawing. Each was empty. A few pieces of rubble and rotting wood. The deeper they went the more Telamon's unease deepened. He expected such a place to smell, but the stench grew more oppressive, reminiscent of a corpse house or a battlefield where the dead had been left unburied. Cassandra was murmuring some Celtic prayer. Telamon turned.

"I didn't think you believed in the gods."

"On occasions like this I certainly do!" she snapped. "That smell!" She pulled a face. "You know what I'm thinking?"

"I can guess." Telamon entered the last chamber and looked around. "I've seen enough!"

They went back to the cellar steps and up into the kitchen. Harna still squatted on the floor.

"Do you ever go down there?"

She shook her head.

"When Leonidas died and the officials came from the palace?"

"They didn't ask, I didn't show them."

"Doesn't the smell concern you?"

Harna's eyes crinkled in amusement. "I live in a cesspit and you ask if the cellar smell offends me?"

159

Telamon strode back into the main room. Agathan and Sallus still lounged on a bench, their faces tense, watchful.

"Have you been down to the cellar?" Telamon demanded.

Sallus grimaced, Agathon shook his head. "No need to."

Telamon played with the ring on his finger, moving it backwards and forwards. "Well?" he asked. "Aren't you going to tell me?"

"What can we tell you?" Agathon wailed. "We live and sleep here. Leonidas died here. He was a drunk, he should have been more careful."

"Very well."

Telamon opened his pouch and took out the royal seal. He thrust this into Agathon's face. The soldier immediately leapt to his feet. He took the cartouche, kissed it and handed it back. Sallus followed likewise.

"Now I have your attention," Telamon smiled, "you are both back on duty. I want you to go out into the streets beyond the wall. If you're quick enough, cunning enough, and don't want to spend the rest of your leave digging latrines, you'll catch this beggar . . ."

"Oh, him!" Agathon sneered. "He's been lurking around here, the porter calls him Cyclops."

"Well, you're both brave soldiers," Telamon continued. "Fleet of foot and sharp-eyed members of the Raven Squadron. I want that beggar caught and brought back here unharmed."

"Why?"

"Because I am carrying the king's seal. I have just issued you an order on his behalf. I don't want you back without the beggar."

Agathon gazed at Sallus, who shrugged and spread his hands.

"Not in your own time," Telamon added, "but mine."

Both men hastened towards the door.

"Oh, Agathon!"

The officer turned, hate blazing in his eyes. "What now?"

"Beat that girl again and you'll be clearing latrines as well as digging them!"

Both officers left; the main door of the house opened and slammed shut.

"Well, well, well!" Cassandra stood rubbing her right arm. "You should have been a soldier, Telamon."

160

"I don't like liars and murderers. Shall I tell you what I think happened, Cassandra?" The physician sat down on a bench beneath the window. "Leonidas came to this evil place, with six companions. I suspect they found the treasure. Leonidas killed them and buried their corpses in the cellar – that accounts for the awful stench. Leonidas would have taken the treasure and deserted, but the Persians returned a little faster than he thought. He hastily buried his find and fled. Those two beauties – no." Telamon paused. "Leonidas may not have killed all of them. The beggar Cyclops knows what happened."

"And did our two beauties kill Leonidas?"

"What strikes you about this place?" Telamon asked.

"It's filthy."

"And our two beauties?"

"Pigs could be cleaner. Even from where I sat I could smell them."

"That concerns me," Telamon replied. "Whatever else they may be, they are cavalrymen. They take pride in their appearance. But their tunics are dirty and soiled, their bedchambers are pigpens."

"You mean it's deliberate?"

"Yes, I think it's deliberate, to give the impression of soldiers wallowing in their dirt. They don't want to raise any suspicions: yet outside, at the back of the house, they have clothes, tunics and cloaks washed and drying in the sun. Harna!"

The girl came stumbling through the doorway.

"Those clothes outside, did you wash them?"

She shook her head. "The master did," she replied. "Filled a vat of water."

"Agathon?"

"Yes, helped by Sallus."

Telamon thanked and dismissed her.

"Now, isn't that strange? Leonidas died the night before last and what do our two beauties do? They keep this house as dirty as ever but wash their clothes."

"Perhaps they were soiled, after a night's roistering."

"No, no," Telamon disagreed. "They're covering up a murder."

"So you do think Leonidas was murdered?"

"Oh yes. Agathon and Sallus have his blood on their hands, but proving it is going to be difficult. There is a treasure trove here. They forced Leonidas to share it, then killed him. The problem is, where have they put it? We checked the cellar. I don't think it's there. The loft is too weak. Any digging in the gardens would soon be noticed." Telamon scratched the side of his head. "We know Leonidas told the porter to absent himself. Come with me!"

"They're dangerous!" Cassandra called out.

Telamon turned.

"Sallus and Agathon are dangerous," she repeated. "They're veteran soldiers. We are not, we don't even carry weapons."

Telamon nodded in agreement. He walked into the shabby hallway and pulled open the front door. The noonday heat made him catch his breath: the light breeze had now dropped, the rank-smelling garden lay silent under the sun. Telamon went down the steps and along the pathway. Cassandra, hurrying behind, stumbled where one of the paving stones had sunk. They reached the porter's lodge: the old guardian sat inside on his stool. He reminded Telamon of a tired old satyr, with his long claw-like fingers and hunched back.

"What's happening?" the man grumbled as he got to his feet. "The other two hurried out as if they were being pursued by the Furies."

"They might well be." Telamon stood by the doorway to the lodge and stared back at the crumbling, sombre house. "I wonder . . .?"

Telamon studied the front of the house and walked back up the path. He could see no disturbance, nothing untoward around the steps or in the portico. The wooden pillars were set in baked clay. Telamon recalled Cassandra's warning about the two officers. He opened his purse, returned to the lodge and grasped the porter by the shoulder.

"Take this coin, hurry to the Temple of Hercules. You will find an officer there, Callisthenes."

The old man made to object, but then stared down at the silver glinting in the palm of Telamon's hand.

162

"Go there!" Telamon urged. "And you will have another coin on your return. I will also make sure that this lodge and garden will be yours. You must tell the officer to bring soldiers here without delay."

He pushed the man towards the gate. Cassandra pulled back the bolts and opened it.

"Who shall I say sent me?" The old man turned, gazing mournfully back at his lodge as if he were being deprived of it for life.

"Telamon the royal physician."

He made the porter repeat the message and slammed the gate behind him. Telamon stood with his back to the gate and stared up at the house. Cassandra was right, it had a haunted, malevolent appearance. But where would the treasure be hidden? It would probably be coins, precious stones, bracelets, necklaces, rings, not too heavy. Telamon studied the upper stories, the shuttered lower windows, the shabby door, the portico with its four imitation columns, the steps leading up to it. He stared at the paving-stone path: once it had been broad and smooth with well-laid flagstones, but now only four remained, set out like the four rectangles in Leonidas's drawing.

Telamon hurried across and studied them. He could see where the stones had been shifted; their edges were clear of moss and mud.

"You think it's here, don't you?" Cassandra had followed him. "That's why I stumbled; these paving-stones have been raised. They resemble Leonidas's drawings."

"Yes," Telamon agreed, "they do, four in all. Leonidas wasn't drawing a map, he was doodling. He did find his treasure trove. He wouldn't leave it in the cellar. We know why: sooner or later someone would have started digging and, I think, discovered some grisly corpses. The walls are flaking, so why not out here? He'd raise the flagstones, bury his ill-gotten gains and flee. Years passed and the path became overgrown again until Leonidas returned."

Telamon paused as he heard sounds in the alley, shouts and curses. He hastily walked back up the path and onto the portico. The gate was pushed open. Agathon and Sallus, the beggar pinned between them, came hurrying up the garden path.

Telamon went and sat on the bottom step. The two soldiers thrust the beggarman to his knees. At first glance he appeared an old man, with his shock of unruly grey hair, but the sunburnt face, though lined and drawn, was young-looking: one eye gleamed brightly, the other was covered by a patch kept in place by a piece of cord tied round the man's head. He wore a shabby brown tunic, a piece of rope round the middle: the sandals on his feet, though shabby and tattered, were those worn by Greek infantrymen.

"You are in no danger."

Cyclops's sharp eye studied Telamon.

"You are in no danger," the physician repeated.

The man shook his head as if he couldn't understand.

"He's been talking gibberish!" Agathon snapped. "We trapped him in the alley. He may be a beggar, but he can fight."

Sallus dabbed at a cut lip: angry bruises marked the beggar's right forearm. He also nursed one wrist. Telamon took this gently and felt the bones, moving the hand backwards and forwards.

"A slight sprain," he diagnosed. "A cold compress will soon heal it. I am going to take you inside."

The man gazed fearfully at the house. Telamon was determined not to question him in front of these two assassins.

"What shall we do?" Agathon complained. "And by the way, where's the porter?"

"He said the excitement was too much for him," Cassandra taunted. "I think he's fled."

Telamon jabbed a finger over his shoulder at the house. "You two can stay in there. I want to question Cyclops."

Cursing under their breath, the two cavalrymen went up the steps, slamming the door behind them, Agathon yelling for Harna.

"Don't run away." Telamon leaned forward. "You are only pretending to be an idiot, a madman or even a Persian who doesn't understand Greek, but you're not, are you? You're Greek, probably Macedonian. You're not a cavalryman, you haven't got the legs for it. By the way you walk, you're a hoplite, a foot soldier."

Cyclops sucked his lips as he tried to hide a grin.

"You are in no danger," the physician continued. "My name is Telamon, counsellor and confidant to Alexander the king. If you won't talk to me perhaps I could talk to you. You were a foot soldier in the Macedonian army. Somehow or other, two years ago when Parmenio captured Ephesus, you became involved with that old scoundrel, the cavalry commander Leonidas. He, you and five others quartered in this house. Only the gods know how you became involved. At first it was just an ordinary soldiers' billet, rather shabby, haunted, slightly mysterious. But Leonidas discovered something: that the house was once owned by an assassin, a member of a secret society called the Centaurs. Leonidas always dreamed of discovering treasure: he searched this house from cellar to attic and found it. But Leonidas was greedy." Telamon paused. Cyclops's gaze never faltered. "Oh, yes, Leonidas became greedy: he murdered five of his companions, but you escaped."

The man held a hand up and leaned closer. "Call me Cyclops. At the moment my real name is of little concern. I am Macedonian by birth, a foot soldier, a junior officer in the Shield Bearers regiment." He licked his lips. "I will not talk here."

Telamon and Cassandra followed him down to the porter's lodge. The beggar went round this to the far side so he couldn't be seen from the house. He sat down, leaned against the wall and squinted up at Telamon.

"It's good to speak fluent Greek." He grinned, scratching the stubble on his chin. "I still shave when I can afford the barber's coin. I even thought of going out to the camp, throwing myself at the feet of General Ptolemy."

"What happened?" Telamon demanded.

"Oh, there's no great mystery. It's as you say." Cyclops wiped the sweat from his neck. "Is it possible to have some wine?"

Cassandra went into the lodge and brought back a jug of wine and a cracked cup. She filled this to the brim and thrust it into the beggar's hands. He half-drained it in one gulp and smacked his lips.

"Ah!" he sighed. "Good wine, it tastes like nectar! I'd love that and some cheese, goat's cheese, thick and creamy, with freshly baked bread."

"You'll have all that." Telamon squatted down in front of him. "I am a royal physician, I have influence . . ."

"I couldn't give a damn if you're bedding Queen Olympias!"

Cyclops retorted. "I like your face." He gestured at Cassandra. "What would I do for a night with you!"

"I'd eat you alive!" Cassandra snapped. "I've thrown bigger things out of a bowl!"

Cyclops laughed.

"Why didn't you run?" Telamon asked. "You did before."

Cyclops gestured towards the house. "The ones you sent after me are brutes, but as they brought me back, I thought well, I can't keep skulking in the shadows for the rest of my life." He finished the wine and moved the cup from hand to hand. "True, I was here when Parmenio took Ephesus two years ago. Everything was a mess, you know how it is. You get through the gates, you're ordered not to plunder, so it was girls and the wine shops." He paused. "Leonidas was a drinking companion. He had five men with him. When I came knocking at the gate here, I was greeted like a long-lost brother." He shook his head. "I don't like this bloody house. I never did. You should be here at night and you'll see what I mean. The old porter just shakes his head but there's a presence, a sadness: something hideous happened there. We didn't like the drawings on the walls: centaurs inflicting horrid tortures. There was an altar in the main room, Leonidas had it smashed. It looked blood-stained, as if sacrifices had taken place. The upstairs chambers were no better. I've fought in many a battle, but the House of Medusa was like entering a dusty, narrow valley haunted by demons where nothing green or fresh grows and the vultures circle above you. I used to have nightmares. At first Leonidas laughed. You know what he was like? When he wasn't riding a horse he was drinking or feeling some girl's tits. That house changed him. He became interested in its history, started asking questions. He found some documents in a wall cavity and visited a courtesan, a whore." Cyclops wetted his lips.

"Arella?"

"Yes, something like that." Cyclops scratched his cheek. "She was related to someone who owned the house but she wanted nothing to do with the place, said it was the haunt of blood-suppers and demons. Leonidas claimed the place haunted

166

him, possessed him: it contained hidden treasure and he would have it."

"And you believed him?" Cassandra asked from where she sat on a moss-covered boulder.

"Yes, Red Hair, we did. We searched the house, every mouse-hole, every piece of flea shit. Leonidas became different, sullen and withdrawn. He had the paintings washed off the wall, the plaster chipped away. He kept us here, he didn't want us talking." Cyclops spread his hands. "At last we found it, built into the far cellar wall. A large coffer, a yard long." He let his hands drop. "About nine inches high, bound and padlocked. I've never seen a coffer like that. We broke the lid, and went mad with joy: bags of coins, golden darics, silver drachmae from Greece and Persia, small leather sacks of pearls white as snow: small ingots, precious stones, amethysts, rubies and emeralds. We were getting ready to celebrate when one of the camp marshals came thundering down the lane outside. The Persian army was advancing on Ephesus. Parmenio couldn't hold it: we were to leave everything and retreat, be out of Ephesus by dawn the following morning."

"That's when the killing took place?"

"That's when the killing took place," Cyclops agreed. "Leonidas brought wineskins down to the cellar. Oh, he was all jovial and merry, fixing torches into the wall sconces so it became as bright as day. I only discovered later," he added bitterly, "why he did that. We sat on the ground toasting each other, the treasure in the centre. We worshipped it as we would a god. We all got drunk. Leonidas left, ostensibly to fetch more wine. We discussed how we would divide the treasure, six of us seated in the torchlight, clear targets for Leonidas. The first two died before I even realized."

"One man against so many!" Telamon exclaimed.

"Leonidas didn't bring wine, but a bow and a quiverful of arrows. You've seen the cellar, it's only got one entrance. He had us pinned up against the wall, nowhere to hide. Two shafts!" Cyclops snapped his fingers. "Dead within a few heartbeats. Another sprang up; he took an arrow straight in the heart. Leonidas was moving quickly. He knelt and took aim again and again." Cyclops paused.

Telamon imagined that cold, bleak cellar, the torchlight blazing, the broken coffer, the death-bearing arrows whistling through the air, the thud of their impact, bodies sprawled.

"An arrow took me in the eye," Cyclops continued. "I fell back, rolled over with the pain and shock. When I regained consciousness I peered round. Leonidas had taken care of everyone. He'd slit the throats of the wounded and was now dragging the treasure up the passageway. He'd also started drinking. The pain in my eye and the right side of my head was hideous, as if my entire face was being burnt." He touched his eyepatch. "You're a physician; that arrow should have killed me."

"I have heard of it happening before." Telamon touched the top of his own eye. "An arrow here can pierce the eye and bury itself deep in the bone. If the wound is treated properly, recovery is possible. Anyway, how did you get out?"

"Leonidas was dragging the treasure chest, pushing it with his back to me, he was all huffing and puffing. I got to my feet, he never heard me. I had one thought, to get by him. I was down the cellar and past him. He screamed curses, but somehow or other, only the gods know how, I was up the steps and through the trapdoor. I pushed a table over it and made my escape. My face was drenched with blood, my body lacerated with thorns. In the city all was confusion. The Greek army was withdrawing and I didn't know what to do. Leonidas was well known, it would be his story against mine, if he allowed me to live long enough to tell it. The arrow had become dislodged but its head was still there." He tapped his eyebrow. "Now, like any soldier, I had a devotion to Hercules."

"So you went to the temple?"

Cyclops nodded. "I claimed sanctuary."

"Didn't the priest turn you over to the Persians?"

"I thought he would, but he said he was a Greek first and foremost. I asked for Hercules's help. He was a kind man." The beggar's one good eye brimmed with tears. "Sheltered me. He wasn't a physician but a leech. He took out the arrowhead and what was left of the eye. He treated and cleaned the wound, using a heavy wine to wash it. I lay for days, bandages over my eye. The

168

wound became infected. I had a fever but he cleaned the pus. I was tough and I healed."

"Why didn't you stay there?"

Cyclops shook his head. "The priest wanted me to, but if I were captured, the Persians would crucify me, so I left. He gave me food and some coins: I told him that was enough. I asked him why he helped me." Cyclops squinted his good eye. "He said one day the Macedonians would return. I left and became a beggar. I kept well away from the House of Medusa, and I told no one about what had happened, not even the priest. I just waited. Fortune smiled and the Macedonians returned to Ephesus: I knew if he was still alive, Leonidas would come back here."

Telamon plucked at some grass and threaded it between his fingers. He heard a shout from the house but ignored it.

"You've heard about the murders at the Temple of Hercules?"

The beggar nodded. "A strange business."

"Are there any secret entrances to the temple?" Telamon asked. "Could someone have slipped in?"

Cyclops shook his head. "I helped the old priest. He had other assistants but they weren't very good. Anyway, he liked to keep the temple to himself: built of solid rock, it was. After the riots broke out" – he pulled a face – "I returned, but it was too late. The priest's corpse lay on the steps, clubbed and hacked. I couldn't even recognize his face. I tried to drag the body off for honourable burial but the mob thought I was plundering it so I left it and fled." He shook his head. "I know nothing of what happened there, though the old priest was high in the councils of the Oligarchs. I do know one thing." His head came up, his face transformed by a mischievous smile. "I was going to use what I'd learnt if I surrendered to the camp marshals. The shrine has a silver vase protected by the ring of charcoal. I did ask the priest what it contained: he replied 'Nothing'."

"What!" Telamon exclaimed.

"I didn't believe him, but the priest had a strange ladder made of wood and wire. He'd position one end near the rim of the firepit, the other end resting on the plinth." Telamon recalled the two ledges halfway up the plinth. "He used to go across that to polish the vase. He would always do it when the temple was closed: once I was with him, he kept me close. I glimpsed the inside of the vase: there was nothing."

"So it contained no poison or sacred substance? No relic of the god-man Hercules?"

"Nothing but dust."

Telamon walked away and came back. "So, for two years you pretended to be a beggar in Ephesus?"

"Yes, one among many."

"You know nothing about the bloody faction-fighting between the Democrats and Oligarchs?"

"I heard about the murders, nothing else. Once I was healed, I kept away from the Temple of Hercules."

"Do you know anything about the Centaur?"

Cyclops pulled a face. "I also kept well away from other beggars. The Persians would have paid a bounty for my head. I'll tell you this." Cyclops waggled a finger. "On one of the few occasions I did return to the Temple of Hercules, the Oligarchs were meeting there. Have you seen one of the paintings of the centaurs?" He gestured back at the House of Medusa. "Which Leonidas did not scrape off."

"No, why?"

"According to legend, the centaurs were always surrounded by a swarm of wasps." Cyclops grinned. "Yes, I heard what happened in the Governor's palace last night. Anyway, I was begging in an alley near the temple. One of the Oligarchs came hurrying along, all cloaked and hooded. He paused halfway down the alley and I followed, whining for alms. The Oligarch pulled back his hood, took a chain from around his neck and slipped a cord over in its place."

"And?" Telamon asked.

"I startled him. He spun round. I'm sure a silver wasp hung from that leather cord. If you look at the centaurs painting, you'll notice how those mythical beasts wore the same emblem. Strange, isn't it?"

"Could you recognize the man?"

"No, the alleyway was shadow-filled. He picked up a rock and threw it at me, so I scuttled away."

"Physician!"

Telamon walked round the lodge. Agathon stood on the steps, hands on his hips.

"You have business with us?"

"Oh yes, I do," Telamon whispered. "We have business." He returned and crouched before the beggar. "You," he declared, "are going to help me!"

"Do what?"

"Why, to trap two murderers and dig up Leonidas's treasure!"

Telamon paused, staring at Cyclops. "I wonder why that priest didn't betray you: he was Persia's friend."

"I was only a minnow," Cyclops joked. "Perhaps he would have found it difficult to explain to the Governor why I came to him."

"Did you tell him about this house?"

Cyclops shook his head.

Telamon studied the beggar and recalled the centaur paintings in the Temple of Hercules. Didn't the centaurs only have one eye? Had that old priest, motivated by superstition rather than compassion, viewed the wounded, one-eyed Macedonian as some mysterious emissary of the gods?

Telamon stood up. "It's time!" he murmured.

Chapter 8

———◦◦◦◦———

"After subduing the greater part of Europe, the Amazons possessed themselves also of some cities in Asia, founding the city of Ephesus."

Marcus Junianus Justinus:
Universal History, Book II, Chapter 4

The painting of the centaur in the far corner of the wall just near the window was fading, though the shifting rays of the sun brought it to life. The Centaur looked more like a demon than a mythical animal with its curved horns, bloodshot eye and red, gaping mouth. Its claws were like the talons of an eagle, the muscular body crouched. Ugly head twisted back, the centaur was baying at the sky, the body of a young maiden trapped between its cloven hooves. A cloud of wasps swarmed above the monster's head, while the medallion round its neck also bore a wasp emblem: a hideous nightmare of a creature.

Telamon shifted his gaze. Agathon and Sallus sat on a bench just beneath the window: they lounged as if they had nothing to worry about. Sallus was the weaker character: he kept blinking, chewing the corner of his lips, tapping a sandalled foot on the dusty floor. Cassandra stood behind Telamon, Cyclops near the door. Cassandra had searched for Harna but there was no sign of her.

"What are you going to do, physician?" Agathon taunted. "Speak, sing or dance for us? The day is drawing on and we have other matters to attend to."

"Like your clothes," Telamon asked, "drying out on the bushes beyond?"

"Among other things," Agathon replied.

"Why did you wash them?"

Telamon shifted on the stool. He would have liked to have waited a little longer, but there was no sign of the porter. Telamon was wary lest these two birds of the night fly away.

"Well, we always wash our clothes."

"No, you don't." Telamon picked up his leather satchel and placed it on his lap. "You washed those clothes because you were trying to hide a murder."

"What!"

Sallus would have jumped to his feet, but Agathon held him back. Telamon glanced to where their cloaks were heaped on the floor. Were they preparing to flee rather than return to the camp?

"You don't wash your clothes," Telamon continued. "So I shall tell you what happened here. Leonidas was an assassin as well as a thief. Two years ago he found the Centaurs' treasure buried in the cellar of this house. He meant to take it for himself. However, the Persians suddenly returned. Leonidas slaughtered most of his companions, concealed the treasure and fled."

Agathon and Sallus were now all attention.

"You two brave soldiers are members of his squadron. Sallus is related to one of Leonidas's victims. From the start you would have been suspicious about the fate of your comrades. You reached the conclusion, as any keen searcher would, that something dreadful had happened at the House of Medusa. Leonidas's explanation about all his comrades being trapped and killed by the Persians was unacceptable."

"We did find it suspicious," Agathon protested. "But, there again, Leonidas and the rest became separated."

"No one would doubt Leonidas," Sallus added. "He was known to be a brave warrior."

"So why did you come here with him?" Cassandra asked.

"We don't need to answer your questions, you red-haired bitch!" Agathon taunted. "What are you, a bloody slave? A whore?"

"She asked a good question." Telamon ignored the insult. "Which I now repeat."

Agathon shrugged. "Circumstances! Leonidas invited us and . . ."

174

"And on the night he died? You, Agathon, went into the city with him?"

"Yes, we filled our bellies with wine. Leonidas was drunk. I brought him back here."

"You didn't undress him?"

Agathon smirked.

"Look" – Sallus tried to be placating – "Leonidas was in his cups. He was probably sleepwalking. You've seen the garden. He fell into the pool and drowned himself. We dragged him out."

"Oh no." Telamon shook his head. "This is what really happened. You, Agathon, brought him in through the main gate, took him along the side of the house, across the garden and threw him into that pool."

"What!"

"Leonidas was drunk." Telamon picked at the strap on his leather satchel. "Probably helped into the arms of Morpheus by a light sleeping potion. Both of you put him in the pool, pushed his face down and drowned him."

"But Harna," Agathon retorted. "She saw me bringing Leonidas in."

"No, she saw you bringing Sallus in. He had left the house, climbing down from an upper-storey window at the back: he was waiting for you in the dark. Sallus took Leonidas's cloak, before you both drowned him: he wrapped this about himself and, pretending to be Leonidas, was helped upstairs. The night passed. In the early hours Agathon returned downstairs wrapped in Leonidas's cloak and went out to the pool, where he put it back on the dead man. Afterwards, Agathon slipped to the back of the house and climbed up to his bedchamber."

"Nonsense!" Sallus laughed. "You can't climb a sheer wall!"

"In a house like this you can, with its crumbling bricks; I've climbed more difficult stairs. The porter eventually finds the corpse. You would have preferred him to wait until the morning. However, you send a message to the palace and go back to the pool to make sure there are no traces of your presence there." Telamon spread his hands. "Even if there were, you'd claim any disturbance

175

in the undergrowth was due to you having to pull Leonidas's corpse out of the water."

"Of course," Agathon agreed coolly. "And that's why we washed our clothes?"

"I don't think so," Telamon smiled. "When you drowned Leonidas you were probably fully dressed in tunics, mantles and cloaks. You wouldn't be wearing those in the morning when you pulled the corpse out. Someone might, perhaps, have become suspicious at the mud and slime from the pool which must have stained all your clothes. But I agree." Telamon put the leather satchel down on the floor beside him. "Washing your clothes was a mistake, there was no need for it. If you had been more cunning you would have allowed Harna to do it. Of course you don't really trust her, so you had to make sure. Perfection, sometimes, can be a hideous mistake."

"Is that all the proof you have?" Sallus taunted.

"No. I am a physician who has studied the effects of wine. I have seen men drink so much they can't even walk two paces. I have also treated men and given them a heavy infusion of wine with a sleeping potion."

"What are you implying?" Agathon demanded.

"Well, here we have an old soldier, so drunk he can't even walk along the streets. You have to help him upstairs. You put him on the bed. He should have stayed there until the late hours of the morning. Yet, for some unknown reason, Leonidas gets out of bed, comes downstairs, goes out into the garden, obligingly falls into the pool and drowns himself."

Agathon glared back.

"I asked Harna." Telamon leaned forward. "She described how Leonidas came down those stairs. Oh, he was heavy-footed, breathing noisily, but he never stumbled, never missed his footing. He reaches the bottom, opens the door and goes out." Telamon paused. "This is where it becomes really interesting. Leonidas manages to cross a garden which is overgrown: bramble briars, the curling branches of bushes, the long grass, uneven ground, rubbish and masonry. However, this drunken old soldier, in the dead of night, manages to cross all this, only to fall into a pool.

176

Indeed, I can understand him falling into the pool, but there's no evidence he tried to get out, no shouting, no disturbance, no alarm."

Agathon's head went down.

"I've studied his corpse," Telamon continued. "Not a mark on it! Old battle wounds, but nothing to betray what must have been a stumbling walk, if not a crawl, across an overgrown garden."

"And?"

Telamon smiled. "No one has yet given a good explanation of why the old soldier was there in the first place. You hoped that Leonidas's death would be regretted, but dismissed, as a drunken end to a drunken life."

Agathon sprang to his feet, beckoning at Sallus to follow. "Arrest us! Put us on trial! We'll answer any court martial. The evidence you offer is nothing!"

"Perhaps." Telamon got to his feet too. "But, at the end of it, you won't have the treasure."

Agathon ignored him, moving over to their cloaks. "We don't have any treasure," he retorted over his shoulder.

"Oh yes you do!" Cassandra sang out. "It's hidden beneath the flagstone outside the front door!"

Agathon moved quickly. He picked up the cloak and threw it at Telamon. He and Sallus drew daggers from their war belts. Telamon backed away. He glanced quickly at Cyclops, who stood rooted to the spot. Agathon's face was a mask of fury.

"You're right!" he snarled, jabbing at the air with his dagger. Sallus was moving aside to get round Telamon and strike at Cassandra. "We did murder Leonidas, just like he murdered our comrades. When he returned to Ephesus, we swore, if we could stay with him, we'd keep our suspicions to ourselves."

"Of course," Telamon breathed. "You blackmailed him. You must have known those corpses were still buried in the House of Medusa."

"We were going to share the treasure out," Agathon continued, shifting the dagger from one hand to another. "But we didn't really trust Leonidas. Anyway, he's dead. You and your bitch can keep him company in Hades!"

177

He danced forward. Telamon used the leather satchel to fend off the blow, and grasped his assailant's knife hand. Agathon tried to break free. Telamon dropped the satchel and closed with him, pushing and straining, catching his other hand, watching the dagger being forced up towards his face. He was aware of commotion and cries around him. Sallus had lunged at Cassandra. She, too, was locked in a life-and-death embrace, though Sallus, less confident, had dropped his knife. Telamon glanced despairingly at the door, but Cyclops had disappeared.

Telamon could smell Agathon's body stench, see the veins bulging in his neck, the sweat on his chest. They pushed and shoved like wrestlers, backwards and forwards. Telamon's leg became caught in a cloak; he tried to kick it loose, slipped and stumbled. He crashed to the floor, Agathon on top of him, eyes glittering, forcing the dagger towards Telamon's neck.

As Agathon's lips bared in a grin, Telamon glimpsed a shadow. Agathon's face went slack. He coughed and convulsed, his eyes glazed unseeingly, even as the first drops of blood spurted out of his nose and the corner of his mouth.

Telamon felt him slacken and pushed him off. Agathon rolled away, hand going up, trying to seize the dagger Harna had thrust deep just beneath his neck.

The servant girl stood back, arms folded, face impassive. She glanced quickly at Telamon, but seemed more interested in the death throes of her former master. Telamon rolled over. Cassandra and Sallus were locked like two lovers. The cavalryman had his hands round her throat; she was trying to force hers between his wrists to break his grip. She did so, thrusting Sallus away. The cavalryman glanced quickly at Agathon and ran towards the far window.

The door opened. An arrow whistled, striking Sallus full in the back; he crashed, arms up, against the wall and bounced back like a ball. Cyclops stood in the doorway, a great horn bow in one hand, a quiver of arrows at his feet.

"Thank you!" Telamon gasped. He stumbled towards Cassandra, who sat dazed on the floor. "Are you all right?"

Cassandra's face was white as snow, her eyes red-rimmed and watery. She clutched at her throat, gasping for breath.

"Oh, the gods be thanked!" she breathed.

Telamon heard a sound and looked up. Cyclops had strung another arrow. Before Telamon could even shout a warning, the arrow was loosed and took Harna straight through her throat. She stumbled forward, a look of surprise on her face, before collapsing to her knees over the corpse of Agathon, who lay twisted in a widening pool of blood. Cyclops bent down to pluck up another arrow.

Telamon shoved Cassandra aside and raced towards him. The one-eyed beggar had the arrow clear from the quiver, bringing it up, a long dark shaft, vulture feathers in its flight. Telamon's onrush made him fumble: that short interruption gave the physician more time. As Cyclops brought up the bow, the arrow strung, prepared to pull back, Telamon was on him. He stumbled slightly but his shoulder hit the beggar, knocking bow and arrow out of his hands.

Cyclops retreated. From somewhere a dagger appeared, thin and wicked-looking, with an ugly bone handle. Like any street fighter, Cyclops crouched, shifting the dagger from hand to hand, his one eye glaring at Telamon.

"Don't be a fool," Telamon whispered. "You've done good work."

"It's my treasure," Cyclops retorted. "I was wounded, a beggar for years on the streets of Ephesus. Now what? Arrested as a deserter?"

"I can speak for you," Telamon offered, moving slightly back-wards, eyes watchful.

"Will you?" Cyclops's tone became beseeching. He lowered the dagger then suddenly lunged forward. Telamon met him. Cyclops was no knife man: he struck straight for Telamon's chest but the physician grasped his wrist, punching him with his other hand, clawing at his eyepatch. Locked straining in each other's arms, Telamon and the beggar staggered about like two drunken lovers.

"Cassandra!" Telamon shouted, but she was lying on the ground, red hair shrouding her face. Telamon brought the heel of his hand under his assailant's chin. The beggarman tried to break free as he strained to lift the knife.

There was a crashing outside, shouts, the door was flung open. Cyclops turned. Burly hands seized him by the hair and pulled him away. Telamon fell to his knees: he was aware of soldiers in full armour, swords and shields, the clatter of feet. An officer was there, purple plumed feathers in his helmet.

"Come on, sir," a voice said kindly. "You're a physician, you shouldn't be lying on the floor."

Telamon was helped to his feet. He looked at Cyclops and started in horror. The beggar was kneeling on the floor, hands lashed behind him. A soldier stood above him, and even as Telamon shouted, the sword held above his exposed neck fell in one slicing cut, shearing off the head. Blood spurted out from the decapitated trunk as the head rolled and bounced into a corner. A soldier cursed at the mess it caused, while the executioner kicked the still erect cadaver onto its side.

Telamon turned away, hand to his mouth, trying not to be sick. He was taken gently by the shoulder and pushed onto a stool. Callisthenes crouched before him, helmet in one hand, a piece of wet cloth in the other; he used this to dab the sweat from Telamon's face.

"Are you well, sir?"

Telamon gazed blankly back.

"Dear me! Dear me!" Callisthenes gazed round the room. "How many corpses do we have?" Callisthenes tutted, like the mother of naughty children.

"Is the girl all right?" Telamon demanded.

He glanced over: Cassandra was sitting on a stool, her back to one of the pillars.

"Take care of her, lads!" Callisthenes called. "Fetch a wineskin and watch where you put your hands. Leave her tits and arse alone! She's the good physician's assistant!"

Telamon pointed to the decapitated corpse, its blood spilling out along the dusty floor, like the water of a brook trying to find its course.

"Why did you do that?" he asked wearily.

"Orders, sir," Callisthenes replied smartly. "Martial law is still in force. Any Greek attacking a Persian warrants immediate death.

Any Persian attacking a Greek, immediate death. Anyone drawing a knife against the legitimate authorities . . ."

"Immediate death," Telamon finished the sentence.

"Right, sir, you've got the idea. We were at the Temple of Hercules," Callisthenes continued, getting to his feet, "with our four notables over there."

Meleager, Agis, Peleus and Dion stood in the doorway, staring round in disbelief. Callisthenes stretched out a hand. Telamon grasped it and the captain pulled him to his feet.

"It's worse than a slaughterhouse, sir, let's go out."

He guided Telamon over to the side door. The physician excused himself and went across to Cassandra. She looked more comfortable, the colour returning to her face; her eyes were steady, though she trembled as she grasped the wine cup in her hands. Two of Callisthenes's guards knelt on either side like adoring worshippers in a temple: one of them stretched out his hand to touch her fiery red hair.

"I wouldn't do that, soldier!" Telamon warned. "She regards fingers as a delicacy. Just look after her and she will be well."

He patted Cassandra on the shoulder and followed Callisthenes out into the garden. The captain had found some wine.

"A gift from the porter." He thrust a cup into Telamon's hand. "Now, sir, can you tell me what happened? I'm sure you have a good explanation."

Telamon told him. Callisthenes squatted before him, legs crossed like a scholar before his teacher. When Telamon had finished, Callisthenes shook his head, whistling under his breath.

"I thought Cyclops was one of us," Telamon murmured. "But you can't blame the poor bastard, his greed got the better of him."

Callisthenes was staring at the house. "We'll take the corpses out. The king's orders were quite explicit: they're to be exposed in the marketplace, strung up on gibbets as a warning to the rest."

"Not the girl," Telamon broke in. "She was an innocent." He opened his purse and tossed a coin at the captain, who caught it deftly. "Give her a decent burial!"

Callisthenes agreed, and clambered to his feet, wiping the dirt

181

from his legs and hands. "I'll set fire to this blood-drenched place, but first . . .!"

A short while later Telamon and Cassandra, the four Ephesian dignitaries beside them, the porter standing on his stool peering over their heads, watched as Callisthenes's men began to raise the great flagstones in front of the house. Under the first two was nothing but gravel and dirt: under the third, the ground had been freshly dug, and it was the same under the last. Two large clinking sacks stained with mud were dragged out, the cords cut, the contents emptied onto the ground.

The Ephesians exclaimed in surprise. The sun caught the gold and silver, the precious jewels, the bracelets and necklaces, a shimmering mass of treasure.

Callisthenes recognized the danger, and immediately ordered the sacks to be refilled. "Keep your eyes off it, lads!" He pointed to the corpses laid out in a row outside the main door. "This is tainted treasure!"

The men stared at the corpses and shuffled uneasily. Harna looked grotesque, the arrow still embedded in her body. Agathon's and Sallus's cadavers were soaked in blood. The beggar's corpse had been dragged by the heels, leaving a streak of blood: as a macabre joke, someone had placed the severed head on his chest.

"Take the treasure back to the palace," Telamon ordered. "But to the victors the spoils!" He picked up a bag of coins and weighed it in his hands. "This is for the porter." He threw it at Callisthenes.

"We were looking for you!"

The physician turned. Agis and his companions walked over.

"We were at the temple when the message arrived," Agis explained, his face pale and sweat-soaked at the grisly scenes he had witnessed. "The king will expose those corpses?" he asked thickly.

"Before dusk," Telamon stared at the sky, "a gibbet will be set up in the main square. The corpses will be displayed as a warning to all. Now, why were you looking for me?"

"The Temple of Hercules has to be purified." Dion spoke up.

182

"The coals have to be doused, the silver vase replaced. The king wants you to inspect it again."

"Alexander can read minds," Telamon smiled.

"I cannot stay," Peleus added pompously. "I have other duties." He swaggered off. A young man crouched near the gate got up to greet him. Peleus put an arm round his shoulder and they both minced away.

"Peleus does like his young men," Agis breathed. "But come!"

They walked out of the garden, down the alley and onto the main thoroughfare, the Avenue of the Goddess, which swept down into the city. The broad paved highway was lined by sycamore and palm trees, and every so often a soaring white statue of the Goddess Artemis in different poses. Before each statue the citizens had placed baskets of flowers and fruit, which were now being pilfered by the beggars. Agis tried to question Telamon about what had happened at the House of Medusa, but the physician felt weak, his stomach agitated, and he was more concerned about Cassandra, who remained white-faced and tight-lipped.

As they walked Telamon became aware of the presence of Macedon: soldiers lounged in side streets or in the small parks. A squadron of cavalry trotted by, feathered helmets bright in the afternoon sun. Telamon's companions drew strange glances: the spectacle of such inveterate enemies, walking with the Macedonian, was a rare sight.

The city seemed quiet enough. Merchants and farmers had returned. Carts and hand-barrows thronged the avenue. People of various nationalities went about their business. Nubians, in their bright coloured cloaks, rubbed shoulders with fair-haired Scythians dressed in the skins of wild animals. Egyptians and Libyans, Canaanites, Greeks and Phoenicians, even a gaggle of merchants from Carthage. They thronged about in a variety of different clothing and glinting jewellery, the air permeated with strange perfumes and smells.

They left the avenue and entered the city proper, going under one of the great gatehouses manned by Macedonian archers and shield-bearers. The tumult of the city greeted Telamon like a hot wave. He felt giddy, slightly nauseous. The houses stood packed

183

together, intersected by narrow alleyways or broad avenues of black basalt. Beggars whined for alms. A group of Libyan dancers twisted and turned to eerie music while a little boy begged spectators for a coin. Fire-eaters and tumblers, leechers, quacks, acrobats and story-tellers, all touted for custom. The tricksters, the Scorpion and Wizard men, sold precious stones from Mount Sinai or lucky charms from beyond the Third Cataract on the Nile. They passed small temples dedicated to strange-sounding gods, around which circled different processions: men and women in saffron robes, their cheeks deeply rouged, shook sistra and tambourines, dancing like dream-walkers in a trance, eyes heavy, mouths half-open. Telamon tried to ask questions, but the din was deafening. They had to stand aside as one procession snaked out of a market-place: a young woman sitting in a palanquin borne by four sweating Nubians. She was naked except for a thin, white gauze veil; on her head, a bull's mask, its horns sweeping up. Young girls ran before her carrying bowls of steaming incense while others threw rose petals. The smell of rotting meat from the palanquin was so offensive Telamon stopped, hand to his mouth.

"Master, we need some shade," Cassandra whispered. "I feel so tired."

"Come this way."

Agis plucked at Telamon's arm and led him up a side street. They brushed aside a story-teller shouting how he had travelled beyond the eastern rim of the world, been chased by men who could turn into the shape of hyenas. How griffins with human heads and black winged panthers had stalked him. How he had seen temples of gold and silver. The story-teller tried to grasp Cassandra's arm, but Telamon pushed him away.

Agis turned sharp right and led them into an eating-house. Telamon, pleased to be away from the din, stared round the courtyard. A broad square, with porticoed walks on either side and a shimmering pool in the centre. On the far side a wide range of trees, sycamore, acacia, terebinth, date and palm, provided both shade and shelter for the weary customers.

"I know an even quieter place."

Agis led them into the kitchen, a fragrance-filled room where freshly slaughtered geese, chickens and ducks hung from bowls, plates arranged beneath them to catch the blood. Just outside the kitchen door stood a trellised fence covered by creeping plants, near which was a range of earthenware stoves packed with wood and charcoal and topped with grills on which pieces of quail, antelope, beef, duck, partridge and chicken were roasting merrily. Two little girls, completely naked, ran up and down, a bucket in one hand, a ladle in the other, to baste the meat with a variety of herbal sauces. Clouds of smoke wafted the savoury smells towards them. Telamon realized how hungry he was.

This area of the eating-house was reserved for special guests. Beyond the eating area lay a small paradise, watered by a canal to keep the grass, flowers and shrubs fresh and sweet-smelling.

Agis was recognized by the owner, who led them across to a shady spot beneath a cluster of palm trees where trestle tables, benches and stools had been placed. Wine and water were served. Telamon told Agis what he would like to eat, and turned to Cassandra.

"Are you well?" he whispered.

"I feel a bit faint." She blinked and dabbed the corner of her mouth. "So much blood! Death came so quickly!" She snapped her fingers. "Why did Cyclops turn against us?"

"A moment's decision," Telamon replied. "A fickle wish." He stretched across and picked up Cassandra's goblet, tasted it and handed it to her. "The best Chian," he whispered. "It washes the mouth, gladdens the heart and settles the stomach: it does not leave you heavy-headed."

Cassandra sipped while Telamon picked up his own goblet and stared round. He felt rather self-conscious under the cold, hard stare of these Ephesian dignitaries.

"Do you find it difficult?" he asked.

Meleager raised his eyebrows.

"I mean, a few days ago you were at each other's throats."

"As the House of Medusa proves," Meleager retorted, "that is a human condition not peculiar to Ephesus."

"What happened there?" Agis demanded. "After all, Meleager and I are now principal magistrates of the city."

185

Telamon sighed, sipped his wine, and gave a brief account of what had occurred. They heard him out: Telamon only told them what he wanted, no more.

"It's an ancient story," Meleager said. "The Centaurs were a religious sect: they worshipped some hideous goddess, the Destroyer." He shook his head in wonderment. "I never thought the House of Medusa was so important."

"Leonidas did," Cassandra remarked.

"That's because he was looking for treasure," Agis commented.

They paused as servants brought across the food: bream in cheese and oil, served on wooden platters, wedges of garlic cheese and slices of roast hare on fresh leaves and covered with black pepper and olive oil. As they ate the conversation was desultory. Cassandra became more lively, pausing halfway through her meal to leave them, as she put it, "to make herself more presentable". Telamon's stomach settled; he felt the weariness slip away. He also became acutely aware of the tension between Meleager and Agis, with Dion quietly fanning the flames. It was muted enough, but manifested itself in sharp comments, retorts and references to the past which only they could understand.

"Arella." Telamon pushed away what was left of his food and picked up his wine goblet. "An influential young woman?"

"She was very skilled in love-making," Dion declared, "and surrounded herself with an aura of mystery which only increased her allure."

"Did she confide in anybody?"

"Perhaps her maid."

"There was one person," Dion offered. "The woman who trained her, a retired courtesan who calls herself Basileia, Queen of the Moabites. She still owns a house near the Perfume Quarter. From what I can gather Arella often visited her."

"I want to speak to her," Telamon said.

"She doesn't meet strangers."

"She won't be meeting a stranger," Telamon replied, "but the personal envoy of the king. We are going to the Temple of Hercules, yes?" Telamon gestured at the servants standing round the stoves. "Pay one of those a coin to take a message to this Queen of the Moabites: the King of Macedon's representative wishes to meet her at the Temple of Hercules. She either comes or I'll have her arrested."

Agis made to object. "You're the principal magistrate in the city," Telamon retorted. "Murders have been committed. The king himself was threatened. Arella is part of all this."

"Yes, she is," Agis agreed. "Or was. Now she's no more than a dead fish by her swimming pool."

"Yes, that's right," Telamon agreed.

Agis looked at Meleager as if about to issue an order. Meleager stared coolly back and returned to picking crumbs from his platter. Agis sighed and rose. He went across and talked to the proprietor; two of the servants donned their sandals and left. Agis sauntered back across the grass.

"The Queen of the Moabites," he said, taking his seat, "will not be able to solve the mystery of the Centaur or the murders in the temple."

"When I was a boy," Telamon replied, "Aristotle set me a mystery. He challenged me to take hold of both ends of a piece of string and, without letting go, tie a knot in the middle of the string."

"And could you?"

Telamon nodded.

"How?" Meleager asked.

"Ah, that's for you to find out," Telamon teased. "But I did do it! It's the same with this mystery. There's a way of resolving it. Every murderer makes a mistake. I'm sure the Centaur has. Now, I wish to ask you questions, and prefer to do so here than in the presence of witnesses. Did any of you approach that temple while Demades and his companions were in the sanctuary?"

His question was greeted with a sharp denial.

"And Arella?"

"I have visited her," Dion offered. "I will not lie, though I'd prefer my wife not to know that."

"Did Arella ever reveal anything?"

"She had one golden rule: Arella never discussed religion or politics."

187

"Was Hesiod a customer?"

"No," Dion retorted sharply. "Hesiod was like Peleus." He tapped his wine cup. "He had his own peculiar tastes."

"And the priest at the temple?" Telamon did not tell them what he'd learnt from Cyclops.

"The priest was killed by the mob," Agis remarked. "His assassin cannot be traced."

"In which case, gentlemen," Telamon got to his feet, "the Temple of Hercules waits."

By the time they reached the small square which fronted the temple, Callisthenes and his guards had returned. The great doors of Lebanese cedar were opened, as were those beyond the porter's lodge. Once again, Telamon entered the dark, musty sanctuary. He stood for a while staring at the soaring pillar of Hercules, the gloomy aisles beyond the pillars. The temple floor was still stained from the blood-letting. Telamon noticed that the charcoal fire was beginning to die, most of it turning to a white feathery ash with the occasional glowing coal.

"Callisthenes?" he called.

The captain of the guard came smartly in.

"The treasure from the House of Medusa has been taken to the palace," Callisthenes said quickly. "Aristander himself received it. He seemed rather annoyed that he hadn't discovered it himself."

Aye, Telamon thought, and he'll comfort himself with a few trinkets.

"I gave the porter the coins," Callisthenes continued. "The king has ordered the House of Medusa, once darkness has fallen, to be razed to the ground and its soil soaked with salt."

Telamon pointed to the charcoal. "I want this charcoal collected, placed in leather sheets and taken to the palace."

"Why's that?" Agis demanded.

"I want it sifted. I will do it myself. In the meantime" – Telamon gestured at Cassandra – "let's walk round this temple again."

While the Ephesians stood by the doorway talking among themselves, Telamon and Cassandra walked around the fire-pit.

188

"I am tired," Cassandra moaned, "of places like this. First, the House of Medusa, now this cold bleak temple which still smells like a slaughter-yard."

Telamon paused and chucked her gently under her chin. "Are you well?"

Cassandra's eyes were bright, her face composed. "Do you wish to examine me, physician?" she asked cheekily. "Oh, by the way, how did you resolve Aristotle's puzzle about the string?"

"Ah." Telamon smiled. "I crossed my arms and picked up each end. When I unfolded my arms a knot was formed. But don't tell anyone."

"How long did that take you?" she teased.

"Modesty forbids a reply." Telamon gestured round the temple. "This is going to be more difficult. Look around, Cassandra." He pointed to a dark, oily patch. "I found the corpse burnt to a cinder here. Only the gods know how he died. Around here" – he gestured towards the pillars – "Demades and the rest, together with their Macedonian guard, died, all clubbed twice, on the side of the head and in the front."

Cassandra shivered and rubbed her arms.

"The only exception was Demades's servant Socrates. He was found near the door behind the statue at the rear of the temple, his face and arms clawed as if by a great cat."

"Or a centaur's talons?"

"Or a centaur's talons," Telamon agreed. "Some wine and food remained, both untainted. No weapons were found," he continued. "Nothing remarkable. From what I understand Demades was agitated, wary, fearful: his servant Socrates spent a great deal of the time near the temple doors, staring out as if expecting to meet or see someone. Now he could have been doing that on his master's behalf, though from the little I've learnt Socrates himself was agitated." Telamon stood away and looked up at the great stone face of Hercules. "The windows are too high and narrow for an intruder to enter."

"And this rear door?" Cassandra pointed behind the statue.

"That was bolted and sealed with the king's seal: it hadn't been opened for many a day, though the bolts were recently oiled. The main doors were also locked. Aristander held the key. Yet all these men died quietly. No alarm was raised, no screams heard."

"Where was Socrates's corpse?"

Telamon led her round the statue and pointed at the paved floor near the rear door. "Just there."

The physician walked back and stared at the silver vase, restored to its plinth. Telamon reckoned it must be at least a hundred years old, kept burnished by successive priests.

"And that," he murmured, "reminds me of something."

He went out into the portico and called Callisthenes over.

"The priest's house?"

"It's all boarded up, it was ransacked," the captain replied. "Come, I'll show you."

He led them off the steps and down a narrow alleyway. The priest's dwelling stood at the end, protected by a high brick wall. Its front gate hung askew. Inside, the cobbled forecourt was littered with wood and broken pottery. The fountain had been smashed, the water bubbling up, encrusted with dirt. The outside of the house, once a pleasant place, showed the blackened stains of fire. The plants growing up the wall had been torn down or burnt. The front door had been refitted, with wooden bars nailed across. Callisthenes drew his sword and prised these free. Telamon and Cassandra stepped inside. Again a scene of destruction: the tiled floor had been dug up, the walls fire-scorched.

"Everything was taken," Callisthenes said. "The pillagers helped themselves."

Telamon entered the kitchen. Pots and jugs had been either smashed or stolen, the small movable stove overturned. The main room showed similar destruction. Telamon noticed a drawing on the far wall and went across: although marred by the fire, the painting still held its colours.

"It's a map of the temple interior," he remarked. "Look, there are the pillars, the stone plinth, the ring of charcoal, the silver vase."

"What's this?" Cassandra pointed to a scene which depicted the shadowy aisles of the temple. Telamon peered closer. He could make out a dark shape between the two pillars, half-man and half-horse.

190

"A centaur!" he exclaimed. "I wonder what that means? What it symbolizes?"

He was about to continue when the wail of a conch horn shattered the silence.

Chapter 9

"Apelles painted an equestrian portrait of Alexander: in which the painting of the horse did not satisfy the King."

Quintus Curtius Rufus:
History of Alexander the Great, Book II, Chapter 6

T he scene outside the house took Telamon's breath away. He didn't know whether to be surprised or laugh out loud.

A woman was walking, or rather waddling, up the path, a mound of bubbling flesh. She reminded Telamon of a bloated toad. Perfume billowed out from her goffered gown, and the clinking of the trinkets around her neck, wrists and ankles proclaimed her to be Basileia, Queen of the Moabites. She was dressed in a splendid linen robe of many colours. A dark-blue stiffened shawl draped her shoulders, a brilliant carnelian necklace circled her fleshy throat: her multiple chins kept bouncing off this, and her eyes were almost hidden in rolls of flesh. She pursed her mouth as if she had filled her fat cheeks with vinegar and was about to spit. She shuffled along on high-heeled shoes, a fly-whisk in one hand, a small parasol in the other. Her escort was equally macabre, covered in silver paint from shaven head to toe, even their loincloths and sandals: only their eyes and lips were free of the paint. Two were armed with clubs and swords, others carried great pink ostrich plumes which they wafted over their mistress, sending out clouds of perfume on every side. A dwarf walked in front tinkling a bell. He was dressed in imitation of the armour of a Greek hoplite, though his cuirass and kilt were pink, as was the horsehair crest in the helmet he carried under one arm.

"Make way," he bawled, "for Basileia, Queen of the Moabites!"

Callisthenes tried to stifle his laughter, but was unable to and walked back into the house, shoulders shaking. Cassandra, too, realized she had forgotten something and fled back in. Telamon chewed the corner of his lips. The strange procession stopped before him. The dwarf punched him on the knee.

"Are you the one who sent for my mistress?"

Telamon bent down and picked him up: the dwarf dropped his helmet and screeched, legs kicking.

"I am the one," Telamon replied, put him back on the ground and bowed to Basileia: her shrewd eyes, like two black buttons, crinkled in pleasure; her lips, not so pursed, gaped to reveal gold–studded teeth.

"I am Basileia." Her voice was soft. "You must be Telamon, envoy of Alexander of Macedon. I am not used to . . ."

"Madam, I know what you are not used to." Telamon stood aside and gestured at the house. "But I need to talk to you about a mutual acquaintance."

The four bodyguards were staring at Telamon, bodies slightly forward as if ready to spring in defence of their mistress. Basileia turned and chattered in a tongue Telamon couldn't understand. One of the bodyguard ran back down the lane and returned carrying a large cushioned chair. He glowered at Telamon as he brushed by him and entered the house. Basileia then processed in with all the dignity of a princess.

The servant placed the chair in the main room. Callisthenes had now composed himself, standing close to Cassandra. Basileia dismissed both with a look of contempt. Telamon found a rather battered stool, brought it across and sat before her.

"I am glad you have come, madam," he began. "I appreciate you are a woman of importance, your days must be very busy."

"I am used to flattery, physician. I have now passed my fiftieth summer."

Basileia shook her head in a rattle of jewellery, the amethyst earrings bouncing on the fleshy lobes. Every time she moved, Telamon caught her fragrance, a mixture of cassia, myrrh and frankincense mingled with the sweetness of crushed roses and lilies.

"In my time, Macedonian," she continued, gesturing at her

angry dwarf and bodyguard to stand well back; she stretched out plump fingers, so fat Telamon wondered if she could ever take her rings off. "In my time, this hand has been kissed by princes and generals. Men used to kill themselves when I withdrew my favours."

"True beauty always remains," Telamon replied tactfully.

Basileia stretched out and touched his cheek. "You look sad, Macedonian, but, there, in a place like this anyone would look sad. Looted, was it, during the recent troubles? It must be the priest's house? Ah yes." Her finger came up. "I heard he had been killed. I knew him once."

"And you were untouched?" Telamon asked.

"I have a bodyguard of sixteen mercenaries," Basileia lisped. "Scythian cut-throats. No looter would dare come near my gates."

"Arella?" Telamon asked. "You knew her?"

Basileia moved her fat rump, turning her head slightly. "I cannot say." Her voice quavered.

"You can say, mistress. I wish to be your friend and treat you with the greatest of dignity. I want you to be the king's friend."

Basileia moved her head, shoulders relaxing.

"Arella is dead," Telamon continued. "Others have been murdered."

"Ephesus was full of corpses."

"This is different," Telamon persisted. "It is the king's wish." Basileia's head went down. "Clear the room!" she shouted. "Clear the room!"

Telamon looked over his shoulder and nodded at Callisthenes and Cassandra who, hands over their mouths, hurried out followed by Basileia's servants.

"I was born in Moab," the fat lady began. "A kingdom in Canaan. When I was fourteen I was sold to Edomites who brought me to Ephesus. They trained me to be a flautist and a dancer. Men would stare at me, paw my breasts, pinch my buttocks. I was fortunate. I was taken up by a professional courtesan as her maid. She trained me in all the arts. Anything" – she smiled at Telamon – "anything a man wants, I can give. Even men well past their prime suddenly found their powers restored. I assumed the title of Queen of the Moabites. In those days Ephesus was a lawless place. The citizens were fighting among themselves and the city gangs terrorized civic life."

"The Centaurs?" Telamon asked.

"One gang of cut-throats among others, though they were faster, more cunning and ruthless. They showed no mercy, no compassion. I will be honest, I used them myself. This temple was one of their favourite shrines and meeting places."

"The Temple of Hercules?"

"Oh yes, Macedonian. The priest who was killed? He was once a Centaur. He was only an acolyte then, a chapel priest to those brigands."

"So that's why!" Telamon exclaimed.

"What?"

Telamon told her about what had happened at the House of Medusa.

"Cyclops was very fortunate," Basileia chuckled, her many chins quivering. "He may have come here by accident, but if he had known, the priest would have been most interested in that treasure."

"Did you know about it?" Telamon asked.

"Oh yes, that old ruffian Leonidas visited me. He'd found some documents at the House of Medusa which linked me to the Centaurs. Of course I said I couldn't help him, but, there again, he was a Macedonian officer. I didn't like the way he kept rubbing the hilt of his sword, so I sent him to Arella." Basileia ran a finger round her carmined lip. "When the Centaurs were crushed, Arella's father, Malli, brought her to me to look after. I raised the girl," she added proudly, "to become the finest whore in Ephesus." Basileia's eyes filled with tears. "And now she's dead," she quavered in a sing-song voice. "All that beauty gone!"

"Arella helped Leonidas?" Telamon asked.

"Of course she did. I told Leonidas about her family background: how the House of Medusa used to be the meeting place of assassins."

"Weren't either of you interested in the treasure?"

"Treasure?" Basileia mocked. "Treasure? It's not treasure we want, Macedonian, it's power over men."

196

"Did Arella have that power?"

"She courted the great and the good, the high and the mighty." Basileia's eyes became watchful. "She belonged to neither party. She said when you wrap your legs around a man, he's only a man, be he Persian or Greek, aristocrat or commoner."

"Why was she murdered? Come on, answer!" Telamon demanded sharply. "Secondly, during the time Demandes and his companions took sanctuary in the temple, why was Arella seen outside?"

"She may have been curious."

"I am becoming curious, madam, and angry. You were Arella's confidante. You can tell me here, or in the presence of Aristander, the king's Master of Secrets."

"She was worried," Basileia gabbled. "We courtesans, Macedonian, like power. A stranger approached Arella. He came in the dead of night, stole into her bedchamber. He wore a hideous mask, sat on the bed and threatened her. Arella was terrified. The threats turned to promises, of power and wealth beyond all imagining, on one condition: Arella would have to bestow her favours on a person he had chosen."

"Who was this?"

Basileia held her hands up as if in prayer. "I truly don't know, Macedonian. I swear that's the truth. Arella never revealed the name."

"Why did she accept?"

"The visitor called himself the Centaur. He said he would leave half a talent of gold in my hands as surety, as proof that his word was good."

"And did the gold arrive?"

"Yes, mysteriously, at my house. The man who brought it simply handed the pack pony over to my guards and left. I have no description of him."

"When did all this happen?"

Basileia's fingers flew to her lips; her black eyes disappeared into folds of flesh. "All very quickly," she murmured. "The panic began shortly after Alexander's victory at the Granicus."

"And did Arella tell you anything else?"

197

"She was troubled. Someone was pestering her — but," Basileia lifted one shoulder elegantly, "that is part of our life, to be pestered by men whom we do not like." She waved her fat fingers in front of her mouth. "Oh dear!" she murmured. "I have not talked for so long for many a day. I will need to bathe my throat in honey. What do you recommend, physician?"

"Honey," Telamon replied. He felt like adding "and fast for forty days", but bit his tongue.

"Ah, that's what she said." Basileia raised her hands. "I asked Arella about the man she was supposed to favour: she replied she'd rather drink a cup of hemlock than the loving cup with him."

"What did she mean?"

Basileia pulled a face. "Nothing, except that she didn't like the man her visitor had chosen."

"Was it someone in Demades's group? Perhaps the leader himself?"

Basileia's head went down. Telamon grasped her hand, raised it to his lips and kissed it.

"You can tell me more, can't you?"

Basileia glanced coyly at him from under thickly painted eyebrows. "Arella didn't like Demades. He had pestered her, oh, many months ago, for favours, but she had refused. Demades was like a dog on heat — presents, visiting her house — but Arella would have nothing to do with him."

"And the fat scribe, Hesiod?"

"Yes, I wondered what he was doing with my favourite girl." Basileia licked her lips. "Not a man for the ladies, was Hesiod, but perhaps . . .?"

"Could he have been Arella's midnight visitor?"

"He may have been." This self-styled Queen of the Moabites picked up the fly-whisk and waved it before her face. "I am only a retired courtesan," she simpered. "Before you Macedonians came marching bravely in, I thought the old days had returned: sudden, death murder . . ."

"And the Centaur?" Telamon asked.

"Ah yes, the Centaur. Arella told me about him. She didn't

know his name: one of her clients, the Persian Rabinus, who was burnt alive in his cell, used to hint that he knew."

"When you arrived here," Telamon asked, "you saw Agis, Meleager and the rest? Was there any relationship between them and Arella?"

Basileia sucked on her lips.

"You have been so accommodating," Telamon said sweetly. "I hope I can praise you to the king."

"The lawyer Dion." The words came out fast; Basileia was agitated. "You see, on the day Arella died, I sent a messenger to Dion's house, but he wasn't there."

"Why should you send a messenger?"

"Dion is married, but he does like the ladies. I have certain beauties under my wing whom I guard like the apple of my eye and offer to select customers. Dion wasn't there. Agis was just coming away from the lawyer's house. My messenger, a trusty man, continued on to Arella's house, but by the time he arrived" – her eyes again filled with tears – "my little one's residence was all aflame. Anyway, my servant saw a man running through the small garden: he was certain it was Dion."

Telamon's head came up at sounds from outside: raised voices, Aristander's high-pitched tones. The Master of the King's Secrets swept into the house. Basileia knew who he was and immediately started quivering: a bead of perspiration ran down her painted face, fingers all a-flutter. She smiled ingratiatingly as Aristander stood over her, studying her from head to toe as if she were a monstrosity in some travelling troupe.

"Ah, Basileia, Queen of the Moabites." Aristander caught her plump hand and held it up. "This nail polish, it's blood-red?"

"My own concoction," she simpered.

Aristander let the hand fall and plucked at the finely embroidered shawl, tapping one of her earrings with his finger. Basileia did not object.

"You must come to my house," she cooed. "I could show you my wardrobe: robes, sandals and necklaces."

Aristander's hand went to the oil-drenched wig on her head.

"Please!" she begged.

"That's enough!" Telamon got to his feet. He grasped Aristander's wrist: those cruel, cold eyes glared back. "Don't humiliate her!"

"It's you I want words with," Aristander sniffed. "There's something rotten here. Let's go to the window."

He guided Telamon across. "I heard about the business at the House of Medusa." Aristander's tongue went in and out like a lizard's basking in the sun. "So much blood, so many corpses! I've arranged for them to be placed on the scaffold outside with a placard posted above. Alexander is very pleased with the treasure: it's a month's pay for the entire army. He's warned those thieves in the secretariat not one coin is to go missing." Aristander looked back to where the Queen of the Moabites sat on her chair staring nervously before her. "What business do you have with that mound of fat? Show me her wardrobe, indeed! I'm not even her size – though I'd love to get my hands on that carnelian necklace."

"Are the lovely boys here?"

"Yes, outside baiting the soldiers and staring at the corpses. Now, I've got something interesting to tell you. First, this morning I visited the cell where Rabinus died. Ye gods, there was nothing left of the poor man. A hunk of flesh, all black and shrivelled. However, he drew something on the wall before he died. It was like this." Aristander wetted a finger and drew a triangle on the wall.

"What does that mean?"

"I don't know," Aristander retorted. "You're the one who studied with Aristotle. Isn't the triangle a symbol for the Divine? One of those mysterious signs? Well, it looked like a triangle," he added mischievously. "Or it could be a capital 'D'."

"Ah, Dion?"

"Yes, Dion. Now for the second matter," Aristander continued, "Dion visited Arella on the day she died, and I've also visited Demades's widow to question her about last night's assault on the king. She was all penitent and tearful. She thought I'd come to take her head. Now, she admitted Meleager had arranged for her to come to the palace. However, the previous night, a mysterious visitor came stealing into her bedchamber, who informed her that Alexander himself had ordered the deaths of Demades and the rest."

"That's a lie!"

"Yes, I know it is. But our midnight visitor sowed the seed of murder in her mind and told her how it could be done."

"And finally?" Telamon asked. "There is something else?"

"The king has issued a proclamation about last night's events. The killing of the guard, the release of those wasps. I've been through the palace. Alexander is correct; you'd think Olympias lived there with its secret entrances, galleries, cellars and shadowy porticoes. Anyone could have entered the palace. During the chaos our friends outside might have indulged in mischief."

"You have been busy!"

"Oh yes," Aristander replied. "By the way, the king wants to see you. He wants to know how he can take Miletus as Artemis the Goddess prophesied! He also wants to discover if that message written by the madman who burnt the Temple of Artemis contains anything useful."

"May I go?" Basileia called out.

"Stay where you are, you fat bitch," Aristander retorted, "until my friend and I have finished with you!"

"Will you arrest Dion?" Telamon asked.

Aristander shook his head. "Not enough evidence, as yet, but in time, who knows? Finally, Alexander had one of his anxiety attacks this morning."

"I've told him not to drink so much wine."

"He's fearful of assassination," Aristander murmured. "He dreamed about his father last night, going into that ampitheatre, the assassin leaping forward. He's wondering what to do next . . ."

Telamon closed his eyes. Alexander was becoming bored with Ephesus: when cooped up he would laze about before throwing himself into frenetic activity.

"He also wants the Centaur captured and crucified," Aristander continued blithely, clapping Telamon on the shoulder. "The gods be thanked! He holds you responsible for all this, not me!"

Aristander waggled his fingers in farewell and swaggered back across the room. He slapped the Queen of the Moabites on her plump shoulder and went through the doorway, shouting for his guards.

"I so fear that man." Basileia nursed her bruised flesh.

"You have nothing to fear."

Telamon went and closed the battered door. The painting on the wall caught his gaze.

"I have one thing to tell you," Basileia whispered, "in gratitude for what you've done for me."

Telamon sat on the stool. Basileia looked fearfully over her shoulder.

"The politics of this city are a deep and dirty pool," she continued. "All forms of loathsome creatures swim beneath its surface. Agis and Meleager are half-brothers with a hatred for each other. Dion's no better; a man with a savage heart and a black soul. Peleus" – she made a pouting movement with her mouth – "vicious and mean. They love the struggle for power. Dion was a client of Arella."

"And Agis?"

"A heart as cold as ice. I'll tell you something." She leaned forward in a jingle of jewellery and gust of perfume. "Did you know Agis is your king's spy?"

"What!" Telamon exclaimed.

"Of course," Basileia simpered. "One dog watching another! How do you think Parmenio got into Ephesus two years ago? Who stirred the mob up after the news of Alexander's victory at the Granicus? Who sowed dissension among the Persians? Agis holds the whip hand. Did you know the Persians distrusted him? When Alexander landed at the Hellespont and marched on Troy, the news arrived here in Ephesus. Agis went into hiding. Lord Mithra –" She laughed softly at Telamon's surprise. "I know a little more than you think. He sent the Cowled Ones, the King of King's professional killers, into Ephesus, to hunt him down. Agis entrusted his daughter to relatives and hid out in the wastelands. He only reappeared after Alexander's victory at the Granicus."

Telamon whistled under his breath and stared at the painting on the wall.

"You must not reveal your source, but it might be useful to speculate."

Basileia's fingers caressed Telamon's wrist: the physician was so surprised by her news that he didn't withdraw his hand

"I must be gone."

Telamon absent-mindedly got to his feet. He kissed the Queen of the Moabites' hand. She left before he even noticed it, too busy reflecting carefully on what she had told him.

"Are you love-smitten?"

He glanced up. Cassandra leaned against the door jamb.

"I saw the moving mountain. She's left with her strange escort."

"Come in! Come in!" Telamon led her across to the far corner lest any of Aristander's eavesdroppers be lurking near the door. "She told me something very interesting. Alexander has a spy in Ephesus."

"That's hardly surprising."

"No, it's Agis. I'd like to have a word with him in private. Ask him to come in."

A short while later Cassandra ushered the Ephesian in.

"You've kept us waiting long." Agis sniffed. "You always know when that fat whore's been anywhere, she must bathe herself in perfume. She needs to, she sweats like a camel."

"I want to ask you a question," Telamon said. "You share the same father as Meleager?"

"I thought he'd tell you that." The Ephesian walked closer, kicking at a shard of pottery.

"Yet you lead opposing parties?"

"Fate, destiny," Agis retorted.

"But you were paid by Macedon?"

Agis smiled coyly and rubbed the side of his face. "Meleager was paid by the Persians. I received subsidies from Greece, be it Athens or be it Macedon."

"But the Persians hated you?"

"Well, of course they did! I led a party opposed to their rule. They tolerated me; as long as they couldn't convict me of treason, I was safe."

"But they would have liked to have taken your head?"

"Aye and stuck it on a pole along with Hesiod's, Dion's, Peleus's and those of other members of my party. The Persians were strange rulers. You could call them benevolent despots. As long as you weren't caught doing something wrong, you were safe. The trick was never to be caught."

"But you could still suffer an accident?"

Agis gestured at the ceiling. "Accident, physician? Oh yes, I was nearly the victim of a number of accidents. Once I decided to inspect the building work at the Temple of Artemis: a roof collapsed, or rather a beam with some plaster on it. I narrowly escaped. On another occasion one of my warehouses caught fire while I was inside. Again I escaped."

"And the murders?"

"Oh, we Democrats kill Oligarchs, Oligarchs kill Democrats. Ask Dion. I have survived three assassination attempts. One, a flask of wine laced with poison." Agis stood ticking the points off on his fingers, as if he were counting his money rather than revealing how close he had been to violent death. "And then there was the assault in the marketplace. An assassin, hooded and masked, but he struck at the wrong person. Finally, a beggar who thrust out his bowl in one hand, a dagger in the other."

"What happened to him?"

"I was coming back from a hunt, down near the Purple Gates. I drew my sword and killed him."

"And did the Persians come hunting you?"

"Yes, that's when I decided to leave Ephesus for a while. The Macedonians were coming. Alexander was marching towards the Granicus. The Persians realized I would stir up as much trouble as I could." Agis's dark face broke into a smile. "I didn't disappoint them."

"And now you will live peacably with Meleager and his party?"

"Meleager's party doesn't exist," Agis jibed. "And Meleager – well, he's only a shadow of what he used to be. The true power in Ephesus is Macedon."

"And when Macedon goes it will be Agis?"

Agis just smiled and shrugged.

★   ★   ★

The green, fertile paradise, the showpiece of the Governor's palace garden, was thronged with people. Alexander's companions, Ptolemy, Seleucus, Hephaestion and Amyntas, lounged under the spreading branches of a sycamore tree. The beautiful smooth green lawn, watered by fountains, was ringed by members of the Royals. The soldiers sweated profusely in their purple-grey corselets, war kilts of the same colour, greaves and marching boots, white – plumed Corinthian helmets on their heads. Chamberlains and courtiers thronged about. Cooks brought out food, jugs and goblets of wine. Alexander was seated in full dress armour on his black warhorse Bucephalus, in one hand a sword, in the other a jewelled orb which was supposed to stand for Zeus's thunderbolt. He had bathed, washed and shaved, his red-gold hair carefully coiffed. The king surveyed the turmoil he had caused, a faraway look in his eyes. He seemed totally unaware of the clatter, the screech of peacocks, the barking of hounds from a nearby stable-yard. Even when Telamon approached, knocking aside a chamberlain who tried to block his path, Alexander didn't move.

"I wouldn't interrupt if I were you!" Ptolemy yelled.

Telamon stretched out his hand for Bucephalus to nuzzle. Apelles the painter had erected a great wooden screen, its surface specially prepared, on which he was drawing a charcoal outline of Alexander. He was covered in paint from head to toe. The area around him was littered with torn pieces of parchment, brushes, empty pots: the great trestle table beside him was covered with palettes, knives, brushes, sticks of charcoal, styli and inkpots. The artist kept walking up and down, staring at Alexander.

"Been like this for hours!" Ptolemy bawled.

Apelles looked worried; he seemed relieved by Telamon's arrival. The painter gestured at him. Telamon went across.

"I can't decide," the painter whispered, "whether the king should be mounted, seated on a throne, or standing like a general. Above all, I can't capture the look on his face, it's changeable."

"It always has been," Telamon replied. "His moods come and go in the blink of an eye."

"I heard that!"

Alexander dropped both orb and sword and swung himself off

Bucephalus: the black warhorse immediately turned, nudging his master. Alexander seized the reins and talked softly, stroking the white starburst on Bucephalus's forehead; he then stripped off the leopardskin saddlecloth, wiping the sweat from the horse with the palm of his hands, still whispering endearments.

"The horse is easy," Apelles murmured. "Alexander's the problem!"

The king called across the grooms and watched them lead his favourite horse away. He then took off his purple armour and scarlet cloak; he threw them on the ground, unstrapping the war kilt and the greaves round his legs.

"Why not try and capture me in battle?" Alexander raised his hand. "And not such a large painting? Perhaps in conflict with the Persians at Granicus, just after I cross the river? I was among them all by myself."

Telamon coughed. Alexander grinned sheepishly.

"Well, not strictly by myself. A few others joined me. Apelles, I want the painting to have that glazed effect. I want you to capture the life, the power that is within me, not like some figure on a vase. The person who sees it must feel they can stretch out their hand and take the sword from my grip – which, of course," Alexander added tartly, "they won't be able to, just as they couldn't in real life."

"It's your expression, sire," Apelles said. "You keep turning your head away, and when you look back, your expression has changed."

"Well that's your problem," Alexander retorted. "Apelles, you are the best. I want your painting to adorn the Temple of Artemis. I want people yet unborn to gaze on it and wonder. I know you won't let me down. Now!"

Alexander took off his sweaty tunic; dressed only in his loincloth and sandals, he marched up and down.

"Clear this mess up! Have some wine, Apelles, I'll walk you back to your house. On the way we can discuss the best paints to use. I have certain ideas. Perhaps we won't be using Bucephalus?" He gestured at the table littered with paint pots. "Some of those colours are much too bright. I have a few ideas about dulling them and making them more lifelike." He gestured at the broad screen. "I'm not too sure whether it should be indoors or outdoors. Light can distort paintings."

Telamon stared at Apelles, who bit back his smile. The physician was happy Cassandra was not present. She would have hooted with laughter at Alexander, as always, giving orders to the greatest painter in all of Greece.

"Now don't sulk."

Apelles stared in bemusement.

"Don't sulk," Alexander repeated, "and don't leave without me. Telamon, I want to have words with you."

He grasped the physician by the arm and led him across the lawn to the shimmering pool of purity. Its lotus blossoms were now open, exuding their own fragrance as they captured the heat. Alexander took off his loincloth and sandals and jumped into the pool. He swam two lengths and came out shaking himself like a dog. Pages hurried over with a robe. Alexander put this on, slipping his feet into fresh sandals.

"Let's have some wine."

They re-entered the palace, Alexander bellowing at his companions not to bother Apelles. Guards followed at a respectful distance, Alexander took Telamon into the royal quarters, slamming the door behind him. He gestured at the great map spread out across the floor.

"I found this in the Governor's archives."

Alexander went across to the table and filled two goblets, sniffed at the wine and watched Telamon sip.

"Am I now the royal taster?"

Alexander grinned and pointed to the cloth which had covered the jug and goblets.

"The door to my chambers is always guarded: sometimes you cannot even see my guards. More importantly, I filled that jug myself and left the cloth in a certain way, a piece of red thread on top: it hasn't been disturbed."

"Do you fear assassination?"

"Kings always fear assassination. That bloody woman and her bloody dagger! She nearly did Darius's work for him."

"Were you warned?"

Alexander moved his head slightly sideways, a favourite gesture whenever he was thinking.

"You were warned, weren't you? By your spies? You were far too calm and reasonable."

"Which spies?" Alexander teased.

"Agis, Dion or Peleus?"

"Oh yes, they're all spies." Alexander gulped at the wine. "Father paid them to cause unrest and so did I. Agis warned me to be careful with Demades's widow."

"You trust them all?"

"I don't trust anybody," Alexander retorted. "Except you, Hephaestion and Mother." He sighed noisily. "And I've just received a letter from her: she doesn't like General Antipater whom I left in Macedon to guard her. He complains about her and she complains about him."

"But, of course, Mother always wins?"

"Mothers always do." Alexander smiled. "One tear of Olympias is worth more than a thousand letters from General Antipater."

Still quaffing his wine, Alexander walked to the map, gesturing for Telamon to follow. It was a rectangle of canvas about three yards long and two yards wide, a faithful picture of Darius's empire. River boundaries were marked, as were principal cities and the royal road which connected Ephesus with Persepolis in the east and the coastal ports to the west. Alexander knelt down.

"I wish the cartographer who did this worked for me. Look, Telamon, there's the river Granicus, the royal road, Troy, Abydos." He gestured down the western coastline of the Persian Empire. "And here's Miletus, a principal port. Now, the Governor's agreed to hand it over to me, but the man's a born liar. Like any Milesian, all mouth and no dick! He'll close the gates against me. Miletus is well fortified. Notice how the cartographer depicts it, ringed by three walls. Behind these lie the city and the Lion Port, its entrance protected by this islet" – Alexander tapped the map – "on which an impregnable fortress has been built. I need Miletus if I want to bring in fresh troops, or if I have to leave in a hurry. Moreover, if I control Miletus, I control most of the coastline." He gulped at the wine and patted Telamon on the shoulder. "Oh, by the way, I heard about your success at the House of Medusa. You should be more careful, you could have been killed and where would I be then, eh? Ah well, at least I gained something from the Centaur. I am despatching some of the pearls to Mother. I also found a beautiful brooch and a ring: I have sent them to your red-haired woman."

"She's not my woman, but I'm grateful."

"So you should be." Alexander poked him in the chest. "Just be careful, that's all." He peered closer, strange eyes dancing with mischief. "You are not to die before me, Telamon. I have also issued that proclamation. But am I going to capture the person responsible for the massacre in the Temple of Hercules? How can I prove Artemis wishes my painting to be in her temple? More importantly, how am I going to take Miletus? Do you have any ideas, physician?"

Telamon stared down at the map. He had been to Miletus twice in his life. He had seen its defences; the high, powerful walls, the formidable gates guarded by watchtowers.

"I have siege machinery," Alexander explained, "but you know what the real problem is, Telamon? I only have a hundred and sixty triremes, manned by Athenians whom I don't trust as far as I can spit; they're further up the coast. The Persians, however, possess a fleet of five hundred first-class warships."

"Who's in command of the garrison at Miletus?"

"Our old friend, the Rhodian mercenary Memnon. That's why I know the Governor will refuse to let us in."

Telamon closed his eyes and groaned. Memnon hated Alexander with a consummate passion. Now military adviser to Darius, Memnon constantly warned the Persian king not to engage Alexander in battle, but to wear him down with long sieges and a scorched-earth policy. It now looked as if Memnon was going to have his way.

"He won't come out and fight, will he?" Telamon murmured. "Memnon will close the gates and man the walls. If you take one wall, he'll fall back on the second, then the third. If you enter the city you'll have to take every street, house by house, room by room. Memnon, if he wishes, can evacuate by sea with the Persian fleet."

"Its admiral has recently crushed a revolt in Egypt," Alexander replied. "According to our spies, he's making use of the good sailing weather, his warships will be off Miletus soon."

"The Persian fleet can dock there?"

"No, no, the harbour's too small," Alexander said impatiently. "But they will be able to supply Memnon with arms, food, whatever he needs, as well as reinforcements. What I want to resolve, is how do we take care of the Persian fleet?"

Alexander squatted cross-legged on the map, staring down at Miletus. "How do you weaken a fleet, Telamon?"

"Send out your own warships."

"I don't trust them and we haven't got enough."

"Pray for a storm?"

"What's that line from Euripides?" Alexander replied, puckering his lip. "Ah, that's it: 'You talked madness before but this is raving lunacy.' How can I take it?" Alexander taunted. "Think, Telamon! I could pray for a storm but the gods may not reply. I have a fleet which is outnumbered and untrustworthy."

"Perhaps you can't take Miletus? Perhaps just besiege it? Let it wither like grapes on the vine?"

"That does not become me," Alexander whispered. "I am the new Achilles." He continued, quoting from the *Iliad*: "'To be always the best in battle and pre-eminent beyond all others.' I have said I will take Miletus, so I shall take Miletus. My father took Ephesus but lost it. I shall keep it, and every one of Darius's cities."

"So that some day," Telamon murmured, also quoting from the *Iliad*, "'Let them say of him, he is better by far than his father.'"

Alexander lifted his head. "You think that's the key to all this, don't you? To prove that I am a better man than my father? If Philip can have his statue in the Temple of Artemis then why can't Alexander have his painting? But I am not Philip," Alexander continued as if talking to himself. "I am not Parmenio. I am Zeus's son. I am the god's own offspring. I shall keep Ephesus and take Miletus, but how?"

He nudged Telamon viciously in the ribs. The physician struck back, knocking the king's arm away. "I am your man in peace and war," Telamon warned, "but I am not your slave!"

"No you are not." Alexander patted him on the shoulder and sprang to his feet. "But I've given you puzzles to solve, Telamon, and solve them you will. Now, wait there. I am going to get dressed and then we'll walk Apelles back to his house."

Chapter 10

"Alexander, however, who was well aware of how the Ephesian populace, given the opportunity to hunt for guilty men . . . would, out of hatred, kill the innocent . . . called a halt."

Arrian: *The Campaigns of Alexander*, Book I, Chapter 18

Telamon waited in the main chamber while Alexander went down a short passage leading to his private bedroom. From outside he could hear the sound of marching feet, the clash of cymbals, the liquid notes of flutes, as musicians and dancers prepared for the evening banquet. He went to the window and glanced out. Hephaestion was standing beneath a fig tree staring up at the royal quarters. When he realized Telamon had seen him, he moved deeper into the shadows.

"Ever watchful," Telamon murmured.

Hephaestion, the king's lanky friend, Patroclus to Alexander's Achilles, hovered over his royal master as a mother would a child, especially when rumours of assassins came thick and fast. Telamon walked round the chamber. He almost tripped over the horn bow and quiver of arrows which had fallen from a recess. He picked these up, put them back and returned to the map. He knelt down and stared at the port of Miletus, the river Maeander which debouched into the gulf of Mycale, and the islet of Lade. He studied the map, tracing it with his fingers. From the bedchamber Alexander began to sing, a Macedonian battle hymn to the war god Eynalius. Telamon grasped a scrap of parchmant and stylus. He drew a crude map of Miletus and the surrounding countryside. He jumped as Alexander, soft-footed as a cat, touched him on the shoulder.

213

"A fair likeness," the king murmured. "What do you suggest, general?"

"I am a physician." Telamon stared down at the map. "But the Persian fleet is on its way. Hundreds of triremes, warships with three banks of oars, capable of carrying a full crew and a horde of soldiers." Telamon recalled his own sea journeys around the islands, the violent storms, the sickness and disease. "And we have a hundred and sixty warships?"

"That's right. I've ordered my admiral to take up position off the island of Lade, not to meet the Persians in battle but to seal the entrance to the port. He should be in position soon." Alexander's voice became clipped. Telamon suspected the king wasn't telling him everything.

"Won't the Persians force their way in?" Telamon asked.

"No, no, they won't, it's too dangerous."

"And the gulf of Mycale, a mountain range hems in the coast?"

"Very mountainous, apart from the Maeander estuary." Alexander tapped the makeshift map with his stubby finger.

"Isn't it strange?" Telamon murmured. "In Carthage I met a physician, a Phoenician. He had this strange medical theory, how the heart pumped blood while the brain sent messages to different parts of the body: he couldn't prove it, but he was a great talker. We used to go down and sit on the clifftops overlooking the sea; the sky and the water of Carthage, especially at sunrise and sunset, turns a haunting deep purple."

"Yes, I've heard of that," Alexander commented.

"Well one day," Telamon continued, "two Phoenician warships brought in a merchant vessel they'd found drifting at sea. The crew had died of thirst and hunger. They must have become becalmed or lost, besieged by the elements. Now, my Lord King, you can lay siege to a city," Telamon murmured, "but can you lay siege to a hundred ships?"

Alexander pushed Telamon aside and stared down at the map. He knelt, fists clenched, like a gambler waiting for the final throw of the dice which would bring him victory.

"Telamon, you and your stories! You and your stories!"

Face flushed with excitement, Alexander sprang to his feet. A

214

knock came at the door, and Aristander slipped in like a shadow.

"Just when I'm happy," Alexander murmured. "You haven't brought more letters from Mother?"

Aristander glared bitchily at Telamon: he always resented the physician's closeness to the king. "I have been busy on your affairs, my lord, making you a rich man. Certain properties now go to you."

"What are you talking about?" Alexander demanded crossly, picking up his mantle.

"The confiscated property of Hesiod, Arella and the rest," Aristander replied. "More surprisingly, Demades's servant Socrates died a very, very rich man. I have traced his gold and silver deposits to merchants near the Peacock Gate. Over the last few years he acquired a small fortune."

"Demades his master was a very wealthy man," Alexander retorted. "His servant was bound to share his prosperity. I welcome the wealth more than the news. Is that all?"

Aristander, crestfallen, stepped back.

"Now, now!" Alexander said. "No time for sulking, Aristander. You can come with us, we're going for a walk."

The king almost charged through the door. Outside, members of the Guards regiment mingled with the chorus. Alexander pushed his way through, clapping his hands. Aristander raised his eyes heavenwards and extended a hand like a woman would to her husband.

"Shall we walk, Telamon?"

The physician ignored him even as Alexander, realizing they had not kept up with him, came charging back.

"Come on! Come on!"

Aristander and Telamon hastened to obey. Outside, the royal companions Hephaestion, Ptolemy and Amyntas were talking to Agis and Apelles. The painter had changed and attempted to wash some of the paint from his hands and face. Alexander interrupted them. He linked arms with Apelles and Agis as if both were boon companions.

"He's imitating his father," Aristander whispered. "Philip

215

always made a point of escorting honoured guests back to their houses."

"I heard that!" Alexander shouted. "Now, come on!"

Ptolemy, walking behind Telamon, imitated the king by taking the arms of Seleucus and Amyntas. They passed through the Governor's garden.

"I want to show you something," Alexander announced.

They crossed the lawn to a garden pavilion, a little columned hall decorated with bunches of black grapes with green leaves and red stems. Around the ceilings a garland of blue and white water lily petals had been painted. The fluted columns were, alternately, blue and red: the door frame was white picked out in blue, the floor of polished wood.

"I rather like this." Alexander stood admiring the building. "Apelles, draw a picture of it and send it to my mother!" He didn't wait for an answer, but continued onto the path leading to the main gate.

"You don't look too well, Apelles," Alexander declared for all to hear. "You have scratches on your face and hands. You are too clumsy with a knife. Telamon will advise you always to clean your wounds with a tincture of myrrh. Why are you holding your stomach? Do you have bladder problems?"

Poor Apelles could only stutter in reply. Telamon heard Ptolemy's suppressed laughter.

"And I notice your wrist isn't as supple as it could be. What do you recommend, Telamon?" he shouted over his shoulder.

"Arnica," the physician replied.

"I am glad you've come." Alexander turned to Agis. "You should have brought your little girl. What's her name?"

"Rhoda, my lord." Agis looked distinctly uncomfortable at being so close to the king.

"Ah, Rhoda, yes, a beautiful name! Now look, Agis, when I leave Ephesus you will be chief magistrate. I want no more fighting. Democracy must reign in the city, as it will in all other cities liberated from the Persian yoke. I want elected officials, proper law courts and no blood feuds. You can tell the Ephesians that I have dispensed with the taxes they used to pay to the Persians but I want a levy imposed for the Temple of Artemis and a contribution to my war chest."

They were now through the main gates. More guards joined them, flanking the king's party on either side.

"Ptolemy, I know you're laughing at me," Alexander called back. "You always did giggle. Do you have any ideas how to deal with the Persian fleet off Miletus?"

When Ptolemy didn't answer, Alexander turned to Apelles, insisting he use light brown when he painted the human form. Telamon gazed up at the sky, the blue touched with light pink as the sun began to set. The shadows from the cypress and plane trees on either side spread longer, the breeze turned cool and refreshing. Alexander was still chattering when the first arrow zipped over his head.

The second one hit him full in the chest and sent him staggering back into Telamon's arms. Agis tried to catch him as he fell. Telamon laid the king down and, like the rest, stared in horrified silence.

The king had his eyes closed, but then opened them. He was a little pale and had bitten the corner of his lip. Telamon stared in disbelief even as guards recovered their wits and ran towards the trees.

"You were hit by an arrow," Telamon declared.

He saw the mark on the king's dark-green tunic, the arrow lying on the path, its broken-off ugly barbed warhead next to it.

Alexander's companions regained their wits. Orders were shouted: the guards ringed the royal party, locking their rounded shields. A conch horn brayed the alarm. Telamon felt Alexander's chest. The king knocked his hand away. Telamon picked up the arrow: long and dark, made out of the finest cornel wood with vulture feathers for the flight. The broken point contained a cruel barb, like a fish-hook, making it nigh impossible to pull from human flesh. Telamon handed it to Alexander who placed the barb between finger and thumb, turning it so the polished metal caught the light.

The guards who had been searching for the hidden assassin returned, shaking their heads. Taking off their feathered helmets, they breathlessly announced they could find no one, the assassin had disappeared. The press around Alexander grew jostling and noisy. Agis had broken free and was sitting in the shade of a tree to compose himself. Aristander, screaming at the guards to keep their shields up, ordered a general retreat back to the palace. Another soldier came running up with the arrow which had spun over their heads, the same sort as the one which had struck the king. Telamon examined both and saw the "C", the sign of the Centaur, burnt into the side of each shaft. Alexander grabbed them and told everyone to stand back. He then raised his hands in the direction of the setting sun.

"Lord Zeus Almighty! Maker and Creator of all! Listen to your son! I give thanks and reverence to you for sending your daughter Artemis, with her sacred shield, to protect me against the malice of my enemies!"

Alexander turned to the assembled throng. The colour had returned to his cheeks, his eyes sparkled. "I was walking and I was talking," he declared, his voice carrying. "The gods be my witness! I saw the arrow speeding towards me. I smelt a most fragrant perfume and glimpsed, as if it were a shower of gold, the divine Artemis come between me and that death-bearing point. I saw her shield raised. I witnessed the malice of my enemies frustrated. Let the news be proclaimed throughout all Ephesus: Artemis has saved Alexander! Artemis, who was present at my birth, has shown sign of her favour. All hail to Artemis, Lady of the Ephesians!"

His words were greeted with a roar of approval. Soldiers clattered swords against shields. Telamon could only gaze speechlessly at the king, who held the arrows as if they were the thunderbolts of Zeus. Ptolemy gaped in amazement. Fat, blond-haired Seleucus simply scratched his head and stared up at the sky. Aristander, very nervous, was screeching that the king should return to the palace. Alexander, however, linking his arm through Apelles's and calling for Agis, proudly declared that, with Artemis by his side, whom could he fear?

"Did you make this yourself?"

Telamon and Cassandra were dining in their own chamber.

From the palace below rose the sound of Alexander's celebration banquet, the melody of flute and harp, the laughter and shouts of the king's guests. The smell of cooking pervaded the entire palace. Aristander had insisted cellars and passages be both searched and closely guarded. Telamon had excused himself, claiming fatigue. Alexander had blithely accepted this. Cassandra, because of the deaths in the kitchens, had gone down to cook their own food; the royal servants had been only too pleased at her assistance.

"You are truly a woman of many parts," Telamon exclaimed. "How did you find both Lesbian and Rhodian wine?"

"I'm trying to make you feel at home," Cassandra replied. "Didn't Aristotle say 'Rhodian wine is truly sound and pleasant but Lesbian is sweeter'?"

"Who told you that?"

"Ptolemy did, he's becoming friendlier."

"Be prudent," Telamon warned. "Ptolemy acts cynical but he's hungry for power. Never forget he regards himself as Alexander's half-brother. I don't want you drawn into his scheming!"

"Do he and Alexander share the same father?"

"Ptolemy believes they do. Philip was certainly free with his favours. Anyway, where did you learn to cook? I thought you were a temple healer in Thebes?"

"I was," Cassandra retorted. "But believe me, the cooking was terrible: everything tasted like cat meat. One day a patient was brought in, a very curious case: he fancied himself as a wrestler, had drunk too much and dislocated his hip in a fight. How would you have dealt with it, Master?" she asked sweetly.

"I am not your master," Telamon retorted. "I would have bound the patient's arms by his side, put a broad soft strap round his legs just above the knee, but not too close: the legs to be kept three finger-breadths apart. Similar bands would be placed round his ankles then he would be gently suspended, head downwards, about six feet off the ground."

Cassandra nodded. "Why is that?"

"In that position the weight of his body tends to reduce the dislocation. You then put your forearm between the patient's thighs and very quickly rest your weight on his suspended body. A dexterous twist of the forearm" – Telamon imitated the motion – "is all that is needed. The dislocated bone slips back into its socket with a crack like a whip. Bandages are applied, the patient is gently lifted down and restored to his bed."

Cassandra clapped her hands. "Have you done it yourself?"

Telamon nodded. "You have to be quick, and the patient mustn't be too old."

"My guest was fairly young," Cassandra continued, a dreamy look in her eyes. "I was the one who pushed the dislocated bone back. He stayed in the temple for a while: he was a cook and taught me everything he knew." She gestured at the now clean platters. "Honey-glazed shrimps, tuna steak, pancakes with honey and sesame seeds."

Telamon patted his stomach. "I'm glad to be dining with you and not downstairs. It will be one of Alexander's drinking parties. They'll be supping strong wine as if it's water and wake with headaches. So, look at the bright side." He sighed. "Tomorrow will be quiet."

"When do we leave?" Cassandra asked.

"I don't know. Alexander is dedicated to one celebration after another. He wants to show the Ephesians how Artemis has favoured him."

"Is Aristander at the feast? When I saw him earlier he was all shaking and trembling after the attack on the king."

Telamon shook his head. "Aristander is dining with his chorus. He'll be wearing his favourite blond wig, his face painted like an Athenian courtesan. He'll ask the "lovely lads" to deliver a speech from one of Euripides's plays and, when he's really drunk, join them in bawling out raucous hymns in a tongue no one else understands."

Cassandra, who had drunk copiously, laughed and almost rolled off the couch separated from Telamon by two small acacia-wood tables. She had dressed in her best, a brightly coloured goffered linen robe with silver sandals. She wore the brooch and ring the king had sent her. Telamon studied her curiously, fascinated by her changing moods.

220

"Did you tend to those still suffering from the wasp attack?" he asked self-consciously.

"Oh yes, they'll heal soon enough."

"What are you doing talking to Ptolemy?"

"You're not jealous, Master?"

"No I am not! Ptolemy is mischievous. What does he want?"

"He's curious about whether we found more treasure and kept it for ourselves. You know what he's like."

"He's a cynic."

"Not after Artemis saved our noble leader." Cassandra picked up the wine jug and refilled their cups. "Everyone was astounded by the king's escape. Hephaestion, when he learnt about it, had a panic attack. I've never seen a man so distraught. Are he and Alexander lovers?"

"No." Telamon sipped from his wine and plucked a grape from a bowl, thought again and put it back. "Theirs is a friendship of souls."

"In other words," Cassandra teased, "if Alexander said the sky was black Hephaestion would agree?" Yet," she sighed, "it truly was a miraculous escape!"

From below came the clash of arms. Cassandra started. Telamon waved her back.

"Alexander and his companions are doing a war dance. Wait a while and you'll hear their battle hymn."

"I'm thinking about that arrow," Cassandra retorted. "Could it have been broken, splintered, before it was loosed?"

"Possibly." Telamon shook his head. "But the arrow hit the king's chest, it should have drawn blood. Loosed from a horn bow such a shaft can wreak hideous damage. I just don't believe in miracles."

"Will Alexander catch the attacker?"

"Aristander's agents are already busy on it. Agis was with us. Meleager, Dion, Peleus, even Basileia, Queen of the Moabites, will have to account for where they were."

"It could have been a hired assassin?"

"No." Telamon sat up on the couch. He placed his wine cup on the table. "A hired assassin is too dangerous. He can take the money then betray the person who hired him to the king for an even more fabulous sum. Moreover, if he had been caught, Alexander's bodyguard would have flayed him alive, and that's before they crucified him."

"Whoever it was knew the king was leaving the palace?"

"I discussed that with Aristander. For the last few days the king has escorted Apelles back to his house, surrounded by guards, and nothing has happened. All our assassin had to do was discover that Apelles had visited the palace and conclude that, at some time in the evening, Alexander would take his usual stroll. Do you know something, Cassandra? No." He held a hand up. "You are not sharing my couch. You have drunk too much and so have I, tomorrow we'd regret it! I have a feeling we'll solve this, not by evidence but by logic."

"Oh, don't be so engimatic." Cassandra flounced back on her couch. "And, by the way," she added impishly, "have you solved that mystery, the confession of the man who burnt the temple?"

"Not yet." Telamon picked up his wine cup and cradled it. "But I am interested in one dead man: I think I'll begin with him." He winked at Cassandra. "Socrates, Demades's servant."

Nectara, wife of Dion the lawyer, abruptly woke up. She didn't know if the clattering was from her dream or elsewhere. She peered round the bedchamber: two night-lights, capped oil-lamps, glowed in their wall niches. The silver carvings on the two great chests caught the glint of flame. Nectara's eyes grew accustomed to the gloom. She pushed back the linen sheets and the heavy wool wrap placed over her, as sometimes the nights grew cool. Was that sound from deep in the house or from the passageway outside?

Nectara's bedchamber was on the second storey, overlooking the fountain court. She crouched for a while listening: all the worries of the previous day returned. Her husband Dion, who prided himself so much on his own subtlety and wit, on his cunning stratagems and the influence he could exercise, was deeply troubled. Nectara had expected it to be so different. During the time of the Oligarchs, she and her husband had lived in the shadows, ever fearful of the arrival of Persian soldiers at the dead of night, the assassin's dagger or the poisoned flask of wine. Now the Macedonians had arrived, Dion had assured her things would change.

Nectara eased herself off the jointed bedstead and pulled back the veil protecting against moths and flies. She opened the shuttered window. The sky was already growing lighter, the stars beginning to fade. Red shots of light showed daybreak was imminent.

Dion had drunk deeply last night, sitting in his writing chamber, poring over parchments, lips moving soundlessly as if talking to some invisible presence. She wondered what secrets concerned him. Dion had grown very close to Hesiod, that ubiquitous scribe with his secret comings and goings and whispers behind closed doors. She caught her breath. Hesiod had been killed, brutally murdered in that whore's elegant mansion. Nectara pulled back her night-black hair and absent-mindedly picked up a clasp to keep it in place. She'd always hated Arella, resenting Dion's deep affection for a common whore. Very rarely now did Nectara welcome her husband into her own quarters: when he did come, sometimes he'd forget himself and whisper that prostitute's name. Ah well, the whore too was dead; Nectara could rejoice at that when she met the other women to discuss the affairs of the city.

The cold breeze chilled her skin. She closed the shutters: as she did so, she glimpsed, from across the fountain court, a sliver of light from her husband's writing chamber. Was Dion still down there?

Nectara took a thick woollen mantle from its peg and draped it over her shoulders. She was fearful, not superstitious; wary of the terrors of the night, a feeling of brooding danger. She should go down and question Dion; she must encourage him to talk, like he used to in years gone by, about their plans for the future. Perhaps Dion would forget the bloody politics of the city? He was a skilful lawyer, a brilliant orator. What did he want with the likes of Agis and Meleager?

Nectara took an oil-lamp, put on her sandals and walked out of the chamber, down the stairs into the courtyard. The early morning air was brisk and cold. She welcomed the sound of the tinkling fountain, the smell of roses and lilies from the flower baskets, the savoury fragrance from the herb garden. She entered the portico. The door to the men's quarters was unlocked. She opened this and went down the passage, a narrow gloomy tunnel which led to her husband's quarters. Dion himself had supervised its building, his writing office on the ground floor, a small bed-chamber above: it also boasted a flat roof where Dion, during the fragrant months, could enjoy the view of the city or watch the sun rise. Would he return to that? Or would he be too busy with secret meetings and subtle plots?

"Dion!"

Nectara did not wish to startle her husband. She approached the door and knocked. "Dion! It's me, Nectara! I wish to talk to you!"

No reply, nothing but a slight creaking. She tried the latch. It was locked. Nectara stood biting her lip. If her husband did not wish to be disturbed, he always called out, not this oppressive silence.

Nectara went back along the passageway and out into the courtyard. The writing office had a window on this side and on the wall overlooking the herb garden; both were shuttered.

She tried to peer through a crack. She could see her husband's desk: oil-lamps still glowed there.

"Dion!" Nectara's alarm became edged with panic. "Dion, what's the matter? Dion!" she repeated. "Dion! Oh, Dion, please open the door!"

Beads of sweat broke out on her forehead, her stomach clenched, she found it difficult to breathe. Unspoken fears and unnamed terrors confronted her. She decided to wait no longer but ran across the courtyard, took down the conch horn and blew a long throaty blast, raising the alarm. So panic-struck was she that she blew again and gazed up at the windows. Here and there a glow of light appeared; the chamberlain and servants had been roused. Nectara lowered the horn but she found it difficult to stay still; her body trembled as at the onset of a fever.

"Mistress, mistress, what is it?" The chamberlain came out of a doorway in the far corner of the courtyard, a blanket wrapped round his shoulders.

"My husband." Nectara pointed to the shuttered windows. "I can't rouse him. He won't answer the door."

"Perhaps he's asleep?" the chamberlain tried to reassure her.

"See for yourself!" she urged.

The chamberlain was now joined by heavy-eyed, tousled-headed servants. They, too, beat upon doors and shutters, growing alarmed at the lack of response. Nectara sat on a garden bench, aware of the fragrant scent of the roses and the lotus blossom near the fountain pool. Was she dreaming? Was this a nightmare?

"Mistress." The chamberlain stood over her. He had gone back to his chamber and put on a cloak, heavy sandals on his feet. "Your husband must be in the chamber. The oil-lamps still burn. We must force an entry. The shutters are the easiest . . ."

Nectara nodded. She sat, hands clenched, eyes closed, hearing the sound of breaking wood, followed by shouts and exclamations. The servants were now in the room. Her heart skipped a beat, she felt as if she was going to vomit. Something was not right, yet she was unable to move. She heard the bolts on her husband's writing chamber being pulled, the slap of sandalled feet along the passage-way and across the courtyard.

"Mistress." The chamberlain crouched before her, his face grey and anxious: his eyes told her everything. "Mistress, your husband is dead."

Nectara opened her mouth to speak, but all she could manage was a strange gargling sound.

"You'd best come!"

Nectara made to refuse. Two of her maids appeared: she stretched out a hand and they gently helped her to her feet. Nectara walked down the passage. It seemed to take an age.

The door was half open, the light pouring out. Nectara stepped into her husband's office. She refused to look to her left but gazed at the desk, the coffers and stools, the great high-backed writing chair. Her maids were stifling their sobs. Nectara turned her head and screamed in terror at the hideous sight. Her husband Dion, dressed in a tunic, one sandal on, the other half off, was gently swaying, his neck turning, twisting, in the cruel noose which bound it, the other end tied to an iron clasp in the rafter from which oil–lamps had once hung.

Nectara gazed in disbelief. All she was aware of was her husband's face, hideous in death, a slightly blueish tinge to the skin, eyes popping, tongue thrusting out. His neck was twisted, hands and feet hanging loose, the overturned stool kicked away in his death throes. She recalled the creaking she'd heard and realized its horrid source. She opened her mouth to scream but her husband's body was moving, the chamber was moving: Nectara closed her eyes and fell in a dead faint.

Telamon and Cassandra, accompanied by Aristander, reached Dion's house just after dawn to discover the period of mourning had already begun. Plates of food were laid out in the doorway for the messenger from Hades. Dark cloths hung from the windows which, like the doors, had been flung open to allow the soul of the dead free passage into the Underworld. Servants sat in the courtyard, clothes rent, dust and ash staining hair and face. The sound of a woman's keening, a heart-rending cry, echoed across the courtyard. No water splashed in the fountains, the baskets of flowers had been removed. Pots of water were placed in doorways so visitors could purify themselves on entering and leaving.

"Suicide or murder?" Aristander bluntly asked as they were led into the house and down to the hall: a luxurious place, its columns brightly painted, hunting scenes on the walls; costly furniture tastefully arranged around the small polished banqueting tables.

"For the sake of the dead," Telamon whispered, "keep your voice down and your speculations to yourself!"

They were greeted by the chamberlain, who explained that the Lady Nectara had retired to her bedchamber, overcome by the horror of it all. Telamon murmured his condolences and asked to view the corpse.

"Has it been taken down?" Aristander asked brusquely. The chamberlain, a dark-faced Libyan, glared back at such a breach of etiquette.

"I think it's best if we introduce ourselves properly," Telamon intervened. He explained that they had been sent on the express command of the king. The chamberlain was appeased, especially when Telamon handed over a generous donation, as all mourners were expected to, so the servants could hold a lavish funeral feast for their master.

"Has the corpse been removed?" Telamon queried.

The chamberlain shook his head. "The Lady Nectara fainted. I was going to have the master's body cut down but then I thought, I thought . . ." His voice trailed away.

"You remembered the law?" Telamon prompted. "That a victim of unexpected death be left where it is."

"Yes, yes, that's right." The chamberlain's gaze refused to meet his.

"We received your message," the physician continued, "that your master had hanged himself. Do you think it was suicide?"

The man rubbed his eyes, dragging his fingers down his face, streaking the ash which stained it.

"I do not think my master – you see, I was his steward," he began haltingly.

"Your master was not a man to take his own life?" Telamon murmured.

"He was a just man in many ways," the chamberlain confessed. "At times very hard, but why should he take his own life? He was wealthy, powerful."

"Were there any visitors to the house last night?"

"Not that I know of."

"Did anything strange occur?"

"My master was withdrawn. He and his wife dined alone, a light meal, and afterwards he returned to his writing office. He drank more wine there, he retired to bed, but . . ."

"He came down again?" Telamon asked.

"Yes, yes, he must have."

Explaining what had happened, the chamberlain led them down to the office. Inside Telamon gazed around. The room was large, whitewashed, no paintings; a few coloured cloths decorated the walls. An austere chamber: a desk littered with manuscripts, inkpots and styli, behind it a chair pushed slightly back. A bench under one

227

window, stools, coffers and chests. Telamon tried to concentrate on the ordinary. He glimpsed Dion's corpse out of the corner of his eye, hanging so forlornly at the end of a long tarred rope: that would have to wait.

"Was there any sign of violence? Someone breaking in? Have his papers and coffers been disturbed?"

"I have already searched," the chamberlain replied. "Nothing!"

Telamon stood in the doorway. The writing table faced him, the chair behind it. He glanced towards the windows, one in the far wall, the other in the wall to his right. Both were now open. A servant stood outside each of these, as the chamberlain explained, to keep the curious away.

"Who removed the shutters?" Aristander demanded.

"We had to. See how heavy the door is."

"The place stinks of death," Cassandra murmured.

Telamon didn't reply. He stared up at the twisted, grotesque face, the rictus of death that had transformed Dion's saturnine features.

"I have seen many corpses," he whispered, "yet the horror of death never diminishes."

He studied the rope. The noose was tied tightly, the knot, just under Dion's right ear, pushing the head to one side. The rope hung tight and taut in the clasp. Telamon stared again at the gaping mouth, the protruding tongue and jutting lips, the whole jaw forward, the half-open eyes staring sightlessly down. Telamon touched the man's hand: ice cold, fingers curled.

"He's been dead some time. The flesh has no warmth, the muscles are hardening."

He crouched down, ignoring the urine which stained the bare ankles and the floor beneath. The thong of one sandal had slipped; it dangled loose, making the scene even more eerie.

"Why the urine?" Aristander demanded.

"He'd drunk a lot of wine." Telamon gestured back at the table. "The bladder would be full, and empties during violent death."

He asked the chamberlain to bring fresh water and towels, and the man hurried off. Telamon picked up the high-legged stool. Cassandra held this as he climbed on.

"I am about the same height as Dion," Telamon murmured, stretching his hands up to the beam. "Yes, I can tie the knot in the clasp. I put the noose round my neck, tighten it and kick away the stool." He snapped his fingers. "Aristander, you carry a knife?"

The Master of Secrets brought out a thin-bladed knife and handed it to Telamon, who grasped the rope.

"Right!" he ordered. "I will cut through this. Cassandra, Aristander, grasp the corpse, lower it to the floor!"

Aristander was reluctant: Cassandra elbowed him aside and grasped the corpse just above the knees. Telamon cut through the rope and Cassandra lowered the corpse to the ground. The noose round the neck was tightly tied in a double knot under the right ear. Telamon wrinkled his nose at the smell of death, the hint of corruption. He loosened the noose, and the corpse gave off a gasp of air through the half-opened mouth. Aristander jumped back.

"Nothing but trapped air," Telamon declared.

He examined Dion's face, the mottled hue of the cheeks, the protuberant eyes, clenched jaw, swollen tongue held tightly between the teeth. Telamon noticed the dry saliva stain along the chin.

"He was slightly sick: that could be due to shock."

"Did he commit suicide?" Cassandra asked.

Telamon pushed up the man's tunic, examining his thighs and legs before turning his attention to the wrists and fingers.

"I can see no sign of ligature or binding."

Telamon rolled the corpse over, ignoring the smell as gas trapped in the belly escaped. He examined the back but, apart from small scars and cuts, spots and pimples, found nothing untoward. Telamon felt the muscles hardening in the rigor of death. He rolled the corpse over, pulled the tunic down and studied the sandals. The one hanging loose was due to a weak thong which had snapped. Telamon couldn't decide whether this was caused by something which had happened before death or simply an accident. Again he checked the hair, massaging the scalp.

"I can find no contusion or blow," he announced. "Cassandra, examine the wine carefully."

She went across to the desk; Aristander was already sifting through the papers littered there. Telamon stood upon the stool to rehearse how this clever lawyer had taken his own life.

"He would find it easy," he murmured. "This clasp is made of iron, embedded deep in the timber, secure enough to hold his weight." He pretended to put a noose over his neck, tighten it, stood for a while on the stool then jumped down.

The chamberlain returned with a jug of water, a bowl and a towel. Telamon once again examined the corpse, paying particular attention to the fingernails. He noticed the calluses and ink-stains on the man's right hand.

"Your master was busy writing last night?"

"Oh yes, sir. He was working on the steward's accounts. He had neglected them due to the recent troubles."

"I can find nothing here," Aristander declared crossly; he ignored the hiss of disapproval from the chamberlain as he collected the manuscripts together into a pile on the middle of the desk. Cassandra stood by the window sniffing at both jug and cup.

"It's a very light wine," she called over. "I detect nothing wrong." She smiled impishly at Aristander. "Perhaps you can taste it for us?"

"I'll do that, sir," the chamberlain offered. "I brought that wine and cup myself."

He walked across, filled the cup and raised it, saluting the corpse.

"You don't have to," Telamon warned. "It should be checked."

"We are all under suspicion," the chamberlain retorted, his dusty, tear-stained face breaking into a wan smile. "When a master dies, his servants are always suspected, whatever the circumstances."

Before Telamon could object he lifted the cup and drained it in one gulp. The chamberlain coughed, spluttered, then smiled.

"I always taste the wine my master drinks. I detect nothing wrong."

"Do tell me," Telamon warned, "if you feel unwell."

"Must he do that?" The chamberlain pointed at Aristander, who had now opened a coffer and was going through other papers.

"He carries the king's seal."

"I also have my bodyguard outside!" Aristander snapped, not raising his head. "I will do what I want and go where I want in this house. Oh, by the way physician" – the Master of the King's Secrets gestured at the corpse – "was it suicide or murder?"

"It must be suicide," the chamberlain declared.

Telamon tapped his sandalled foot against the stone floor. "There are no secret entrances?"

"No." The chamberlain shook his head. "Just the door and the windows."

Telamon went across, opened the door and examined the lintel as well as the thick hinges, four in number, which held the heavy cedarwood in place. Next he studied the intricate lock and the inside bolts, both top and bottom.

"Undisturbed," he commented. "I would like to see outside."

The chamberlain led him out. "I still feel no ill effects," he confided. "Why, sir, did you expect anything?"

Telamon paused halfway down the passage. "You're sure the doors and shutters were firmly closed?"

"Locked and bolted," the chamberlain confirmed. "Come, I'll show you."

When they entered the courtyard Agis and Peleus were there, deep in conversation with some servants. They broke off as Telamon came out.

"What's happened?" Agis demanded. Peleus hung back, looking darkly at the physician as if he held him responsible for his colleague's sudden death.

"You knew the victim better than I did," Telamon retorted. "Would Dion take his own life?"

"Anybody else's," Agis declared, "but no! Dion loved power, the beat and pulse of the city, the intrigue, the conspiracies. He was happiest when he was scheming."

"Did he say anything to you which might alert you to him being threatened or blackmailed?"

"He was a little withdrawn." Peleus spoke up. "Taciturn, rather clipped in his manner and attitude. I thought he was grieving for Hesiod." He lowered his voice. "Or even Arella."

"The king sent us the news," Agis confided.

"When did you last see Dion?" Telamon demanded.

Agis blew his cheeks out. "Yesterday morning, after the feast."

"And in the evening?" the physician asked.

"I was at home with my daughter Rhoda. My servants will attest that I worked late – and before you ask Peleus," Agis sneered, "he was keeping the company of his pretty boys." He turned slightly. "Isn't that right, Peleus?"

"My affairs are my business," his companion replied. "Dion was of our party. I considered him a friend. Now I would like to pay my respects."

Telamon let them go. He walked across the courtyard and examined the shutters lying on the ground. Each consisted of two heavy slats of wood with a clasp on the inside which held the bar across; both bars were still in place. Telamon then examined the hinges on the side of each shutter: these were of thick coarse leather, held in place by bronze clasps.

"You found these secure?"

"Oh yes, sir," the chamberlain agreed. "We took off both shutters, pulled them away, left them lying here and entered my master's chamber."

Telamon scrutinized the hinges and shutters as well as the lintels of both windows. The frames were secure, though the wood had splintered where the bronze clasps had been pulled out.

"What do you suspect?" Cassandra asked.

"Nothing."

Telamon walked into the herb garden, crouched down and sniffed at the fragrant plants.

"No one could go through that door," Cassandra declared. "The servants say the shutters were secure, closed and barred."

"Why did the Lady Nectara come down?" Telamon shouted to the chamberlain.

"She doesn't know, sir. She thought she heard a noise, that could have been a door banging or" – the chamberlain shrugged – "a wandering fox. Sir, may we remove the corpse? The day will prove hot, it must be dressed."

Telamon agreed, got to his feet and went back into the courtyard. Agis and Peleus had disappeared. Aristander was there clutching a bundle of manuscripts. He hurried over, eyes glittering with excitement.

"I've discovered something!" he whispered. "Something very interesting indeed!"

Chapter 11

"Meanwhile Alexander remained in Ephesus, offered sacrifice to Artemis, and held a ceremonial parade of his troops fully equipped and in battle order."

Arrian: *The Campaigns of Alexander*, Book I, Chapter 18

The paradise of the King of Kings in Persepolis was a place of cool, green beauty. It comprised parks, orchards and hunting preserves as well as vine-covered arbours where Darius and his courtiers could shelter from the heat of the sun. Special grottoes and groves had been laid out and given special names: the Garden of Rebirth with its mandrake, poppy and cornflower growing round the edges of clear pools; the Garden of Dreams where water lilies and pomegranate flowers flourished; the Garden of Healing where the plants and shrubs beloved of the royal physicians thrived in specially imported soil; the Garden of Delight, where vegetables for the royal kitchen were nourished: cucumbers, lettuces, garlic, onions, water melon, lentils and marrow. In spring, when the sun was not too hot, Darius's favourite pastime was to gather his falconers and go hunting along the edge of the marshes at the far end of his paradise.

On that particular day Darius was alone with Lord Mithra. The king was dressed in his hunting garb covered with a resplendent robe, his soft hands protected by jewelled gauntlets. On his wrist perched his favourite peregrine falcon, an exquisitely beautiful bird with dark, wine-coloured plumage, a cruel beak and powerful talons. Darius stood by a small birdtable on which diced meat had been placed. He stared out across the water, head slightly cocked to one side as if listening for some sound. The peregrine, trained to

235

obey its master, perched still, only moving slightly, shaking the gaudily embroidered jesses and making the minute bells give off their own peculiar tinkling sound. Lord Mithra was dressed in a white goffered robe, an embroidered shawl over his shoulder: with his shaven head he reminded Darius of an Egyptian priest.

The King of Kings muttered endearments to the peregrine while he studied this Keeper of the Royal Secrets. In many ways Lord Mithra also reminded him of a falcon with his deep-set eyes, high cheekbones, sharp-edged nose and, above all, that dark brooding gaze, as if Mithra's body were in one place but his soul in another. Behind the king and his closest adviser, in the shadow of date and palm trees, stood the Cowled Ones, garbed in dark clothes, armed with shields, scimitars and garrotte cords, Lord Mithra's personal bodyguard: the king trusted these even more than he did his own elite regiment of Immortals. From the thick rushes on the edge of the marsh echoed the cry of waterfowl; the peregrine stirred restlessly.

"No, be calm, my beauty." Darius picked up a juicy piece of meat and held it in the palm of his hand. The peregrine moved, a swift jabbing movement, and the meat was gone.

"Messages from Ephesus?"

"I have had messages from Ephesus, my lord," Mithra agreed.

"So soon? So fast?"

Mithra chuckled. "The fish may have gone but my net still stays. Our spy the Centaur leaves messages at a wine booth outside the Purple Gate."

Darius nodded. Once that message was collected and secretly hurried away, it would eventually reach the Persian courier service: the most skilled riders, on the finest horses in the empire, would race along the great road bringing news about the Macedonian barbarian in his city of Ephesus.

Darius ground his teeth in rage. *His* city of Ephesus! Taken from him as swiftly as the peregrine had seized that piece of meat.

"Do not distress yourself, my lord. Ephesus is a net: silken, cloying, but it still holds fast." Lord Mithra stepped forward and crushed a small plant with the toe of his sandal. "Alexander and his barbarians are not used to such opulence: the fresh food, the

236

fragrant fruit, the heavy, dark wine of Chios. They feast and they revel while Miletus is being reinforced and our fleet aims like an arrow for the Lion Port."

"What will happen?" Darius demanded.

"Our spy is brief. He mentioned two assaults on the Macedonian. Both failed."

"Ahirman really protects the Macedonian," Darius breathed.

"What one gains in one place," Mithra replied, "can be lost in another. Alexander is too busy with his painter Apelles. He is trying to convince the citizens that he is truly god-born. He has issued proclamations that his protector, Artemis, has saved him from sudden death. He has ordered civic receptions, banquets, marches and parades. He'll dally in the net for a long time while Miletus is reinforced and our fleet takes up position."

"What else?" Darius asked.

"The Macedonian has been made a fool of. He offered protection to those sheltering in the Temple of Hercules and his word was proved futile. He was attacked in his own palace, made to flee for his life, his servants killed, his so-called invincibility weakened."

"Yet he caught Rabinus?"

"And Rabinus is dead, my lord, as are his wife and children."

Darius nodded. The deaths of innocents did not concern him. Rabinus was a chief scribe. He could have fled or, if unable to, taken his own life. The punishment for such treason was both hideous and swift. The man had died and so had his family, a warning to any others who might contemplate failing the King of Kings.

"What will happen now?"

"If I am correct" – Mithra drew closer and studied the peregrine – "Alexander will dally in Ephesus. The Centaur will harass him. Miletus will grow stronger by the day and our fleet will dock. Alexander will realize his mistake but it will be too late. He will march to Miletus and lay siege, but the city, supplied from the sea, will hold out. Alexander's fleet, no more than a hundred and sixty warships, will be scattered. The barbarian will lose an important port: those cities which have gone over to him, Ephesus included, will rise in revolt . . ."

237

A waterfowl burst from the reeds and streaked up into the sky. Darius released the peregrine in pursuit; the predator rose high above its quarry. Darius watched its death-dealing plunge. In his mind's eye he saw himself, falling like a thunderbolt from heaven on the Macedonian invader.

Telamon, sweaty and dusty, stood in a deserted stableyard and gazed despairingly at the mound of grey-white ash which Callisthenes and his men had brought from the Temple of Hercules. The cinders had lost all heat; nothing more than a dirty pile of refuse.

"Like a body without a soul," Telamon murmured.

He looked across at Cassandra. She mumbled some reply, eyes flashing angrily above the mask wrapped across her nose and mouth. She lifted a gloved hand and pulled the damp cloth down.

"Must we do this?" she wailed.

"We have no choice."

Telamon glared at the heap of ash. He had spent most of the day reflecting on Dion's murder. Now the noonday heat had eased, he had come down here to sift through the charcoal which had once ringed the shrine in the Temple of Hercules. Both he and Cassandra were dressed like beggars in their dirtiest robes, as well as stout marching boots. They had borrowed mattocks, rakes and hoes from the gardeners. Callisthenes, looking like a grey ghost in the dust, had cheerfully announced that the cart was his gift to them, and stamped off to clean his mouth with wine.

Cassandra leaned on the rake and glared across the courtyard. "All we need now is our conquering hero to come marching in!"

"Hush!"

Cassandra shook her head. "I will not hush. Telamon, was he like that as a boy? He really does believe Artemis has saved him! Celebrations throughout the city! Prisoners being pardoned! Athletics competitions arranged! Plays put on at the theatre! Later on today, the entire army will parade along the Avenue of Artemis from one city gate to another."

Telamon balanced the rake in his hand and pulled down his own face mask. He went across, picked up a waterskin, undid the stopper and, lifting it up, squirted some into his mouth. He handed it to Cassandra.

"He was always like this," he confessed. "Ever changeable. A trait inherited from Mother. The great general, the great painter, the arrogant prince, the humble, laughing friend."

He took the waterskin back.

"Always remember this, Cassandra. Alexander is first and foremost an actor, a brilliant actor, which, I think, makes him a brilliant soldier and general – as well," he added bitterly, "as a very cunning bastard. I can't understand him. Miletus has closed its gates against us. The Persian fleet is on its way but he stays in Ephesus, drinking, eating and playing at soldiers. Ah well, let's start on this."

"Have you understood that message yet?" Cassandra asked. "The one the madman wrote after he burnt the Temple of Artemis?"

"Don't mention it!" Telamon snapped.

He pulled the mask over his mouth and nose and advanced threateningly on the mound of ash. Clouds of dust rose to water their eyes and cloak their bodies in grey.

"We look like ghosts," Cassandra coughed, pulling down the face mask and stepping away: the dust billowed across the courtyard.

"No, no," Telamon murmured taking the waterskin again. "This ash contains ghosts. It may provide some clue to the murders."

"Where's the silver vase?"

"Alexander wants to examine it."

"You mean keep it!"

Telamon pressed a finger against her lips. "Cassandra, you come from Thebes. Alexander burnt Thebes and massacred thousands. I know that, he knows that. He allows your little jokes, but he's ever changeable. He prides himself on his chivalry to women but, being Alexander, he can always make an exception to the rule." Telamon pointed to the bed of ash which carpeted the courtyard. "I'll make a mark. You go through the ash on the left, I'll sift the rest."

"What are we looking for?"

239

"Anything that shouldn't be there."

"But it's ash!"

Telamon paused. A dog howled in a nearby courtyard, followed by the shouts of its handlers.

"Alexander was supposed to go hunting today. I wouldn't be surprised if he comes here himself. Look, Cassandra, anything you find strange" – Telamon pointed to a wooden chest near the wall – "put it in there."

They began their search. Now and again Cassandra rested to gulp fresh air, wash her face and rinse her mouth with water; Telamon did likewise. Cassandra's moans were soon replaced by exclamations of surprise as she found something and put it in the coffer. She tried to draw Telamon into discussion but he waved her away. Most of the ash was nothing but cinder. Callisthenes had assured him that they had taken everything out.

"We left the pit like an empty bowl," the captain informed Telamon. "Not a pebble, not an ash remains."

Something caught his eye and Telamon picked it up. What looked like hardened, shrivelled leather, the top of a sack re-inforced with string which, because of its thickness, had not been consumed by fire. Other items were found: pieces of metal, a fragment of wood shrivelled and burnt, no more than two inches long. Telamon picked this up and examined it curiously.

"Most of it was burnt by the fire," he murmured. "This must have been oak."

He waved away the dirt and recalled the scene in the garden. Alexander seated on Bucephalus, Apelles walking round, the king dismounting, Bucephalus being led away by the grooms. Telamon had noticed the hoofprints left by Alexander's favourite horse: in shape and symmetry, they were very similar to the wounds inflicted on those slain in the Temple of Hercules.

"It wasn't a horse," Telamon murmured. "Nor was it some bloody-eyed centaur."

He took the items he had found across to the chest and continued. At last they were finished: Cassandra cursing, shaking herself like a dog. They broached a fresh waterskin, removed their masks, washed faces and hands and rinsed their mouths. Telamon

240

showed Cassandra how to swallow water and bring it back through her nose.

"We'll go for a swim later," he added.

"Naked?" Cassandra teased. "Together? Oh Master, what will people say?"

"That we are two very dirty individuals. Now, let's see what we've found."

Telamon emptied the contents of the chest on to the cobbles. Cassandra had found similar strips of leather, hardened and blackened by the fire.

"What are you playing at?"

Telamon spun round. Alexander, dressed in a tunic, hunting boots up to his knees, a whip in one hand, an apple in the other, came sauntering across the yard.

"Ever cautious," Telamon whispered. "I knew he would come. He's up to something. Cassandra, keep a polite tongue in your head."

Alexander paused before the carpet of ash, then glanced at his physician. "You both look like shades from Hades. Callisthenes told me about this. What are you doing, Telamon?"

He came across, bit at the apple but spat the contents out and threw the half-eaten fruit away.

"By the bollocks of a bull, everything tastes of ash!" He winked at Cassandra. "The fiery redhead, with a large mouth and ever-clacking tongue." He leaned over and took a wisp of her hair, rubbing it between his fingers. "Mother has reddish hair. They say she had some Celtic blood. She wasn't always called Olympias, her real name was Myrtale. She assumed her second name after one of Philip's great victories. Are you well, Cassandra?"

"Now I am in your presence, sire, yes of course!" Cassandra bowed.

Alexander stepped back, head slightly to one side, as if deciding whether Cassandra was being submissive or insolent.

"Ptolemy likes you."

"No sire, Ptolemy would like to ride me, that's what he said."

Alexander laughed. He approached Telamon, kissed him on each cheek and wiped the dust on the back of his hand. The

241

different colours of the king's eyes were now more noticeable. He kept clicking his tongue.

"My lord, you are agitated?"

"My lord is not agitated." Alexander tossed the whip from one hand to the other. "My lord Alexander is plotting. I have come looking for you, Telamon. We are going to have a parade tonight."

"Followed by a banquet."

Alexander grinned. "That's the plan. I'll give you fair warning, so don't repeat this. Have your medicine satchels packed and all your personal possessions ready."

"For what?"

"You'll see."

"Have you examined the vase?" Cassandra asked. "The one from the Temple of Hercules?"

Alexander took a step closer. Telamon smelt that strange perfume which the king's body always exuded. The physician held his breath; Alexander was in a most peculiar mood.

"I have examined it." Alexander whispered like a fellow conspirator, "and I have weighed it." He glanced out of the corner of his eye at Telamon. "I have also had it studied by silversmiths. I'm going to have it cut open." He spread his hands. "I think the vase contains another vase, an ancient one, probably from the time of Hercules. To preserve it, it's been given a heavy coating of silver. The craftsmen I've hired said they can discover if this is true." He smiled at them. "Ingenious, yes? That's why the vase is empty! In one sense it didn't contain anything, but in another it did, something hidden away, kept secret. That's why it was protected" – he gestured at the carpet of ash – "by a ring of fire."

He pushed by them and crouched down before the items they had taken from the ash. He picked these up, examined them curiously and sniffed.

"You do have an explanation, Telamon?"

He got up, grasped Cassandra's arm, his other hand resting on Telamon's shoulder. "Let's go for a little walk."

They left the courtyard and entered a small vegetable garden, square herb plots dissected by trellised fences. They found a turf seat. Alexander sat down, Telamon and Cassandra on either side.

"Well?" he asked.

"Bucephalus!" Telamon replied.

"You've been talking to my horse?"

"No, sire, examining his hoofprints."

"Ah yes, the imprint on the grass. Very much the same as the wounds on the victims in the Temple of Hercules. You're not going to accuse a horse of murder?"

"Nor a centaur." Telamon sighed. "This is what I suspect happened. No one entered that temple. No secret passage exists. The rear door was bolted and sealed. I don't believe the gods came down to wreak vengeance or some Persian demon from hell stalked that bloody shrine. Demades was there with six of his companions and one Macedonian soldier. People were allowed to come in and out of the shrine; visiting relatives, the curious . . .''

"But they were searched for arms?"

"Of course they were. Callisthenes is a good soldier. He would look for daggers, swords, bows and arrows. What he didn't look for was a heavy piece of bronze moulded in the shape of a horseshoe."

"What?" Alexander exclaimed.

"That could be carried in a wallet," Telamon explained. "While a small oak stick, even a walking cane, would not be seen as dangerous. What I suspect is that both items were taken into the temple and given to the assassin."

"And who was he?" Alexander was excited.

"I'm not sure."

Alexander watched a swallow dive above the flowerbeds.

"Let me finish my story. The piece of oak, probably no more than a foot long, as well as the bronze horseshoe, was given to the murderer."

"Ah, I see," Alexander interrupted. "The bronze could be screwed or clasped to the piece of wood?"

"Precisely," Telamon agreed. "Forming a very powerful war club. Bronze is very heavy, oak reliable. The horseshoe was secured to the wood by some clasp or bolt. The assassin could hide it away in the darkness of the temple."

"That's possible."

"It's the truth," Cassandra declared, eyes glowing with pride. "Telamon is a sharp observer."

"And that's why I like him," Alexander teased back. "But having a war club," he continued, "does not mean eight strong men died. Remember what Callisthenes said?"

"Food and wine were taken into the temple," Telamon continued. "Once the assassin had a club, all he needed were four other things: a skin of wine, one of oil, sleeping powders in a small phial and one other small item I'll describe later."

"There was some oil in the temple," Alexander declared. "Kept in jars near the door."

"Yes, that could have been used. We can't blame Callisthenes for what happened. They needed wine to drink. The oil could be used for food, light or for easing cramped muscles. Whatever, in the end, all the assassin had to conceal was a makeshift club, a small phial of powder, and perhaps some horsehair: he was going to need that to leave an evil stench to make us think some bloody-eyed centaur had visited the temple. The assassin wanted to create an aura of mystery. He knew the temple was sealed and guarded. On the last night, the keys were taken by Aristander: he decided to strike then."

"Why?" Cassandra interrupted. "Why didn't he murder the victims before?"

"I'm not sure. Perhaps he was waiting for something, a message perhaps? I am afraid that part" – Telamon smiled thinly – "of the painting is still covered in dust."

The physician paused. He was still uncertain, but he was beginning to perceive the hideous events in that sombre temple during the hours of darkness.

"Imagine yourself there," he continued. "The doors are sealed. The light pouring through the windows dies: oil-lamps are lit to provide light and warmth. The circle of charcoal also affords some comfort. Demades and his associates are uneasy. Tomorrow morning they are going to leave the temple. They are still suspicious. Probably some of them lost loved ones in the recent massacre. They haven't yet" – he nudged Alexander slightly – "experienced the power of Macedon . . ."

244

"No, but their assassin will experience his vengeance!"

"They're tense, excited, wondering what tomorrow will bring," Telamon explained. "The Macedonian soldier provides some security. He probably kept to himself. Anyway, the wine is served."

"Who by?" Alexander asked.

"Why, by the servant of course, Socrates."

"So he's the assassin?"

"Yes, I think he is. He pours eight cups, the sleeping potion mixed in seven. All solicitous, Socrates serves both the wine and the food. He sits back and waits. The wine alone would make them sleepy, but the effect of the powder brings unconsciousness. The temple grows silent. No one is awake, bodies sprawl here and there, stretched out in sleep. Socrates acts . . ."

"But why him?" Alexander interrupted testily.

"I don't know. I shall come to that. Socrates takes his makeshift war club. He moves from one victim to another. A blow to the side of the head and one to the face. Those poor men died in their sleep; their fate proves the proverb, 'Sleep is the brother of Death'. The temple sanctuary is now a butcher's yard. Socrates, however, has to find out what's in the silver vase. He has to take it down, but how can he cross the fire?"

"He took one of the corpses, didn't he?" Cassandra spoke up.

"That's right. Socrates is past caring about decency. He drags a corpse over, throws it on top of the coals and creates a human bridge. He quickly crosses and removes the vase. He is as surprised as anyone to discover there's nothing in it. He puts the vase down. The sanctuary now reeks with the tang of blood and the smell of burning flesh, but Socrates has not yet finished. He drags the burnt corpse off the coals. The air is bitter-sweet with the rancid smell of human fat. Socrates takes some oil, douses the corpse and sets it alight: that will deepen the mystery. When the temple is opened, no one will be able to understand either how the vase was taken down or why a corpse was burnt to blackened ash."

"But Socrates must have been frightened? He couldn't pose," Alexander demanded, "as the sole survivor?"

"Oh, but he could, and would have done, but for the subtle

double-cross. Cassandra found a lump of burnt metal, probably no larger than the clay cast of a cat's paw. Once it was a claw."

"Easily smuggled in," Cassandra added. "Wrapped in a cloth, it could be passed from hand to hand."

"Ah!" Alexander sighed. "The other item?"

"This is only conjecture," Telamon continued, "but I suspect Socrates was going to act as follows. He scratched his arms and his face to give the impression that some enemies, two or three, all in disguise, stole into the temple. The rest were killed while asleep: Socrates fought back. The others received death wounds, he was simply clawed and scarred. Remember his corpse was found near the rear door behind the statue."

"Socrates was going to open that, wasn't he?" Alexander asked.

"Yes," Telamon agreed. "You can imagine the scene in the dead of night, or the early hours. The temple walls are thick, the front doors double-barred and locked. Socrates was going to break your seal, pull back the bolts on the small postern door and run screaming into the night. The guards outside would be surprised: due to the thickness of the walls, they would have heard or smelt nothing untoward. The windows are high and narrow. Socrates could act the bemused, terrified servant who had done his best to protect his master. He would point to his own wounds, tell some hideous tale, and probably would be believed. Oh yes," Telamon murmured, "Socrates was very clever, even to the small claws he smuggled in, at the bottom of food baskets or even slipped from hand to hand.

"Afterwards Socrates had a few remaining tasks to do." Telamon pointed to the charred remains. "He threw the claws, the oilskin, the bronze horseshoe club and its wooden handle in among the charcoal . . ."

"And he'd clean the wine cups, wouldn't he?" Cassandra asked.

"Yes, he would clean and refill them and the jug of wine, remove any trace of them being tainted. Socrates, however, had made one fatal error: he trusted the person he worked for outside the temple." Telamon raised a hand. "No, don't ask me who. Not yet! This person had smuggled in the wine and oil, the claws, the bronze club, stick and sleeping potion. Socrates didn't realize the claw was laced with a deadly poison. He himself was trapped. The real assassin had

246

no intention of allowing him to live. The poison was probably something herbal or snake venom. Yes." Telamon rubbed his eyes. "That was obvious, but who would suspect Socrates had poisoned himself? His death only deepened the mystery. It increased the impression of something demonic happening in that temple." Telamon paused. "At first the poison would have no effect. Then the shooting pains would begin, like scorching fire: Socrates staggers to the door but it's too late: he collapses and dies."

"Would people have believed him?" Cassandra asked.

"I would have," Alexander declared. "A sleeping potion can't be traced."

"These heinous murders," Telamon explained, "contain a hideous paradox. I considered it to be the perfect crime, one that couldn't be resolved. However, the paradox springs from the very fact Socrates was not allowed to finish what he planned. If he hadn't been betrayed by his colleague outside, he would have been able to explain himself logically and convincingly." Telamon rubbed his hands together. "Remember the rear door of the temple was bolted from the inside. Socrates, if he had been given time, could have drawn those bolts, so recently oiled, probably by himself. He would have alleged the door was made to look as if it was secure but the assailant, or assailants, simply pushed hard to gain entrance. Or, indeed, one of the victims admitted the attackers but was killed to silence his mouth. Whatever, Socrates would have staggered out, screaming murder, raising the alarm. Who could disbelieve him? He'd got rid of any weapons. Only the gods know what he would have said, but why should a faithful, unarmed servant be suspect? He'd pass the blame on to the Democrats . . ."

"Or," Alexander interrupted, clapping his hands, "he would have blamed the Macedonians; we broke in and killed them, and the soldier inside was in our pay."

"Possibly," Telamon agreed.

"But that's dangerous," Cassandra declared.

"Oh yes. Socrates took a risk, but, I suspect, the prospect of his reward outweighed any fear." Telamon smiled. "Remember, we'll never know how Socrates planned to explain himself, but I am sure it would have been convincing."

"And the vase?" Alexander asked.

"There might have been something inside, but I doubt it. The vase is irrelevant: the real assassin must have been very pleased with the result. A Macedonian soldier, together with leading Ephesians, has been killed: Alexander's promises are proved to be worthless, his apparent invincibility questioned, as if the gods themselves had decided to intervene against him." Telamon grinned. "And that includes your ancestor Hercules. With one stroke, the Centaur questioned who was the real master of Ephesus."

"But why?" The king got to his feet. "Why Socrates? Why should he turn against his master? Kill members of a party of which he had been a member? What profit was there in this?"

"A great deal." Telamon rose. He crossed to a small pool and trailed his fingers through the cool water, knocking away the floating lotus blossoms. The sunshine was now comfortable. Telamon stared at the fountain, carved in the shape of a satyr carrying a jug on its shoulder.

"Aristander suspects Dion." Alexander walked over and sat on the edge of the fountain. "He discovered love letters between the lawyer and his whore, as well as detailed drawings of the Temple of Hercules."

"They could have been drawn by anyone," Telamon replied. "While love letters don't prove Dion was the Centaur."

"But there's more," Alexander insisted. "Dion was seen at the courtesan's house at the time she was killed and her place put to the torch. There's the mark Rabinus left on his prison cell: the Greek capital 'D'. It must have been Dion." Alexander snatched a clump of grass. "He became frightened of capture and committed suicide."

"Did he?" Telamon asked. "I wonder." The physician picked up a lotus and sniffed at it. "You ask what profit?" He watched a small sparrow alight on the arm of the statue. "Socrates was like any man, he had his weaknesses. We know he was heavily bribed: gold and silver banked away. More importantly, Socrates was in love. Worse that that, infatuated with Arella. Basileia told me how Demades pursued the courtesan, hoping to gain her favours. To do that he'd use his servant to take presents: diamonds, perfumes, sacks of gold and silver, all the precious luxuries Arella loved. Only she turned him away."

"So Socrates fell in love with Arella?" Cassandra asked, coming across and crouching on the grass. She ignored Alexander, intently watching the physician.

"Yes, Socrates became infatuated. But" – Telamon paused – "and this is where it becomes interesting: before we arrived in Ephesus there was a spy, an assassin, called the Centaur, yes?"

Alexander agreed.

"But a Centaur is two creatures, half-man, half-horse."

"You're saying the Centaur is two individuals?"

"*Was* two individuals. Socrates was certainly one of them. Only Apollo knows the name of the person who controlled him: Dion, Peleus, Agis, Meleager? One of those, but as yet I have no evidence, it's pure conjecture."

Telamon paused as a braying trumpet cut through the warm afternoon air, followed by more shrill blasts.

"Oh, just ignore that," Alexander said. "We're preparing for our great parade through Ephesus: the troops are assembling in the fields outside." The king rubbed a piece of grass through his fingers. "I'm much more interested in this. So, whoever controlled Socrates loosed those arrows at me, persuaded Demades's widow to bring that dagger to the feast, released those wasps, killed that guard . . ."

"Could it have been Dion?" Cassandra asked.

"As Aristotle said, all things are possible." Telamon washed his hands in the water from the fountain. "Arella is still the key to all this, that's why she was murdered. Before Demades took refuge at the Temple of Hercules, the two Centaurs met, Socrates and this mysterious person. Socrates was told how he would carry out the murders, and was given assurances that the materials he needed would be smuggled in, either by someone in disguise or by Arella. We know she was seen around the temple."

"But why should Socrates agree?" Alexander demanded.

"Three reasons. First, it was part of his task. Socrates was paid not only by Demades but also by the Persians. Secondly, he was heavily bribed: we know that from what Aristander told us . . ."

"And thirdly?"

"He was given assurances that, if he carried out the murders, he would be rewarded with the charms of Arella."

"I don't believe that," Alexander scoffed.

"I do." Cassandra was eager to challenge the king. "Most men, apart from this physician, have their brains where their penis hangs."

"Does that include me?" Alexander narrowed his eyes.

"No, sire, you are a king." Telamon closed his eyes at the sarcasm in Cassandra's voice. "You are above such mortal matters."

Alexander's lips puckered in a smile. "Your temper is as fiery as your hair. You do remind me of Mother. Continue, Telamon."

"I agree with Cassandra. Socrates was already a killer, a Persian spy, a man who could be bought and sold. But his infatuation must have been intense, increased by Arella's refusal."

"What proof do you have of this?"

"I know from Basileia that Arella was visited at night by a mysterious stranger, bribed with the offer of more power, influence and money. She would also have been threatened: Arella had kept company with leading Persians, including the Governor. Arella didn't tell Basileia the name of the person she was supposed to favour but she did crack a joke: she claimed that on the whole, she'd prefer to drink a cup of hemlock."

Alexander laughed. "I see the joke." The king plucked the piece of grass from his lips. "She was referring to Socrates's great namesake, the philosopher who was forced to drink poison in Athens?"

"Arella agreed," Telamon continued. "But Socrates would need assurances: that's why he stood near the temple door. He was waiting for her. She would come, quickly whisper sweet promises, and the die would be cast. For all we know, Arella may have smuggled what Socrates needed into the Temple of Hercules. Socrates would have trusted his true master, the Centaur: they had plotted and murdered before, shared the wealth from Persepolis, so why should something go wrong now? The Master Centaur, however, had other plans. Socrates went into the dark. Arella's mouth had to be closed once and for all. She was probably relieved at Socrates's death but, like her kind, arrogant. As long as she kept her mouth closed and was discreet, Arella could weather a change of government. She was not part of the bloody politics of the city. She thought she could survive."

"So the Centaur paid her a murderous visit?" Alexander asked.

"It would be so easy. He turned up at the gate, was recognized and allowed in. The rest is how I've described it."

Again a bray of trumpets and the sound of horses neighing, men shouting, in the distant courtyard.

"We have two hours yet," Alexander declared. "Continue!"

"While the Centaur was busy massacring Arella's household, along came Hesiod, the ubiquitous fat scribe."

"Did Hesiod suspect something?" Alexander asked.

"Yes, I think he did. He was following the same path we are now walking, and he wanted to discover how much Arella knew. Hesiod was a powerful official. He must have had people in his pay. Perhaps they glimpsed Arella in the marketplace or on the temple steps. Our scribe would be curious. Arella was also friendly with the Persian Rabinus. Hesiod may have arrived at her house to question her, or try a little blackmail. He chose the wrong time and the wrong place: the Centaur killed him."

"Do you think Dion's suicide was really murder?" Alexander asked.

"I am reflecting on that. In Ephesus two factions are at each other's throats. Murder, bribery and corruption are rife, shifting alliances a way of life: Arella and Hesiod were casualties of this."

"The same could be said for Dion?"

"Perhaps. It certainly applies to Rabinus. The Persian was stupid, he should have fled: his capture is a powerful testimony to the charms of Arella."

"If she had survived," Alexander grinned, "I would certainly have entertained her." He ignored Cassandra's sharp bark of laughter.

"The Centaur was fully trusted by the Persians," Telamon continued. "He certainly visited their palace and learnt all its secret galleries and passages."

"Do you think the Persian governor knew the true identity of the Centaur?"

"I doubt it, whatever Rabinus said. The Master Centaur would come here in disguise. He was the Lord Mithra's agent; the Governor would be wary, even frightened of him, agree to anything he wanted. He wouldn't know his name, he was simply showing off to Rabinus."

"Then why should Rabinus make that mark on the wall as if he was naming Dion?"

Telamon flicked the dust off his wrist. "My lord, have you ever visited the House of Glass in Corinth? It's a piece of madness, a folly, the work of an insane glass-smith. He built a small room and spent a fortune covering the walls with mirrors."

"Ah yes, I have heard of it."

"I was curious, I visited it. If you stay long enough, you become dizzy. You begin to wonder what is a reflection and what is the reality. The Master Centaur played a similar game. He was protecting himself. He wouldn't give his name to the Governor, but maybe Dion's was offered, to confuse and create suspicion. Perhaps Dion's so-called suicide was really murder."

"But the evidence," the king remarked, "indicates suicide."

"That's what the Master Centaur wants us to believe. He may even be planning to flee."

"May he now?" Alexander got to his feet. "I have a little surprise for everybody, even you, Telamon! Just make sure everything is packed and ready to go."

"I understand," the physician asked, "that the blood book of the principal families of Ephesus is kept in the Temple of Artemis. Will you ask the priestess's permission for me to consult it?"

"Better still," the king grinned. "Soon you will be closer to the Temple of Artemis than you think." Alexander grasped Telamon's shoulder and gazed long and hard at him. "You have done well, physician, though there's little evidence for what you allege." He gestured at the pile of ash, the scorched items lying in the courtyard. "You will need more than that."

"I know," Telamon replied. "It's more a matter of logic than evidence."

252

"Logic?" Alexander walked away. He gestured at one of the overhanging roofs of the palace. "Do you remember, physician, how we studied logic? I never thought logic would put a man on a cross high against the sky!"

The sun was setting, its last light glinting on the silver-plated obelisks, statues, and the golden cornices of temples and mansions. Telamon, standing behind Alexander, stared out across the great square. The far side was densely packed, as was the entire Avenue of Artemis which stretched down to the Purple Gate through which the Macedonian army would march. Alexander was present with all his entourage and the principal priestesses of Artemis as well as civic dignitaries including Agis, Meleager and Peleus. Ptolemy, Seleucus, Hephaestion, Amyntas, Antipater, Parmenio: all the leading generals of Alexander's army stood on the steps, resplendent in their purple-grey dress armour, golden cloths round their necks, purple sashes about their waists. Silver-fringed scarlet cloaks hung elegantly over their shoulders, their legs were encased in shimmering greaves, calfskin marching boots on their feet. They stood like Greek heroes, plumed helmets under one arm, in their right hand the silver-encrusted baton, a sign of their pre-eminent rank.

Alexander appeared to be what he wanted to appear: the golden god-man, the glorious Captain-General who had come across the Hellespont to liberate all Greek cities from the Persian yoke. Around his red-gold hair a silver wreath, on his chest a gold-embossed cuirass with the face of Medusa on a medallion in the centre, a snow-white war kilt fringed with gold hanging over silver-embossed greaves and purple boots; the king stood on the lower step facing across the great concourse. Telamon was intrigued by the man standing next to Alexander, dressed in a simple robe and tunic: the physician recognized the balding, round-faced, sly-eyed Eumenes, head of the army secretariat. On Alexander's left Aristander leaned on a silver-topped walking cane, the leader of his chorus holding a parasol to protect his master's balding head against the sun.

Alexander raised his hand, fist clenched: the crowd, which

253

included a number of Aristander's agents, roared their approval, sending the pigeons whirling up into the sky. The distance was too great, the crowd too dense, for any speeches.

Alexander was posing like an actor in a play, depending on gestures rather than words. In the far corner of the forecourt stood a group of trumpeters, salpinxes at the ready, standard-bearers and messengers beside them.

"Oh, Artemis be praised!" Cassandra moaned. "Master, how long will this go on?"

"Till Alexander is satisfied."

"What's he plotting?" Cassandra insisted. "What's the use of such a parade followed by one of his stupid banquets? Tomorrow, more parades," she added wearily, "more feasting. Isn't he arranging games to honour his father's memory, hiring troupes of actors?"

Telamon simply nodded in agreement.

Alexander raised his arm as a sign that the parade should begin. The trumpets rang out and the Macedonian army began its parade in full battle array. To greet them Alexander went down and mounted Bucephalus; the groom handed up a magnificent war helmet. Alexander put this on and drew his sword. He raised it in one glittering arc, to be greeted with fresh roars of approval.

The army passed by. First the Foot Companions, regiments of infantry resplendent in their purple cloaks, sashes of a similar colour round their waists, on their heads bronze Boetian helmets, the rim jutting out above the eyes and a long sweep at the back protecting the nape of the neck. White feathers, or plumes of horsehair, distinguished the officers.

The regiments were a magnificent sight in their different-coloured cuirasses: each soldier carried a shield and spear, sword belts round their waists. Squadrons of Companion cavalry followed behind, the horses specially groomed. Each squadron was again distinguished by a different colour – purple and yellow, red and gold – while the saddlecloths of the officers were animal pelts: bear, jaguar or panther. After these, further troops of horse, their riders wearing simple armour and strangely carved helmets fashioned out of animal skins. These were not greeted with roars of approval, as the Ephesians recognized the Thracian and Thessalian mercenaries whose reputation for savagery was well known. Other mercenaries followed: lightly garbed Cretan archers, Agrianian footmen. After these the elite corps of the Macedonian army: the Guards regiments, or Shield Bearers, with their Phrygian helmets, rounded shields, short spears. Finally the Phalangists or Pike Men, Alexander's striking force, lightly armed, wearing only tunic, boots and the Macedonian flat hat or causia: their real weapon was the eighteen-foot sarissa, the long pike or javelin. These were greeted by fresh shouts of approval. Alexander once again raised his sword in salute. Even Telamon, though he had seen the sight many a time, marvelled at the military precision of these crack troops: they now delighted the crowd by forming and re-forming into different wedges, phalanxes, small squads of deep wedges, forming the arrowhead or diamond formation, their performance greeted by showers of flowers and rose petals. Once they had finished, the crack phalanx deliberately chosen for this display passed on. The rear of the column was brought up by Alexander's favourite squadron of cavalry. Like the king's, their saddlecloths were leopardskins, the harness and bridle of gleaming black leather with silver studs: red plumes nodding between the horse's ears. These, too, executed manoeuvres to the delight of the crowd, and then passed on. Telamon gazed bemused. Squadrons of light horse, not to mention the engineers with their siege machinery, were missing. He was going to ask Alexander where they were when heralds moved along the avenue, proclaiming a fresh parade the following evening when Alexander would display more of his military might.

Once they had left, trumpets brayed and the crowds along the avenue and across the square broke up, teeming back into the city to continue the festivities in market squares, wine booths and beer shops: not to forget, as Cassandra archly remarked, "the many brothels, as plentiful as pimples on a beggar's arse".

Telamon, distracted, heard sounds behind him. The broad sweeping steps of Artemis's temple were being ringed by a file of Guards, helmets on, shields up, swords drawn. They surrounded the invited guests. The priestesses and other civic dignitaries were

255

politely allowed through this ring of steel; the rest, including the king's companions, Meleager, Agis and Peleus, were ordered to stay. Peleus began to object, shouting stridently, silenced abruptly by an officer raising his sword.

Alexander dismounted, came through the ring of guardsmen, and clapped his hands for silence. He gestured at those remaining to join him at the foot of the steps. Eumenes, a sly smile on his fat oily face, appeared carrying a small leather sack. Alexander, his face stone-hard, dipped into this and gave each person, including Telamon, a small scroll.

"You can read it later," he declared. "I want no objections! There'll be no feasting tonight. The army now lies outside the south-west gate of Ephesus. My scouts are taking sealed orders to all my commanders. The men will not be dismissed to barracks: there will be no more feasting and banqueting!"

"Why?" Ptolemy demanded.

"We advance quickly on Miletus, a forced march through the dark. There will be no debate, no question: everyone here is to leave immediately!"

Chapter 12

———⇒◦○◦⇐———

"Alexander, falling suddenly upon the enemy with his incensed army, possessed himself immediately . . . of the outward town."

Quintus Curtius Rufus:
History of Alexander Book II, Chapter 6

"The ceaseless twinkling laughter of the waves of the sea."

"Poetry?" Ptolemy urged his horse closer to Alexander's. "Did you compose that?"

"No, Ptolemy, I wish I had. Telamon, do you recognize the line?"

"Words are physic in a distempered mind," the physician replied.

Alexander threw his head back and laughed, steadying his mount against the buffeting wind which swept the clifftop.

"Tell Ptolemy which play we're quoting from."

"Aeschylus," Telamon explained. "*Prometheus Bound.*"

"Never heard of it," Ptolemy retorted, shading his eyes against the sun. "What *I* would like to see bound is the Persian fleet."

Telamon stared out at the sinister shapes dark against the horizon; low in the water, sails furled, the massed fleet of the Persian Empire now stood off the gulf of Mycale. Below the royal party clustered on the clifftop lay the city of Miletus, the marble-white of its temples and civic buildings gleaming in the late afternoon sun. Columns of smoke wafted out over these towards the sea. Telamon moved his horse so he could glimpse the Macedonian camp.

Alexander was jubilant. He pulled his horse away and, shouting at Telamon to join him, cantered further down the cliff, oblivious to its crumbling edge.

"I can see better from here!" he exclaimed. "I caught them unawares, didn't I, Telamon?"

"You caught everybody unawares, my lord."

Telamon, wary of the dizzying drop, dismounted, led his horse away and hobbled it. He sat down and looked over the waving green grass, its moving mass of many-coloured irises and poppies. Alexander had indeed caught them all unawares. The planned processions, banquets, receptions, games and theatre presentations had all been a mask to hide his true intentions. Fast as a cobra, Alexander had struck at Miletus. His hundred and sixty triremes, under the command of Admiral Nicanor, had occupied the island of Lade, sealing the mouth of the great Lion Port of Miletus. On board the triremes were thousands of Thracian and Thessalian mercenaries. Nicanor's orders were explicit: to hold Lade and seal the port. The admiral had been successful. Lade had been fortified: Nicanor's triremes, lashed together, prows facing out to sea, formed an effective wall against the Persian fleet, which had arrived too late.

A shadow fell across the grass. Telamon glanced up; Alexander, leading his horse, was smiling down at him. Telamon looked over his shoulder at the other commanders, still clustered at the cliff edge pointing out to sea.

"They still think the Persian's fleet's a danger." Alexander smiled and crouched down. He plucked an iris and examined it curiously. "I didn't know you'd read Aeschylus's play."

"I saw it performed in Syracuse."

"You prefer watching plays to marching?" Alexander teased.

Telamon rubbed his eyes. "It wasn't a march," he complained. "It was a charge."

Alexander, his eyes full of mischief, crouched like a schoolboy twirling the iris between his fingers. "And what a charge, eh, Telamon?"

The physician glanced away. He would never forget it. The cavalry on the flanks, the infantry moving at double pace through the Maeander river valley, the starlit skies, the full moon, nightingales singing from distant copses. Alexander riding up and down the columns, shouting encouragement, urging everyone to move faster.

"The quicker we march, lads," he shouted, "the sooner we get there! We'll surprise Miletus!"

"And what about their ladies?" someone had shouted back.

"I'll leave that to you!" Alexander retorted.

Through the night, column after column, phalanx after phalanx, squadrons of horse, carts loaded with provisions and armour: everything pouring at a rapid pace towards Miletus. Behind the army, a stream of scouts and camp marshals driving on would-be deserters, the weak, the tired, the lazy. Telamon had ridden with the royal party. Cassandra, thankfully, had been allowed to sit in one of the carts. Alexander acted like a man possessed. He refused to stop to eat or drink, ordering waterskins to be passed along the columns of dusty, marching men. Ptolemy and the rest, of course, had tried to argue. Meleager, Agis and Peleus had complained bitterly, but Alexander was insistent. His plans were well laid: squadrons of horse, he declared, were already within striking distance of Miletus: Macedonian engineers and their siege equipment lay a mere walk away, hidden in copses within sight of the city.

The following morning his army, moving so quickly, surprised the city of Miletus. The first ring of walls was seized, its defenders driven back to the great gates, soaring walls and towers of Miletus's second line of defence. The Macedonians were elated by Alexander's strategy, which brought plunder, food and wine. The king allowed them to refresh themselves and immediately sent his siege weapons to pound the second wall either side of its main gate.

"What are you thinking, Telamon?"

The physician shrugged. Alexander handed him a wineskin.

"I can't think. My backside's numb, my thighs ache, my back feels as if I've been lashed."

"It was the only way," Alexander replied. "I had to pretend to be lazing in the sun. I gave that impression." He took the wineskin back, rinsed his throat and spat the wine out. "I wanted to take the spy unawares, Darius unawares, Memnon unawares and, above all, the Persian fleet unawares. If I'd been a little faster I might even have taken the second line of defence. My advance commanders tell me the Milesians mistakenly thought they were Greek mercenaries coming to join Memnon. Well" – Alexander got to his feet – "I certainly spoilt his breakfast, didn't I? Come on, Telamon, I'll show you the sights."

They left their horses and went back to the clifftop. "Thank Apollo Aristander's not here," Alexander murmured. "He can't stand heights. Are those Ephesians comfortable?"

"They're sharing a house."

"Good!"

Alexander wiped his bare feet on the grass. He was dressed in a simple brown tunic, sword belt strapped round his waist. He looked as fresh as the morning, hair washed, face shaven and oiled. The consummate actor, Telamon thought: Alexander was now playing the cunning general, a role he had watched Philip perform so well.

"Come on!" Alexander grasped Telamon's hand. "You won't fall!"

They went back to the edge of the cliff and stared down at Miletus.

"You see." Alexander pointed down. "The walls are shaped like a horseshoe, three in all, fortified to protect their archers. Towers jut out slightly so their bowmen can fire down if our men get too close. The gates are reinforced and they've probably built another wall behind them. The ground is too hard to mine so I'll have to hole one of the walls. I remember what Philip told me: concentrate on one spot, two at the very most."

Telamon followed the king's directions.

"I wish I had a siege machine which could fire from here," Alexander whispered. "It's a beautiful place, isn't it," he added sadly. "I don't want to burn it. It's a city of blood, mind you, Telamon. Have your read your Herodotus? When the first Greeks came here they brought no women, but married the local girls whose menfolk they'd murdered. The Milesians still have a law forbidding Milesian women to sit at table with their husbands or address them by name."

260

He stared out at the Persian warships; brooding, threatening shapes. "Last time the Persians won. Do you know the story?"

Telamon shook his head.

"The Greek fleet went out to meet the Persians, who defeated them, captured the city, burnt it to the ground and enslaved its inhabitants. The news shocked Athens. A playwright produced a drama, *The Capture of Miletus*, and the entire audience burst into tears. The author was heavily fined and the Athenians forbade anyone ever to put the play on again."

"Miletus seems to have recovered," Telamon replied. "New buildings . . ."

"Can you make out the one with the soaring columns? That's their great theatre. Next to it, with the golden-topped obelisk, can you see it?"

Telamon couldn't, but he agreed.

"That's the Temple of Athena." Alexander, excited, dragged him even closer and pointed. "And the great temple close to the harbour? That's their Delphinium, dedicated to Apollo the Dolphin God."

"Will the Milesians surrender?" Telamon asked.

"I don't think so. We're going to have to fight our way in. Oh, look at the sea, Telamon. In the sunlight it looks wine-coloured, no mist, nothing."

"Except black smoke," Telamon added.

Alexander caught the edge in his voice. "That's war. Some of the people fought back, fires start."

Telamon shifted his gaze to the outer part of the town, now occupied by the Macedonian army. A great, sprawling camp. He could make out individuals, pavilions, and the great swathe of devastated earth which separated the edge of the camp from the second wall of the city.

The rest of their companions, led by Ptolemy, joined them.

"What are we going to do?" Ptolemy was still angry at being taken by surprise. "The Persians are out there!"

"Aye," Alexander replied. "And we are here!"

A bird keened. Telamon stared up at the cloudless sky. He was glad to be here; it was cool and fresh, far enough away from the heat, dirt and smoke of the camp.

"Is that a hawk?" Alexander asked, following Telamon's gaze. "Or an eagle?"

"I heard a report" – Parmenio, the grizzled veteran commander from Philip's days pushed his way forward, knocking Telamon aside – "that an eagle was seen resting on the prow of one of our ships. I take that as a sign: Zeus is with us. Our fleet should sail out to meet the Persians. We shall defeat them at sea."

"I disagree." Alexander was still watching the bird high in the sky. "If the eagle was resting on one of our ships, Zeus is telling us we should stay on land and defeat the Persian navy from the shore."

"And how can we do that?" Ptolemy demanded.

"No." Alexander shook his head, eyes screwed up against the sun. "I don't think it's an eagle, it must be a hawk or a buzzard."

"I couldn't care if it's bloody Icarus!" Ptolemy growled. "Alexander, hundreds of Persian warships prowl the sea. They are full of soldiers. If they move in . . .?"

"They are full of soldiers," Alexander agreed. "And the Persian ships are manned by the best seamen in the Middle Sea, from Phoenicia and Cyprus. There are too many of them," the king continued. "Our fleet is too small, and it's manned by Athenians. I don't trust them at all." He paused. "If we stay on land we can defeat the Persians at sea."

"How?" Parmenio and Ptolemy spoke in unison.

Alexander stretched out and tweaked the tip of Ptolemy's nose. He gazed round at his commanders.

"Look at you," he teased. "All ready for a fight. Want another Granicus? It won't be like that, not this time."

"Why don't you just tell us what you're going to do?" Ptolemy demanded. "You're like a woman . . .!" The insult died on his lips.

Alexander's smile disappeared.

"I mean . . ."

"I know what you mean." Alexander pointed to their horses, nibbling at the grass. "Everything under the sun needs to eat and drink. Imagine, Ptolemy, you are a commander of a Persian warship. You have hundreds of men on board, sailors, marines, soldiers. Where do they go to relieve themselves?"

"Put their bums over the side."

262

"So the ships won't be too clean, will they?" Alexander retorted. "If they stay out there much longer, and the wind changes, we'll be able to smell them. And what do you eat?" he continued. "You can't light fires. Hard rations, biscuits, stale bread, dried meat?"

"The Persians will love that," Seleucus laughed.

"And what do you drink?" Alexander persisted. "Watered wine?"

"Well, water."

"Of course," Alexander breathed. "You are a Persian soldier in cramped quarters, filthy conditions. You eat iron rations, your lips and mouth are caked with brine, the sun is hot and you want to drink. So where do you go?"

Ptolemy blushed with embarrassment.

"Come on, Ptolemy," Alexander teased. "Where do you go?"

"Into shore," Parmenio declared. "To seek fresh water."

"And where do you go to get water for so many men? Come on, we all know. An estuary or river mouth: the only one round here is the Maeander, and that's firmly held by our troops."

Alexander's commanders looked crestfallen. The king clapped his hands, dancing from foot to foot like a boy who has played a trick on his friends.

"Can't you see? The Persians can't get into Miletus because we've blocked the harbour mouth. They can sail up and down to their hearts' content while they broil under the sun. I tell you this." Alexander pointed a finger. "I give the Persian fleet two days at the most, then it will leave, to clean, re-victual and fill its water jars. The Milesians" – he pointed out to the city – "are on their own! Well," he grinned, "until we join them!"

An hour later Alexander and his companions, protected by a screen of scouts, galloped back into the Macedonian camp. The contrast to the grassy, flower-covered clifftop was stark. The outer part of Miletus had been taken, every house occupied by Alexander's soldiers. The streets were strewn with rubbish and remnants of the fierce hand-to-hand fighting. The soldiers themselves were in good heart despite their exhausting march. They had found fresh supplies and a little plunder. Alexander had assured them that, within days, they would be able to stroll along the Lion harbour and drink their wine in the shade of its palm trees.

Alexander had taken over a large, wealthy mansion just inside the first wall of the city, set in grounds with pleasant orchards. Telamon and Cassandra had been given a small chamber at the back. When Telamon arrived, Cassandra was lying on a cot bed: they had done their best to clean the room and the small ante-chamber where Telamon could meet his patients.

"There's some food on the chest, covered by a cloth," she mumbled without turning round. "I stole it from the royal quartermaster. He's only got eyes for my breasts so my hands could do what they wanted."

Telamon took off his dirty tunic. He picked up a wet rag and wiped the dust and sweat from his body. "Have you any patients?" he asked.

"Have I got patience?" Cassandra teased.

"You know what I mean."

Cassandra rolled over and sat on the edge of the cot. "Minor cuts and bruises. If the great conqueror has his way we'll soon be busy enough, eh? What's all this madness?" she asked crossly.

"Alexander's madness," Telamon replied, opening a small chest and taking out a clean tunic. "Formidable cunning and ruthless speed, tricks he learnt from his parents. While we were at Ephesus, Alexander secretly despatched troops to the coast. Nicanor's ships picked them up and they sailed for Lade. At the same time, squadrons of cavalry, engineers with their siege machinery, were sent out and hidden as close to Miletus as possible."

"And now?" Cassandra rubbed her eyes. "What will happen now?"

"Alexander's siege engineers are ranged against the second wall. The great assault will happen," Telamon snapped his fingers, "in the twinkling of an eye! It could come now or tomorrow."

Cassandra was watching curiously; her green, cat-like eyes were red-rimmed and ringed with black shadows from lack of sleep.

"I know you, Telamon."

"Then you know more than I do."

"We've been here, what, two days? And you've been wrapped

264

in a cloak of secrecy." She gestured at the window. "You stood there for an hour this morning, just staring out. You know who the Centaur is, don't you?"

"I suspect." Telamon sat on the edge of her bed. "One or two obstacles still lie in the way. Like a tally of figures, I keep adding them up wrongly."

"Would Socrates have done that for the love of a woman?"

"Paris sacrificed Troy because of Helen's golden locks. I was in love once," Telamon continued. "I wonder what I would have done. Anything, I suppose."

"Could you love me?"

Telamon got up and walked to the window.

"Could you love the Red Hair?" Cassandra teased.

Telamon turned and stared at her.

"You are becoming part of me, Cassandra, little by little, day by day. You don't complain. You keep up a commentary which puts Alexander in perspective." He smiled. "You are as good a physician as I am, but we are at war. Alexander is going to force a breach in that wall."

The smile faded from Cassandra's face. "Oh no!" She half rose. Telamon gestured her back. "He won't take you with him?"

Telamon nodded. "I'm his personal physician. Alexander will take medicine from few people. He was wounded at the Granicus, it could happen again. Don't worry. I'll keep close to Black Cleitus, my eyes closed and my shield up. Cassandra, what's the matter?"

The young woman jumped up, shaking her head. "I have business to do. The quartermaster said I could have some more chicken."

She was out of the room before Telamon could stop her. He stood brooding for a while, sighed, and returned to the jottings he had made the previous evening. Outside a soldier was singing softly about the love of his life in some dark forest many miles away. Telamon sat down on the stool and studied the manuscript, his mind confused. He'd studied the confession of the madman who had burnt the Temple of Artemis. He recalled that other temple, cold and dark: those sprawling corpses, Socrates moving like a demon, outside the masked figure of his master, the true assassin.

Telamon closed his eyes. Another image; Alexander walking out of the palace gates, the arrow hitting his chest.

Telamon turned all these images over in his mind. The shadows grew longer, the sun began to set. Cassandra returned with more food. The sounds of the house drifted by; in the distance, the cacaphony of the camp. Telamon was curious. The battering against the walls seemed to have ceased, the ominous whistle of catapults and siege machinery; now there was only the occasional trumpet call, shouts, neighing from the horse lines.

Telamon retired early that evening, still thinking about what he had seen and learnt. He could clearly see the face of the Centaur, but how was he to prove his guilt? He was aware of the night growing cold.

Cassandra moved about, lighting a brazier, pulling a blanket over him. She leaned down, lips only a few inches from his face.

"The great conqueror," she whispered, "is planning something. Everything is quiet."

Telamon smiled sleepily. "I suspect so myself. Cassandra, bolt the door and rest. We're going to need it."

He drifted into sleep. Now and again he was roused by sounds from the house, once or twice the clatter of horses and carts. When a hammering on the door sent him leaping from his bed, Telamon stared at the grey dawn light seeping through the shutters.

"Open up!" Alexander called.

Cassandra moved on her bed. Telamon pulled back the bolts.

"Refreshed and ready, Telamon?"

"What for?" the physician snapped.

"Battle!"

The king was dressed as a Foot Companion, a gleaming cuirass across his chest, a black and red war kilt, greaves of dull bronze. He had his sword belt on; his cloak, fastened round his neck, was thrown back over his shoulders. He carried a Phrygian helmet with two white plumes on either side. Telamon was aware of other figures behind the king.

"Come!" Alexander beckoned, his voice devoid of all humour. "It's time once again!"

Telamon recognized the ominous invitation as well as its

266

timing. Alexander was planning a dawn offensive. He intended to breach the walls of Miletus. The physician hastily dressed, grabbed his motley collection of armour. Cassandra was now awake. She helped Telamon arm for battle, muttering and cursing as she pulled at thongs and hastily tied the straps of the war kilt. She clapped greaves on his legs and rose to survey her handiwork.

"I would like to say," she said grimly, face hidden in the shadows, "that you are like a true Hector, but of course he was killed, wasn't he?" She picked up the Phrygian helmet and thrust it into Telamon's hand. "Your marching boots are well tied. Don't forget, your sword on your left side and keep your shield up." She kissed him quickly on the cheek. "May the gods protect you, physician Telamon! Now you'd best go."

Telamon took the rounded shield and stepped into the silent street. Alexander and his commanders were waiting in a blaze of torchlight at the far end. Telamon joined them, as did others. Some were sleepy, others still questioning; Alexander refused to answer. He led them through the streets, a screen of guards going before him. They passed different units making their way up. They breasted a steep hill and paused.

Telamon caught his breath. War had changed that part of Miletus. All the houses, shops and tenements stretching up to the second curtain wall had been levelled. The area before it had been turned to wasteland, now dominated by a long line of siege machinery: catapults, mangonels, stone-throwing machines, battering rams, bolt-shooting catapults and soaring siege towers which contained more engines of war. Against the early morning sky these stark, death-bearing siege machines looked like hideous creatures from the Underworld. They crouched along that desolate land, ready to drag down the walls of Miletus.

Already the engineers were busy. Catapults were being loaded, the wheels of siege towers oiled. Specially trained archers manned the bolt-shooting catapults, which operated on twisted horsehair anchored in a wooden frame and reinforced with metal plates; they possessed the power to loose great jagged bolts, lances, balls of fire or huge boulders. Telamon surveyed the walls: the odd pinprick of light glowed, but the Milesians seemed unaware of what was happening.

"They don't expect a dawn attack," Alexander remarked, jumping like a boy from foot to foot. "And the Persian fleet has withdrawn, probably gone back to Samos for fresh water."

Telamon looked down the battle line: at least forty or fifty siege machines and, behind them, formed in rank after rank, foot soldiers. The Royal Guards brigade had the place of honour in the front. Further down the hill came the neigh of horses, the clop of hooves, the shouts of cavalry officers. Telamon recognized Alexander's plan. A breach would be formed, the foot soldiers would pour through to create an ever-widening gap, or seize a gate, so the cavalry could sweep up into the town.

The air was now rent by the creak of machines, the winch of ropes, the groans and gasps of men as they loaded these hideous and very accurate throwing machines. The sounds must have reached the Milesians. More pinpricks of light appeared on the crenellated walls. The dawn breeze caught the wail of a conch horn, but Alexander was already moving, the captain of his engineers eager for orders.

"At the first blast," Alexander shouted, "use the bolts to clear the parapets! Then" – he pointed to a place to the right of the main gate – "create a hole there! On my sign, let the Furies be released!"

Scouts carrying torches ran up and down the lines. The siege machinery was primed, the great throwing arms pulled back. The huge catapults were loaded, the battering rams at the foot of the siege towers moved backwards and forwards. Already archers were firing into the platforms above. Alexander turned to his trumpeter, his head and shoulders draped in the skin of a black panther. The king raised his hand, lips soundlessly moving as he uttered some prayer.

"Now!" he shouted.

The salpinx gave a long wailing blast. All along the line rose the shouts of the captains of engineers in each unit.

"Aim! Loose! Fill!"

The silence was riven by a blood-chilling crashing and twanging as the catapults and mangonels were released. A hideous whistling sound cut through the air as a hail of stones, jagged bolts and bundles of fire were loosed at the walls of Miletus. Some smacked vainly against hard stone, others fell too short, but in the main the engineers had calculated accurately. Damage was done. A scream-ing figure, clothes on fire, fell from the walls. Spirals of smoke rose as the burning pitch landed on wooden walkways or ladders.

Trumpet calls echoed from the city, followed by the wail of conch horns. Figures appeared on the parapet walls to expose themselves to the deadly rain Alexander had loosed. Javelins and balls of fire smashed into the stonework. The target was a line of no more than twenty yards, which included a gatehouse and a stretch of wall on either side.

The Milesians, unable to cope with such a constant hail of destruction, were unaware of Alexander's other tactics. Agrianian footmen raced forward with bundles of faggots and wood; the great ditch was hastily filled, a makeshift bridge thrown across. The powerful battering rams were pushed forward, flanked on either side by hundreds of Cretan archers; these kept up a steady rain of fire against those defenders who had escaped the avalanche of death-bearing missiles. The battering rams, protected in their leather-covered sheds, reached the wall. The men inside swung the huge metal-capped bolt backwards and forwards against the walls. The besieged tried to retaliate with burning oil and brands of fire, but the top of that wall had already been severely damaged and cleared of defenders. The Cretan archers, specially chosen for their marksmanship, kept up their deadly hail. Alexander's siege ma-chines now turned their attention away from the wall above the battering rams and concentrated their fire further down.

The sun rose quickly. The air throbbed with the twang of cords and the eerie whistling of deadly bolts. Screams from the city cut through the hissing of arrows and the ominous crashing of battering rams. The Macedonians suffered casualties: Cretan archers, caught by bolts, slingshots or arrows, would suddenly jump back or stagger away clutching blood-spouting wounds. A side gate opened and the Milesians attempted a sortie, but a phalanx of guardsmen raced forward to confront them so they hastily withdrew. Clouds of dust wafted backwards and forwards. The air was rank with the smell of pitch and burning sulphur, the acrid, sickening smell of smouldering flesh.

Alexander's foot soldiers inched forward. The king himself, ignoring all warnings, stood in the front line. He seemed oblivious to any other part of the battlefield except where his battering rams were hammering away. Beneath his helmet Alexander's face was now covered in a fine chalky dust. He had his shield up, sword drawn, and beside him the towering figure of his personal bodyguard, Black Cleitus, distinguished by the furry bear pelt slung across his shoulder. Behind him, his companions, Ptolemy, Seleucus and Amyntas: each was eager to follow their king, be the first in the city. Pride of place, however, was given to Hephaestion. Black Cleitus protected Alexander's left, Hephaestion would guard his right. Telamon stood in the group behind the king.

The battering rams became hidden by a white haze of dust. "It must be now!" Alexander whispered over his shoulder. "If my mathematics are correct – the thickness of the wall, the force of that machinery. What I don't want" – he pointed to the battlements above the clouds of dust – "is for the Milesians to reinforce those. Oh, the gods grant it!"

As if in answer, there rose a thunderous crash from the battle line. Fresh clouds of grey dust billowed up. A Cretan archer raced back towards Alexander, but a sling shot took him in the head and sent him sprawling, coughing blood. Another, more fortunate, reached the king, eyes jubilant in his dusty face.

"The battering rams are through! They are being withdrawn!"

"Eynalius! Eynalius! Eynalius!"

Alexander raised his sword and chanted the battle paean to the ancient Macedonians' god of war; the sound was taken up by others. Alexander leapt forward like a deer. Telamon was carried forward by the rush, sword slippery in his sweaty palm. He was aware of the ground racing beneath him, clouds of dust stinging his eyes and mouth. A Cretan archer who had taken an arrow in his cheek tried to clutch Alexander's leg but was pushed aside, trampled by the royal party. More bodies lay twisted in grotesque positions beside blood-soaked, severed limbs. They reached the battering rams under their great mantlets. The air was rank with the

270

smell of burning oil. The cheery, blackened faces of the engineers greeted them. Some nursed wounds, others were laying down planks of wood, makeshift bridges. Alexander and his party poured over these into the breach up against the line of armed hoplites waiting to meet them.

Alexander led the attack. The opposing force, a mixture of mercenaries and townspeople, afforded little resistance against the sheer savagery and speed of the Macedonians, who fought shield to shield, sword arms rising and falling like threshers winnowing corn. The Macedonian line held. Eyes glared at Telamon through great plumed helmets, men collapsed, kicked, stabbed, pushed aside. Being in the second line, Telamon could only pray that no one would force their way through. One man did, but he was immediately cut down. The Macedonian phalanx, now strengthened, moved across the rubble six deep: they formed an arc, then a wedge with the king at the apex. Behind them the engineers were busy, pulling away other portions of the wall. A group of Guards detached themselves and raced towards a postern gate. The Milesians defended this in a screech of steel, war cries, shouts and screams of pain.

The line of helmets Telamon had glimpsed when he'd first reached the wall was retreating. They were now into the second part of the city, a market square bounded by temples and civic buildings. The Macedonians' salpinxes rang out, a sign to stop, to consolidate.

Telamon glanced over his shoulder. The walls were at least ten yards behind him; the breach had been widened. Macedonian cavalry were pouring through the postern gate, which had been seized. They thundered into the square, pouring down the streets which led off it. The attack had taken the city by surprise. Telamon recognized Alexander's tactics: if his cavalry moved fast enough, they'd breach the third line of defence, force the gates into the heart of the city and seize the Lion Port.

For a while the Macedonian battle lines jostled and moved backwards and forwards. An order was given to break ranks. Alexander came running back, his face splattered with blood, helmet and cuirass dented. Splashes of red stained his hand and

271

sword arm, but otherwise he and his companions had sustained only minor knocks and bruises. The Guards regiments which had first forced the entry hastily divided into two, retreating to either side of the square. Fresh regiments, preceded by scouts, Agrianian footmen, lightly armed peltists and archers, poured across the square into the side streets where the Milesians and Memnon's mercenaries were busily throwing up makeshift barricades.

Telamon went across to a horse trough, took off his helmet and washed his face. He stared round: here and there fires had started, belching clouds of black smoke as houses burnt. The screams from the streets and main avenue were heart-rending. Alexander stood in the market square, surrounded by officers and advisers. A general advance was ordered. More Macedonian troops were pouring through the main gates, which had been cleared and opened. Messengers came hastening back. Telamon went across. Alexander, squatting on steps leading up to a temple, was wiping his face with a wet rag, issuing orders to different units.

"Telamon, I have no further need of you. You are well?"

The king got to his feet as Hephaestion pushed through with a wineskin. Alexander lifted this and squeezed a mouthful between his lips.

"We have seized the gates of the city!" an officer shouted. "The port is ours!"

"Alexander, look!"

Hephaestion grabbed the king's arm and pulled him round. From a side street came a white-bearded man, in one hand a garland, in the other a branch of palm leaves. He was escorted on either side by two other dignitaries. The Guards officer who led them forced them to kneel at Alexander's feet.

"City elders," the officer remarked. "Now we're in, they want to give us the city."

Alexander threw the wineskin to Hephaestion, grabbed the palm branch and garland of flowers from the old man's hand, tossed them to the ground and stamped on them. The envoy's face turned grey with terror: white spittle stained the corners of his mouth. He stretched out his hands.

"My lord, we beg for mercy. The Greek mercenaries have

withdrawn. All that is left to resist your might are civilians, men, women and children."

"Memnon!" Alexander barked. "Where's Memnon?"

"He left with the Persian fleet. He said the chances for the city were poor. Your ships block the harbour, the Persians ran short of food and water."

"I know that," Alexander taunted. He paused at a hideous scream from a nearby house.

"Mercy, please!" the envoy repeated. "Will Alexander of Macedon do what Persia once did? Raze us to the ground?"

Again the scream.

"Hephaestion!" The king pointed across the marketplace in the direction of a house where soldiers were breaking down the door. "Tell those lads to withdraw! Ptolemy, Amyntas, have trumpeters and camp marshals ride through the streets! Issue a proclamation of peace! Miletus is now ours. Its inhabitants are my subjects. Martial law is to be imposed. No more plundering, pillaging, raping or killing, on pain of death!"

His commanders hurried off. Alexander picked up the wineskin, which Hephaestion had left on the ground. He helped the dignitaries to their feet. They grew voluble in their thanks and praise.

"You should have opened your gates immediately," the king declared. "Now go back to your homes, no one will hurt you."

Already the sound of fighting was dying. The bray of trumpets cut across it, then the shouts of officers and marshals as the king's terms were publicized. A messenger ran up, a Cretan archer, face blackened, arms red with blood to the elbows, tunic torn. He had pillaged a valuable shield showing the Bull of Minos on a silver medallion in the centre.

"Message from General Parmenio, sir." The Cretan squinted one eye at the king. "The city is now ours. Of the Persian fleet there's no sign." The Cretan's face widened in a black-toothed smile. "The mercenaries have broken and fled. Most of them floated out on their shields to rocky islets in the harbour. Parmenio has ordered Admiral Nicanor to send warships against them, with ladders slashed to the prows."

273

The king took the shield from the Cretan. "Where did you find this, soldier?"

"Just lying in the street, sir."

"You're a liar!" Alexander tossed it back. "But it's yours. Take a message to General Parmenio. Tell him to offer the mercenaries amnesty provided they take an oath of loyalty to me and enter my service."

"But, after the Granicus –" the Cretan spluttered.

"That was a mistake," Alexander retorted. "There'll be no more Greeks killing Greeks. Give my message to General Parmenio. Tell him to drink a cup of wine."

The archer turned away.

"Oh, and by the way" – the king called him back – "tell Parmenio I was right about the eagle! He'll know what I mean."

Chapter 13

"Alexander had also several encounters with Darius's lieutenants whom he conquered, not so much by his arms, as by the terror of his name."

Marcus Junianus Justianus:
Universal History Book XI, Chapter 6

"**I** mprobable possibilities are always preferred to probable impossibilities." Alexander paused and turned, goblet in hand. "Do you remember that, Telamon? One of Aristotle's lectures at Mieza?"

"I remember it," the physician replied. "I didn't understand what he meant then, and I still don't. Nor do I understand why you're quoting it now, except it makes you sound intelligent."

"But there's no one here to impress." Alexander gestured round the empty Temple of Apollo. "Only the fading sunlight through the windows" – he gestured behind him – "a statue of Apollo the Hunter and these lonely pillars. Look at them, Telamon, they're in the Egyptian style with acanthus leaves at the top and bottom. It's a dark place, isn't it? One of the oldest temples in the city, or so they say." Alexander's voice echoed through the cavernous sanctuary.

"It's a gloomy place," Telamon agreed. "All temples are gloomy." He stared around this small shrine to Apollo which stood on the main avenue leading down to the Lion Port. "Why did you quote Aristotle?"

Alexander sipped from his wine and swayed drunkenly. He was dressed in a golden tunic edged with purple, a red mantle slung casually over his shoulders. He still wore his greaves and marching sandals, though he had washed and shaved and his barber had dressed his hair.

"Because they thought it was impossible for me to take Miletus and we have! The Persian fleet has gone. The mercenaries have surrendered. The day is done. Darkness falls. Now for the night," Alexander continued, quoting from the *Iliad*. "We shall keep watch on ourselves, and tomorrow early, before dawn manifests itself, we shall arm ourselves and rouse the spiteful God of War." He strolled towards Telamon, a slightly tipsy walk. "They said I couldn't do it, Telamon, and I did!" he whispered. "I beat off the Persian fleet without sending one ship out to sea. I took a three-walled city." Alexander sipped from his goblet.

Telamon stared at the shadows around them.

"Are they all outside?" Alexander asked sharply.

"They are," the physician replied. "And, Alexander, you're not as drunk as you pretend. You can fool them . . ."

"But I can't fool you?"

"Only for a while."

Alexander spread his hands. "Well, you asked for this audience. Why?"

"I'll begin with your quotation from Aristotle and the difference between" – Telamon chose his words carefully – "improbable possibilities and probable impossibilities."

"Oh dear!" Alexander sat at the base of a pillar. "Come and sit on the floor with me, Telamon, like we used to do when we were boys. What's on your mind?"

"Cassandra and I have been busy with the wounded."

"Are there many?"

"We lost about two hundred men, killed. We have fifty wounded who will die and about a hundred who will walk again."

"And you have used your magic?" Alexander teased.

"I did what I could. I was very interested in the arrow wounds."

Alexander's head went to one side.

"Do you know, sire" – Telamon wetted his lips – "I went among the wounded. I never came across one soldier who was fortunate enough to be hit by an arrow whose barb somehow snapped off so only the blunt shaft struck his chest."

"Really?"

"Truly," Telamon replied. "Some of the Cretan archers were badly burnt. I talked to their commander about shafts, arrowheads and the force of a bow. I asked had he ever heard of a man being struck by an arrow whose barb, being weakened, snaps at the moment of impact and causes no wound."

"And?"

"He laughed at me, sire. Said it was impossible, until he recalled something and became all subdued."

Alexander tapped his foot against the paved floor. Telamon stared into the aisle: on the far wall someone had painted Apollo the Hunter with bow stretched, arrow notched. "That's appropriate," he remarked, pointing it out.

Alexander smiled at him. "Have you deciphered that message? The confession of the madman who burnt my Temple of Artemis?"

"Oh yes." Telamon opened his wallet and drew out a piece of parchment. "It contains an anagram. The original Greek reads:

"Σγω σμοδω, εγω ειμω, πιαφαλλαδ, αλφα και ομεγα παντων. Ο του α θανυτου παιδος και δ υιος θεου"

which can be translated: "I am, alternately, the Beginning and the End of all things, the child of the Immortal and the son of God". However, if you arrange certain letters in the same message, it may read:

"Σγω ειμιν Αλεξανδροδ, όυιοδ θεου, όπαιδοδ φιλιπου και Ολγπιαε"

which can be translated: "I am Alexander, the son of God, the child of Philip and Olympias".' Telamon shrugged. "Of course that could be dismissed as trickery, but it's the best . . ."

"No, no," Alexander interrupted, face bright with excitement. "I will claim the madman burnt the temple but, in his own way,

277

with what the priests call the Divine Madness, recognized his real reason for burning it was that Artemis had left to attend my God-given birth – a pretty play on words, but it'll suffice. Yes, yes, that will do to shut the arrogant mouths of these Ephesians. More importantly, you know who the Centaur is, don't you?" Alexander's head came up. "That's why you wanted to see me. Why Peleus, Agis and Meleager are waiting outside with my officers. So, all this business about archers' arrows?"

"Oh, don't play the innocent!" Telamon snapped. "The day you left the palace to walk Apelles home, why wasn't Hephaestion there? He's your shadow."

"He was busy elsewhere." Alexander's face had a brazen look. He narrowed red-rimmed eyes and clicked his tongue.

"That's right," Telamon agreed. "Try and imitate your mother, but it doesn't frighten me. Alexander, I shall tell you what happened. Late that afternoon you took me into your quarters. You left me with a map while you went and changed. I wandered round your chamber. I noticed a horn bow and a quiver of arrows. They were there because you and Hephaestion were planning something. You wanted to impress the Ephesians, prove that you were under the special protection of Artemis. You felt insulted at their rejection of your offer to refurbish the temple. You remembered the hidden sneers when you mentioned the story of how the Goddess had attended your birth."

"Their lack of generosity," Alexander replied slowly, "did cut me to the heart."

"So you and Hephaestion arranged a little pantomime to convince them. On that particular afternoon you went out. No Cleitus guarded you, even though an assassin lurked in Ephesus. You were determined to seek your own justice, to show those arrogant Ephesians a thing or two. Hephaestion was your accomplice. He left the palace just before you did and hid in the trees, armed with a bow and two arrows. The first he loosed over your head – that always puzzled me. Why should a careful assassin miss such an easy target on a clear summer afternoon? He then shot his second arrow, but this was different, its arrowhead had been removed. You were holding it in your hand, and beneath your tunic you wore a thick leather vest. I noticed that, after you'd been struck, you made no attempt to examine the skin beneath it."

Alexander, head down, stared into his wine cup.

"Hephaestion looses his arrow, the blunted shaft hits you in the chest. It causes no wound. You fall to the ground and, as you do so, place the arrowhead nearby, as if it had snapped off. Artemis had come between you and the death-bearing shaft, protecting you with her shield."

Alexander's shoulders were shaking: he glanced up, tears of laughter in his eyes.

"It's a lovely story," he whispered. "Oh, Telamon, you're far too sharp for your own good. Can't I have my little fable? Can't I play my little games?"

"Sire, if you want to be the thunderbolt of Zeus, have Artemis as your grandmother and Apollo as your second cousin, and that makes you happy, then it makes me happy. I would only become concerned if you truly believed it." He paused. "That you were saved by Artemis was a probable impossibility: trickery, on the other hand, however improbable, was still possible . . ."

Alexander, still shaking with laughter, wiped the tears from his cheeks.

"Clever, wasn't it?"

"It could have been very stupid. If Hephaestion had missed? If the blunted shaft had hit you in the eye?"

"He's a master bowman," Alexander retorted, getting to his feet. "We didn't harm anyone. The Ephesians love me for it and the story will be told for time immemorial."

"If you had taken me into your confidence," Telamon also got up, "I would have been able to unmask the Centaur earlier. Only this afternoon, as I walked among the wounded, did I realize the trick you had staged. Alexander, if you weren't a soldier or a general, you could have won the plaudits of all Greece as an actor."

"I must remember that." He tapped Telamon gently on the cheek. "If we lose the next battle, you, I, Hephaestion, and the Red Hair with the big mouth should start our own acting troupe and wander the cities of Greece. Well, I'm hungry, I wish to celebrate. They're waiting outside, aren't they? Let's have the actors in. Apollo's temple is a good stage. Let's face the truth and be done with it. Oh, Telamon!"

The physician turned at the door.

"Just Hephaestion. Tell him to come armed and have three guards standing outside the door."

Telamon pulled back the bolts and opened the temple door. The king's companions stood on the porch. Agis, Peleus and Meleager were sitting on the top step, staring out across the empty market square. Telamon called Hephaestion over and whispered instructions. A short while later the king's companion brought in the three Ephesians.

Alexander welcomed them and accepted their congratulations. He sat on the floor, his back to a pillar, still cradling the wine cup. He gestured that they sit before him. Hephaestion, dressed in his battle armour, quietly withdrew his sword and stood behind the Ephesians. Telamon sat on Alexander's right.

"Why are we here?" Agis began. "My lord, you have won a great victory, but our departure from Ephesus was summary and hasty: we were kidnapped, abducted . . ."

"Shut up!" Telamon interrupted. Agis's swarthy face flushed with anger.

"You were brought here," Telamon continued, "because the king could not trust you. He had good cause to keep his plan secret, especially from you, Agis."

The Democrat would have sprung to his feet, but Hephaestion pressed him gently on the shoulder.

"What is this?" Peleus had lost his smug arrogance: his cruel eyes were watchful, like some wild cat trapped in a corner.

"What is this?" Telamon mimicked. "Why, sir" – he gestured at Agis – "he is the Centaur, the assassin, the Persian spy."

"This is ridiculous!"

Again Agis would have leapt to his feet but Hephaestion, a look of confusion in his eyes, pressed the flat of his sword against the Democrat's face. Alexander drained his cup noisily and threw it into the darkness where it clattered and clanged.

"My Lord King, this is arrant nonsense!" Agis spluttered. Peleus sat stunned, but Meleager had a knowing look in his eyes. Telamon wondered if he'd always suspected the truth.

"What proof?" Agis demanded. "What evidence? If I am guilty then put me on trial!"

"You are on trial," Telamon retorted. "Do you not know the Macedonian law? The king hears cases and his word is a just verdict."

"That's true," Alexander agreed, studying Agis as he would an opponent on the drill ground, as if seeing him for the first time. "My father Philip once tried two brigands. As usual, he was drunk. He sent one Greek brigand to run from Macedon and the other to chase him."

Alexander laughed. The three Ephesians just stared back.

"So, Agis, you will listen. If I believe the case goes against you, I shall crucify you outside the Peacock Gate of Ephesus."

"What evidence?"

"Aristotle claimed," Telamon replied, "truth has a beginning, a middle and an end: all three must co-exist in a truth. Your father, Agis, was Ephesian, an Ionian Greek, but your mother was Persian. I have seen the blood book in the archives at the Temple of Artemis. Your father divorced your mother just after your birth, and married Mcleager's. Your mother later committed suicide, hanged herself from the rafters of her own house."

Agis's face remained composed.

"It's a long-forgotten fact," Telamon continued, "but it explains your hatred for your father, for your half-brother and for anything Greek. You were six; you spent a great deal of your childhood outside Ephesus with your mother's kinsfolk. You are fluent in Persian, perhaps more Persian than the Persians themselves. Your father later brought you back to Ephesus. According to the temple books, you began to pay sacrifice to Artemis at the age of eight or nine. By then you had learnt to mask your hatred. You became a successful merchant and, like your half-brother here, entered the politics of the city. The Persian court noted your rise to power. The Lord Mithra is always on the lookout for men who might further Persia's cause, particularly in the west. The court of Macedon was preparing for war, uttering threats that, one day, the Macedonian king would bring fire and sword to the Persian territories." Telamon stared at Meleager. "You must have known some of this?"

"I did," the Oligarch replied slowly. "But, as you say, Agis wore a mask. He left my father's household and returned years later. My father felt regrets . . ."

"My father felt nothing!" Agis interrupted. "No guilt at driving his legitimate wife to suicide and rejecting his own flesh and blood for so many years!"

"And you hated him so much," Meleager retorted, "you kept it well hidden. Our father fell ill. The physicians say he died of an infection, a fever. Did you have a hand in it?"

Agis glanced at Telamon. "My father received his just desserts, as I will, as you all shall! You said, physician, that truth has a beginning, a middle and an end?"

"So it does. Your father died, the rancour between you and your half-brother became public knowledge. The past was forgotten. People considered it political, the ever-continuing war in the councils of Ephesus. You, Agis, are two people: the public face and the private man. Your business enterprises prospered, and why shouldn't they, financed by Persian gold and silver, given information about which commodities were in short demand, which harvests were plentiful? In return, your value to the Persian court increased by the year. You proved to be more than just a source of information, but their principal spy in Ephesus, more important than its governor. You became wealthy and rose high in the ranks of the Democrats until you were their leader. A ruthless man, you dominated the likes of Peleus, Dion and Hesiod while secretly carrying out the instructions of your masters in Persepolis."

"Divide and rule," Meleager broke in.

"Yes," Telamon agreed. "Divide and rule. Time and again Demades and the Oligarchs would attempt a reconciliation, try to bring about a lasting peace. Time and again it was frustrated."

"That's true." Peleus had recovered his wits. "You, Agis, were always at the forefront of our party for accepting such pleas for peace."

282

"But it never happened," Telamon continued. "Agis stirred up the blood feud through secret assassination, to keep the fire burning and the hatred bubbling. An Oligarch was killed, a Democrat assassinated. In truth, it wasn't one party waging war against the other, only Agis carrying out his master's instructions, venting his hate against a city he despised."

"But how?" Meleager asked. "Demades believed there was a traitor on our councils but not theirs."

"Oh, there was," Telamon replied. "Agis studied the history of Ephesus. He learnt about the Centaurs, the secret society of assassins which thrived when he was a youth. He took their title, inherited their bloody mantle, though he had to be careful. The whereabouts of a Democrat politician, someone he had marked down for death, was easy, but how could he decide which Oligarch to strike? More importantly, how could he learn what discussions were taking place among the Oligarchs of Ephesus?"

Telamon paused and glanced sideways at Alexander: he was sitting, eyes closed, head to one side, listening intently.

"The Centaur is a hybrid creature," Telamon explained, "two in one: half-man, half-horse. Agis needed a helper. Someone he could rely on among the Oligarchs. Like a wolf stalking a sheepfold, he searched for a weakness and found it. What better person than Socrates, servant to Demades, leader of the Oligarchs?"

"Impossible!" Agis scoffed.

"I don't think so." Meleager spoke up. "Socrates had ideas above his station: a man who liked to dabble in politics."

"From the little I know of Socrates," Telamon declared, "he was a man with a weakness for perfumed flesh. When his master tried to win the favour of the courtesan Arella, Socrates was truly smitten."

"Did he betray us for her?" Meleager asked.

"The betrayal took place much earlier. Socrates liked the gold and silver to finance his amorous pursuits: he relished power, and being a traitor gave him power among these influential citizens, the Oligarchs who looked down on him. In truth, the Centaur was two people: Agis the master, Socrates the servant."

"Would Socrates know Agis's identity?" Peleus asked.

Telamon shook his head. "You're secretive, Agis. You would

meet Socrates in disguise, in the shadows. You would threaten and cajole, bribe and corrupt. Which Oligarch should be marked down? Where would he be vulnerable? Who would carry out the murder? What were Demades and the rest discussing?" Telamon pointed into a darkened aisle. "The meetings would take place well away from the light. Socrates would never glimpse his true master. I suspect each wore a medallion, a sign of mutual recognition. At such meetings, mischief was planned."

"That's right," Peleus agreed. "Hesiod always used to marvel at how much Agis knew about the Oligarchs' plans. Even when Alexander marched on Ephesus, Agis knew which Oligarch was hiding where, who had arms."

"I am sure he did." Telamon held Agis's gaze. "You manipulated and manoeuvred, slithering like a snake through the bloody politics of Ephesus, stirring up one side against the other, leaving the Persians in control. You must have enjoyed the game. You played so many roles: the wily Democrat, the powerful opponent of the Oligarchs, the Greek who looked for liberation and the restoration of liberties. Secretly, you were the Persian, faithful to his masters, exacting vengeance for all the hurt and humiliation heaped on your mother and her son. Time passed. Macedon threatened. Parmenio came and left. You intensified your bloody work. You were well known to the Persian Governor. He'd be under strict instruction from Lord Mithra to give you every aid and comfort. You would know all the secret entrances into the palace, the dark galleries and corners where the Governor and you could meet. In truth, not even he knew your real identity. Other times, to confuse him, you would use the Temple of Hercules. Socrates would be your messenger and you both waged a savage war. Eventually the news of our victory at Granicus swept through Ephesus." Telamon stared down at the statue of Apollo. "I wonder if you knew before anyone else? What an opportunity to continue the feud. To eliminate opponents. Entire families were marked down for death. You and your cronies massacred your opponents. Only the gods know how many years will pass before the wounds heal."

"Then I arrived," Alexander intervened harshly. "I brought your blood-letting to an end."

"Macedon was a new opponent," Telamon said. "The Oligarchs were weakened, destroyed as a political party. However, your masters in Persepolis had more work for you."

Telamon started as the door was flung open. Aristander, looking aggrieved, came bustling in.

"Stay out!" Alexander barked, spots of anger high on his cheeks. "This does not concern you, magician!"

Aristander flapped his hands. Alexander made to rise threateningly, and he fled back through the door.

"Demades and the leaders of the Oligarchs," Telamon continued, "took refuge in the Temple of Hercules. Alexander promised them their lives and safety. To you it was a once-in-a-lifetime opportunity: to kill Demades and the other Oligarch leaders as well as bringing Macedon's promise into disrepute, to make our king a mockery and his word appear hollow. Above all, it was time for you to bid farewell to Socrates. If there was no party of Oligarchs, no Persians, what did you need of him? Socrates was a venal man. He might become dangerous. You decide to sweep the board with one throw."

"Arella?" Meleager broke in.

"What about her?" Peleus snarled.

"Demades, before he fled," Meleager explained, "was growing very concerned about his servant. Socrates was sly, cunning. Demades probably trusted him until he died. Yet, as I said, he was concerned."

"Explain," Telamon asked.

"Demades claimed Socrates had become distracted over something. Since the massacre in the Temple of Hercules, I have listened to the gossip, and your questions . . ."

"You are correct," Telamon intervened. "Demades had tried to win Arella's favour, only to be rebuffed. He had used his servant as his envoy. Socrates, too, became infatuated with her: that was his distraction. In the normal course of events Arella would never have bestowed her favours on a mere servant. Socrates raised the matter with his true master and the plot was formed. You, Agis" – Telamon pointed at the Democrat, who gazed stonily back – "cajoled, bribed and threatened Arella."

"How?" The question was impudent.

"Oh, in disguise, at the dead of night. Arella agreed to bestow her favours on Socrates. In turn, Socrates would carry out your orders for the bloody massacre at the Temple of Hercules."

"Ridiculous!" Peleus snapped.

"No, no, it isn't." Alexander shook his head, rubbing his hands together. "Listen to my physician. He has studied all the symptoms and he'll tell you the cause."

"I'll be brief," Telamon assured them. "Arella was greedy for power, wealth and influence. Agis promised these."

"But Arella didn't know," Meleager asked, "the real price Socrates had to pay for her favours?"

"No. Agis learnt from Socrates about Demades's plan to come out of hiding and seek sanctuary. The plot was laid then: Socrates was bribed, but would ask for proof. Agis turned to Arella, who was compelled to accept and secretly visited the temple to offer Socrates reassurance. She was seen near the Temple of Hercules."

"And the murders?"

Telamon pithily described the same conclusions he had given the king and Cassandra. That Socrates had been secretly armed: his use of the sleeping powders, the murders, and how he believed he would escape through the rear door, claiming others had slipped in. How his own death by poisoning had only deepened the mystery.

"Have you proof of this?" Agis demanded: he swallowed quickly, his neck coated in perspiration.

"We found the fragments: a piece of bronze, the blackened staff, scraps of twisted leather. Socrates buried them deep in the charcoal. I have no real evidence, not for your handiwork there, but later on . . ."

Telamon paused. From beyond the doorway he could hear Aristander's voice, still screeching protests.

"Ignore him," Alexander whispered. "His pride is being hurt. He's got other tasks." He glanced at Telamon. "Hunting down the wealth Memnon and his party left in Miletus."

Telamon made himself more comfortable. "You had further work to do, Agis. Arella's mouth had to be closed. You must have been wary lest she had left papers, evidence of what had been

286

planned. She had to die, her house burnt to cinders. Like any courtesan, Arella would spend the afternoon preparing herself for some favoured client: bathing in the pool, sleeping, painting her face, perfuming her body. On the day she died, you made your presence felt. You knocked at the gate to her house: the porter peered through the grille and saw Agis, now the most important citizen in Ephesus. How could he refuse admittance? He opened the gate and you stepped through. The man turned to push back the bolts. You struck him once, with a club similar to the one Socrates used. You then undid the bolts and left the door off the latch, just in case someone else arrived and raised the alarm on receiving no answer. Once inside, you probably disguised yourself and hastened across the garden. Arella and her maid were killed, the house soaked in oil. You were about to fire it and leave when Hesiod arrived."

"I know why." Peleus spoke up. "Hesiod was growing curious. He'd always believed a spy among the Oligarchs was giving us information. He'd also heard about Arella being seen near the Temple of Hercules. She was noted for her beauty," he added contemptuously, "and her greed. Hesiod would be curious to know why she went there."

"And?" Telamon asked.

"Hesiod was as furtive as a rat," Peleus explained. "Arella bestowed her favours on the rich and powerful, which included the Persian Governor and his principal scribe Rabinus, captured in her house. Hesiod wanted to be popular, win favour with the Macedonians. Arella might be a rich source of information, of tittle-tattle and gossip, open to threats, cajolery or bribery."

"True," Telamon agreed. "But Hesiod was killed and the house torched. You, Agis, made your escape."

"But I was visiting Dion's house that day. Ask his wife, his servants."

"Were you?" Telamon replied. "As you left Arella's house you saw your colleague, the lawyer, come hurrying across the grounds. He was on the same errand as Hesiod. He wanted to question Arella. He didn't see you, and so you seized the opportunity."

"What opportunity?"

"You presented yourself at Dion's house. You must have known Aristander would ask where you all were the afternoon Arella was killed. It would appear that Agis, the busy leader, was visiting one of his colleagues. No one ever asked you the purpose of the visit, or where you had been before. You used Dion then, as you did later."

"I did all this on my own?"

"Why not? You are Agis, the chief magistrate. You enjoy the favour of the king. You can go where you wish. I'm sure there is some tavern or house outside the city where messages from your masters in Persepolis could be left. After Arella's murder, you returned to other business. During the Persian rule you often visited the Governor's palace at Ephesus. You would know all about the secret passageways, how the wasps built their nests in the cellars or eaves. Quite a nuisance, as was our imprisonment of Rabinus. He really should have fled. He had been caught at Arella's house and would have to be silenced. You came to the palace as the king's guest. You have a royal pass. It would be easy for you to conceal a club, to find that guardsman sleeping in the deserted portico, kill him and hide his body. Your heart was set on mischief and malice, on causing as much confusion and chaos as possible. You secretly encouraged Demades's widow to strike at the king, but warned Alexander about what might happen."

"As you are paid to by me," Alexander broke in. "You, like the rest, received my gold. You were my spy here, along with other Democrats. You were trusted . . ."

"You used that trust," Telamon explained, "to rouse Demades's widow and, at the same time, portray yourself as the saviour of the king. During the chaos at that banquet, you slipped down to the cellars beneath the kitchen. The wasps' nests were prepared. You simply pushed them through the gap at the bottom of the kitchen wall, shattering them with your club, your own hands and face being protected, then you fled. Those wasps rose in swarms, agitated, and struck at the innocents in the kitchen. More deaths occurred, more shame for our king. You visited Rabinus's cell, slipping through the shadows: it would take no more than a few heartbeats to empty a skin of oil through the grille and throw in a lighted rag. Rabinus is trapped. He dies, silenced for ever. Anything he may know about the Centaur, about the Lord Mithra's spy in Ephesus, dies with him."

"But he drew something on the wall." Alexander spoke up. "Aristander thought it was a triangle, or a capital 'D' for Dion."

"Perhaps he did," Telamon replied. "Or was he drawing an 'A' for Agis? Or, knowing what a clever liar you are, had you given the Governor Dion's name as the Centaur to create a diversion? Is that what Rabinus thought in his death throes? A good night's work, eh, Agis? The king almost killed. One of his soldiers executed. Chaos among the kitchen servants and Rabinus silenced."

"It could have been Dion," Agis retorted, voice measured, eyes serene, "Meleager or Peleus."

"That's what you wanted me to think. Peleus, no." Telamon shook his head. "Meleager perhaps: that's why he was not marked down for destruction during the massacres. He could be portrayed as a man not to be trusted, with a burning sense of grievance. You and I know Aristander suspected Dion, so you struck again. Dion was becoming agitated. Perhaps he entertained his own suspicions. On the night he died you visited him. You would talk, lull him into a sense of security. You came stealthily by night to discuss secret matters. Perhaps Dion was flattered. He'd offer some wine. You poured it, but mixed in the same potion your other victims had drunk in the Temple of Hercules. The conversation continued. You were safe if anyone came in, you could slip away. Dion fell asleep. You put the noose about his neck and tied the end of the rope around a hook in the beam. Dion, drugged, couldn't resist. He was choked to death. You remove your wine cup, toss what's left in Dion's out of the window, clean it and put it back. The door was locked and bolted. You left through the window . . ."

"But the shutters were barred!" Peleus broke in. "Everyone was talking about that."

"Oh, that's easy enough to arrange," Telamon replied. "The shutters are fastened by leather hinges, clasped to the lintel by strong bronze studs. Before he left, Agis closed one shutter, bringing the bar down. He then removed the other shutter, plucking out the brass studs on one side: it would hang down, the two boards being held together by the wooden bar. Agis climbed through the window and

289

swung the entire shutter back into position, pushing in the brass stud so it looked exactly like the other; closed and barred. This would require some force, but the chamberlain did say Dion's wife was roused by a knocking. Of course, it helped Agis, and he must have known this, that the door to Dion's writing chamber was sturdy, bolted and locked. So the following morning, the servants did what anyone would do: they removed the shutters to break into the room. Any trace of Agis's handiwork, footprints or signs that one of the shutters had been disturbed, was lost. Dion also appeared to have been involved in the massacre at the Temple of Hercules. Perhaps he did make some drawings as he speculated on the mystery. Or Agis could have left them, or Dion could have drawn them up at Agis's request. Whatever, the finger of suspicion points at Dion, but now he's dead, apparently a suicide."

"I suspected one of you was a spy." Alexander got to his feet. He walked to the door and pulled across a bolt. He came back, measuring his footsteps along the paved floor. "That's why I plucked you from Ephesus and brought you to Miletus; lest any of you pass information either to this city or to your Persian master." He sat down.

"But my Lord King" – Agis spread his hands – "where is the proof of this? I was with you that day the assassin loosed two shafts at you and the Goddess protected you."

"We now know who loosed those shafts," Telamon replied.

Agis lowered his hands.

"True," Telamon admitted, "it did confuse me for a while. As for proof, I shall give you my proof. First, we know the massacre at the Temple of Hercules was the work of the Centaur, yet all the men there died. However, the murders continued: there had to be two assassins. Secondly, Meleager was in hiding. He might be suspect, but at that time he didn't have the strength, the resources, to plan and plot such a massacre. Thirdly, you are of Persian birth, powerful and rich. You have the means as well as the strength to carry out such tasks."

"Is this evidence?" Agis scoffed.

"Fourthly," Telamon continued, "you made a mistake. You talked of Arella lying like some dead fish on the edge of her pool.

How did you know she was killed there? Her corpse was found burnt in her house. You allegedly never visited her, either before or after her death, and the details of her murder were not publicized."

"That's true," Meleager declared. "I recall those words."

"Finally, we come to Dion. Here, Agis, catch!"

Telamon drew a piece of rope from beneath his mantle and threw it across. Agis was surprised, but he caught it.

"You are left-handed. Of all your colleagues, only you are left-handed."

"And?" Agis asked, surprised.

"Pass me the rope back." Agis did so. "Dion was right-handed." Telamon wrapped the rope round his neck. "If I were fastening a noose, because I am right-handed, the knot would go against my left ear. If I were left-handed, it would go beneath my right. Dion was right-handed, but the noose was beneath his right ear."

"Perhaps he was drunk!" If Hephaestion had not been standing behind him, Agis would have jumped to his feet. Telamon was aware of how cold and dark the temple was growing.

"We have other proof." Telamon steeled himself for the lie. "On the night Dion was murdered you were seen near his house."

"That's impossible! It was . . ." Agis closed his eyes.

"Why is it impossible?" Telamon asked. "Is it because you were in disguise? Or the night was pitch black? Did you also know my servant Cassandra saw you wandering the palace, the night of the banquet, by yourself?"

"How could she?"

"Or that Basileia, Queen of the Moabites, possesses evidence you visited Arella the day she died?"

"These are all lies," Agis spluttered, "not evidence."

"You haven't denied the allegations."

"I do deny them."

"Did you know that you were all plucked from Ephesus," Telamon continued matter-of-factly, "so your houses could be searched? Your families interrogated?"

"Not Rhoda!" Agis was like a man stricken, face pale and sweat-soaked.

"Oh yes, Rhoda," Alexander broke in. "She'll have to be

questioned. Everything you own, Agis, will be sifted and winnowed. Every chamber, every coffer, every chest. When we have the proof, I will apply the law of Persia. Not only you will die on the cross, but every single member of your family."

Agis's head went down.

"How long will it take?" Alexander continued. "Days? Weeks? Months? But we'll find more evidence, more proof. You will stay here, Agis, heavy with chains. Perhaps we'll bring your daughter to visit you? To make her beg you to tell the truth?"

Agis's head came up, tears in his eyes.

"I was born, I am" — he began softly — "of Persian birth. I hated my father. I hated Ephesus and everything within it. My mother hanged herself so I decided to take retribution, to exact my own vengeance. It is as you say. I am the servant of the Lord Mithra. I took your gold, Macedonian, but I accepted the Lord Mithra's favour and protection. As I grew older and more powerful, my storehouses grew and my treasure chests filled to the brim. I stirred up murder. Oh," he whispered, "it was so good to watch the great ones of Ephesus fall by the sword and poison! The blood feud became common. Of course," he laughed sharply, "like everything, it grew difficult. I rose to be leader of the Democrats. Demades sent out peace-feelers, and that's how I met Socrates, a man with a secret life, a hunger for perfumed flesh and the wherewithal to buy it. He fell like a ripe apple into my hands. I always met him secretly in a darkened place, my face and voice disguised by a mask. We each wore the emblem of the Centaur, a wasp on a chain. I promised Socrates gold by the cup. At first he was reluctant, but it became so easy and he was caught."

"Did he suspect your identity?"

Agis gnawed at his lower lip. "I confused him over my true identity: it may have been a case of Democrat against Oligarch, Democrat against Democrat, or Oligarch against Oligarch: after all there was little love lost within each party. Socrates told me what he knew. He helped me single out individuals marked down for death: who would be where at certain times."

"Did you commit the murders?" Telamon demanded.

292

"At first, yes. All my handiwork, physician. Socrates eventually played his part."

"And Persia?"

"The Lord Mithra was delighted: Greek against Greek, leaving his governor free to rule and administer the city. The Persians financed me with gold and silver, intimated which commodities to invest in, which trading ventures would be profitable. I was a son to Lord Mithra: only he knew my name. Publicly I played the hero of the Democrats and commoners of Ephesus." Agis cleared his throat. "I protected my public reputation as Persia's enemy, as did Lord Mithra, with bungled accidents and attempts to assassinate me. Socrates also murdered. He liked it. A servant of the nobles, he rejoiced at having their blood on his hands. I remembered my history and recalled the stories about the Centaurs, so I took their name . . ."

"And continued to wreak bloody havoc?"

"Of course." Agis had a strange, secretive look in his eyes. "Parmenio came and went, then the Macedonians returned. The news of your victory at the Granicus surprised everyone: it was time for a change. Socrates told me that Demades was becoming suspicious about a traitor in his ranks. Little, fat Hesiod was also becoming curious. The Lord Mithra was quite clear: Ephesus would fall into Alexander's hands but I was to cause as much chaos as possible. And that was easy," he added with a touch of sadness. "The Oligarchs were marked down for destruction. I sent secret warnings to Meleager, not because of any blood tie, but to create suspicion. Demades and his party fled to the Temple of Hercules. I saw my opportunity to continue the blood feud, to sustain it even under Macedonian rule. Above all, I could demonstrate that Alexander's word meant nothing. Demades had to die, he was suspicious, and I was tiring of Socrates, who was becoming more importunate by the day. When his master became infatuated with Arella, so did Socrates. You are correct, physician, I exploited that. If Arella had asked, Socrates would have plucked the moon from the sky for her. She was a wilful, greedy bitch. I bribed and threatened her to respond." He paused. "I knew a great deal about Arella: she did not want to be marked down as a Persian sympathizer. Just after Demades and his party fled to the temple, I gave Socrates instructions. I told him that Arella would smuggle small items in."

"And Socrates agreed?"

"Of course. Arella had promised him her favours. I swore she would even visit him in the temple to guarantee my word. Socrates was committed. I told him that one afternoon, he must look for a given sign and, that same night, commit the murders. He was also given strict instructions. He was to use the bronze claw once everything was ready. The plan was to open the rear door of the temple, to create the impression that it had been entered and all those within had been brutally attacked: Socrates had been fortunate enough to escape with a few scratches and raise the alarm. The fool never suspected."

"The poison?" Telamon asked.

"It worked quickly." Agis stared into the darkness. "Little more than a few heartbeats, certainly within the hour. Even if Socrates had managed to open the door, he would have died later. The potion was noxious, a mixture of poisonous plants mingled with crushed almonds, a deadly concoction. You can buy whatever poison you want in Ephesus."

"So, instead of Socrates escaping," Alexander put in sharply, "you created a most mysterious murder?"

"Yes, better than I ever thought."

"And the silver vase?" Telamon asked. "Why did you tell him to take that down?"

"I wanted to make sure it contained nothing. Socrates, and sometimes myself, would visit the Temple of Hercules in disguise to receive messages or payment from the Persian governor. The priest became suspicious about Rabinus's visits. Socrates told me he had learnt that from Demades."

"Ah, I see." Telamon moved restlessly. "So that's why the priest had to die and the vase be inspected. He wouldn't be the first temple guardian to keep precious manuscripts within some sacred vase or urn."

"Socrates was told to burn everything inside, though I suspect,"

Agis added, "it was empty. The priest was marked down, he was meddling and nosy."

"Did you want Demades to go to the temple?"

"Yes," Agis replied.

"So," Alexander said, "the massacres began: some Oligarchs were rounded up, but you used Socrates to urge Demades and the rest to go into sanctuary at the temple. Socrates, being a mere servant, would be safe on the streets, scurrying here and there with messages to Demades's colleagues. Once they were there, they were trapped, like hens in a coop."

Agis stared unblinking at the king.

"And Arella the courtesan?" Telamon asked.

"Ah well." Agis pulled a face. "She knew too much. Rabinus had babbled to her. So I went to her house and killed her as you described. Hesiod also arrived. He had to die: with his snooping eyes and prying ways, he couldn't be trusted. Curiosity can be a dangerous vice."

"And the same for Dion?"

"Yes, he was becoming alarmed. He thought he was under suspicion. Hesiod had also babbled to him about a traitor in our ranks. Why shouldn't Dion be killed? I had no more need of him. We were of the same party but, in my eyes, he was no better than the rest. I agreed to visit him at night to avert suspicion. I slipped over his garden wall and came secretly into his writing chamber. I brought some drawings, rough sketches of the Temple of Hercules. After I had killed him, I put these among his papers. I noticed how secure the door was, so I bolted and locked it from the inside."

Agis was apparently keen on a full confession. Telamon could guess the reason why.

"I killed him as you said. Dion didn't know much, but he was beginning to question certain things, particularly where I was during the banquet at the Governor's palace; the night I visited him he asked me about that. By then I had already decided on his death. He poured us wine; unobtrusively I mixed in some sleeping potion, then I hanged him. I was in a hurry, I didn't think about the knots." Agis seemed to be talking to himself. "I shuttered and barred one window, and for the other, I did as you described." He

295

smiled. "A common enough trick among housebreakers in Ephesus. After all, I have been a magistrate there."

"And the night at the palace?" Telamon asked. "The king's banquet?"

"Oh, I sowed the idea in the mind of Demades's widow. I visited her shortly after her husband's murder. Like a serpent in the darkness, I suggested she should seek revenge and described how she could do it."

"Then, to protect yourself," Telamon asked, "you told Alexander but continued your mischief?"

"I knew the Governor's palace like the palm of my hand," Agis scoffed. "Entrances exist you still don't know about. I would go there and the Governor would see me at my time and in my place. I knew all about the wasps, the deserted courtyards, and, of course, I had the Macedonian king's pass. I knew Rabinus was taken. He had to die. I was searching for him when I met the soldier, hiding from his companions with his jug of wine. I used the club concealed on my person, the same type Socrates used in the temple, an innocent-looking wooden pole with a bronze head clasped to it. I talked to the soldier for a while: I learnt which dungeon Rabinus was in, then I killed him. Later that night, when the alarm was raised, I left with Dion and slipped away. I moved two wasps' nests and threw them into the kitchen. If you hold them gently enough, there's no real danger, and I protected my hands and face. I also took some oil, a wineskin full of it, and poured it into Rabinus's cell and thrust in the fiery rags." Agis shrugged. "If you know the palace, it was so easy: secret passageways, dark porticoes and shadowy courtyards. Everyone was milling about, it took no longer than it would to walk a mile."

"Did the Governor know who you really were?" Telamon interrupted.

"Of course not. I gave him Dion's name to confuse matters."

"You must have been alarmed," Telamon demanded, "when that hidden archer loosed arrows at the king?"

"Not really," Agis sighed. "As you will find out, there are more Persian spies in Ephesus than you think. The Lord Mithra might have hired someone else, I thought."

"Was the king's death one of your tasks?"

Agis sprang to his feet. Hephaestion's sword came up to the back of his neck.

"Where are you going?" Alexander asked quietly.

Agis went down on his knees. "I beg for my . . .!"

"Not your life!" the king said. "That is mine!"

"Then for a quick death!" Agis retorted. "And the life of my daughter Rhoda. She bears no blame."

Alexander's face had turned an ivory sheen, his lips a bloodless line. "Why should I show you mercy?"

"Because I have confessed," Agis declared.

"And?" Alexander asked.

"I can give you further information."

"Give it."

"I am glad you are searching our houses." Agis allowed himself a broad smile. "I can supply you with a list of Persian agents in Ephesus. At the top of the list will be Peleus."

The other Democrat sprang to his feet, hands fluttering. Agis didn't even spare him a glance.

"Peleus has been bound both body and soul, and so was Dion: the same goes for that fat bitch the Queen of the Moabites. Bring me a stylus and a wax tablet; I'll give you the names of the rest!"

"You won't find my name on that list," Meleager interrupted.

Agis nodded in agreement. "I told a lie," he confessed. "I spared Meleager to create suspicion. Of all the Ephesians, he is the most honourable. An Oligarch, yes, but he never took Persian gold. He's no great love of Macedon either but, in his own way, he's honourable." Agis stretched out his hands towards his half-brother. "If the king agrees, take Rhoda as your own daughter."

Meleager looked at the king, who nodded imperceptibly. Meleager grasped Agis's hand. Alexander rose to his feet and leaned against the pillar.

"Hephaestion, take Agis away. He has one hour to write out his list. Peleus is to be taken to the city gates, stripped of his mantle and sandals, given a staff, a day's water and some food. He is exiled from Ephesus for life."

Peleus started to object, but Hephaestion was already walking to the door to allow in more guards. The temple was cleared. Only Telamon, Alexander and Meleager remained.

"What is your sentence?" Telamon asked.

The king glanced up.

"Meleager, you are chief magistrate of Ephesus, the Archon, but its garrison remains under my orders and those of its commander. You are to go back to that city and stamp my authority on it. The blood feud will end. The Temple of Hercules is to be razed to the ground and rebuilt. Agis's house and daughter are yours: the rest of his wealth is mine. Now you may go!"

Meleager walked to the door.

"Oh, Meleager!"

The Oligarch turned.

"Apelles's painting will be finished. It is to be placed in the new Temple of Artemis, in pride of place." He snapped his fingers at Telamon. "The madman's confession, the incendiary who burnt it to the ground? Telamon, explain to Meleager what you have found."

Telamon explained how the arsonist's confession contained an anagram, a veiled prophecy to Alexander's birth which Artemis had attended.

"But, but that could be . . .?" Meleager's objection died on his lips. He sighed. "It will, my lord, be done as you wish. The temple once housed your father's statue; now it will hold your painting, a true likeness of Alexander the God. But my lord," Meleager added, "Agis?"

The king gazed stonily back. Meleager, embarrassed, shuffled his feet and disappeared through the door. From outside came Aristander's screech of annoyance.

"Keep everyone out!" Alexander shouted, stretching out his hand for Telamon to grasp. When the physician did, the king pulled him close and kissed him on both cheeks.

"I shall not forget." Alexander stood back. "Agis will confess. He'll tell me what the Persians plan next, where they will stand and fight."

"And when he's told everything he can?" Telamon asked.

"Enough blood's been spilt," Alexander whispered. "See to it, Telamon. After the sun sets, take him a cup of hemlock, he's to drink it. This godless man can go down to Hades and tell those in the darkness that I sent him there!"

Author's Note

———◦◦◦◦———

The events at Ephesus in the summer of 334 BC and Alexander's brilliant seizure of the powerful port of Miletus are as described in this novel. The civil war in Ephesus was probably the most bitter Alexander ever encountered in his campaigns in Asia Minor, and this gave me the idea for this novel. According to the sources, Alexander allowed the bloodbath to continue for a while before intervening and bringing the street-fighting to an end. As for the attack on Miletus, the primary sources which exist, especially Arrian, simply describe Alexander as "passing through" Miletus's first line of defence unchecked: this suggests an attack as sudden and brutal as any blitzkreig of modern warfare. Alexander's neutralization of the Persian navy is also accurately described. He blocked the port with his own small squadrons while his land troops cut off the only available supply of fresh water: the Persian fleet was forced to retire and Miletus fell. Memnon escaped, but many of his troops swam out to small rocky islands in the harbour, only to be offered, and accept, honourable terms for surrender.

The medical theories and treatment mentioned in this novel are based on extracts from Hippocrates of Cos's notebooks as well as other primary sources. Greek physicians may not have understood the full complexity of the human body, but they were keen observers of it. Physicians such as Telamon did travel the known world acquiring knowledge from different sources.

Alexander is a chameleon-like figure. He was a consummate actor who deliberately misled both his own court and the enemy. He did this at the battle of the Granicus, and again in his brilliant campaign against Miletus. One of Hegel's great figures of history, Alexander was a shooting star whose life and exploits still fascinate

301

us thousands of years after his death. He was deeply influenced by his parents: his filial relationship can be succinctly described as one of love and hate. He adored both Philip and Olympias but their constant feuding wreaked its psychological effects on him. Alexander was a Greek who wanted to be a Persian, a man who believed in democracy but could be as autocratic as any emperor. Alexander could be generous to a fault, forgiving and compassionate but, when his mood changed, could strike with a savage ruthlessness. The utter destruction of Thebes and Memnon's mercenaries at the Granicus illustrate Alexander's darker side. Sometimes he could be childlike, trusting and innocent; he regarded life as one great adventure.

Alexander's relationship with the painter Apelles, as described here, is based on primary sources. During his stay at Ephesus Apelles painted Alexander's picture. Apelles is now reckoned to be one of the great artists of the ancient world; Alexander considered himself to be his equal and constantly harangued the painter on his technique. Eventually Apelles sharply rebuked Alexander, pointing out that his own assistants were laughing at the Macedonian king's lack of artistic knowledge. Alexander took the rebuke in good part and allowed Apelles to display his genius without constant criticism. Alexander truly believed in the legend that the Temple of Artemis at Ephesus had been burnt down by an arsonist on the night of his birth. He became deeply upset when the new government of Ephesus resisted his generous offer to rebuild the temple from his own treasury, but never retaliated.

Alexander was a loyal friend and companion. Once he gave his word, he kept it. He did restore democratic rule in Ephesus and tried not to interfere. He had a passion for poetry, particularly Homer's *Iliad* and, thanks to his tutor Aristotle, a deep interest in the natural world. He could be superstitious to the point of being neurotic but, as at Miletus, displayed a personal bravery and courage which is breathtaking. His genius as a general and leader has, perhaps, never been surpassed, yet he also had a vein of self-mockery, even humility. His drinking has been the subject of much debate. Some authorities, such as Curtius Rufus, claim he was a drunkard given to homicidal rages. Aristobulus, his close friend, quoted by Arrian, claims that Alexander's long drinking sessions arose not so much from his love of wine, but out of comradeship for his friends. Whatever, Alexander had his faults and failings, and wine brought these out. Perhaps that explains Alexander's continued fascination for us: not just his great victories and exploits, but his personality which, at times, could sum up the best and worst in humanity.

Paul C. Doherty